GH00865341

A Fragment of

Moonswood

Tracey Mathias

Tracey Mathias

Canfield Dragon Press

Published by Canfield Dragon Press

ISBN 9780993275517

Canfield Dragon Press

www.traceymathias.com

Cover illustration © Tim Mathias, 2015

for my parents

Contents

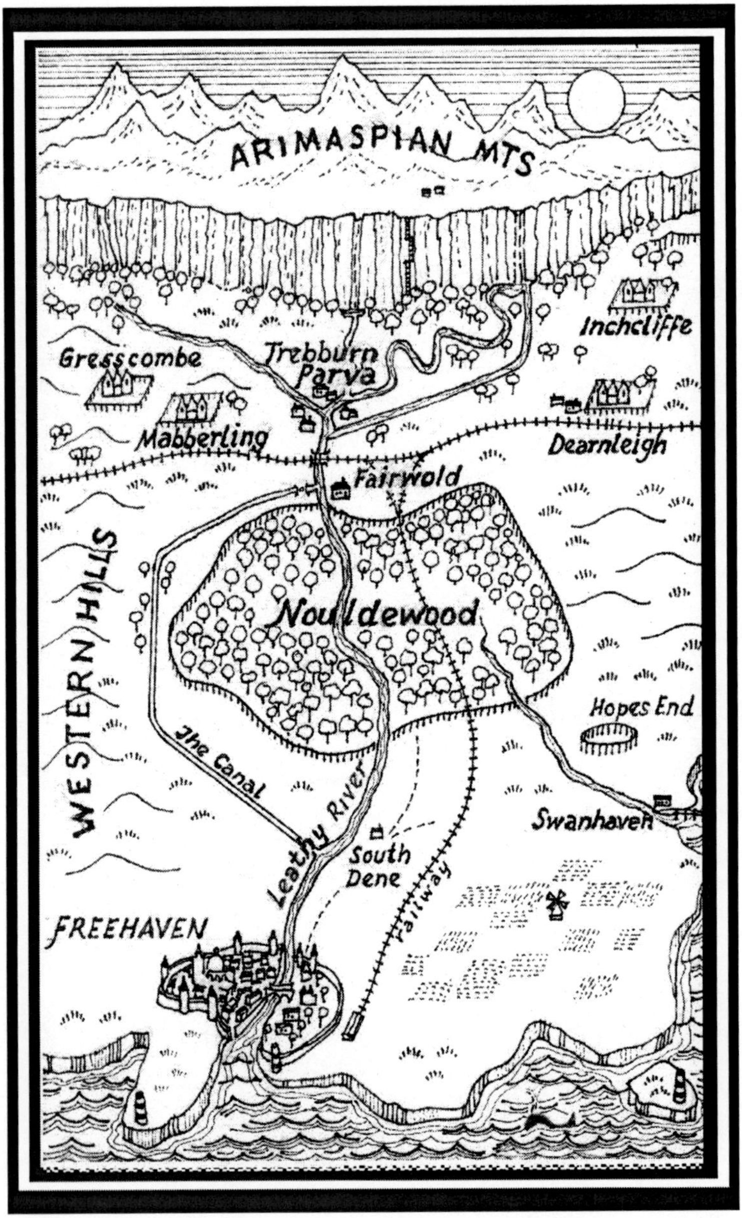

ARIMASPIAN MTS
Inchcliffe
Gresscombe
Trebburn
Parva
Mabberling
Dearnleigh
Fairwold
WESTERN HILLS
Nouldewood
Hopes End
The Canal
Leathy River
Swanhaven
South
Dene
railway
FREEHAVEN

Chamboleyne and the Children

Tal was running hard, hurtling down the rocky path. He leapt a corner, slid, and fell headlong. *No time to stop*. Scrambling up, he risked a shout -

'Gaia!'

- but his voice carried too loud and too far in the clear air, and he didn't dare call again. He pelted on, skidding down the last steep turn onto level scrubby ground where a dozen goats were browsing the spiky bushes. Beyond them was a long crest of rocks where his sister was sitting, with her back turned to him, the goats and the mountains above.

Tal swore silently and glanced back over his shoulder. The thing that had set him running was still there, smudged against the brilliant white of the high snowfields and the clear blue sky above them. Two columns of grey smoke, rising into the air: it didn't make *sense*, but he couldn't doubt what he was seeing. He swallowed the sudden salt taste of fear, and set off at a run across the stony ground, startling the goats as he hurtled past them. Reaching the rocks, he scrambled up to the high flat stone where Gaia sat.

She had her knees drawn up to her chest and her arms huddled round them, because the air was always cold up here, above the clouds - even in Melisto with a strong summer sun burning overhead. She was staring down towards the unknown land far below, the forbidden country that she would never visit. When she was little, she had asked their mother, 'What's down there?' and Mai had said, 'It's just another part of Assalay. We don't go there.'

'What's it like?' Gaia had insisted.

'I don't know. We don't go there.'

But Gaia still wanted to know, and she went on trying to see. For most of the year, it was hopeless. In autumn, winter and spring, clouds as thick as goats' hair blankets hung heavy around the shoulders of the mountain, hiding the land below. It was only in summer, usually, that the cloud thinned into a wavering mist, letting her see a strange land of brilliant green... Usually. Not this year. This year, the clouds had hardly cleared at all, and when they did it was only for a heartbeat, too briefly for her to see anything.

There! She caught a flash of colour far below, but as she leaned forward to look, Tal grabbed her shoulder.

'You're meant to be *watching*, Gaia!'

He forced her round to face back up the mountains. The smudgy columns of smoke still drifted in the bright air and she stared in disbelief.

'But... They don't come in summer!'

'They do now.' Tal hauled her to her feet. 'Let's get this lot safe, shall we? *If* we can.'

She nodded, dry-mouthed. They slid down the rock, gathered the flock and started down the steep path towards home. The goats were restless: flinching at shadows and slight sounds, sniffing the air with flared nostrils. At the first bend in the path, Gaia glanced up to check the drifting lines of ominous grey again. Was she imagining it, or were they nearer now?

'Tal?' she said, and she could see from the grimness in his face that he had realised it too. 'Keep going,' he said. 'Just keep going,' but an instant later a shadow swooped across them and a sickening, retching stench of burnt meat rolled through the air.

Gaia clutched at Tal's hand as the green-grey dragon flew above their heads. It glided away from the face of the mountain on spread wings, banked, turned and flew back again. It was lower this time: close enough for them to feel the wind of its flight, to choke on the rank meat stink of its breath, to see the narrow yellow eyes above the long snout. Gaia closed her eyes, tensed for the savage agony of fire: the smell of roasted flesh, the screaming of burning goats, her own screaming...

'Look,' Tal whispered. She opened her eyes. The dragon was soaring upwards to land on a high pinnacle of rock above the path. It was restless at first, swaying its ugly head, swinging its tail and picking up one clawed foot after another, but slowly it hunkered down on its giant haunches and lowered its head against its scaly chest. It blinked, and yawned out a cloud of grey smoke.

'It's going to sleep, isn't it?' Tal mouthed.

'Think so.' Gaia wrinkled her nose. 'Smells as if it's just eaten.'

'Let's go then. *Quietly*.'

Gaia tugged at the goats, but they were stubborn with fear and refused to budge. Tal murmured the call that he usually sang out loud to gather them at evening - 'Come away, come away!' - and at last they started to move, but they were skittish: jostling one another in the narrow track, shoving, pushing, and finally breaking into a panicked run. Trapped among them, Tal and Gaia ran too.

They were making too much noise, Tal knew: hooves clattering against rock, dislodged stones tumbling and smashing, his own heart thundering. 'Slow down!' he hissed, but it was impossible; he could only keep running, every nerve alert for the searing breath of the roused dragon at his back. The track zig-zagged steeply down and down, and at last widened out onto the open ground above the village. The goats scattered. Tal stopped and looked back. No dragon.

'Well?' He glared at Gaia.

'What d'you mean? *Well?*'

'How about *sorry*, Gaia? You were meant to be watching!'

'Arctos' sake! Nothing's ever *your* fault, is it, Tal?'

They stared furiously at one another, dark-eyed. 'I'm going to find Mum,' Tal said at last. 'Bring the goats.'

He hurried down towards the village, and Gaia trudged across the open slope to gather the scattered flock. As she rounded them up, a dark-haired, skinny boy, barefoot and ragged, with two shabby goats at his side, came running down the track.

'Jason!' Gaia ran to meet him. 'Are you alright? There was a dragon!'

'Saw it.'

'I didn't,' she admitted. 'I was meant to be watching...'

'Don't tell me. You were looking the wrong way.' He gave a quick smile, bright as clear sun on a mountainside, and she half smiled back, but the memory - the swooping shadow, the stench, the terror - was too vivid for laughter.

'Hey.' Jason touched her hand lightly. 'No-one's eaten. Come on.'

They drove the goats along the rutted path into the village. Just past the crowded market-place, they found Tal with Mai. 'We're fine, Mum,' he was saying. 'There was only one dragon. He flew overhead...'

'Overhead!'

3

Tal glanced briefly at Gaia, a *don't tell her* look. 'Not very close. Anyway, he wouldn't have been interested in us. He'd already eaten.'

'I know.' Mai's face was grim. 'He took one of Selene's goats.'

'That's bad luck,' Tal said quietly. Gaia said nothing, but she was watching the horror in her mind: the shocking attack out of a friendly summer sky: scorching breath, and snatching claws and the high screaming of terrified goats. She shivered.

'It's alright.' Mai put an arm round Gaia's shoulders. 'Nobody's hurt, or… Just one goat. It could be worse.'

'But why was it here at all?' Gaia asked.

'No-one knows.' There was a dizzy, bewildered look in Mai's eyes. 'No-one's *ever* seen a dragon in summer before.' She stared up at the sky above the mountains, and shook her head. 'You can't go back up today. Let's go home and eat. Have you got any food, Jason?'

Jason gestured up at the mountain. 'Was going to find myself some berries or something.'

'Better share with us, then,' Mai said, and they continued along the track, past houses whose stones had darkened and crumbled with age. Their house was the last in the village. Beyond it was stony ground, bounded by a low wall, and beyond that a cliff that plummeted down and down until it disappeared from sight in the cloud. A gap in the wall led to the top of the rickety wooden ladders that were the only link with the country below. Last summer, Jason had dared Gaia to do the unthinkable thing.

'Climb down the ladder a bit. I will if you will.' They had been caught, already through the gap and sitting uncertainly at the top of the unimaginable drop, by Gaia's great-uncle Ambrose. He had ushered them calmly back onto safe ground before he had let them see how furious he was.

'*We don't go off the mountains.* You know the story of Chamboleyne,' he had raged. 'What in the name of moonshine were you thinking of?' Gaia, who had never known Ambrose so angry, had been ashamed and frightened, and even Jason had looked abashed. And Mai, when Ambrose had told her, had been angry too, but also scared and so upset, that Gaia still felt hot-faced, remembering it now as she followed her mother up the uneven stone steps into the dwelling-room of the house.

4

Mai opened the cracked clay pot which held the round flat loaves that she made a couple of times each moon. She peered inside. 'Have you got your lunch, Gaia?'

'Tal has.'

'Good.' Mai took two loaves out of the jar, paused for a moment, put one back and replaced the lid. 'Give this to Jason.'

'What about you?' Gaia said.

'Oh…' Mai waved the question away. 'I'm not that hungry. I'll eat later.'

'Mum?' Gaia lifted the lid off the jar, and opened the big wooden bin which held their precious supplies of grain. There were only a handful of loaves in the jar, and a sprinkling of broken grains and floury dust at the bottom of the bin.

'I was just trying to make it last,' Mai said. 'It'll be fine. The next market's at full moon.'

Fine if the dragon doesn't come again, Gaia thought. But what if it's there tomorrow, and the day after, and the day after, and we can't graze the goats? No goats means no cheese and no wool: nothing to trade, and that means no bread…

'Gaia,' Mai said. 'Let's worry about tomorrow tomorrow, shall we?'

'Fine.' Gaia took a loaf out of the jar and handed it to Mai. 'Let's worry about tomorrow tomorrow.'

There was a strange holiday feeling about that afternoon. They turned the goats loose to browse on the sparse bushes below the house, and sat at the foot of the stone steps, with the sun on their faces. Mai brought her spinning outside, while Tal carved an old length of wood, singing softly to himself. Jason scratched a grid in the dust, gathered a handful of small grey and brown stones and flicked one of them at Gaia, who was leaning against the warm house wall with her eyes closed.

'Want a game of goats and dragons?'

'Alright. I'll be goats.' She knelt by the grid, set out the stones, and manoeuvred them from one side to the other, while Jason's stone dragons tried to snatch them. They played a couple of long, closely fought games, arguing furiously about the rules, and afterwards they lay side by side on the ground, staring up at the sky, watching the clouds gather. A few large splashes of rain fell. Jason clambered to his feet.

'Better be off.'

'You can stay,' Mai said. 'You're always welcome.'

'S'alright.' He called his goats and set off for the tumbledown house where he lived alone. Gaia watched him go: a solitary figure, between the old houses. Under the heavy clouds and the rain and the looming mountains, the little village looked lost and sad. As night closed in, she and Tal gathered the goats, milked them, and penned them safely in the lower room of the house; then they climbed the steps, and shut the door on the rainy evening. A chill had fallen with the darkness and they wrapped themselves in goats' hair blankets and sat at the cold hearth.

'Tell us a story, Mum,' said Tal.

'Which one?'

'You choose.'

Mai picked up her spindle and a handful of wool, drew out a thread and set the spindle turning, teasing the wool into an even yarn.

'This is the story of Chamboleyne and the children,' she said at last. 'A long time ago…'

'*How* long?' Gaia demanded.

'Oh, shut up, Gaia,' said Tal. 'Just listen.'

'A long time ago,' Mai said, '- and no-one knows when, Gaia - the people in these mountains kept goats, like us, and the goats were life for them, as they are for us. They gave milk and meat for food, wool and skins for warmth, and dung for the fire. It was a hard life. Harder than ours has been, but maybe not harder than it will be soon.' She fell silent, and for a moment Gaia thought that she had forgotten the story, but then she went on.

'Well. Life was quiet as well as hard. The villagers watched the moons and the seasons pass, and everything was always the same - until one day, one year, in the last quarter of Arctos. The days were short and cold, and the winter snow was still deep on the high mountains. A group of goatherds had taken their flocks to find what food they could in one of the lower valleys, and as they shivered and stamped their feet and blew on their fingers, they saw a little group of travellers, dark against the snow on the mountains above.

'The travellers stumbled down the steep slope from the snowfields into the valley, and the villagers saw to their astonishment that, apart from the tall, gaunt man who was leading them, they were all children, the oldest a girl of about thirteen. They were half frozen and half starved, weak and exhausted from the impossible journey across the mountains.

'"Help us," said the man.

'The villagers brought them home, and built fires to warm them. They gave them food, and the children ate eagerly, but the man who had led them waved the food aside.

'"Let me speak first." His voice was weak and the villagers had to lean close to hear him. "I am Chamboleyne. You don't need to know who these children are. All you need to know is that they have been - are - in great danger. But I think - I hope - they could be safe here, if you take them in, and care for them as your own. If you do that, and if they never leave this mountainside, they may be saved."

'"What will you give us in return?" asked one of the goatherds.

'"I can offer you nothing," Chamboleyne said. "Nothing, except our weakness and our need."

'"And danger?' asked the man. 'Might we be in danger too, if we took them?'

'"I can't deny that," said Chamboleyne. "But if you turn us away, you send us to our deaths. The winter is fierce, and we have no strength left." He hesitated before he spoke again. "For my sake. I beg you… Save them for my sake. I have done the worst of things, and the only way I can repair it is by bringing these children to safety. Save them, and you save me. Save them, and one day they may save you."

'The villagers quarrelled about what to do, but they were kind to the children anyway; wrapping them in blankets and laying them on beds of heather to sleep. Chamboleyne sat listening to the argument, too worn out to say more. He watched the children sleep, then he closed his own eyes, and died where he sat.

'Early next morning, six men carried his body to a high ledge, to be picked clean by eagles and dragons. As they returned (still arguing about what to do with the children), one of them slipped, and grabbed at a piece of rock. It came loose in his hand, fell to the ground, and shattered. The broken fragments glittered in the winter sun - and that was how our gold was found.

'Well, after that, the arguments stopped. Chamboleyne and his children had brought the village luck, and that's one thing you don't turn away. In the spring, a travelling trader from the lowlands came to the village, and after him, more and more: their eyes so full of the glitter of gold that they didn't even see the children.

'So the years of gold began. We bought good things then: rich food, fine furniture and clothes. The lowlanders built the ladders so they could trade more easily with us, but we remember Chamboleyne's warning. Many strangers have climbed up. None of us has climbed down, and none of us ever will.'

The gloomy light had almost gone. Mai picked up another handful of wool from the basket and ran the yarn through her seeing fingers. 'That's the end,' she said, 'Go to sleep.'

That isn't the end, Gaia thought. If the story had ended there, where Mai always stopped it, everything would still be alright. In the darkness she told herself the real ending. After many years, finding gold had become more and more difficult and dangerous. There were no more miraculous glittering showers from the cliff. The miners had had to work their way deep into the mountains, cutting gold from the rock walls of caverns and tunnels. Before Gaia was born, even those hard-to-work seams had been exhausted, and the miners had searched desperately for others. Gaia could remember - very dimly, from her early childhood - the men setting off at dawn and returning weary and empty-handed at dusk, to swap grimly humorous accounts of narrow escapes from falling rocks. And then there had been the giant fall, and the end of the golden dream.

So much for Chamboleyne's luck. Chamboleyne's luck had crashed to dust and disaster and death. So many deaths: hardly any child in the village had a living father. Gaia closed her eyes tight, trying to remember her own father, Athanasius, but as usual she could catch only fleeting glimpses - as if someone had opened a door and slammed it shut again a moment later. She could never see his face: it remained a blank. But she knew he had looked like her (just as Tal looked so uncannily like Mai). 'Your father's child,' people always said to her, fondly and sadly, and sometimes Gaia caught her mother looking at her with an odd intensity, and couldn't be sure if Mai was seeing her or the man who would never return from the collapsed mine under the cliffs.

She sighed and turned under her itchy blanket.

'Gaia? What's the matter?' Mai's voice sounded hollow and sad in the darkness. Maybe she, too, had been silently telling the tragedy that had followed the happy ending.

'Nothing,' Gaia lied.

The moon cleared a cloud; through the high window, a shaft of yellow-white light fell into the room. Melisto: bright warm moon: bringer of sweet things: goddess of the late summer. In a few days, she would be full, and the day after that, Gaia would be thirteen. The same age as the girl in the story, and like her, destined to go nowhere but this narrow ledge of rock where the village sat. She turned restlessly again.

'Sleep,' said Mai. She started to sing softly.

Far above the summer pastures,
Golden in the setting sun,
Fly the flocks that tell you, dearest,
I'll be home when day is done.

Far above the snowy mountains,
In the endless autumn sky,
Pale the moon that tells you, dearest,
I'll be home at even tide.

Gaia pressed her fingers against her ears to shut out the song, because no-one was coming home; not today, not tomorrow. Not ever.

The Amulet

The summer dragon disappeared as suddenly and strangely as it had come. After a few days of grazing the goats safely below the village, Gaia and Tal felt confident enough to take them up into the mountains to feed as usual - though Gaia spent her time anxiously scanning the empty skies, and snatching only quick glances down the mountain. There was no glimpse of the land below; the clouds were as thick as they had been all summer.

Today was the day of the full moon market: there would be no going up the mountains, and no need to get up early. She stretched out under her blankets, watching the dust in the sunlight and listening to Tal singing outside.

'High above you when you're sleeping
In the silent winter night,
Hangs the single star...

'Get *off*, you wretched animal! You can't eat that!'

Gaia rolled out of bed, crossed the room, and called down from the doorway, 'Who can't eat what?'

'Snowfall. Chewing my bag. Should have left her to the dragon.' He shoved through the milling goats, climbed the steps into the house, and set the brimming milking pail on the table.

'I'm going to take them for water,' he said. 'Mum said, can you stay here? To help get some stuff ready for market. She's just helping Ambrose. She won't be long.' He ran back down the steps, and drove the goats towards the stream: Gaia could still hear him after he was out of sight, calling, 'Come away, come away,' through the clear morning air.

Left alone in the house, she drank some milk, tidied the blankets and sat down on the steps to wait for Mai. The air grew warmer and the shadows shortened, but Mai didn't come. Gaia got up and went back inside.

Mai's loom stood in its usual place against the wall, with an unfinished length of cloth stretched across it; brown and cream wools interwoven in alternating stripes. Patterned cloth always went to market: only that was *today* and if this cloth wasn't finished, there would be one less thing to barter for their vital supplies of grain, firewood and winter fodder. Gaia looked out of the door again. The shadows were even shorter and there was still no sign of Mai.

She went back to the loom. Weaving was Mai's job, but Gaia had watched her, every day of her life, and seen how it was done. She picked up the shuttle that carried the thread, balanced its weight in her hand, and tugged at one of the wooden battens that pulled forward alternate sets of warp threads. She fed the shuttle through them, adding another line of weft to the cloth, pressed it down, wiped her sweaty hands on her skirt, pulled forward the other warp threads, added another row, another, and another...

'*Gaia!* What on earth are you doing?'

She dropped the shuttle. Mai was staring at her from the doorway.

'I was just...' She faltered into silence as she looked at what she had done, and saw what her mother was seeing. Mai's weaving was neat and regular. Hers was a mess: too loose here; too tight there; the wool fluffy, lumpy and grubby where she had undone and rewoven some of the rows.

'What did you think you were doing?' Mai asked again. 'It's ruined. I can't trade *this!*' She started to unravel the cloth, tearing at the spoiled wool while Gaia stood, dumb and useless, staring at the mess of torn threads on the floor. Tal came whistling up the steps, shoved open the door, and fell silent.

'What's going on?'

'Gaia,' said Mai. 'Thought she'd finish the weaving, and *look* at it.' Her face was tight with anger, but there was fear in it too: she looked like someone walking the sheer edge of a long fall.

'I was trying to *help!*' Gaia pushed blindly past Tal and out of the house. She ran across the rough ground below the village, and up the slope to the rocks where the openings to the old mine workings loomed dark and silent. She stopped there. There was nowhere else to go. *Nowhere:* just this narrow rocky world where whatever she touched seemed to crumble to dust. She sat down on a boulder and hid her face in her hands.

'Gaia?' Tal's voice roused her. 'You alright?'

'Go away,' she said, hating him: steady, capable Tal who would never have thought of interfering with Mum's weaving, but who would have done it properly if he had.

He sat down next to her. 'Mum's calmed down a bit. She knows you were only trying to help.'

'*Trying* to help.' Gaia kicked at the ground. 'Sometimes I hate it here. Don't you?'

He looked at her blankly. 'I've never really thought about it. I mean...'

'I *know*. Here's all there is. Oh, forget it. We should go.'

From all over the village, people were hurrying down to the gap in the clifftop wall, and she and Tal got up from the stone, and walked down the slope to join them. A knot of villagers had already gathered around the sealed sacks of goods which had been winched up the cliff on the old pulleys next to the ladders. Jason was with them.

'You alright, Gaia?' he said.

'*Don't ask,*' mouthed Tal.

'Gaia?' Jason asked again.

'Nothing,' she muttered, but he touched her hand and winked at her, and she thought, *at least there's Jason*, and felt comforted. They sat side by side on the warm stones of the wall, waiting, until the top of the ladder began to shudder and sway, and a fat man climbed into sight. His baggy shirt was streaked with dirt and drenched in sweat. He clambered off the ladder, breathing deeply, and wiped his forehead with his sleeve. Ambrose stepped forward to greet him.

'Mr Rackin. Happy full moon.'

'Ambrose.' Rackin gave a curt nod and bent to check the seals on the bags. 'Right. You can bring this lot up.' He watched wordlessly as the villagers shouldered the bundles, and trudged after them along the track to the market. Gaia, carrying a load of firewood, glanced back at him, puzzled. Rackin was usually friendly enough, but today he was grim as midwinter, and she felt uneasy as she dropped her bundle on the market floor, and went with Tal to join Mai.

The market had been a grand building once: in the golden time. Now, it was as broken and sad as the rest of the village. Gaia tried to imagine how it must have been when the timber posts had not been so weathered that their elaborate carvings were almost worn away; when the roof had not leaked; when the black slate paving had not been cracked and splintered. And when - most difficult of all to imagine - the villagers gathered here had been proud and confident miners with gold to sell, not shabby goatherds waiting nervously for a bad-tempered trader to announce his terms.

'Right,' said Rackin. 'Here's the deal. Half a luneweight of grain for a cheese; a weight for a blanket or hide. A load of firewood...'

His words were drowned by frightened protests. 'You can't... It's not... that's half what you gave before...' Mai, white-faced, was reckoning up the scanty pile of goods at her feet. The ruined blanket was not there, and Gaia looked away, unable to meet her mother's panicked eyes.

Ambrose spoke above the other voices. 'Mr Rackin, please. Let me explain...'

'*No!*' Rackin interrupted him. 'Let *me* explain. Last year was bad; this one's a disaster. It's rained all summer. The fields are full of drowned wheat. I have trouble selling your smelly cheeses and your itchy blankets at the best of times. No one's going to want them now. They've hardly enough to buy *bread.*' He looked round at the silent, shocked faces. 'I'm doing you a favour. Take it or leave it.'

Ambrose spread his hands. 'What choice do we have?'

'Then let's get this done.' Rackin turned to Cassie's mother, and ran a quick, calculating eye over the cloth and cheese she had spread on the market floor.

'Two bags of grain, two loads of firewood.'

She gasped. 'That's all?'

'I'm not bargaining.' Rackin made to move away, but she called him back. She bundled up her cloth and cheeses and he fetched the meagre goods that he had offered in exchange: two small hempen sacks of grain, and tied bundles of firewood. *Three moons,* Gaia thought: that's got to last *three moons*. It's not *possible...*

'Gaia!' Jason touched her arm softly.

She frowned at him. 'What are you doing here?' Jason never traded. His shabby goats gave enough milk for his own needs, but there was never enough left over for cheese-making. He had never learned to spin or weave, either, and simply swapped his goats' wool for bread or firewood with the other villagers.

13

He winked, beckoned her aside, and opened the leather bag slung over his shoulder. It was stuffed to bursting with plump golden grains of wheat. Gaia reached into the bag and pinched a couple of the hard grains between her fingers.

'Where did you get that?'

'Where d'you think?'

'What? Rackin *gave* it to you?'

He gave a snort of mirthless laughter. 'That's likely, isn't it? I *nicked* it, stupid.'

'Jason!'

'Listen, Gaia. I wouldn't steal from anyone up here: you know that. But from a fat git like Rackin who's got more than he needs? Who makes money out of dealing hard with people who can't afford it? I don't see the problem with that.'

'But... What if he'd caught you?'

'He didn't. Did he?' Jason grinned.

She grinned back at him. *'Honestly.* You've got a nerve.' She glanced over her shoulder. Rackin was talking to Mai. 'I better go. And you better keep that bag shut.'

She hurried away. Tal was packing cheeses, while Mai folded a length of cloth. She gave Gaia a quick look. 'Help Tal, please Gaia.' There was a taut quietness in her voice, a hundred things that she wasn't saying. Silently, Gaia knelt next to Tal to help. When everything was ready, Rackin laid out his price: two sacks of grain and a load of firewood.

'Is that *all?*' Gaia stared.

'Shut up,' Tal told her. He shouldered the firewood, while Mai picked up one sack of grain and handed the other to Gaia. At home, they emptied the grain sacks into the wooden barrel. It was still barely half full.

'Mum,' Gaia said. 'How're we going to manage?'

Mai shut the lid. 'We'll manage. We'll forage what we can. Fish. Birds. Berries.'

Tal nodded. 'There'll be lots we can find. For the next couple of moons, anyway.'

'And I'll make as much cloth as I can, before the Hesperal market,' Mai said.

'Mum,' Gaia said in a small voice. 'I'm sorry about the weaving.'

'Oh, Gaia.' Mai put an arm around her shoulders. 'Don't worry. It wouldn't have made much difference. And we'll be alright.'

Gaia looked at her doubtfully.

'I mean it. If the worst happens, there's still this.' Mai knelt at the cold hearth, pulled out a loose stone at the back of the chimney, reached into the hollow space behind it, and took out a small bundle, roughly wrapped in dirty leather.

'What's that?' Tal leaned forward to see.

Mai laid the bundle on the table and folded back the leather. Two small bars of gold gleamed in the late sunlight. They seemed to fill the room with warm brightness.

'I've been saving these.' Mai trailed one finger across the shining metal, and Gaia understood. Her father had dug and smelted the gold: it was precious because it bore the touch of his hands.

'I think it's time to use them, though,' Mai said. 'We'll buy provisions for the winter, and in spring there'll be a new flock of kids. We'll make as much cheese as we can. I'll teach you to weave, Gaia.' She smiled and Gaia smiled back, but she was thinking, what if next year's bad too, and we've used up the gold? What then?

Mai rewrapped the gold, knelt to put it away, and looked up at Gaia. 'It's your birthday tomorrow.'

'Yes.'

Mai sighed. 'Thirteen. A special age. We'd have had a big party, once, with a feast, and presents, and dancing. But now...'

'I don't mind,' Gaia said. 'Especially about the dancing.'

Mai laughed and got to her feet. She was holding something. 'This is all I've got for you. But happy birthday, anyway.'

She passed Gaia a leather pouch, rough and crumbly with age, and fastened with a long drawstring. Gaia undid the string, and felt inside the bag. There was just one thing in it: something square and flat. She slid it onto the palm of her hand.

It was a piece of soft white stone. Veins glittered through it like caught moonlight. One face was as smooth as new-fallen snow; the other was engraved with a pattern of flowing lines. Gaia traced her fingers along the carvings. After a long time, she looked up at Mai.

'What is it?'

'The amulet. It's a kind of charm. For luck. It's been in your father's family for as long as anyone can remember. There's a story about it: that it will bring the family glory and wealth and greatness.'

Tal snorted. 'It hasn't exactly worked, then, has it?'

Mai laughed. 'Not exactly. Really, Gaia, I think it's just an old and pretty thing, with an old and pretty tale attached to it.'

'It's lovely,' Gaia said. She traced her fingers along the carvings again. 'Is it honestly mine?'

'Yes,' Mai said. 'It's always given to the oldest child in each generation. It's a birthright, more than a present. It's been meant for you since you were born.'

'Where did it come from? What sort of stone is it? And do the carvings mean anything?'

'I don't know. I've told you everything I know about it. Those other things...' Mai shook her head. 'I don't think anyone has known those for a long time.'

Gaia tucked the amulet into its pouch, drew the string tight and hung it around her neck. There was a strange comfort in its slight weight against her body.

Parhelion

A high, wordless cry jolted Gaia out of sleep, to complete, terrified alertness. Heart pounding, dry-mouthed, she sat up. A faint light filtered through the window: not the steady serene silver of moonlight, but a sinister red flickering.

'What's happening?'

'What was that noise?'

Mai and Tal were awake now too. The scream came again.

'The goats!' Tal flung himself to the door and wrenched it open, Gaia and Mai crowding behind him. The goats were out, not shut safely away beneath the house... then time and place slipped, and Gaia was outside too, running with the flock as great flying beasts dived and swooped out of the darkness on leathery wings, and she ran and ran, helpless in the heart of the fire...

She woke again. Properly this time: out of the nightmare. There was no sound, except the echo of her own thudding heart. The big autumn moon shone steadily, flooding the room with divine light. 'The moons watch you,' Mai had told her, when she was a little girl, waking from bad dreams. Gaia murmured the prayer that Mai had taught her.

Let me not be hidden from the sky,
But always lie
Where I may see
The moons, who through the seasons watch for me.

But the words wouldn't dispel the terror of the dream, and she knew she wouldn't dare sleep again that night. It was freezing: her breath wreathed like smoke in the silver light, but she was already wearing all her clothes under her blanket, so there was nothing to be done about that, or about the emptiness gnawing at her stomach. Shivering and hungry, she waited unhappily for dawn.

17

The nightmare still haunted her in the morning, as she and Tal laboured up path where they had fled from the summer dragon. Now, in Brumas, the mountainside was white and crunchy with frost, and the high peaks were lost in stormy cloud. Gaia and Tal stopped where a crevice between two big rocks provided some shelter from the wind, and turned the goats loose to browse. Close by, a stream poured over smooth rocks into a deep brown pool.

'Better try and catch some fish.' Tal knelt, rolled up his sleeve and plunged his hand into the water, swearing at the cold.

'Shall I try?' Gaia asked.

'Not now. Pick some berries. Take over when I've frozen to death.'

She gave a half smile, and crouched down among the spiky, dry-leaved bushes to look for garberries: the small sour fruits that glowed like embers in the undergrowth. She was searching a tangle of twisted grey stems when Tal shouted, 'Gaia! Look!'

He was pointing away from the mountains. Gaia stood and squinted into the distant cloud.

'What? I can't see anything.'

'It's gone now... Wait! There!'

Tiny and indistinct, a far-off flying shape hovered briefly into sight above the clouds and disappeared again.

'What was *that?*' asked Tal.

'Don't know. A dragon?'

'Didn't look like one.' He strained his eyes for a moment longer, and shrugged. 'It's gone now, anyway. I got a couple of fish. Any berries?'

'Hardly any.' She showed him the pitiful handful of berries at the bottom of her bag. 'There were loads yesterday. Someone must have got here first.'

'Jason.' Tal gestured up the slope: Jason was making his way downhill, the two scruffy goats bounding around him.

'Hey,' Gaia said as he reached them. 'What happened to all the berries that were here yesterday?'

He smiled his quick smile and opened his bag. It was full of glowing garberries. 'You need to get up earlier, Gaia.'

'Huh. Well, if you've got them all, there's no point me looking anymore.' She flopped down in the shelter of the overhanging rocks

18

and Jason sat next to her. Tal knelt by the pool again to try for another fish.

'Had my nightmare last night,' Gaia told Jason.

'The dragons?'

She nodded.

'Scary,' he said. 'But only a dream.'

'I know.' She smiled: Jason could always make things seem better. Leaning back against the rock she took the amulet out of its pouch. Since her birthday she had held it in every spare moment, feeling its size and weight in her hand, and tracing the engraved lines with her fingers. Her hands knew it intimately now: she could have recognised it with her eyes closed. But no amount of studying would explain what it was, where it had come from or what it could *do*. Its promises of wealth, glory and greatness seemed a mockery in these thin days of foraging for wild food, and watching how quickly the grain in the bin was being used up. *What use are you*, she wondered, but it just lay, silent, lovely, in her hand.

'Your amulet, Gaia?' asked Jason. 'Found out what it does yet?'

'No. Maybe nothing...

'Gaia!' Tal shouted.

The strange flying object had risen above the clouds again. It was close enough now for them to see a mass of wings above a silver crescent, like a new moon lying on its back. It was flying straight towards the mountain. As they watched, a deep *boom* rose from the village and shuddered in the air. Gaia felt cold coursing through her. She had heard that sound once before, when she had been very small and Tal just a baby, and after it there had been frightened shouting and frightened silences, and grim faces, and Dad had never come home...

'*Gaia!*' Tal tugged at her hand. 'That was the gong. We've got to go.'

Chasing the goats, they ran down the mountain, through the village and into the market square - and stopped short in astonishment. The square was full of colour. That was Gaia's first impression: brilliant colours that she had only seen before in the distant movement of light: the white of far-off snow; the indigo of a vanishing rainbow; the divine silver of moonlight.

'Who are they?' Tal whispered.

They were two dozen strangers, standing in ranks under the dilapidated arches. They wore powdered silver wigs, silk coats of indigo with silver braiding, white britches and stockings, and shiny black shoes with silver buckles. Despite their finery, their faces were sweaty and their hands filthy from the long climb up the ladders.

'Who on earth?' asked Tal again.

Gaia didn't answer. She was watching Ambrose talking to one of the strangers: it was impossible to hear what they were saying, but Ambrose's face was as sombre as a mountainside shadowed by storm clouds. One of the strangers gave an order to the others, and they turned and marched out of the square towards the clifftop. The villagers surged after them in a curious, apprehensive crowd, but Ambrose sank down onto a bench and stared at the cracked stone floor. Gaia crossed the square and sat next to him.

'Ambrose?' she whispered. 'What is it?'

'Gaia.' He took her hands in his. 'I've been hoping this wouldn't happen. It's Parhelion.'

'What's Parhelion?'

Ambrose gave a weak smile. 'Not what. Who. Lord Parhelion.'

He looked up and Gaia followed his gaze. A gilded silver basket born by hundreds of harnessed eagles was descending rapidly towards the clifftop. 'Who's Lord Parhelion? And what's he doing here?'

'He's Lord of the Arimaspian Mountains, which gives him the right to take tribute from us. That's why he's here.'

'What's tribute?' Gaia asked.

'A payment. For the privilege of being allowed to live here.' Ambrose glanced at the broken-down village and the barren ground beyond, and gave a wry smile. 'I thought - hoped - he'd leave us alone. We paid his father well, in the golden days, but once the mines were closed we weren't worth the journey. Only the old Lord's dead now, and rumour says that this one's going through his fortune as fast as fire through straw. Which means, sadly for us, Gaia, that he's looking for money wherever he can get it.' He gazed up at the descending craft. 'I must go and receive him. Come.'

They walked down the slope to the open space at the cliff's edge. Parhelion's men stood in a circle around a silver cloth laid out on the rough ground, watched by the gathered villagers. As Gaia and Ambrose reached the crowd, the air trembled, shuddered, and was suddenly full of the wind of hundreds of beating wings. The flying carriage swooped low above their heads and banked in a sharp turn. It hovered briefly and descended; the basket settled lightly on the ground, and the eagles landed around it, shaking out their wings. Parhelion's men ripped open the sacks that lay piled at the top of the cliff, and flung dozens of dead rabbits to the birds, which bounced and strained against their harnesses; snapping at one another; tearing at the bloodied meat with sharp beaks and talons.

Gaia looked away. Tal was standing close to Mai at the other side of the crowd. There was no sign of Jason. In the carriage, a big, well-fed man was watching with a cold smile as the eagles fought and fed. He wore a flowing silver wig that reached his shoulders, and a long coat of purple silk embroidered with silver thread. When the birds had finished their savage meal, he climbed out of the carriage, and gazed round the desolate village. Ambrose let go of Gaia's hand, walked to the edge of the silver cloth, and lowered himself to kneel stiffly on the hard ground with his head bowed.

'My Lord,' he began. 'I bid you welcome…'

He was interrupted by a shout of 'Oy! Thief!' and Gaia's breath turned to ice in her throat, as two of Parhelion's men pushed past Ambrose, dragging Jason with them. They flung him to the ground at Parhelion's feet. His satchel burst open, and a shower of tiny red fruits scattered like sparks: bouncing and rolling and finally falling still. Jason struggled to his knees. One of the men pushed him down again and put a foot on his neck.

'Stealing rabbits, my Lord,' he said.

'Chain him. Take him when you leave.' Parhelion turned toward the village.

'No!' Gaia stepped forward and stood in his path; he tried to sidestep her, but she moved and blocked his way again, looking him full in the face, meeting his gaze with angry eyes.

'It's not fair,' she said. 'It's only a rabbit, and you've got hundreds. And if you can feed eagles why can't you…'

'Gaia.' Ambrose took her arm and moved her gently aside. He bowed to Parhelion. 'My Lord, please. His parents are dead; his father in the disaster; his mother soon after, and the times are hard; hungry; he…'

'Do you not know the law?' Parhelion cut across him. 'The penalty for stealing is enslavement. Are you expecting me to break the statutes of the republic?'

'No; but to be merciful, My Lord. Your father…' Ambrose began, but Parhelion had already turned away, and was striding up the village track. His men shepherded the villagers after him up to the market place, but Gaia ducked out of sight behind a pillar, slipped away, and hurried back to the clifftop. She found Jason sitting on the ground next to the carriage, his wrists and ankles shackled. He gave her a fleeting smile and a wink, but he was hollow-eyed and shivering. She tugged at the heavy chains on his wrists. The links were too thick to break or even bend.

'No good. Tried that.' Jason gave her another lopsided smile, and shivered again. She sat down next to him, pressing close to shelter him from the biting wind howling down from the mountains: though she knew that it was fear as much as cold that was making him tremble. They sat in silence for a while, then he nudged her.

'Gaia,' he said, and she looked up to see Mai running down the slope towards them.

'You need to come home, Gaia.' Mai looked at Jason, and pressed her hands to her mouth. 'I'm *sorry*. They said, we all have to go home and wait.'

'Go,' Jason said. But as Gaia stood, he reached up, clumsily because of the chains, and caught her hand in both of his, and said her name again. She crouched down and hugged him, holding him close, feeling fury and fear surging through her like fire. 'Hey,' he whispered. 'I'll be fine.'

'I know,' she said, except she didn't believe it and she could tell that he didn't either.

'Look after the goats for me.'

'Yes.'

'Go on. You better go.' He pushed her gently away. She stood. She didn't want to turn away from him, so she walked backwards up the slope, holding his gaze, until she reached the outskirts of the village. She paused then, and as she stared back at him, he raised one shackled hand in an awkward farewell.

After that she couldn't look at him without crying. She turned away and stumbled after Mai, along the path home, and up the steps into the shadowed room where Tal was already waiting. Gaia sat down at the table and hid her face in her hands.

'I've been thinking, Mum,' Tal said. 'This tribute...'

'Yes.' Even through her own tears Gaia could hear Mai's voice shaking.

'You said we'd have to give him goats or gold. But what about the amulet?'

Gaia raised her head. 'No!'

'It makes *sense*, Gaia,' Tal said. 'We can't afford to lose the goats. And we know we can trade the gold, but we don't know if Rackin would take the amulet. And if not...'

'Shut up. I *know*.' Gaia reached into the pouch for the amulet, laid it on the table, and traced her finger sadly along the carvings. 'It's just ... I feel as if I *belong* to it.'

'Arctos' sake,' Tal muttered. Mai sat next to Gaia and took her hands. 'Your father felt like that too. I don't want to lose it either, Gaia. Only...

'Only Tal's right, isn't he?' Gaia's voice was dull with tears. Jason *and* her amulet: both loved, both lost on the same day. She cradled the fragment of polished stone, while Mai held her, and Tal paced to and fro in front of the empty hearth. At last the door was flung open, and Parhelion strode into the room, followed by a small rat-featured man with clever eyes.

'Well, Scrimp?' said Parhelion.

The small man fumbled through the yellowed, dog-eared pages of a large leather book. 'The head of the household is Athanasius, my Lord.'

'Athanasius is dead,' said Mai.

'*Another* one.' Parhelion tutted impatiently. 'Correct the book, Scrimp.'

Scrimp had already fished pen and ink out of his coat pocket, and was scratching out an entry in the heavy book, and writing new words in a small even script. Parhelion waited irritably, his eyes wandering round the bare room with a look of resentful disappointment. When Scrimp had finished writing, Parhelion asked, 'How much?'

'Last time it was five seraphs, my Lord, but...'

'*Five* seraphs?' Mai swallowed.

'Or goods to the same value,' Scrimp said.

Mai glanced at Gaia. 'You don't have to.'

'No. I do.' Gaia stepped forward and offered the amulet to Scrimp with the smooth face up. He took it, studied it doubtfully and turned it over. Shock washed across his narrow face and he darted a sharp look at Gaia. 'Where …?'

'Let *me* see that!' Parhelion held out his hand, and Scrimp passed the amulet to him. Against the white silk of his gloves, it looked shabby and worn, a little scrap of nothing. His eyes darkened.

'Are you making fun of me?'

'It's very old, my Lord,' Mai stammered. 'It…'

'Old and worthless *junk!*' Parhelion flung the amulet aside. It skittered across the floor and under the table, and Gaia dived to rescue it. Warm relief swept through her; but Mai was stammering,

'I'm sorry, My Lord. We have goats…'

'*Goats!* Do you know how many *stinking* goats I've been given today?' Parhelion shook his head scornfully, and ran his gaze around the room again. His eyes rested on Tal, holding Mai's arm, and Gaia: crouching on the floor, clutching the amulet in her clenched hand. She thought of Jason, chained and shaking, and returned his look with all the fury she could muster.

'I'll take the boy,' Parhelion said. 'And the girl. Despite her swansprite's eyes. Nothing else you've got is worth *anything.*'

'*No!*' Mai broke free of Tal, fell to her knees at the hearth, and tugged out the loose stone. She scrambled up with the package in her hand and shook the gold from its leather wrapping. Both bars fell with a heavy clunk onto the table.

Parhelion's eyes gleamed. He snapped his fingers, and Scrimp picked up the gold, stowed it in his satchel with his heavy book, and fastened the buckles, giving Gaia a long searching look.

'Come, Scrimp!' Parhelion snapped his fingers again, strode to the door and flung it open. Afternoon was fading now and the daylight had almost gone. Grey storm clouds swaddled the mountains and wind and heavy rain swept across the village. Lightning split the sky with a clap of thunder.

'We can't *fly* in this, my Lord,' Scrimp began, but Parhelion had already pulled his cloak closely round himself and was hurrying out into the pouring rain. Scrimp gave a last wondering look back at Gaia, and followed him, stumbling on the wet steps.

Parhelion

From the doorway, Gaia, Tal and Mai watched them go. As they reached the track, lightning crashed again, and high overhead there was a chaos of giant swooping wings and fire. Parhelion stared wildly up at the dragons, and then at Gaia. 'You!' he shouted. 'This was you...'

Scrimp dragged at his arm; yelled, 'Hurry, my Lord!' and they began to run again. Slipping and sliding on the wet ground, fighting the wind and the blinding rain, they reached the carriage and scrambled aboard. The eagles struggled into the stormy air. As they lifted off there was a white glare of lightning, and Gaia glimpsed Parhelion clutching at Scrimp in terror while the gilded wickerwork burned silver beneath them. Then they were gone: vanished into the storm and the falling night.

An Unlucky Game of Cards

'Let's get inside,' said Tal. 'It's freezing out here.' They retreated into the house and he slammed the door against the storm, guided Mai to her seat at the fire and wrapped a blanket round her shoulders. She caught his hand and tugged him close: he let her hold him for a moment, then freed himself gently, and knelt to light a fire, blowing the first glow into a weak blaze. Reaching for his satchel, he took out the morning's fish, slit them open, and laid them on the grill over the flames. In the dripping oil, the fire sizzled and flared.

'Gaia? You had some garberries, didn't you?' Gaia opened her bag, took out a berry, and rolled it between her finger and thumb; remembering the scattered berries on the path, and Jason's cold hands clutching hers.

'I should fetch Jason's goats.'

'You'll get soaked,' Tal said.

'I promised.'

She wrapped a scarf around her head and slipped outside. The storm had moved away: lightning reflected from the high snowfields and the thunder had died to a distant rumble. But the rain was still falling heavily and the wind snatched at her as she rounded the corner of the house. Head down, she fought through the weather to Jason's house, climbed the steps and pushed open the door.

For a moment she hesitated on the threshold, imagining him stepping out of the shadows. But the silent, cold room had the feeling of somewhere long abandoned. Gaia stepped inside, picked up a blanket from the floor, and held it to her face. The very faint scent of Jason that it carried was like an ancient memory.

Feeling her way through the darkness, she found the grain bin, lifted the lid and dipped her hands into the grain he had stolen from Rackin. She cried then, tears falling warm on her hands, because she could picture him so clearly, grinning and triumphant after pulling that trick. She had laughed at him for it. But now he had tried it again with Parhelion, and that had been a *stupid* thing to do, because those rabbits had been too well-guarded, and Parhelion was a man without mercy.

She ran another handful of grain through her fingers. *If I'd told him he was an idiot, stealing from Rackin, would he have left those rabbits alone?*

But it was done, and he was gone, and there was nothing to do about it, and no sense leaving things that could be useful. She poured the grain into the blanket, twisted it into a bundle and slung it over her shoulder. Shutting the door on the empty shadows, she fetched Jason's goats from the cellar, dragged them home through the rain and penned them with their own flock. As she came out of the goathouse, she saw Ambrose, hesitating at the foot of the steps.

'Ambrose!'

He turned towards her, peering through the rainy darkness. '*Gaia!* Thank all the moons and stars. Is... Tal...?'

'He's here,' she said quickly. 'Mum had some gold left. Just two pieces. I thought it might not be enough...' Her voice broke a little with remembered fear.

'It's alright, Gaia,' Ambrose said, but she shook her head, because Jason was gone, *and* the gold that Mai had been keeping to buy grain and fodder and firewood to see them through the winter. Ambrose caught hold of her hand.

'Ambrose!' she exclaimed. You're freezing. Have you been outside all evening?'

'I've been visiting people.' He sounded old and defeated, and she imagined him, trudging through the storm, from one sad house to another, with only pity to offer. She led him up the steps, out of the wind and rain into the shelter of the house. Tal looked up from the fireside and smiled a welcome through a haze of fishy smoke. Mai stood up and put her arms round Ambrose. She guided him into her own chair, and wrapped her blanket round him.

'Mai,' he said. 'He took so many children. Not just Jason. Cassie. Lal's twins, Alex...'

'Oh, Ambrose.' Mai crouched down and took his hands between her own. They sat in silence, holding hands, comforting one another.

'Um...' Tal said. This fish is ready.'

Ambrose raised his head, and smiled.

'Well done, Tal. Let's eat. And look: moonlight on us, too.' He gestured at the window. The storm had passed, leaving a clear sky where Brumas, sad misty god of the mid-Autumn, shone almost full. They gathered round the table in the white light.

'Only Brumas,' Ambrose said. 'It's still too early for dragons. Dragons today; a dragon in the summer: it makes you think something's gone wrong with the world. What's the matter, Gaia?'

'The dragons.' Gaia ran her finger round her plate. 'I think... I think Parhelion said *I* made them come. And he said I had a...a *swansprite's* eyes. What does that mean?'

'Nothing,' Ambrose reached across the table and patted her hand. 'Nothing. Just that he didn't like the way you were looking at him.'

'But what's a swansprite?' Gaia persisted.

'It's just a lowland superstition...'

Tell me, Ambrose.'

'Oh, Gaia.' Ambrose sighed. 'Alright. In the lowlands they believe some people can channel the power of the moons, to control things no ordinary person can control. Animals, the weather, illness. And they say that they can call down evil on anyone they hate.'

'I hated Parhelion,' Gaia said. 'Because of Jason. If I could have summoned dragons to him, I would have. But I don't think I did.'

'I don't think so either,' said Ambrose. 'I think the dragons saw one of their own and came to greet him. After all, what else is Parhelion but a dragon in a man's skin?'

The moonlight dimmed and lightened again as a last wisp of storm cloud drifted across it. 'You might have brought the dragons, Gaia,' Tal said. 'That might be what the amulet does.'

'The amulet!' Ambrose looked enquiringly at Mai.

'I've given it to Gaia. She's thirteen now, remember.'

'Of course. Can I see it, Gaia?'

Gaia took out the slender white square and placed it in Ambrose's hand. It gleamed palely in the moonlight and he traced the carving with a gnarled forefinger. 'I'm glad you remembered to give it to her, Mai.' He smiled. 'I remember when Athanasius first had it. He kept asking *what's it for?* He was like that, your dad. Very *practical*.'

'A swansprite's thing,' said Tal. 'Maybe that's what it is.'

'It's not,' Gaia said.

'How do you *know*?'

28

'It just doesn't feel like it.' The amulet was mysterious and strange, but she had never felt any stirring in it, none of the immense energy that must be needed to change things that the moons ruled.

'But Mum told us it was powerful,' argued Tal.

'Only in the right place,' said Ambrose.

They turned to him in surprise.

'It has power,' he said, as if he was reciting words that were engraved on his memory, like the symbols on the amulet. 'To bring our family greatness and glory and honour. But its power will only be revealed when it's read in the right place. That's the story, anyway.'

'Read?' Gaia said. 'What does it say?'

Ambrose shook his head. 'I don't know. I don't know where the right place is, either. Somebody must have done, once, I suppose, but that's all lost now.' He got up, stiffly, from the table. 'I must be going. Will one of you walk with me, a little way?'

'I will.' Gaia jumped up and wrapped her shawl round her shoulders. They stepped out into the moonlight together.

'Mai seemed tired tonight,' said Ambrose, when they were far enough from the door not to be heard.

'She's worried. And she'll be more worried now, after today, won't she?'

'I'm afraid so.' He stopped, leaning on his stick, and gazed sadly at the village. Moonlight silvered his grey hair and deepened the lines on his face. 'Maybe you'll find the secret of the amulet, Gaia. Sweet heavens, we could do with some luck, now more than ever. Goodnight, my dear. Don't come any further.'

She watched him making his heavy way along the path, then she took out the amulet and held it tightly. It was as if she could feel the warmth of her father's fingers on it, and the touch of all the generations before him ... There was a comfort in it but no power. And how could she read it in the right place, when no-one knew where that was; when no-one could read it at all?

Parhelion's eagles battled the violent winds. Again and again, the driver begged his Lordship to put down somewhere, anywhere; just to wait for the weather to ease. But Parhelion was more afraid of the dragons than the storm: he imagined them, still chasing him, just out of sight behind the sheets of rain. So he commanded his driver to fly on, until finally the storm passed, leaving the sky peaceful and empty. Below them, the moon glimmered on water, and they saw the faint points of light that meant a town.

Over the din of the eagles' beating wings, Parhelion bellowed to his driver. 'Where's that?'

'Trebburn, my Lord.'

'Lanneret's town.'

'Even so, we should land, my Lord. The birds won't fly much further.'

'Very well.' Parhelion leaned back in his seat. The carriage banked and swooped down over a wide market-place; narrow, dark streets; a substantial house whose lights reflected off the river, and finally landed with a squelch in the muddy waterlogged garden of a waterside tavern. Soaked and shivering, Parhelion followed Scrimp across the wet garden, and through a back door into a dingy corridor. From a closed room at the far end came the muffled roar of conversation and laughter.

'A coarse place,' Parhelion muttered.

'But shelter for the night, my Lord.' Scrimp bustled along the corridor and opened the door, releasing the smells of spilt wine, hot food and sweat; the din of laughter and argument; the heat of a smoky fire. Parhelion pressed a handkerchief to his nose as he picked his way after Scrimp through the crowded room, and a trail of whispering broke out behind them. 'He's not. He can't be... He *is*. That's silver in his coat...'

They pushed their way to the bar.

'Good evening,' Scrimp said.

The landlord, preoccupied with an argument between two men that looked as if it might turn into a fight, ignored him.

'His *Lordship* and I require accommodation for the night.'

The landlord whipped round. His eyes flickered over Parhelion's cloak: its noble indigo was barely visible in the half light, but the silver threads running through it caught the faint glimmer of a guttering candle on the bar and shimmered like strands of moonlight.

'My Lord,' the landlord stammered. 'Welcome... My name's Casker, my Lord, and I... I bid you welcome to the Roaring Dragon.'

Parhelion started and looked wildly over his shoulder.

'It's the name of the *inn*, my Lord.' Scrimp rolled his eyes. 'Lord Parhelion and I were caught in the storm. We require beds for the night, and a private parlour for our dinner.'

'Yes sir! My Lord.' It was market day, and all the rooms were taken, but no-one would protest at being turned out for an emergency like this. 'But… this is our only sitting room… I'll clear a space for you.'

Casker vaulted over the bar, and chivvied the drinkers away from the fireside, silencing their protests with a fierce whisper of *'Parhelion!'* Arguments and laughter died into an awed murmur as Parhelion and Scrimp took their seats. On his way back to the bar, Casker gave a fleeting smile. 'Well, well,' he thought. 'Never been this polite in here before. Let's hope we can keep it going till morning…'

'Do you have any decent wine?' Parhelion's voice rang strong and complaining across the room.

'Oh… My Lord… yes…' Casker fumbled under the bar.

'Give him the Castellan, Casker. It's the only drinkable stuff you've got.' The speaker was a big man: well-dressed and handsome, despite an old scar on one cheek. He approached Parhelion's table and bowed to him.

'Welcome to Trebburn, my Lord. My name's Braggley. I trade here.' He bowed again. Parhelion regarded him coldly.

'May I buy you a bottle of wine, my Lord?' Braggley went on. 'Casker gets the Castellan de Brulemel especially for me. The rest of the cellar… well, I'd best not say what *that* tastes of.' He laughed. Parhelion looked at him coldly again.

'Oh, and if you'd do me the honour, I've a guest wing that's all yours for the night. I live just across the river.'

Parhelion remembered the solid house on the opposite bank. It would have to be better than the Roaring Dragon. He had never stayed in a place like this, and he didn't want to now, if it could be avoided. He nodded. 'Much obliged.'

'A pleasure. Ah, and here's the Castellan. Thanks, Casker.' Braggley took the bottle, uncorked it and filled two glasses to the brim.

'I won't, thank you.' Scrimp pushed his glass primly aside. Parhelion lifted his, sniffed, sipped, and looked at Braggley in surprise. This *was* a good wine; one that he wouldn't have been surprised to find on the best tables in Freehaven. Braggley grinned.

'Good, isn't it?'

Parhelion nodded and swallowed a long draft of the heady, rich wine. He gestured Braggley graciously into an empty chair, pushed Scrimp's glass towards him, and began to relax. Over the second bottle, he became talkative, and Braggley took a pack of cards out of his pocket and riffled through them, carelessly. 'D'you play, my Lord?'

'My Lord…' murmured Scrimp.

'Don't be boring, Scrimp. A bore,' Parhelion said to Braggley. 'My Treasurer is a bore. Yes. I play.'

'Shemmy?' Braggley threw five golden serafs onto the table.

'Ah,' said Parhelion. 'I'm somewhat short of ready cash…' He picked up Scrimp's satchel and fumbled inside it. 'I could put this on the table.' He pulled out one of the ingots that Mai had given him. Braggley whistled.

'That's fine,' he said. 'May I?'

Parhelion handed him the gold, and Braggley turned it over, watching the rich gleam of the metal in the leaping firelight. 'Where did this come from?'

'Up in the mountains.'

Braggley looked at him in surprise. 'I thought those mines closed down years ago?'

'They did, yes, but one of my vassals had kept this. The only gold I got today.' He scowled. 'I had to take most of my tribute in goats and slaves.'

'Slaves?' Braggley lifted his glass casually.

'Children,' said Parhelion. 'Skinny, but tough enough. You'll see them at the market in a couple of days.'

'I look forward to it. Shall we play?'

Parhelion woke to watery daylight, an insistent tapping at his door and Scrimp's thin voice scraping at his eardrums. 'My Lord?'

'Go away!'

'It's getting late, my Lord. I understand that you agreed to take Mr Braggley hunting this morning?'

Parhelion groaned, queasy at the thought of feathers and fur and blood. 'Alright. I'm coming.' He rolled out of bed, crossed to the window and peered across the rain-pitted river to the ramshackle garden of the Roaring Dragon. That gold. Had he really lost it? Both pieces? He leaned his forehead against the cool glass. He didn't look forward to explaining that to Scrimp. He dressed gloomily, and descended the stairs. In the hall, a common-looking person accosted him.

'Morning, my Lord! That was quite a night.'

Parhelion shuddered.

'Feeling a bit fragile?' Braggley laughed, and Parhelion shuddered again. Last night he had thought of this man as his new best friend: rough around the edges, perhaps, but a decent sort, the salt of the earth. He had even offered to introduce Braggley to his mother - a thought that now sent him into a stomach-twisting panic. He looked wildly at Scrimp. *Get me out of this.* His Treasurer looked back at him with perfect dry understanding.

'I'm afraid we should be leaving, My Lord. Pressing business in Freehaven.'

'Of course.' Parhelion gave a silent sigh of relief. Scrimp was a bore, but he had his uses. 'Order the carriage, would you?'

'Already done, my Lord.' Scrimp nodded out of the window. The carriage flew low across the river and came to a perfect landing on the lawn. With an icy farewell to Braggley, Parhelion followed Scrimp out into the rain, across the damp grass and into the carriage.

From his study window, Braggley watched the eagle carriage soar skywards and out of sight. As it disappeared into the heavy clouds, he chuckled, and picked up one of the two gold ingots from his desk. It felt satisfyingly weighty, but he cared more for the scribbled IOU tucked into his pocket. He doubted Parhelion would even remember writing it.

A few mornings later, Braggley sauntered through the narrow town streets to the market-place. Parhelion's men were instantly identifiable in their indigo livery, standing guard over some scrawny goats and half a dozen dark-haired children in chains. Braggley narrowed his eyes and studied the children. 'Nice,' he murmured, and having no further business that morning, he wandered on his way, glancing occasionally, thoughtfully, up at the mountains as he went.

Disaster

Tal was up early to do the milking. He hurried through the ice-laden air, hands and face stinging from the cold, and in the shelter under the house, he huddled among the goats for warmth. He tried out a tune as he milked, until raised voices from the room above made him stop. He sighed. Mum and Gaia were arguing again.

'What d'you mean, it's *going* to be alright? It's *already* not alright!' Gaia's words rang with anger. Mai spoke too quietly for him to make out her reply, but he could hear the tightness in her voice.

'I mean,' Gaia shouted, 'there's never enough to eat! We're always hungry. Tal *cries* sometimes because he's so hungry.'

He stood up, knocking the milking stool over. Again, he couldn't hear Mai's answer.

'Yes, he does, Mum,' Gaia shouted. 'You just haven't noticed. *Arctos!* If Dad was still alive… He wouldn't just have sat here saying *no, you can't leave the mountain, it's forbidden…*'

Tal shoved through the goats, hurtled up the steps into the house, and hit Gaia, hard, an open-palmed slap across her cheek that made his own skin sting. 'Shut up!' he almost screamed. 'Just shut up!'

There were tears of pain in her eyes, but when she spoke her voice was ice-cold. 'Face it, Tal. She's not going to get us through this.' She pushed past him and slammed the door behind her. Mai dropped into her chair and covered her face with her hands. Tal knelt in front of her and touched her softly.

'Mum?'

'I'm sorry,' she said. 'I'm sorry. I'm so sorry…'

'No! *You've* got nothing to be sorry for. She's the one who should be sorry; she's got no right…'

'Look at you, though.' Mai closed her hand round his thin wrist. 'I can feel all your bones. Do you really cry because you're hungry?'

He'd have hit Gaia again if she'd been standing there. 'Once,' he mumbled. 'We were out late. That's all. It's fine. It's just *winter.*'

'Oh, *Tal.*' She held him close; it was a long time before she let him go and gave him a little push. 'Go on. Better get those goats out while the daylight lasts.'

Gaia was sitting on the wall at the clifftop, her back to the house. Tal ran to her, grabbed her and turned her to face him. 'Don't you dare, ever, *ever*, say anything like that to Mum again!' Without waiting for her, he ran back up the slope, fetched the goats, and started out for the pasture, keeping in the middle of the flock to ward off the cold.

Hesperal, last of the autumn moons, had brought bitter winds and storms, and the summer pastures were covered in deep snow now. Tal took the winter route: through the village, past the old mine, and up a steep path by a falling stream that had frozen into a waterfall of ice. At the top of the path, he paused to catch his breath. Gaia had followed him and she caught up with him while he was resting.

'Sorry,' she said.

'It's not me you need to apologise to.'

He looked down at the village: the houses seemed tiny and unprotected against the vastness of the hills and the cold sky.

'I know,' Gaia said. 'Shall I go and see her now?'

'No time.'

She looked disappointed, and he thought, *serves her right. Let her wait.* In silence, they took the long walk that brought them down into a lonely valley, so enclosed that all you could see from it were the high snowfields; the changing clouds in the cold sky; and the straggling lines of migrating birds beating the difficult passage through the winds that raged around the mountain tops.

Shut in and silent, this valley always made Gaia feel edgy, and today it was worse because all she wanted to do was go and make her peace with Mai. The day dragged past. Slowly, the sky lightened to a midday blue that was almost white. Slowly it darkened again. Gaia pulled Jason's blanket tight around her shoulders.

'It's getting late, Tal.'

'I know.' He raised his voice to call the goats and they set off for home: scrambling up out of the valley, trudging across the snow-covered upland and down into the last valley before the village. Ahead of them now lay one more steep climb, a slippery descent of the waterfall path, and a fast walk home. Tal plodded steadily up the slope, eyes firmly on his feet and the next step. But Gaia set off too fast and halfway up she stopped to catch her breath, glancing ahead to see how far she still had to go.

A drench of fear washed through her, colder than the evening and the wind and the snow. There was a smudge on the sky: a cloud of drifting black rising into the dusk.

'Tal!' she screamed. Tal stopped, stared, and began to run, the excited goats leaping around him. She flung herself after him, struggling up the difficult hill, stumbling over sharp stones and tough thorny roots. Dimly, she realised that he had crested the slope. He yelled, 'Gaia!' and she took the last few steps at a trembling run, halted next to him, and stared down in disbelief at the village.

The market was ablaze. White-hearted flame savaged through its timbered columns and roofs, and as they watched, one side of the building swayed and collapsed. A shower of sparks billowed orange into the closing evening.

'There's no-one fighting it,' Gaia whispered. That was the real horror, because the market was a precious place and no-one in the village would willingly leave it to burn. 'Where is everyone?'

'I don't know. Come on, Gaia. *Run!*'

They skidded down the icy path alongside the waterfall and pelted into the village; passed the blazing market place, turned onto the homeward track, and juddered to a halt. Every house here had been burned: low flames flickered and smoke wreathed among their fallen stones and blackened timbers. Tal met Gaia's horrified eyes wordlessly. They started to run again, their feet kicking up drifting black ash from the path.

Home was destroyed: burned to a ruin. Tal ran to the bottom of the steps and yelled, 'Mum!' His voice echoed from the cliffs, but the only answer from the house was the faint hiss and murmur of fire. Gaia pushed past him, and climbed up to the doorway. In the sad light of dying flames and falling evening, she stared at the wreckage of the house. The floorboards and beams had burned through and collapsed into the cellar. Most of the roof had fallen in and as she watched, one of the last big rafters gave way and crashed onto the debris below, bringing down an avalanche of slates.

'Get down, Gaia,' Tal said from behind her. 'It's not safe.'

They stumbled down the steps, rounded the house, and peered into the cellar, but there was nothing there except smouldering timbers and shattered slates. Tal turned away and stared back up the track. The village stood desolate. Fading fires flickered in the dark houses, and there was a deep silence, broken only by the occasional fall of stone and slate. Gaia caught hold of Tal's hand.

'Tal. Where *is* she?'

'I don't know.' He pulled free of her, cupped his hands to his mouth and yelled: 'Mum! Mum!' His voice echoed into the vast darkness and died away. He tilted his head to listen. Above the small snuffling of the goats breathing and the whisper of dying fires, he heard stumbling footsteps, and through the shifting half light of the flames he saw Ambrose hurrying towards them along the track. They ran to meet him, and he flung his arms round them and held them close.

'Thank heavens, you two. I thought…'

'Ambrose. Where's Mum?' Gaia wriggled out of his embrace and stared at him. There was a bleak sadness in the heavy stoop of his shoulders. 'Is she …Is she…?'

'She's alive,' he said. But his voice was desolate, and she felt scared and not comforted. 'Come inside. I'll tell you.' He led them through the ruined village and up the rough slope to a low opening in the rocky cliff.

'Ambrose, this is the *mine!*' Gaia took a step back. This was a dark and hallowed place; a place of death and memory where no-one ever went. If he meant them to go in *here*, then their world had surely been smashed to pieces.

'There's nowhere else,' Ambrose said. 'It's alright. We're only just inside, in the moonsight, and it's sheltered, and safe. There's room for the goats.'

Gaia gripped Tal's hand as they ducked through the opening into a low chamber hollowed out from the rock. It was sheltered from the wind, but damp and cold despite the weak fire that was filling the air with a bitter smoke. A few familiar figures crouched at the fireside: Ambrose's wife, Alma; old Thea; three children. But no-one else.

'Ambrose?' Alma peered through the smoky darkness. 'Who's that?'

'Gaia and Tal.'

'*Ambrose,*' Gaia said again. 'What happened? Where is everyone? Where's *Mum?*'

'They've been taken.' Ambrose wiped his hand over his face. 'There was an attack. They came up the ladders. There was no time to sound the alarm.'

'Who?'

'Slavers,' said Ambrose. 'They took anyone they could sell. They left me and Alma and Thea because we're too old. But they took Mai and the others and all the children they could find. I couldn't keep them safe. I'm sorry.' His voice sounded full of tears. *Ambrose crying*: it was the most frightening thing Gaia had ever heard. 'I'll just have one more look,' he said, and he ducked back out into the darkness.

Alma stood up and took Gaia and Tal's hands. 'Come and get warm,' she said, and Gaia let herself be led to the fire. She ate without tasting anything, and when she lay down on the stone floor it was a long time before she could sleep. She watched the changing patterns of moonlight; unable to frame a single thought, except *I didn't say sorry.*

She woke next morning to the ache of hard stone beneath her, grey daylight falling at an unfamiliar angle – and the savage memory of what had happened. Tal was already awake, sitting with his head on his knees, staring at nothing.

'Tal?' she said.

'Should do the goats.' He got up without looking at her and buried himself among the flock at the back of the cave. When Tal milked, he whistled or sang, always: but today he was dumb, and his silence battered Gaia's ears like the howling of a winter storm. Unable to bear it, she blundered out of the cave. Day had dawned, but the light was heavy and yellow; a few solitary snowflakes drifted in the air. Ambrose was climbing the path from the village, driving a handful of cream and black goats. A dragon soared high overhead and they scattered in panic across the rocky ground. Ambrose stared at them helplessly. Gaia went to him and put her hand on his arm.

'I'll help you round them up.'

'Thanks, Gaia.'

'Where's Selene? They're hers, aren't they?'

He nodded. 'They've been out all night. That's why they're so scared.' He met Gaia's eyes. 'I can't find her. She must have been taken too.'

They stayed around the mine all morning, sheltering inside whenever the snow became too heavy, coming out into the clear air to escape the suffocating smoke whenever the weather eased. Towards midday, Gaia was sitting with Ambrose on the broad stone at the mine's entrance; remembering the day when she had sat and raged here, when her biggest trouble in the world had been a piece of ruined weaving, and Mum's angry disappointment. The memory was shattered by the clamorous peal of the market bell. She clutched Ambrose's arm.

'What's that?'

For a moment he looked as alarmed as her, then he relaxed. 'Of course. Full moon. It's Rackin. Come.'

They found Rackin at the market place, wrapped in a huge fur coat that made him look bigger than ever. He was staring at the chaos of fallen tiles and smouldering beams which here and there still flickered into flame.

'Dragon's teeth, Ambrose. What have you done here?'

'Not us,' said Ambrose. 'Slavers. They came yesterday. They took almost everyone.'

'Dragon's teeth,' said Rackin again. 'Who were they?'

'I don't know. There was a big man. Taller than you, dark-haired...'

'Scar on his cheek?'

Ambrose nodded, and Rackin blew out a long breath that curled like freezing smoke. 'Braggley. Sweet heavens. I'm sorry, Ambrose. You're a cussed lot up here, but you didn't deserve that.' He gave a long look at the ruins of the market place and the broken empty village beyond. 'What now? Where will you go?'

'Go? Nowhere. We'll stay.'

'Ambrose, that's *madness*. I'll come back in spring and find you dead from cold and hunger. You *have* to leave.'

'No.' Ambrose shook his head. 'There's hunger in the lowlands, you told us that yourself. You think they'll help us - needy strangers with nothing to give? And if anyone comes back, I have to be here for them.'

'No-one escapes from Braggley, Ambrose, and slaves are rarely freed. You'll wait a long time to see any of them again.' Rackin sighed. 'You're right, though; there's little charity in the lowlands these days. Still, it's got to be better than staying here. It's freezing already; you've nowhere to live…'

'Our ancestors lived in the caves. We'll do that. We'll salvage whatever's left in the houses, we have our goats…'

'And fodder? Fuel? Grain?'

'We'll gather what we can before the heavy snows.'

Rackin glanced at the leaden sky. 'You haven't got much time.'

'No. So, forgive me if I say farewell and set to work.' Ambrose bowed and turned away.

'Wait!' Rackin called him back. 'You're a fool, Ambrose, but you're a good man, and Braggley's an evil…' He spat into the embers of the fire. 'I don't want to see you beaten by him. Fetch whoever's left. Send them to carry the goods up. There's wheat, straw and wood. Enough to keep a few of you going till spring, if you're careful.'

'But we can't…'

'I know you can't pay. I'll wait. Till you discover gold again.' He grinned. 'Salvage, huh? Need a hand?'

'I… Mr Rackin…'

'Call me John. Let's get to work.'

They worked hard all afternoon, Rackin like a strong giant bear in their midst: cheering and encouraging them, carrying the heaviest loads. Before the moon was up, the mine had been transformed. Rough shelves built of rescued stones and timber carried the few unbroken storage jars they had found, brimming with Rackin's gifted grain. Straw and firewood were stacked against the wall. The empty sacks had been stuffed with heather to make rough mattresses. A good fire was burning. Rackin, surveying the rocky chamber, and the little circle around the fire, smiled. 'Could be worse. You stand a chance now, anyway.'

'Thank you, John,' said Ambrose. 'And… It's very late for you to go down the ladders now. We can't offer much of a full moon celebration, but you're welcome to stay.'

'Gladly.' Rackin settled himself next to Tal. They ate a simple meal, and Ambrose told the story of Chamboleyne and the children. In the silence that followed, Gaia fell straight into an exhausted sleep, but only to dream of Mai as she had last seen her, broken and in tears at the end of that unforgivable argument. It was an unbearable dream, and she forced herself awake from it, to find Ambrose and Rackin talking quietly over the dying fire.

'Where will he have taken them, John?'

'Braggley lives at Trebburn Parva. To the market there, I guess.'

'Is there any way I could get them back?'

'You'd have to buy them, and' - he glanced round the rocky chamber - 'you've nothing here that's worth that kind of money. You couldn't afford *one* of them.'

'So I've lost them,' said Ambrose hopelessly.

Gaia sat up. 'What about my amulet?'

'Gaia,' said Ambrose. 'Go back to sleep.'

She ignored him, tipped the slender square out of its pouch and held it out to Rackin.

'Here. What do you think? It's old, and there's a story that it's precious.'

'You lot and your stories,' murmured Rackin. 'Let me look.' He turned the amulet gently in his big hands, squinting at it in the firelight. 'Moonswood,' he murmured.

'*Moonswood?*' Gaia asked. 'I thought it was stone. It doesn't look like wood.'

'It's not really wood,' Rackin explained. 'It's ancient tree sap, turned hard. More like stone than wood.'

'Moonswood. Is it precious?'

'Rare enough.' Rackin held it closer to the firelight. 'Funny little thing. Is that *writing?*'

'Can you read it?' Gaia asked.

Rackin shook his head. 'Can't make it out.' He frowned. 'It's not my sort of thing. Corn, cloth, cheese: I can put a price on those as quick as blinking. But this... I haven't the first idea. And no-one in Trebburn trades in anything like this. The only place to sell it would be Freehaven. I'm sorry.'

He handed the amulet back to Gaia, and Ambrose said, 'Never mind, Gaia. It was a good idea. Go back to sleep now.'

She gave the moonswood square to Rackin again. 'Couldn't you take it to Freehaven?'

'Out of my patch, I'm afraid. I don't trade that far.'

'So how can *I* get there?'

'No, Gaia,' said Ambrose. 'You don't leave the mountain.'

41

She rounded on him, furious. 'Because of what a dead man said, hundreds of years ago? Because once upon a time he brought us luck? *Look* at us, Ambrose.' She gestured round the dim smoky cave. 'Where's his luck now?'

Ambrose didn't answer, and she said to Rackin, 'What do you think?'

'About - what's his name? - Chamboleyne?' Rackin hesitated. 'I think you're right. I'm sorry, Ambrose; I'm a guest, I know; it's not my place. But she is right, isn't she? He's dead and gone, and you've had no luck for a long time.' He turned to Gaia. 'As to going to Freehaven... I don't know. It's full of ifs. *If* you get there, *if* that amulet's worth anything, *if* you manage to sell it, *if* the people who bought Mai are prepared to sell her back to you... It's a slim chance.'

'But it *is* a chance,' she insisted. 'Isn't it?'

'Yes,' he admitted. 'And the only one that I can see.'

'Then I'm going,' she said. 'With you, John, if you'll take me as far as Trebburn, and with your blessing, Ambrose, if you'll give it to me. But I'm going anyway.'

The Only Chance

'Gaia!'

She had woken a dozen times in the night, thinking it must be time, only to find herself still wrapped in silence and darkness. But now there was a faint grey tinge in the sky, Rackin was whispering her awake, and Ambrose was busy over the fire. Gaia pushed back her blankets and shivered. It was just before dawn: bitter cold, the coldest hour of the day.

'Here. This'll warm you.' Ambrose handed her a bowl of hot porridge made with fresh milk and a handful of grain. He must have got up in the cold and dark to make this for her. Warmth flooded through her, and sadness, because she had fought him for what she wanted, and won, and would be leaving him. She put the empty bowl down, stood and put her arms round him.

'You do understand, don't you, Ambrose?'

He held her in a tight hug. 'I understand. Go with my blessing, and I'll pray the moons to keep you safe, and that you find her... Maybe that amulet will be some use at last.' He let her go, and glanced at the grey square of the cave entrance. 'Almost light. You said you needed to leave early, didn't you, John?'

'Yes,' Rackin said. 'If we're to stand any chance of catching them up at Trebburn. You ready, Gaia?'

She swallowed hard against the dry sickness in her mouth, fastened her cloak around her shoulders and crouched down next to Tal. He was still sleeping and she put one hand on him very softly.

'Wake him,' Ambrose said. 'Think how you'd feel, if it was you, and you woke to find he'd gone.'

She tightened her grip on Tal's arm, and whispered his name. He started awake. Unhappiness clouded his eyes, and she realised that she'd woken him from a dream in which the day before yesterday had never happened.

'What?' He blinked at the grey light. ''S'early. What's wrong?'

'Nothing. Just... Tal... I'm going away.'

43

That woke him: he sat up, wide-eyed. *What?*

'I'm going to Trebburn, with John.' Her voice shook with the hugeness of what she was saying. 'I hope I might see Mum. At least find out who she's been sold to. Then,' she took a deep breath, 'I'm going to Freehaven. To sell the amulet. To buy Mum's freedom.'

He looked at her blankly. 'But... Parhelion said it was junk.'

'Scrimp didn't think so. I could tell. And he was a lot cleverer than Parhelion. And John says it's moonswood.'

'Moonswood? He blinked at her, baffled. 'Anyway. You can't *leave*. What about Chamboleyne?'

'Chamboleyne's just a story, Tal.'

'*No...*' He looked at Ambrose, who had told them the story, all their lives; just last night: *we don't leave the mountain*. But Ambrose said nothing. Tal nodded slowly. He climbed out of his blankets, shoved his feet into his boots, and bent over them to tie the laces. 'So.' His voice was muffled and not quite steady. 'When do we start?'

'You're not coming, Tal!'

'You're not going without me!'

'You're *not* coming. *Tell* him, Ambrose,' she said, but Ambrose simply smiled and handed Tal some breakfast, and she understood that he had foreseen this, and wanted it.

'Oh no.' Tal stepped back from the edge of the cliff, looking white and sick. 'I don't think I can do this...'

'No choice,' said Rackin. 'Or rather, there *is* another way, but it's over the mountains. It takes moons, and at this time of year, you'd freeze to death. The climb's not as bad as it looks, once you've got started. I'll go ahead, then I'll probably be able to catch you if you slip...'

'*Probably*,' muttered Tal. 'Great.' He inched back to the cliff's edge and peered over. The two wooden ladders, side by side, were flat to the sheer rock-face which plummeted down and down until it disappeared into the cloud.

'How much further down, once you're in the cloud?'

'About the same again,' said Rackin. 'It's the best part of a morning's climb. And another day and a half to Trebburn. So...'

'So we need to get going.' Tal set his teeth. 'Don't we?'

'Just watch me.' Rackin knelt at the cliff's edge with his back to the drop, gripped the sides of the ladder, and felt with one foot for the first rung. He climbed down a few steps, and grinned up at Tal and Gaia. 'See? Nothing to it. And if a great fat git like me can manage it, it'll be nothing to you two mountain goats. You first, Gaia.'

Gaia swallowed, edged her way to the brink of the cliff, and knelt at the top of the ladder, feeling empty air behind her: the long fall to the cloud and whatever lay beneath it. She clutched onto the poles and shifted one leg downwards. Rackin caught her ankle and guided her foot onto a rung.

'That's it,' he said. 'That's the worst bit. Move down a bit to make space for Tal.'

Gaia took another steadying breath and climbed down a few rungs. Eyes closed, she clung on while Rackin swung himself across the narrow gap onto the parallel ladder, climbed up to guide Tal into place, then down, and back onto the ladder below Gaia.

'Let's get going. And remember: *don't rush*. I know we're in a hurry, but you must only move one hand or foot at a time. And don't look down. Just keep looking at the cliff. Here we go.'

Gaia moved one hand, one foot, the other hand, the other foot. One rung. She moved down again, shifting feet and hands in the same order, staring fixedly at the wet, dark rock of the cliff face in front of her. Her hands were freezing, as if the old wood of the ladder had solid ice at its core. Above her, Tal was counting: *one (hand), two (foot), three (hand), four (foot); one…* Below, Rackin kept up a steady chatter of reassurance. 'Good, good, well done, keep going, not much longer to the first platform…' Down, down, down she went, looking only at the rock and thinking only of the next step. It was a surprise when Rackin reached up to guide her and Tal onto the first platform.

'Time for a rest.'

'I don't need a rest,' Gaia said.

'We rest,' said Rackin firmly.

She shrugged wordless agreement, and they stood for a few moments, shoulder to shoulder because the platform was no bigger than a tabletop. Gaia placed her shaky hands on the rail, and looked down.

'Careful,' warned Rackin. 'That wood's old. Don't put your weight on it.' She stepped back, and he said, 'No-one's done any work on these ladders since the mines closed. Heaven knows how long they'll last now.'

She imagined the ladders falling: big spurs of wood collapsing down the height of the cliff. It would leave the village more solitary than ever: only the dangerous high route that somehow Chamboleyne had managed at the worst time of year would still link it to the rest of the world. She thought, bitterly, that it would have been a good thing if the ladders had already fallen and kept Braggley away.

'Time to move on,' Rackin was saying. 'We'll be going into the cloud soon, and it'll be slippery. Be extra careful.'

They started again. Eyes fixed on the wet rock: down, down, down: hand, foot, hand, foot. Above her, Tal was counting again, and Rackin was still talking cheerfully below. Then a wisp of cloud drifted in front of her face. At the next step, it thickened into a muffling white mist. She was breathing in cold dampness and the rungs were slippery with freezing wet under her hands. She stopped, trying to blink her vision clear. 'John!' she called.

'It's just the cloud. Keep going.'

'Get a move on, Gaia, you're in my way.' Tal had come to a halt above her.

'Alright.' She breathed in, and started again, more slowly than before. Everything was a blind whiteness; she couldn't see the rockface a hand's breadth in front of her, and the cold was savage: the cloud was laden with slivers of ice that stung her hands and face and eyes. She gripped the ladder with numb fingers: down, down, down: until the next platform loomed out of the mist. They huddled in the shelter of Rackin's big body, blowing on frozen hands and shivering, and this time he hurried them on.

'You'll freeze if you rest in the cloud for too long.'

Down, down and down. The mist thinned and half cleared, closed, and cleared again. Gaia glanced down and almost lost her footing, unbalanced by the shock of green and blue far below her. She forced herself to focus on the cliff again, and the monotonous rhythm of descent. Down, down, down....

'Well done.' Rackin lifted her down the last steps, and guided Tal to the ground after her. 'Always a bit scary, the first time...'

'Just a bit,' Tal said, and Gaia sank onto a flat stone, her legs suddenly too shaky to hold her. Arms clenched over her stomach, she looked around. They were in a steep-sided gorge. Behind her, the high wall of rock and its ladders soared up and out of sight into the cloud. Opposite, there was another, lower cliff, above which she could see

46

the leaden sky. A fast-flowing stream tumbled greeny-white along the bottom of the gorge, and an old track, with many missing and broken stones, ran alongside it.

'That's the way they'll have gone.' Rackin pointed along the track. 'We go the other way. Take a bit of time to rest first.'

'No.' Gaia forced herself to her feet. 'I'm fine. Let's go.'

They crossed the river on broad flat stepping-stones, and set off along another old track.

'This was all built when the mines were open,' Rackin told them over his shoulder as he walked. 'Wish I'd seen it then: my dad used to say there were barges and carts up and down here night and day, and people swarming up and down the ladders. Now it's just me who comes here.'

A sad place, thought Gaia, hushed and gloomy; damp with the slow weeping of water. A dying place: except... there was the brilliant green of moss beneath her feet, and slender, feathery, long-leaved plants springing from fissures in the rock, stronger and brighter than the dry grey plants that grew on the mountain. Despite her hurry, she paused to take one of the fronds in her fingers, feeling the softness of the pliant leaves, and the surprising toughness of the thin stalk...

'*Gaia!*' Tal called. She let the springy fern go, and hurried after him. A little further along, the gorge widened. There was a broad pool here. A long boat was moored to the bank and next to it stood two sturdy creatures, bigger and solider than goats, with strangely long ears. Their grey coats were heavy with silver droplets of water.

'My barge, and this is Mabel and Josephine.' Rackin waved at the boat and patted the animals' waterlogged backs. Gaia and Tal looked at him, puzzled. 'Donkeys,' he explained. 'I'll get them fed, and we can be off. On you get.'

They climbed onto the back of the barge while Rackin set to work on the long front deck, pulling straw and harnesses from beneath a tarpaulin cover. 'D'you want a hand?' called Tal.

'Why not?' Rackin grinned, and Tal jumped down and ran along the bank to join him. Gaia watched them untangling ropes, and harnessing the donkeys; then she tilted her head to look up at the winter clouds that hid everything she knew, and felt a lurch in her stomach like falling through empty air.

'Alright, Gaia?' Rackin had come back aft. He cast off the mooring rope. 'We've still got a bit to do up front. Can you steer for now?' He grasped the tiller, and swung it to demonstrate. 'Push right to move the boat left, and left to move right. Nothing to it.'

He grinned reassuringly, and strode back to the foredeck. Gaia gripped the tiller as the donkeys pulled the boat out of the pool into a narrow canal. She steered unsteadily at first, veering from one bank to the other, but by the time Rackin and Tal shuffled back to her along the cabin roof, she was starting to find the knack of it. She shifted to make room for Rackin.

'You keep going. You're doing fine. Show Tal how it's done.'

He ducked into the cabin, reappearing briefly to fling them a couple of fur coats. 'Stick these on. It's cold. Oh, and shout when we get to the locks.' He disappeared inside again, and soon a wisp of pale blue woodsmoke drifted from the cabin chimney.

'Locks?' Gaia wondered.

Tal shrugged. 'Probably be obvious when we get there. Can I try steering now?'

She made way for him at the tiller and watched the strange landscape slip by. At first, the river and canal flowed side by side, but soon, the bottom of the gorge fell steeply away and the river tumbled down it in a series of waterfalls. From here, a stone bridge had been built flat against the cliffside to carry the canal. They travelled along the narrow suspended channel, higher and higher above the river with the cliff towering above them.

'Don't look down,' Tal said.

'No.' This was almost as giddying as coming down the ladders. Gaia stared fixedly ahead, but after a while, the cliff lost height; the bridge came level with the top of it and the canal swung away from the gorge in a long curve. Ahead of them now lay a bleak moorland, empty except for the line of the canal tracking across it.

Rackin shoved open the cabin door. Warm steam billowed out into the sharp air. 'Good,' he said. 'Here already. Let's have lunch.' He handed out slices of bread, and mugs of soup, and pulled the donkeys to a halt.

'Can't we keep going while we eat?' Gaia asked.

He shook his head. 'Donks need a rest. I mean, we're just standing here, but they're pulling the lot of us, and that's no small thing when one of us is me.'

The donkeys grazed at the coarse moorland grass. Gaia and Tal blew the steam from their cups and sipped at the hot soup. Rackin talked as he ate. 'The road along the river is the old route to Trebburn. It goes behind these hills, but the canal cuts across them. They built it in the old days, to take your gold to Trebburn. Must have cost a fortune, but it was worth it then. And now, hopefully, it'll let us make up that two days' start that Braggley's got on us, and you'll see your mum again.'

Gaia swallowed the last mouthful of soup against a sudden tightness in her throat. 'Can we start again, please?'

'Course.' Rackin called, 'Hup!' to the donkeys, and they started a slow amble along the towpath. He stepped into the cabin to put the mugs away and came back out holding a basket. 'Here. Have one.'

Gaia reached into the basket and took out something with smooth burnished red skin that sat neatly in the palm of her hand. 'What is it?'

'It's an apple. Haven't you ever…?' Rackin laughed, frowning at the same time. 'Go on. Eat it.'

She bit into it. Cold sweet piercing juice and crisp flesh burst in her mouth. She took another bite, and another, and another… 'Hang on.' Rackin reached out to take the remains of the apple from her. 'Don't eat the core. It's not so nice. The donks'll have it later. They're not fussy.'

Gaia put the apple core on the cabin roof, and sucked the juice from her fingers: relishing the sweetness, but scared too. There were so many things they didn't know. *Too* many. Feeling dizzy again, she stared silently at the strange moorland. After a while, Rackin pulled the donkeys to a halt at the top of a long hillside. From here, the canal descended the slope in a series of steps, and then cut across a broad valley, bounded in the distance by a range of low hills.

'That's where Trebburn is.' Rackin pointed. 'Just under those hills. About a day's journey across the valley, but we have to get through the locks first.' He jumped down from the barge and they followed him to a deep, narrow basin with gates at either end.

'Is this a lock? How does it work?' asked Tal.

'Easy,' Rackin said. 'You close the far gates - it fills - you take the boat into it - open those sluice gates at the end - it empties and you're down at the next level. Easy, but slow. Here. I'll show you.' He turned the wheel to close the sodden wooden gates at the far end, and they watched the water churning and rising in the lock.

'John,' Gaia said. 'Can't you take us all the way to Freehaven?'

'I told you. I don't trade that far. Don't have a licence.' She frowned at him, and he explained. 'All traders have to buy a licence. Mine only goes as far as Trebburn.'

'Why? I mean, why do you have to have a licence?'

Rackin gave a short laugh. 'Why do you have to do anything? Because the Fellowship says so. Right. That lock's almost full. Let's get back to the barge.'

He strode along the bank, and she half ran to keep up. 'What's the Fellowship?'

He stopped dead, and stared at her open-mouthed. 'You can't not...' His face broke into a broad grin. 'Oh. I get it. You're kidding. Nice one... Hang on.' The grin faded. 'You're not kidding, are you?'

Gaia shook her head.

'By Brumas.' Rackin breathed out a long breath. 'Right. I better explain... Let's just get through this lock first. You steer.'

Gaia climbed aboard and steered the barge into the lock. Rackin and Tal shut the top gates and opened the lower sluices. The water emptied slowly out, and the barge bobbed lower in the lock. Rackin sat on the edge.

'Have you really never heard of the Fellowship?' he asked.

'Don't think so,' said Gaia. Tal shook his head.

'You'd know if you had,' Rackin said. 'They... well... they're in charge. They rule Assalay. Thirteen Lords. Between them they own all the land, and they take taxes and tribute and...'

'Parhelion,' Gaia murmured.

'What?' The boat was halfway down the lock now; he leaned forward to hear her.

'Parhelion,' she called up. 'He came in the middle of Brumas. He took tribute from everyone: goats, and *people*. He took our best friend. Is he one of them?'

Rackin nodded. 'Yes. And a fair example of what they're all...' He checked himself, and glanced uneasily over his shoulder. The winter hillside, with its scrubby yellow grasses and stunted trees, was completely deserted, but even so, he remained silent until the lock had emptied. Then he said, 'Right. Let's get those bottom gates open, Tal, then that's one lock done. Only twenty to go.'

Lock by lock, they brought the barge down the hillside. The afternoon closed in around them, the sky darkening behind clouds that sent flurries of sleet across the valley. As they went, Rackin told them as much as he knew of the Fellowship. 'How long have they ruled? For ever. I mean, they made Assalay. Besides Parhelion? There's' (he counted on his fingers) 'Teredo, Lanneret, Helminth, Malander, Sallender, Philemot, Demersal, Baladine and Querimon, Hallion, Anserine and Filarion. The most important thing - this is really important.' He stopped turning the heavy wheel for a moment and looked at them. 'Don't ever let anyone hear you say anything bad about them. You may think Parhelion's a fool and a coward and a bully, but don't say it to anyone. Even if you think you can trust them. The Fellowship pays good money to anyone who hands over a traitor - and even a joke can count as treachery in their eyes.'

They cleared the last lock at dusk, and Rackin halted the donkeys. 'We won't go any further today.' He jumped ashore to fix the ropes.

'But...' Gaia began.

'The donkeys need a rest, and so do you. Tal can hardly keep his eyes open.'

Gaia gave Tal a fierce look. 'I'm fine,' he said.

Rackin paused with the mooring rope in his hand, and sighed. 'Alright. A bit further. But whoever's not steering has to walk. I won't have the donks pulling more than they need to.'

'I'll walk.' Gaia jumped down onto the towpath, and as night gathered, she trudged alongside Rackin, her head down against the wind and the sleet. She walked half dreaming, watching the light from the cabin windows gleaming on the water and shining silver-grey on the donkeys' backs. Long after nightfall they came to an unlit farmhouse, dark against the darkness.

'We'll stop here,' Rackin said, and she didn't argue. Tal lifted his frozen hands from the tiller and breathed on his fingers. In the cabin, they curled their hands around cups of hot tea sweetened with honey and herbs. Outside, the clouds had passed, and the full moon looked down on them from a clear sky. But the moon was Hesperal, sad goddess of the dying year: there wasn't much comfort in her gaze, and not much to be hoped for from her.

Tal shook her awake next morning, saying, 'Gaia? Where's John? I'm starving.'

51

'I don't know.' She rubbed her eyes, rolled out of her blankets and opened the cabin door. Rackin was standing on the towpath, staring up at the house that they had seen in the darkness. In the grey drizzly daylight, it seemed even more desolate than at night: closed up and sunk in a deep silence.

'Kit!' Rackin shouted.

No-one answered.

Gaia and Tal jumped down from the barge to join him. He gave them a quick glance, and shouted, 'Kit!' again. Again, no-one replied, and swearing under his breath, he trudged round to the back of the house. They followed him into a muddy farmyard, overshadowed by a tall barn. Beyond the yard, deserted, waterlogged fields reached to the cold horizon. The only sound was the steady dripping of water from the eaves. Rackin hammered on the back door, crossed the yard and looked into the barn. It was gloomy and completely empty. He swore again.

'Let's go.' They squelched back through the mud to the barge. Rackin gave the house a last unhappy look as they got underway.

'John?' said Gaia. 'What is it?'

'Friend of mine. Kit. He's lived there all his life. But this year... Well, you might not have noticed, up on the mountains, but the weather... No-one's ever seen anything like it.'

Tal said, 'There was a summer dragon this year.'

'And it's been cloudier than usual,' Gaia added. 'You couldn't see down the mountain.'

'She's always looking down,' said Tal. 'Dying to know what it's like.'

Rackin gave a short bitter laugh. 'I hope you're satisfied, now you've found out. Anyway, the harvest was a disaster...'

'You told us that. At the Melisto market.'

He looked ashamed. 'I was in a foul temper that day. I'd just been here. Kit had been to pay tribute to his Lord.'

'Parhelion?' asked Gaia.

'Lanneret.' Rackin scowled. 'He'd taken his usual tax. No allowance for the fact that the harvest had all but failed.' He gave another glance back at the farmhouse. 'I've been calling to see Kit since. I knew things were bad, but not this bad.'

'Where d'you think he's gone?' asked Tal.

'Trebburn, or some other town, like every other ruined farmer.' Rackin thumped his fist against the cabin roof. 'I should have done something.'

'You couldn't know,' Gaia comforted him.

'I knew enough.' He steered close to the bank. 'Take the tiller. I'm going to walk for a bit.' He climbed heavily ashore and trudged ahead through the grey day and the flurries of sleet. A long time later, he turned back to talk to them.

'That's the road and the river. Over there.' He pointed across the wide flat plain, and Gaia strained her eyes for a straggling band of slavers and their captives, but the road was obviously deserted.

'They'll be at Trebburn by now, Gaia,' Rackin said. 'They were too far ahead for us to catch them on the journey. The only chance is that we'll get there before they're sold.'

Tal walked after that: outpacing the boat, pausing for it to catch up, and striding ahead again. On board, Gaia leaned against the cabin roof and rocked, as if she could shove the boat along. It was so slow; *too* slow. But as the afternoon began to fade, she felt a chill dimness fall across her, and realised that they had crossed the plain and were travelling in the shadow of the low hills on the other side. Not far ahead, she could see the jumbled roofs and walls of a small grey slate and stone town.

'Trebburn.' Rackin looked up at the closing sky, ran to the donkeys, caught hold of their harness and pulled them into a trot. The barge cut faster through the water. They passed outlying houses, walkers on the road, a closed wagon cantering north... Just inside the town walls, they stopped at a landing stage. Rackin moored the barge hastily, flung an armful of straw to the donkeys, and seized Gaia and Tal's hands.

'Quick!'

They pelted through a maze of filthy dark narrow streets and out into the wide market place at the town centre, and Rackin stopped short, let go of their hands and shook his head.

Trebburn

'Too late.' Rackin thumped his fist into the crumbling wall of a crooked house. 'I'm sorry.'

'Are you sure?' Gaia took a step forward. In the dusk, the square looked vast: a hundred times bigger than the market at home. Knots of people stood talking together, muffled in cloaks and scarves against the blowing sleet. At the far end, a small group had gathered around a raised wooden platform.

'I'm sorry,' Rackin said again. 'Yes, I'm sure. That's the slave market.'

He pointed to a latticework of fences that formed dozens of small enclosures, like animal pens. Gaia walked across to them, with Rackin and Tal close behind her. She leaned on a damp wooden fence rail and gazed at the empty chains coiled down on the cobblestones. Reaching out her hand, she imagined holding Mum: the rough cloth of her shawl, the warm solidness of her wrist, the reassuring pressure of her fingers…

'So it's no good. We might as well go home.' Tal looked unhappy and lost, and she realised that he had been depending on this too.

'Not necessarily. Just wait here a moment.' Rackin strode out into the middle of the square and joined one of the huddled groups of townsmen. He talked for a while, gesturing and nodding, turning occasionally to look at Tal and Gaia.

'What's he doing now?' Tal asked.

'I don't know.' Gaia stared across the wide open space. Daylight had almost gone. Big globe lanterns standing at each entrance to the square made pools of brightness in the falling darkness, catching the blowing sleet and lighting the long green banners that flapped in the night wind. The wooden platform stood under one of the lanterns. A larger crowd had gathered there now, and as Gaia watched, two figures dressed in white appeared on the stage. There was a low tremor of drums and above them a slow, sinister tune. Tal raised his head.

'What's that?'

'Don't know.'

They crossed the square, joined the crowd, and wriggled through it to the front row. Tal stared at the musicians - a drummer, a piper and a fiddler - but Gaia just gave them a brief glance before turning to watch what was happening on the stage. The two white-clad figures were dancing, their movements as menacing as the tune that they moved to; but soon other figures burst into the dance, flourishing ribbons of bright red, orange, yellow. The tune turned to triumph. The white figures sank to the floor while the bright colours fluttered over them...

'What do you two think you're doing?' Rackin put one hand firmly on Gaia's shoulder and gripped Tal by the arm. 'I *told* you to stay where you were. You're not safe wandering round on your own. Slavers pick kids up from *everywhere*.'

'Sorry. We just wanted to see...' Gaia gestured towards the stage.

'Well, at least you're safe. Thank Hesperal.' Rackin kept his hands on them as they stood and watched the ending. The music changed from a fast celebratory dance, to a fanfare of victory; on the stage there was a bright flourishing of multi-coloured banners: blue, green, purple, black, scarlet, gold... The dancers bowed; the crowd applauded and wandered away.

'What's it all about?' asked Gaia.

'It's just a dance,' said Rackin.

'Yes, but what does it mean? Is that a fire at the end?'

'No idea.' He steered them through the crowd. 'Come on. We'll go and find some food. And some news, I hope. Any more questions?'

Gaia looked at the crowd hurrying homeward through the blowing sleet and the brilliant green flags billowing in the lantern light.

'What are the flags for?'

'It's Lanneret's town. Emerald's his colour.' He blew on his hands. '*Arctos*, it's cold. Let's get inside.' He guided them back through the twisting alleyways. As they walked, Tal hummed the tune that the musicians had played, and Rackin flashed him a quick smile.

'Sing that one at home, do you?'

Tal shook his head. 'Never heard it before.'

'You've a good ear for a tune, then.'

They stopped outside a house where laughter and talking and light spilled from the windows onto the filthy dark street. A faded sign showing a painted dragon swung creakily above the door. Rackin paused on the threshold.

'There'll be food for you here, and I'll see what I can find out. Just one thing. If anyone asks, you belong to me. Got that?' He pushed open the door and shouldered his way through the noisy crowd inside. They followed close behind him into a low-ceilinged kitchen, full of heat and the rich warm smells of unfamiliar food. A girl was stirring pots, her fair hair hanging sweaty and untidy round her face. Her eyes lit up with a smile of welcome as she saw Rackin.

'Hello, Mr R.'

He smiled back.

'Hello, Tipsy. Could you look after some young friends of mine? We've had a long journey. They could do with some food and a rest.'

The girl nodded. 'Course. Don't you worry. Friends of yours are friends of mine.' She ushered them into chairs near the stove as Rackin made his way back into the bar-room. 'Here. Come and get warm. It's *bitter* out. What's your names? What? Gaia? Tal?' She frowned. 'Funny names.'

'Are they?' Gaia exchanged a quick, puzzled glance with Tal.

'What's it matter? A name's a name.' She smiled again, filled plates with bread and meat and dark green leaves, and set them on the table. Gaia and Tal pulled up their chairs and ate, uncertainly, surprised by the flavours. Tipsy sat opposite them, propping her chin in her hands, and laughed.

'You never eaten spinach'n'bacon before? Here. Try this.' She stood, picked up a jar from the dresser, and froze. The laughter died in her eyes. A heavily-built man, with a deep scar across one cheek, was lounging in the doorway. He swaggered into the kitchen and sat at the table opposite Gaia and Tal, leaning back in his chair with his hands in his pockets.

'Evening, Tipsy.'

Tipsy swallowed. 'Mr Braggley.' Her voice had died to a whisper.

56

Braggley? Furious and frightened, Gaia looked up and met Braggley's gaze. He was studying her and Tal coolly, a faint, interested smile playing around his eyes and mouth.

'Who are your friends, Tipsy?'

'They... they...' she stammered, and Braggley turned impatiently to Gaia.

'Well? Who are you?' He nodded at Tal. '*You* remind me of someone...'

'They're mine,' Rackin said from the doorway, and Gaia felt her taut limbs unknot with relief as he crossed the kitchen to stand behind them, with one hand on Gaia's shoulder and the other on Tal's. Braggley looked at him narrowly.

'Where d'you get them?'

'Took them in payment of a debt,' said Rackin shortly. 'Time to go, you two.'

'Just a moment, John.' Braggley leaned forward across the table. 'You interested in selling? I mean, it's not exactly your trade, is it? And it's no secret you're having a bad year. You could balance the books with these two. I'll give you a fair price.'

'Braggley,' said Rackin. 'I wouldn't sell you a barge rat in a bad winter.' A flicker of anger crossed Braggley's face, but he simply shrugged, said, 'You always were a fool, Rackin,' shoved up from the table, and left, slamming the kitchen door behind him. Rackin let go of Gaia and Tal, picked up the water jug from the table and took a long swallow from it.

'Nasty taste in my mouth.' He held out his hands to warm them at the stove. 'Well, he was certainly selling today. That's what the party in there was about: celebrating a good day's business.' He grimaced and took another long drink from the jug.

'Was it Mum?' Gaia asked. 'And the others?'

'Sounded like it,' said Rackin. 'They were dark-haired. That's pretty unusual around here.'

'Is it?' Gaia ran a hand through her own tangled, damp dark hair.

'So what happened to Mum?' Tal asked.

'That's what we're going to find out now,' said Rackin. 'If we can. This way.' He guided them out along the narrow hall and into the ramshackle waterside garden. Reflections from the huge glittering house on the opposite bank danced on the water. Rackin gave it a gloomy look and spat into the mud, before heading along the puddled riverside path. They stumbled after him: past the backs of tumbledown houses, into a shadowy alleyway that was almost invisible in the darkness, up a short flight of steps, through an archway, and across a yard to a solid, firmly closed door. Rackin tugged the bell-pull, waited a moment, and rang again.

'Alright!' shouted a muffled voice. 'I'm coming… What time of night do you call this?' The door was flung open and a small man peered out at them, a book in one hand and a lantern in the other. Sleet flurried in the yellow light.

'I call it too late for a visit. But I'm here anyway,' said Rackin.

'John,' said the stranger. 'Come in. And…?

'Friends,' said Rackin. 'Gaia and Tal. This is Penn Scrivers. He's the market clerk here.'

Scrivers smiled, half puzzled, half welcoming, and waved them inside, though a dark hall, and into a small room where a couple of old chairs and a worn rug were drawn up close to a blazing hearth.

'What can I do for you, John?'

'Information.' Rackin settled himself into one of the chairs, while Gaia and Tal sat on the hearth rug in the warmth of the fire. 'Braggley was selling slaves here this afternoon, wasn't he?'

Scrivers nodded.

'One of them,' Rackin gestured at Gaia and Tal, 'was their mother.'

Scrivers looked closely at Tal, and nodded again. Rackin shoved back his chair and paced to and fro in front of the hearth. 'Do you know what he did, Penn?' he demanded. 'He went to their village, and burned it to the ground; he took every able-bodied man, woman and child he could find, and left the others to starve or freeze to death. Slave raiding's *illegal*, Penn; you know that; what were you thinking…'

'Hang on,' Scrivers said. 'This wasn't a raid. He was collecting a debt. A game of cards.'

'Parhelion.' Rackin let out a long bitter breath. 'By all the moons… Do one thing for me, Penn. These two want to find their mother. Tell them who bought her.'

'What for?' said Scrivers. 'She's been *legally* sold, John. Someone owns her. That's that.'

'We want to buy her freedom,' said Gaia.

58

Scrivers eyed her from head to toe, and she felt him noticing her shabby woollen tunic and skirt and her worn country boots. 'With what?' he murmured.

'Never mind that,' Rackin said. 'Will you help?'

Scrivers hesitated. 'Alright. *If* I can.' He picked up the lantern again and led them through the dingy hall into a room filled from floor to ceiling with shelves of leather-bound books. A single volume lay on a sloping desk in the middle of the room and he flicked it open, and asked, 'What's her name?'

'Mai Athanasius,' said Gaia.

He raised his eyebrows, ran his finger down the ledger and stopped, poised over an entry at the bottom of a page. Gaia took hold of Tal's hand. She could feel him trembling. Scrivers was still motionless, his finger resting on that one place on the page.

'Well?' said Rackin.

Scrivers shook his head. 'Can't tell you.'

'Why not?' asked Gaia and Tal together. But Rackin had guessed. 'Ah. She was sold to a Fellowship family.'

Scrivers gave a brief, unwilling nod.

'What difference does *that* make?' demanded Gaia.

'It means I have a duty of commercial confidence.' Scrivers closed the book.

'It means the Fellowship guards its secrets,' said Rackin. He folded his arms and leaned back against one of the bookshelves. 'Go on, Penn. It's only a little infringement of the rules.'

Scrivers shook his head.

'Look,' said Rackin. 'I'll lie for you, if need be. I broke in, tied you up and looked it up myself. Will that do?'

'I…' Scrivers hesitated a moment longer, and burst out, 'Oh, very well. Sallender's agent was here. He bought a group of Braggley's slaves. She was one of them.'

'So where would we find her?' asked Gaia.

'Well,' said Rackin. 'That's not so simple. The Sallenders own lands all over Assalay; all the Fellowship families do. There's no way of telling where she's been taken. Or is there?' he asked Scrivers.

'No. If there was, John, I'd tell you. Might as well be hanged for a dragon as an egg. There's nothing more I can do for you.'

They returned to the barge through the narrow dark streets and settled around the cabin table, under the swaying light of a hanging lantern.

'So that's that,' said Rackin. 'We've got as far as we can here. The next thing is for you to get to Freehaven. See if you can sell that amulet.'

'What's the point, if we don't know where she is?' said Tal. He had hoped for more from Scrivers: the information they had been given had left him feeling as lost as before.

'We know which family she's with. There's got to be a way of finding her.' Gaia turned to Rackin. 'Hasn't there?'

He shook his head. 'I don't know, Gaia. I've done all I can... except get you a ride to Freehaven. We'll see about that in the morning. If you're still going?' He looked from her to Tal and back again.

'*I* am,' said Gaia. 'Tal?'

He sighed. The name of a powerful family and a whole country to search. It wasn't much of a start. But he wasn't going to let her go alone. 'Yes,' he said. 'I'd like to know *where* we're going, though.'

'Well, I *can* do something about that. Jump up.' They stood while Rackin lifted the lid of the bench and rummaged in the locker underneath. He pulled out a battered old map that struggled to roll itself up again as he laid it out on the table. 'Stick those cups on the corners... Thanks. Look. This is where we are now...'

They bent over the map. They could see their own mountains - tiny drawings of rocky peaks - and the blue lines of the canal and river flowing down to Trebburn. At Trebburn, three rivers joined and became a wide river that meandered south through low gentle hills, until it reached the sea at Freehaven.

'Right,' said Tal. 'So we just get a boat all the way along the river to Freehaven?'

'Not quite.' Rackin put his finger on a large splodge of dark green on the map, edged by a few sketched trees. 'The Leathy goes through Nouldewood - the forest - here. So you have to take the canal.' He traced it with his forefinger: a loop of blue swinging westwards away from the forest and back east to rejoin the river just before Freehaven. Tal studied the map closely.

60

'But that's daft. The canal goes through all those hills. There must be locks all the way. It must take *moons.*'

'It does.'

'So why not just go through the forest?'

'Can't. It's a prohibited place.' Tal frowned, and he explained. 'There are parts of the country where no-one's allowed. The forest's the main one. There's a valley a long way north of here, too, and there may be others, down south. I don't know.'

'Why?' asked Gaia.

'By order of the Fellowship. And they don't give reasons. But they enforce the rules. Without mercy. If anyone tells you a place is prohibited, stay away from it, alright?' He lifted the cups from the corners of the map and it rattled shut. 'Now, get some sleep, and we'll get down to the river early and see about getting you a ride.'

They woke in the morning to find their mountains completely hidden behind clouds that sent down a cold sleety drizzle. Wrapped in their thick coats, they walked with Rackin to the river quay, where a big, rusty boat, with tall chimneys and slatted wheels on either side, sat heavily in the water. Tal and Gaia perched on a rail while Rackin negotiated with the owners. At last, he called them to join him.

'Gaia, Tal,' he said, 'This is Ben and Elsa, Mr and Mrs Crabbit. They own the Merry Maid: they've agreed to take you to Freehaven, in return for a hand around the boat.'

Crabbit shook their hands. Mrs Crabbit looked at them, sniffed, and pulled her shawl round her thin shoulders. 'Best be getting aboard. We'll be moving soon.' She climbed the ladder up onto the deck. Gaia and Tal lingered on the quay with Rackin.

'John?' Gaia said doubtfully.

'They owe me a favour,' he said. 'They're a bit… well… brisk, but they're honest folk, far as I know.'

Gaia swallowed. 'I wish you could take us.'

He nodded. 'So do I. But it's not to be thought of.' He folded them both in a bear-like hug. 'Good luck. I'll go and see Ambrose soon. Tell him what's happened, make sure they're alright for the winter…'

There was a sharp shout from the boat above them.

'Come on, you two, if you're coming!'

'One last thing,' Rackin said quickly. 'Don't forget what I said about slavers. They look out for kids on their own. Stick with Elsa and Ben, whatever you do.'

He gave them another hug, and let them go. They climbed up onto the deck. Crabbit pulled in the heavy mooring chains, and swung himself up the rusty ladder into the wheelhouse. Clouds of sooty smoke spurted from the chimney, the boat shuddered and the engine spluttered, coughed, and settled into a steady chug-chug-chug. The big wheels began to turn, churning up the grey water. Heavily, the boat pulled away from the quayside and into the centre of the river.

'Gaia!' said Tal. 'We've still got John's coats... ' He ran to the back of the boat and called back, 'John! Your coats!'

Rackin's laugh echoed across the water. 'Keep them!'

'Thanks!' they shouted, although the boat was ploughing on, and they couldn't tell if he had heard them. But they kept waving until they rounded a bend in the river, and Rackin and Trebburn were lost to sight.

'Stop lounging against that rail, you two.' They turned to face Mrs Crabbit. 'There's chores to be done, and they won't do themselves. You - Gaia? Is that your name? - there's a dinner needs cooking. And - you - John says you can handle a boat.'

'His, yes,' said Tal. 'I don't know about this. It's a lot bigger.' There was still that strange shuddering under his feet; puffs of thin sooty cloud blew out of the chimney, and the big wheels kept turning.

Mrs Crabbit sniffed. 'Well, you'd better go and find Mr Crabbit. See if he can teach you. He won't be pleased if you can't lend a hand.'

'I'm quite good at cooking,' Tal offered.

She looked at him through narrowed eyes. 'No cheek, please. Off you go.'

Tal shrugged, crossed the deck, and clambered up into the wheelhouse, while Gaia followed Mrs Crabbit down three steep steps into a dingy galley. The room was dimly lit by the rainy daylight struggling through a small, grimy porthole, and stuffy with the smell of old cooking oil and smoke. Mrs Crabbit dumped a basket of small muddy objects and a basin of water in front of Gaia.

'These need washing and peeling.'

Gaia picked up one of the muddy things and studied it. 'What are they?'

'Turnips.' Mrs Crabbit gave her a disbelieving look. 'You never seen them before? You need to clean them, and ... Oh, look. I'll show you.' She seized a turnip, scrubbed, scraped and chopped it. 'You do the rest. I've other things to attend to.' She sniffed and settled herself in the rocking chair with a bundle of shabby papers, while Gaia washed, scraped and chopped the turnips, her fingers numb in the cold muddy water, the knife clumsy in her hand. When she had finished, Mrs Crabbit stood up from her chair to look, and gave a long disapproving sniff.

'What's wrong?' Gaia asked.

'What isn't? They're not properly clean, you've left bits of skin on this one...and this... and they're all different sizes. Didn't your mother teach you anything about cooking?'

'Yes.' Gaia bit back anger and a dizzying surge of homesickness. 'But we don't have food like this at home.' She turned away quickly to hide her face and banged into a wobbly set of shelves. A gaudy china doll on the top shelf rocked forwards, backwards, forwards again and fell to the floor, smashing to pieces on the hard planking.

'You *stupid....!*' Mrs Crabbit dropped to her knees, gathered up the pieces and tried to fit them together. But the doll had shattered into a hundred tiny fragments. It was too broken to mend. Gaia watched helplessly.

'I'm sorry.'

Mrs Crabbit said nothing. Grim-faced, she swept up the broken china into a dustpan and carried it out to the deck. Gaia stood at the galley door, and watched as she tipped the shattered fragments into the river.

After that, Gaia could do nothing right. In the long days that followed, she smudged the brasswork she was set to polish, left sooty streaks on the linen she washed, and burned every meal she cooked. Mrs Crabbit barely spoke to her, and when she did, every word was loaded with dislike. Gaia longed for Freehaven, but it was still moons away.

Meanwhile, Tal had learned to manage the big boat and he and Mr Crabbit were, if not exactly friends, at least on speaking terms.

One morning towards the end of Hesperal, they were together in the wheelhouse, when Tal noticed a dark mass spanning the river ahead.

'What's that?'

Crabbit took his pipe out of his mouth, said 'Nouldewood,' and put the pipe back again.

Tal screwed up his eyes, but the forest was too far away for him to see it properly. 'Why's it a prohibited place?' he asked.

Crabbit sighed and took his pipe out again. 'By order of the Fellowship.'

'But why?' Tal insisted.

'That's reason enough. And enough questions.'

Downriver

'Look at that.' Gaia pointed to a large white bird with a long neck, holding its wings above its back as it glided along the river. Tal leaned on the rail to watch. They had stopped to buy food at a small riverside town, and he and Gaia were waiting on the jetty for Mrs Crabbit. Gaia had expected to be left aboard with a long list of chores, but obviously Mrs Crabbit felt that she wasn't to be trusted unsupervised, because she had been allowed to come, while Mr Crabbit minded the boat.

'Isn't it lovely? What do you think it is?' She leaned next to Tal and they watched the bird glide closer towards them.

'*Sweet moons preserve us!*' Mrs Crabbit had joined them on the jetty: she was staring at the bird in horror, and sketching the protective sign of the crescent moon in the air, over and over again.

'What's the matter?' Tal asked.

'It's a swan. Don't you know that?'

'A *swan?*' Gaia said. 'Like a *swansprite?*'

'Aye.' Mrs Crabbit shivered. 'Evil birds. Bad luck. You don't see many of them now.'

'But it's beautiful,' Gaia said.

Mrs Crabbit gave Gaia a long suspicious look. 'They're evil birds,' she repeated. 'And the sooner they're wiped out the better. I was bitten by one when I was young.'

She set off up the muddy track away from the river. Gaia shared a swift secret smile with Tal, and they watched the swan drift out of sight into a stand of reeds, before following Mrs Crabbit into the town.

It was a nothing little place, lost in a winter landscape of frozen empty fields and leafless trees. The windy main street was grey and drab, except for the bright scarlet banners which hung along it ('Teredo's town,' Mrs Crabbit explained) and the market was just a handful of wind-blown and rain-sodden stalls. There were some dull pots and pans for sale, a few skinny goats and sheep, and some

65

children (but no-one they knew). Mrs Crabbit made for the food stalls, which all seemed to be selling mud-covered roots. She stopped to haggle at each one, and Gaia and Tal fidgeted, until Mrs Crabbit lost patience with them.

'Oh, you two!' she snapped. 'Go and look round by yourselves. I'll come and find you when I need you.'

They slipped away.

'John said not to hang round on our own,' said Tal.

'I don't care,' said Gaia.

They wandered through the market. All the stalls were the same: except one, almost at the end of the town, which was piled high with berries, leaves and roots that glowed brilliant in the dull day: red, orange, yellow, white and a dozen greens: so bright that they seemed to be lit from within; nothing like the muddy roots on the other stalls.

'Are they for *eating?*' Gaia asked.

The woman behind the stall laughed quietly. 'Aye. Do you want something?'

'Can't.' Gaia shook her head sadly. 'Don't have any money.'

The woman studied their faces. 'You look hungry. Here. Never mind about paying.' She passed them a handful of roots and berries and they ate eagerly. Strong, rich, juicy tastes burst in Gaia's mouth; this was like *nothing* she had eaten before…

She was startled out of delight by the sound of heavy running feet. A man skidded to a halt alongside them. 'Market guards, Sal!' he panted. The woman started, and began to throw sacking over the boxes, feverishly, with shaking hands.

'Go!' she told Gaia and Tal. 'Just *go!*' Tal grabbed Gaia's hand and dragged her away. They watched from the other side of the street as six men in brown coats with a broad slash of scarlet in the sleeves surrounded the stall and pulled off the hastily thrown covers. The woman bolted into an alleyway, but two of the men were on her in an instant. They hauled her away while the others overturned the stall and trod the bright foods into the dirt.

'Why did they take her?' Tal asked Mr Crabbit later.

'She was selling forest produce,' he said. 'From Nouldewood.'

'What'll happen to her?' Tal asked.

'She'll not see moonlight again.'

Two more days on the river brought them close to the edge of Nouldewood. After they had moored on the second night, Tal and Gaia snatched a moment's freedom, sheltering from the rain in the lee of the wheelhouse. Tal squinted through the fading light at the mysterious darkness looming ahead. 'I wonder what it's like. Nouldewood.'

'What?' Gaia wasn't listening. She had taken out the amulet and was turning it over in her hands. 'Do you think it *will* be worth anything?'

He gave up trying to see the forest and glanced down at the little white scrap in her hands: in the dusk, it seemed to glow like the white berries on the forest food stall.

'It must be, mustn't it?' he said. 'John said moonswood was rare, and all those stories... *honour and glory*, and...'

'What's that you've got?' Mrs Crabbit had rounded the corner of the wheelhouse and was looking down at them, sharp and suspicious.

Gaia stuffed the amulet under a fold of her coat. 'Nothing.' She looked Mrs Crabbit squarely in the eyes.

'Yes, you have. What is it?' Mrs Crabbit gripped Gaia's wrist in one bony hand and forced her fingers open with the other. The amulet tumbled to the deck and she snatched it up.

'What's this?'

Gaia tried to keep her voice steady and casual. 'Just an old thing from home. Can I have it back, please?'

Mrs Crabbit turned the amulet over, and traced the carvings with her thin forefinger. 'And John said you had nothing to pay with.' She thrust the moonswood into her pocket and strode towards the galley. Gaia flung Tal a wide-eyed horrified look, jumped to her feet, and tore after her, all the steadiness gone from her voice. 'Give it back! It's mine...'

Mrs Crabbit turned to face her at the top of the galley steps. 'Then it'll do to pay for my broken china.'

She carried on into the galley. Gaia and Tal followed close behind her. 'Please,' Gaia pleaded, 'I will pay for your china, I promise, but please not with that...' Mrs Crabbit ignored her, climbed onto a stool and dropped the amulet into a jar on a high shelf.

'That's *mine!*' Gaia shouted. 'You've no right! Give it *back!*' She reached for the shelf, but it was high above her head; her hands fumbled blindly along it and she knocked over a jar which rolled slowly and fell to the floor with a smash. Fragments of green glass and a shower of dusty white flour scattered everywhere.

'Now look what you've done!' Mrs Crabbit grabbed Gaia's wrists. Tal darted towards the shelf, but Mrs Crabbit kicked the stool over and stood in front of him, blocking his way.

'Ben!' she yelled.

Crabbit put his head round the door. 'What's all the blessed shouting for?'

'They *attacked* me, Ben!'

She pushed Gaia into the narrow storeroom off the galley. Crabbit seized Tal and flung him in too, and Mrs Crabbit hurled the door shut and turned the key in the lock. Gaia hammered her fists uselessly against the door.

'Give it back to me! Give it back!'

Tal put his hands on her shoulders.

'Gaia. Shh...'

She dragged in a shaky breath and looked at him through wet eyes. 'It's all my fault. If I hadn't broken her *stupid* china...'

He shook his head. 'She'd have taken it anyway. Be quiet. I want to find out what they're doing.'

Gaia wiped her nose with the back of her hand. 'How?'

He turned to the door, ran his fingers up and down the planking, found a knot, and wiggled it like a loose tooth until it came free. He put his eye to the hole while Gaia jammed her ear up against the crack of the door.

'What in the name of moonshine was all that about, Elsa?' Crabbit asked.

Mrs Crabbit sniffed. 'They're liars, Ben. They said they had nothing to pay their passage, but they do. I found them with this.'

She reached down the amulet and handed it to him. He studied it doubtfully. 'Just a kid's thing, isn't it?'

'It might not be, Ben. It might be worth something.'

He ran a rough finger along the moonswood. 'S'theirs, though.'

'Oh?' she said. 'And since when was trade good enough we could afford to give free passage to folk who can pay? Anyway, she owes me. For my china. And the flour jar.'

'Daresay.' Crabbit shrugged, handed her the amulet and made his way back out to the deck. Left alone, Mrs Crabbit sat down in the rocking chair and lit a lantern. She sat for a long time, turning over the amulet in the yellow light. Finally, she stood, stowed it carefully, and carried the lantern to her narrow cabin. Darkness fell on the galley.

'Tal!' whispered Gaia. 'Did you see where she put it?'

'One of the dresser drawers.'

'What now? How are we going to get it back? What if…'

'Shh. Stop panicking. Let me think.'

They fell silent and curled up on the floor but neither slept for a long time. Tal rejected one plan after another, while Gaia stared through the tiny window at the moonless sky with hot unhappy eyes, feeling as if she had lost both past and future at a single stroke.

In the morning, Mrs Crabbit unbolted the storeroom door, chivvied Tal up to the wheelhouse, and dumped a load of laundry in front of Gaia. Washing was the best chore, usually, because it was done on deck where Gaia could watch the winter countryside and the journey slip by. But today she would gladly have peeled turnips or polished forks: *anything* to be in the galley with a chance of searching for the amulet.

She dragged the sheets and the washing tub outside. Nouldewood was very close now: she could make out individual trees on the fringe of the dark forest. The remembered taste of the forest food made her stomach growl. There had been no breakfast.

Tal, sent on an errand by Mr Crabbit, sauntered past her and gave her a significant look. On his way back to the wheelhouse, he stopped.

'I'll help you wring that out.'

'It doesn't matter. I can…'

'I need to *talk* to you, Gaia.'

'Oh.' She handed him one end of the soaking icy sheet.

'Any moment now,' he muttered. 'Get ready to go and look for it.'

'What about *her*? What are you going to do?'

'Don't worry about that,' he said, though he looked worried himself. 'Just go…'

'Tal!' Crabbit called from the wheelhouse. Tal thrust the sheet back at Gaia with a quick, anxious smile, and hurried across the deck and up the ladder.

'What was that all about?' Crabbit frowned at him.

'Nothing. Just giving Gaia a hand. Shall I take the wheel?'

'Aye. Might as well. I'll take over before we join the canal.'

Crabbit climbed down to the deck and went to lean on the bow rail, turning up his collar and pulling down his hat against the weather. In the wheelhouse, Tal took a deep breath and peered through the rain. They had almost reached the canal. Not much time. He scanned the river bank. As usual, they were passing through a dreary landscape of dead winter hedges and fields; but, just ahead, there was a thick clump of reeds at the side of the river and, a little way inland, a small copse of trees marooned in the centre of a furrowed field. He took another deep breath, opened the throttle and swung the wheel hard left. The boat leapt forward and rammed with a huge jolt into the muddy river bank. For a moment the big wheels kept spinning, sending up a fountain of silt that sprayed over the deck and the clean sheets. Then, with a grinding sound that set his teeth on edge, they slowed and stopped. The boat was left askew, its bows jammed into the bank; its stern adrift in midstream.

Tal shut off the engine and flung open the wheelhouse door. On the mud-spattered deck, Gaia was struggling up onto her hands and knees. Mrs Crabbit hurtled up from the galley.

'What in the name of moonlight are you doing?' she screamed at Tal. 'Where's Ben?'

Tal jumped down onto the deck. 'He was in the bows... I hope he didn't fall in.' (He hoped he had.)

'Ben!' Mrs Crabbit ran, slithering in the wet mud, round the wheelhouse to the front of the boat.

'Go,' Tal said to Gaia.

'Did you...?'

'Just *go*.' He watched her slip down the galley steps and wondered whether to follow her. But no: best go and keep Mrs Crabbit out of the way for as long as possible. Reluctantly, he rounded the wheelhouse. In the bows, Crabbit was bent double with his arms clutched around his stomach, winded by the jolt of the boat crashing into the bank. He straightened up when he saw Tal.

'What in the name of darkness...?'

'Sorry,' Tal said. 'It was the rain. I couldn't see properly... the next thing I knew we were in the bank.'

'Stupid!' Mrs Crabbit screamed at him. 'You could have *killed* us! We might have *sunk!* We might have lost *everything!* And you!' She rounded on Crabbit. 'What did you think *you* were doing? Leaving him in charge, sneaking off for a quiet smoke...'

Crabbit said, slowly, 'He knows how to handle the boat. He doesn't make stupid mistakes.'

They both stared hard at Tal. 'I've told you,' he said. 'It was the rain.'

'But she sped up too,' Crabbit said. 'Before we hit the bank. Explain that.'

'I don't know,' said Tal. 'I just didn't think. I'm sorry.'

Crabbit shook his head. He took a step closer to Tal, forcing him up against the bow rail. 'That wasn't an accident.'

'It was, honestly...'

'Liar!' He hit Tal, hard, a stinging blow across his face. 'Tell me why...'

'Oh!' Mrs Crabbit shouted. 'Where's your sister?'

The first dresser drawer was a mess of old papers, scraps of cloth, unravelling balls of string, wool and cotton, teaspoons, thimbles, an unopened pack of handkerchiefs and the body of a mouse that seemed to have died of starvation. The second and third drawers were the same. *Impossible.*

Just look. Gaia started to rummage through the muddle, and stopped. This was all wrong. None of these things had been disturbed for *ages.* No-one had shifted them to hide anything here last night. She grabbed the first drawer, pulled it right out of the dresser and fumbled in the space behind it. There was something there, and her fingers knew it as soon as they felt its familiar worn smoothness and curious engravings. She held it fast in her clenched hand for a moment, feeling as if she had been restored to herself. Then she tucked it away and ran up the galley steps. The Crabbits were hurrying towards her. Tal stood behind them, alert, poised for flight. She caught his eye and gave a slight nod.

'Run,' he mouthed, and she shoved past Crabbit, ducked under Mrs Crabbit's outstretched arm, slipped on the mud and grabbed at Tal's hand. They hurtled along the deck, the Crabbits

71

thundering and shouting after them. Tal scrambled onto the stern rail and hauled Gaia up after him.

'Jump!'

Gaia glanced over her shoulder, met Mrs Crabbit's angry eyes, took a gasping breath, and leapt. Freezing green water closed over her head, and for a panicky moment she floundered, dragged down by her heavy waterlogged clothes. Tal heaved her to the surface, and she put all her strength into swimming, struggled to the bank, and crawled out into the muddy reed beds.

Tal hauled her to her feet. 'Run!'

She glanced back. Bickering and getting in one another's way, the Crabbits had unhooked the heavy rope ladder from the stern and were carrying it to the bows. Gaia and Tal paddled through the soggy ground under the reeds, splashed across a flooded meadow, shoved through a thorny hedge, slid down into a flooded drainage ditch and clambered up the other side. A huge bare field lay ahead of them. Tal halted.

'Come *on*.' Gaia pulled at the sleeve of his soaked jacket.

'No.' He gestured at the boat. Crabbit was astride the rail, peering through the rain. 'They'll see us if we cross the field. Got to stay hidden.'

They slithered back into the icy ditch, waded along it and squeezed through another hedge into another ploughed field. In the middle of the bare earth was the leafless copse that Tal had seen from the boat, and a little way beyond that were the first trees of the great forest. Over the soft hiss of the rain, Mrs Crabbit's voice sounded sharply; not far away.

'Well, they must be here somewhere, Ben!' There was a snapping of twigs, a shrill scream, and a splash.

'She's in the ditch!' whispered Gaia.

'Too close. Run for the trees.' Tal tugged at her hand, and they stumbled across the boggy, ridged ground, and into the copse.

'What are you two doing?'

They spun round. A slight fair-haired girl was watching them, intently, from startlingly blue eyes. She was guarding five skinny black pigs which rooted among the fallen leaves on the copse floor. Tal gave her a quick glance, turned to look back across the field, and gasped.

'Gaia! They're at the hedge!'

'We need to hide,' Gaia said.

'In there.' The girl gestured to the big tree in the centre of the copse. There was a narrow hole at the base of the trunk and they crawled through it into the dank hollow inside. Crouching in the cramped space, they heard heavy footfalls on the dead leaves and Mrs Crabbit's sharp voice.

'Have you seen a girl and a boy go this way?'

Gaia clutched Tal.

'Yes,' the girl said. 'No point following though. They went into the forest.'

'Well, that's that, Elsa,' said Ben. 'Best get you back to the boat and dry you off.'

Mrs Crabbit gave a long sniff. 'Well, I hope the Fellowship finds them.'

Footsteps crunched through the leaves again, fainter and fainter. There was a long silence, then the girl said, 'They've gone.' They crawled out of the tree and rubbed the pins and needles out of their legs. 'Thanks.' Gaia shivered.

'You been in the ditch?' the girl asked.

'And the river.' She shivered again.

'You'll catch your deaths.' The girl looked at their dripping clothes and hair, chewing her lip. 'Better come with me.' She rounded up the thin pigs, beckoned Gaia and Tal to follow her and led them across two more muddy fields to a farm in a shallow valley. Opening the gate, she hustled them across the yard, into a barn and up a ladder to a hayloft under the rafters. She picked up a couple of dusty sacks from the floor. 'Wrap yourselves in these. I'll take your clothes and dry them. You can wait here. But be quiet.' She waited at the bottom of the ladder while they undressed, tied their wet clothes into a bundle and dropped them down to her.

'I'll be back later,' she whispered.

'Wait,' Gaia called after her. 'What's your name?'

'Linnet. Be *quiet*.'

She hurried out of the barn, swinging the heavy door shut behind her.

'What's all that about being quiet?' Gaia said.

'No idea.' Tal let out a long breath and flopped flat on a pile of straw. 'That boat... I can't believe I did that...'

Gaia put a hand on the amulet, safely back round her neck. 'Glad you did, though.'

He smiled. The smile became a yawn. He shook himself, yawned again and closed his eyes. Gaia watched him falling asleep. She was tired too, and she curled up alongside him. It wouldn't matter, just to close her eyes for a few moments…

'Well. What have we got here?'

She woke with a start. Blinking into the bright light of a lantern, she made out the figure of a big man standing over them. Linnet hovered behind him, her arms full of their dried clothes.

'I told you, Father. They just needed somewhere to get dry. They'll be moving on soon.' Linnet pushed the clothes into Gaia's hands. Her face was shadowed and unreadable.

'Well, there's no need to keep them in the barn, child.' Linnet's father smiled. 'We'll make them a bed by the kitchen fire.'

He chivvied Linnet ahead of him down the ladder. Gaia and Tal fumbled into their dry clothes in the dark, climbed down from the loft, and followed Linnet and her father into a brick-floored kitchen where a good fire blazed in the hearth, casting moving shadows over the rough whitewashed walls. Linnet's father waved them into chairs at the fireside. He carved slices of dried meat and bread, and poured out steaming mugs of a fruity strong drink. Gaia lifted her cup and breathed in sweetness and spice; through the steam she looked at Linnet, perched pale and silent at the edge of the firelight.

'Going on tomorrow, you said?' Linnet's father was saying. 'It's cold to be travelling. Why not stay awhile? Till Aquilon full moon, say.'

Gaia shook her head. 'Thanks. But we need to be getting on.'

'No. Stay.' He stood up, and kicked a log in the fire; it sent up a sudden flare of flame and sparks. 'I heard about that boat. Ben Crabbit seems to think you did it on purpose. He was talking in the inn… What he'd do if he got his hands on you.'

Gaia darted a frightened glance at Tal. He returned it, wide-eyed.

'Don't worry,' Linnet's father said. 'You can keep your heads down here. I won't say a word. Stay.' It sounded more of a threat than an invitation now. They watched in silence as Linnet made beds for them: pulling eiderdowns and blankets from a chest, and laying them on the floor in front of the fire; flitting from one corner of the room to another like a trapped bird. When they were ready, her father locked the door and put out the lanterns, and he and Linnet climbed the stairs, leaving Gaia and Tal to the dying firelight.

Despite the warmth of the embers and the blankets, a knot of puzzled fear kept Gaia awake for a long time: she had barely slept when she was roused by a voice whispering her name. She opened her eyes to pale grey morning, and Linnet leaning over her, shaking her awake.

'What?'

Linnet shivered.

'Shhh. Listen, you have to go. Now. Before he wakes up.'

'What's going on?' Tal was awake too, rubbing his eyes, and blinking at the faint light.

'You have to go,' Linnet said again. 'All that about staying till Aquilon full moon.' She swallowed. 'That's the day of the Fairwold slave market. He's going to sell you. He's done it before, with stray kids. *Please, now,* before he wakes up.'

Tal was on his feet, heading for the door. Linnet caught his hand.

'That's locked. This way.' She led them across the kitchen, into a chill white-walled dairy where she opened the window above a smooth stone table. 'Go,' she whispered. Tal hauled himself onto the table, squeezed through the window and dropped to the ground beneath. Sitting on the sill, Gaia hesitated.

'What about you?'

'I'll be alright.'

'You could come with us.'

Linnet shook her head. There was a shout from upstairs.

'Linnet?'

'Hurry!' Linnet gave Gaia a push, and she dropped down, landing next to Tal in the grey dawn. Mist drifted across the farmyard, and the country beyond it was lost in dense fog. They ran through the yard, climbed the gate, and crossed the first field. Behind them, someone was shouting and dogs were barking; when they paused to peer back through the gathering mist, they could just make out Linnet's father, standing at the farm gate with three big dogs at his side. Tal squinted through the drifting greyness.

'What's he holding?'

'Our blankets,' Gaia whispered. 'He's letting the dogs smell them.'

Tal paled. '*Run.*'

They stumbled across the next ploughed field, slowed by the furrowed ground and the heavy wet clay. The mist was thicker now: they could see nothing ahead, could hardly see the ground under their feet, but they could still hear the hounds, baying and howling behind them, closing on them. Gaia ran without any sense of where she was going. Then, suddenly, there were drifted leaves beneath her feet, and closely woven branches loomed out of the fog.

They had left the open farmland, and crossed into the forest.

Nouldewood

Gaia stopped running and looked round wildly: behind them, the open fields and capture; ahead, the deep shadows of the place that it was death to enter.

'Tal! We're in the forest!'

'I know!'

'We've got to get out, Tal, this is *Nouldewood*,' John said…'

'I *know*…!' Tal broke off, and spun round at the sound of scuffling and growling and high-pitched yelps of excitement behind them. 'Dogs!' He grabbed Gaia's hand and they ran, panicked and blind: diving deeper into the trees, tripping over tough trailing ivies and the twisted roots of trees, snagging on low branches and brambles; half blinded by springy twigs that whipped into their eyes.

The dogs were closing on them: Tal could hear their big bodies breaking through the undergrowth; he could almost hear them breathing. He dragged Gaia through a thick tangle of branches into a big clearing with a single tree growing at its centre. *Better*, he thought: no more roots and branches to trip and snatch at them: a clear run. But years and years of leaves lay in deep drifts under the tree. Tal sank, instantly, up to his calves, and behind him Gaia stumbled and fell. He hauled her up, and they floundered on, but it was like trying to run in water. The dogs burst howling into the clearing.

'Tree!' Tal shouted. They made it with the dogs on their heels. He shoved Gaia onto the lowest branch and swung himself up after her; the dogs leapt at them with a volley of snarling and snapping. 'Higher!' Tal gasped, and they scrambled further up, well out of reach, and flopped breathless onto a broad branch. Above them, scraps of sky showed between a dense mesh of twigs; below, the dogs barked and scrabbled pointlessly at the tree trunk. Gradually, the barking subsided into growling, and finally into silence.

'Have they gone?' Gaia whispered. Tal leaned over and looked down. As soon as he moved, there was a storm of furious barking from below. He cowered back out of sight.

They waited. The sun rose as a pale disc behind the curtain of snow cloud hanging low in the sky. The thick twigs and branches above them kept Gaia and Tal sheltered from the worst of the wet cold. But the grey morning crept into a grey afternoon, and the dogs were still on guard, still alert to every movement in the branches; and Tal started to lose hope. Sooner or later, hunger and thirst would force him and Gaia down from the tree…

A rustling beneath them made him look down again. The dogs were wading away through the leaves. They pushed through the close growing trees and were lost to sight, but for a while Tal could still hear them, shoving noisily through the forest undergrowth. When he was sure they had gone, he sat up.

'We need to go. Now. While it's still light enough to see.'

'What about Linnet's father?' objected Gaia. 'And the Crabbits?'

'Been thinking about that. We'll go back to the edge of the forest now, and wait for dark. Then we go east.'

'East? How far?'

'All the way round the forest. We're bound to come back to the river sometime, and we can follow it to Freehaven.'

'That'll take ages, won't it? And what's there…?'

'Not sure,' he admitted, trying to remember Rackin's map. 'But the main thing is to get out. You remember what John said about prohibited places.'

They eased out stiff arms and legs, and slithered back down to the ground. Tal set off quickly through the deep leaves, but Gaia called him back. 'Wait, Tal. Look. She had these … that woman at the market.' She pointed to hundreds of small round purple mushrooms, growing in the deeply ridged bark of the tree, picked one, and ate it. 'Try one,' she said, but Tal was gazing upwards, at the fractured glimpses of darkening sky between the branches.

'Come *on*, Gaia. While there's still some light.' He picked a mushroom and put it whole in his mouth. The flood of rich, strong, meaty flavour made him almost sick with hunger. 'Stick some in your pockets. We'll eat them on the way. But we must go.'

They stuffed their pockets, crossed the clearing, plunged back into the tangled wood, and ducked under a trailing vine hung with white berries, flecked with pale green. 'Hang on,' Gaia said. 'They had these too.'

'*Gaia!* We have to get *out.*' Tal kept remembering what Crabbit had said about the woman who had been selling forest food. *She'll not see moonlight again:* it sounded like a repeated chant in his head. The sooner they were out, the better, but it was hard to be sure which way they had run that morning. He swung himself onto the bottom branch of a big tree.

'What are you doing?' Gaia asked.

'Need to see the sun. Work out which way is which.' He climbed swiftly, up above the forest canopy and into open sky. A yellow-grey glimmer showed him where the sun was setting behind the clouds, and he slid down, jumping into the drifted dead leaves under the tree. Gaia was breaking open a brown pod full of orange seeds.

'Try these.'

He swallowed a handful of seeds, his mouth watering at their extraordinary sweetness. 'Bring some,' he said. 'We need to go this way,' and he set off confidently. But it was impossible to follow a straight line: again and again, fallen trees, boggy patches of ground and thick clumps of brambles forced them off track and though they walked until after sundown, they didn't come to the edge of the forest. Finally, they stopped, unable to see to go any further, with thick darkness on either hand under the endless trees, and the clouded night sky overhead.

'We're lost,' said Tal. 'We'd have been out by now if we were going the right way.' He slumped down to the ground, and she sat next to him, on a thick drift of soft dry leaves under another huge tree.

'Let's rest,' she said. 'We can think what to do in the morning.'

He didn't want to stop. But the darkness was so thick you could almost touch it: they would never find their way through it. He agreed, unhappily, and they lay down on the leaves, wrapped in Rackin's thick fur coats, and slept.

The huge idea came to Gaia in the middle of the night. She lay turning it over in her head. It might work. It *would*: it couldn't not. There was nothing against it. Except...

'Are you absolutely mad?' said Tal.

'I think it's a good idea.'

'Let me get this right,' he said. 'First, we find the river. Then - assuming we *can* find it - we don't follow it north. We go south. All the way through the forest.'

'And on to Freehaven,' Gaia said. 'Yes. Why go back? We know who's waiting for us there. And I'm right, aren't I? That's what John's map said: the river runs through the forest and on to Freehaven.' She spread her hands. 'Simple.'

'Yes... except for the tiny problem that we'd be spending... I don't know - a moon? More? - in a place where they'll kill us if they find us. We just need to get out, Gaia. Soon as possible.'

'But if we don't get caught...'

'If!' he shouted. 'That's a big if...'

'Just *listen*,' she insisted. 'If we don't get caught, we can survive in here. There's plenty of food.' She nodded at a sprig of brown berries and a cluster of yellow mushrooms. 'And it's warmer. Remember how cold it was, on the river? We'd freeze outside. If we didn't starve first.'

Tal thought for a long time. 'Where's the sun rising?' he said at last. 'If we try to keep going south, and follow any stream we come to, we might find the river. We might make it.'

'And if we meet someone, we can always say we came in by mistake and...'

'I think,' he said, 'we'd better just not meet anyone.'

The first day was an uneasy one. There were noises everywhere: the trees overhead were full of birdsong and whispering breezes, and the undergrowth rustled with the scuffling and scuttering of tiny creatures. Gradually, they got used to the little sounds, but towards evening, as they crossed a wide clearing, they heard hoofbeats: a big, heavy animal, thundering towards them. Tal had an instant vision of men on horseback: a Fellowship patrol, looking for trespassers in the forest, and there was nowhere to hide except a scrubby bush. He dived under it, pulling Gaia down with him. They tried to burrow into the fallen leaves on the ground, but they could be seen; he knew they could. The hoofbeats came closer, thudding on the soft earth, slowed, and stopped. He closed his eyes.

'Look,' Gaia whispered. 'They're beautiful.'

In the centre of the clearing stood four white deer: a stag and three does. They *were* beautiful: almost shining in the shadows under the trees, as white as the swan on the river, like creatures of moonlight. They stood, unafraid, as Tal and Gaia crawled out from under the bush, and carried on walking. As they left the clearing, Gaia stopped to glance back at the deer, frowned, and picked at something on the bark of a big tree.

'More food?' Tal asked.

'No.' She rolled a blob of something between her fingers: as thick and sticky as honey but clear as water.

'When John explained about moonswood,' she said, 'I didn't really understand what he meant. I think it's this. Set hard. Turned to stone.' She worked the amulet out of its pouch with her other hand: dead as stone, but not stone: something once alive; transfigured; held in time...

Strange and wonderful: and the forest was strange and wonderful too: with its abundance of food; the warmth of fallen leaves; and the sheltering branches that kept out the fierce winter weather which they glimpsed in the skies overhead. Gaia came to think of it as the Moons' wood: a safe and protected place. But - even after days of wandering - they didn't find the river.

They were utterly lost, and had long lost count of the days when they came to a place where the forest was dense and tangled. They had to fight through closely growing trees and brambles and it was impossible to see or think more than a step ahead. So, when they bumped into it, the thing came as a complete surprise.

It was a fence: a high barrier of thick wooden planks which ran as far as they could see in either direction.

'What?' Tal said. 'Here. Give me a leg up. I want to see what's on the other side.' He stood on Gaia's linked hands, heaved himself up, and sat astride the top plank.

'What's there?' she called up to him.

'A sort of road, and another fence, then forest again.'

'What? Hang on, I want to see.'

She reached up her hand and Tal hauled her onto the fence. For a moment she sat next to him, then she jumped down into the leafy ditch on the other side. She clambered out of it onto the roadway, and crouched down, looking at something on the ground.

'Gaia!' Tal hissed. 'Come back.'

'No. Come and look. This is weird.'

'For Arctos' sake, Gaia...' Tal gave a long look left and right, dropped down into the ditch and climbed up onto the road to join her. She was studying a pair of parallel metal rails which ran apparently endlessly in each direction.

'What d'you think these are?' she said.

He didn't answer. He was listening to a distant whisper, far away along the track; and another sound, closer at hand, just behind the fence: the scrunch of leaves and sharp snap of twigs, as if something big and heavy was forcing its way through the forest. Gaia lifted her head.

'What's that?'

The whisper became louder, a rhythmic clatter, mounting into a roar and someone jumped down from the fence, leapt into the roadway beside them, bundled them into the ditch, and piled armfuls of leaves over them. Above the approaching roar, he muttered, 'Keep still. Keep very quiet and very still.'

The roaring thing passed with a whirl of hot wind that set the leaves blowing and scattering. Looking up, Gaia saw a chain of metal boxes on wheels that swept on and disappeared into the dark distant trees, leaving a cloud of hot steam hanging above the roadway.

'Idiots,' said the stranger. 'What did you think you were doing, walking along there?' He stood up, brushed the leaves from his cloak, and glared at them.

'We didn't mean...' Gaia started.

'And why are you in Nouldewood?' the stranger asked. 'Don't you know it's a prohibited place?'

'We came in by mistake...' She stammered to a halt: they were too deep in the forest for that story to be convincing any more. But the stranger didn't look angry now: he was staring at her, puzzled.

'I know you, don't I?'

Gaia shook her head.

'I've seen you somewhere. Where are you from?'

'Arimaspia.'

He whistled. 'That's way north. What are you doing here?'

'We need to get to Freehaven,' Gaia said. 'We thought we could follow the river through the forest.'

'Not a bad idea. But if you don't know your way...' He smiled. 'Come on. I'll see you safely out and onto the Freehaven road.'

No, Tal thought: this was all *wrong:* trusting a stranger in a forbidden place. He looked at Gaia, trying to catch her eye, to mouth a warning. But she looked at him blankly; and anyway this was a bad place to try and run, with its thick undergrowth... Unhappily, he let himself be hefted back over the fence, and fell into step behind the others as they forced a single-file track through the trees.

'What's your name?' Gaia asked the stranger.

'Don't ask,' he said over his shoulder. 'And don't tell me yours. We don't tell names, in the forest.'

'*We?* Are there others...?'

'Don't ask,' he said again. 'I won't share secrets that don't need to be told.'

He pulled back a springy branch and stood aside to let them pass, and while they were waiting for Tal to catch up, Gaia said, 'What about the thing on the road? It was like a metal dragon. What *was* that?'

He laughed. 'You don't stop asking, do you? That was a Fellowship Lord in a hurry, taking the steam road. It's the quick way between Freehaven and the north.'

'We thought that. It's why we came through the forest.'

'Hmm,' he said. 'Except you aren't meant to be in here.'

'Are you?'

He smiled. 'Fair point. I'll keep your secret if you keep mine. Agreed?'

'Agreed,' she said.

They continued in silence, and, late in the afternoon, they stopped to rest above a deep rocky gully. Tal was silent, but Gaia had gathered a handful of unfamiliar berries as they walked, and she picked through them, asking the stranger which ones were good to eat.

'That's fine... Those are good... Leave those...' He broke off and held up a warning hand. 'Shh!'

Gaia darted a frightened glance into the trees.

'Supper.' He pointed across the gully to a flock of fat pigeons roosting on a high branch. Silently, he unslung his bow from his back, fitted an arrow, and let it fly. A pigeon fell heavily to the forest floor while the rest of the flock wheeled away with a clatter of wings. The stranger slung his bow over his shoulder, climbed down into the gully and up into the trees on the other side to look for the pigeon. Tal jumped to his feet.

'Let's go. Now.'

'What? Why…?'

'We've no *idea* who he is, Gaia. He could be taking us to the Fellowship.'

'He saved us from the Fellowship on the steam road.'

'He *said* he did.'

'But he's going to show us the way to Freehaven.'

'We can find the way,' he said. 'We don't *need* anyone else. Look what happened when we trusted people before.'

'You might be wrong,' she said.

'But what if I'm right?'

She stared at him, and nodded slowly. They crept away into the trees: tiptoeing at first, breaking into a run once they were sure they wouldn't be heard. They hurried on until after dark, and when they settled for the night they chose a more hidden resting place than usual. Tal slept shallowly and uneasily, but nothing disturbed them, except a mouse at midnight and birds stirring at dawn, and as they walked on, they heard nothing except the usual sounds of small animals in the undergrowth.

After a hard morning of pushing through a seemingly endless patch of dark-needled evergreens, they paused to rest and eat. As he reached for a mushroom, Tal froze.

'Listen!'

'Is it him?'

'No. No, *listen*. Oh, forget eating. Let's *go.*' He tugged Gaia to her feet and she followed him, bewildered, until she heard it too: the sound they had been waiting for: the soft fall of water over stones. Before long, they came out onto the banks of a tumbling stream, and after a couple of days of following it, they reached a wide river, flowing dark, swift and silent beneath the canopy of trees. Tal punched the air in triumph. 'We've done it, Gaia!'

After that, it was easier. For days, they followed the deep broad river, and, late one afternoon, they saw the unshadowed light of open country ahead. Tal hurried towards it, but Gaia held him back.

'We need to wait for night. We'll be in trouble if we're seen.'

He nodded. He was impatient to be out of the forest, but she was right. They lingered under the trees, stuffing their pockets with as much food as they could carry, until dusk fell.

'We should wait till it's properly dark,' Gaia said. Now that the moment had come, she didn't want to leave the forest. It had been a kind place: had fed and sheltered them, and seen them safely on their way.

'It's dark enough *now*,' Tal said.

She agreed, and followed him sadly out of the trees.

Far away to the east, the stranger lay down to bivouac in the rough shelter of a rocky hollow. He lay gazing at the moon through the branches, half dozing, then woke with a jolt. 'That's it!' he said out loud. A startled flock of roosting birds wheeled away into the darkness. 'That's where I've seen her.' He got up, started to hurry back the way he had come, and stopped short. 'Idiot,' he said to himself. 'That's impossible.' But he knew the evidence of his own eyes. Impossible or not, he had seen what he had seen, and he had to try and find her. He set off again, heading for the river by the fastest possible route.

Gaia and Tal emerged into a white moonlit world. Light snow dusted the empty ploughed fields and the leafless hedges. Ice crystals sparkled in the moonlight. It felt a hundred times colder than it had been in the forest. They huddled into Rackin's furs, shoving freezing hands deep into their pockets and pulling the hoods over their heads.

'What now?' Gaia asked through chattering teeth.

'Keep going downstream, I suppose.' Tal shivered.

Gaia gave a longing look back at the forest. 'Where are we going to shelter?'

'There's bound to be somewhere,' he said uncertainly, and pressing close together to ward off the remorseless cold, they started along the riverside path. They walked all night without finding anywhere to rest, but as daylight broke, they came to a desolate farm by the river that reminded them of Kit's: no smoke rose from the chimney, and the windows were shuttered. They splashed across the icy farmyard to the door.

'There's no-one here,' Gaia said. 'We could rest in the barn. Carry on later.'

Tal nodded. 'It'd do. Shame we can't get into the house though.' He gave the door an angry shove, and it creaked open. They stepped into an empty, cold kitchen. But a fire had been laid in the grate, and a flint lay on the hearth; and upstairs there was a bed with folded blankets.

'Maybe they thought someone might come back,' Gaia guessed, 'and they left stuff ready for them.'

'Maybe.' Tal picked up the flint, struck a spark from it, and slipped it into his pocket. 'Better not light a fire now. Someone might see.' So they curled up, shivering, under the blankets and tried to sleep away the day. After nightfall, they lit the fire in the kitchen and crouched close over it. Next morning, Tal pocketed the flint; they closed the door behind them and set out again.

That was the luckiest find. They spent the next night among a flock of sheep, under the leaky roof of a stone pen. On the third night they walked until long after dark and finally crept into a hay barn in a farmyard, where they slept uneasily, afraid of being found. Morning brought them to a large riverside village where the track became a broad busy road, crowded with carts and wagons heading towards Freehaven.

At midday, hungry and tired, they stopped to rest at the roadside. They had finished their stores of forest food, and Tal took off his coat, lay flat on the riverbank, and peered into the greeny-brown water. It was teeming with big, slow-moving mottled fish, and he rolled up his sleeve, reached both hands in and stirred his fingers. 'Got you!' He lifted a wriggling fish triumphantly out of the water.

'Put that back, son!'

Tal jerked his head up. A man and a boy were standing beside him on the bank.

'*Put it back! Now!*' the man hissed, and in surprise, Tal let go of the big fish. It slipped back into the water with a loud splosh and swam down into the brown depths of the river. He watched it go crossly. It had been a good fish: fat and meaty, with plenty of eating on it.

'Arctos' sake, lad. What did you think you were playing at? Pulling a Fellowship fish out of Querimon's waters, right under his gamekeepers' noses.' The man nodded upstream at a small boat that was being rowed towards them by two men, dressed in brown jackets with a slash of bright yellow across the shoulder.

'A Fellowship fish?'

'You didn't realise? Lucky Alan and I came down for water just now. You'd have been in a heap of trouble if they'd caught you with it. Try for a little grey one next time. They're allowed.'

'Thanks.' Tal blinked, dizzy as if the riverbank had tipped up underneath him. The man stooped to fill a leather bottle with water.

'Heading for Freehaven?'

'Yes,' said Gaia.

'Want a lift? We've got room.' He gestured at a large horse-drawn wagon which seemed to be full of children, and a smaller donkey cart, standing at the roadside.

'We're fine, thanks,' Tal said.

'Don't be daft,' said the man. 'You'll be late, if you walk it. It's past full moon already. Not long to go.'

'Till what?' asked Gaia.

'Carnival. That's why you're going, isn't it?'

Almost Carnival; already the third quarter of Himalios. Moons had slipped past them while they had been wandering in the forest. They had missed Tal's birthday. *Carnival.* Gaia felt a surge of homesickness: in the village they would celebrate by gathering round a fire and Ambrose would tell the story of Pelon the fire thief. It would be a sad celebration this year with almost everyone gone.

Almost the end of the year. They had been travelling long enough: it was time to be getting on, but Tal repeated, 'We're fine,' and turned away. Gaia ran after him.

'Let's go with them.'

'No. Look what happened before when we thought people were helping us.'

'I know, but...' She looked up at the sky. The clouds were thick and heavy, and it was starting to sleet again. 'We've been lucky so far: finding places to sleep. What happens when we can't?'

He shook his head and stared hard at the sleet pitting the water, and the big prohibited fish moving about under the surface.

Alan and his father filled the last of their water bottles, and carried them back to the carts at the roadside.

'Still space for you,' the man called. 'Coming?'

Gaia made up her mind.

'Yes!'

Without waiting for Tal, she hurried across the frozen ground and let Alan help her up into the cart.

The Road to Freehaven

Tal swore, ran after the cart, grabbed hold, and swung himself onto it. He gave Gaia a furious look. You couldn't trust *anyone*: definitely not strangers you'd just met by the roadside. But it was too late for that. She was blabbering to Alan.

'I'm Gaia, and he's Tal.'

Alan frowned. 'Gaia and Tal? Where are you from?'

'North,' Tal said quickly.

'From the back of beyond, Dad reckoned, if you don't know about the food prohibitions.'

'I don't even know what that means,' Gaia said.

'Simple enough.' Alan shrugged. 'There's some food ordinary folk can't eat, only members of the Fellowship. They're tricky to remember, but you need to. Like Dad said, you'll get into trouble if you're caught with a prohibited food. Take fish, for example...'

By the end of the afternoon, they had moved from fish, through frogs ('Simple; you can eat any of them. Only they're a bit disgusting...') and onto ducks ('complicated. They're used for plumage as well as meat, so it sort of depends whether it's winter or summer... you better double check with Dad.') Before they could start on animals, they pulled up outside a farmstead, where the farmer invited them in to eat by the kitchen stove. Gaia shot Tal a *'told you'* look which he returned with a scowl. 'You don't know you can trust them,' he whispered to her as they settled to sleep.

'We're warm, and fed, and *getting there*. What more do you want, Tal?'

They were getting there. By the beginning of Himalios last quarter they were only a few days out of Freehaven. The road was crowded with other travellers, mostly ordinary folk making their way to the city for the holiday, but at midday they were startled by a sudden flourish of trumpets behind them. Alan - who had been telling them what to expect in Freehaven - stopped talking instantly, and

89

pulled the cart hurriedly to the roadside, just in time to clear the way for four horses, draped in gold cloth and ridden by gold-clad trumpeters who were calling that insistent fanfare over and over again. Gaia watched open-mouthed, but Alan hissed 'Don't stare!' and she dropped her gaze and caught only fleeting glimpses of the shining procession as it passed. The trumpeters were followed by four more horsemen, bearing banners of gold; a gold carriage whose horses' manes and tails were dyed gold; four more flag bearers and four more trumpeters. When they had passed, Gaia raised her eyes and stared after them: a gleam of brilliance against the falling snow, and the grey winter sky and fields.

'What was that?' she asked Alan.

'Lord Malander, of course. Going to Freehaven for Carnival.'

Later that day, they heard trumpets again, and Demersal's retinue swept past them, a brief flowering of rich burgundy in the grey-white evening. Next morning, a fanfare on the river heralded Lord Hallion's ship with magenta sails and a long magenta banner flying from its mast; and the following afternoon, processions of bright yellow and scarlet rode by, like brilliant birds chasing one another's tails. 'Querimon and Teredo,' Alan told them. 'And close your eyes, now. Go on.'

Gaia put her hands over her face. She felt the cart travel round a long bend. 'Look,' Alan said, and she lowered her hands to see a vast city lying before them.

'Freehaven.' Alan pulled the cart to a halt at the back of a long queue of carts waiting to pass through a high stone gate that spanned the road ahead of them.

Gaia stood up in the cart and stared at the city. On the steep hill to the east of the river, huge houses stood in immense walled gardens: they were built of white stone, and their roofs shone myriad colours: blue, turquoise, emerald, gold, yellow, orange: like a fallen and scattered rainbow. On the western side of the river a tall tower and a silver dome stood high above a mass of smaller buildings. A wall ran all round the city, and built against it, close to the road where the carts were waiting, was a shabby camp of makeshift tents.

'What's that?' Gaia asked.

'Just people who can't get in.' Alan gave the camp a quick, careless glance.

'Why can't...' Gaia began, but Tal was tugging at her arm.

'Gaia! Look at the *river!*'

She turned to look down at the wide river, still flowing close by the road, closed her eyes, shook her head, and looked again. The water was a swirling kaleidoscope of brilliant colours: blue, turquoise, emerald, gold, yellow, orange...: flowing about and around one another. 'The Fellowship colours,' Alan said. 'For Carnival.' As the cart edged forward, Gaia stared at the river: so mesmerised by the colours that she hardly noticed the call of trumpets behind them, the panicked jostle of carts trying to get out of the way, and the clatter of hooves as four horsemen rode past with streaming banners of brilliant lapis blue. 'Sallender!' Alan whispered, and Gaia felt a jolt in her stomach that left her unable to speak.

'Sallender? Did you say *Sallender?*' demanded Tal.

Alan nodded.

Tal was out of the cart in a heartbeat, dodging through the crowd after the brilliant blue horsemen and the carriage they were escorting. Gaia hurtled after him. They reached the arched gateway as Sallender's retinue passed through it onto a wide street hung with multi-coloured banners. They tried to follow, but a man dressed in pale grey livery stepped out of the shadows under the arch and blocked their way.

'Papers.' He held out his hand. Along the street, the first horsemen turned onto a side road and out of sight. The carriage lumbered after them.

'What do you mean, papers?' Gaia asked.

The guard sighed. 'You can't come into Freehaven without papers. Didn't you know that?'

The last of Sallender's horsemen were turning the corner. In another instant they would be lost for good in the huge city. Tal made a break for it: ducking past the guard and flinging himself towards the street, but two other grey-liveried men had seized him before he was out of the shadow of the arch.

'Try that again,' said the guard, 'and you'll be in real trouble. Now get out of here.'

They slunk back along the road. Alan was still waiting in the queue of traffic, closer to the gate. 'What happened?' he asked. They explained, and he looked at them with scathing disbelief. 'Didn't you *realise* you have to have papers?' He dug into his pocket and pulled out a folded square of parchment with a seal in orange wax.

Gaia shook her head. 'Where can we get them?'

'You can't. You have to apply before you come.' Alan shoved the parchment back in his pocket. Ahead, the queue had started to move. 'Hang around here if you want a lift back. We'll be leaving when Carnival's over.' He geed up the donkey and drove off. Gaia and Tal stood in the road and watched him go.

'So what now?' Tal asked bleakly. 'If we can't even get *into* Freehaven...'

'I know. I don't know.'

Gaia turned away and stared at the wisp of smoke rising from a smouldering fire among the rough tents under the walls. *The people who can't get in.* She stepped off the road, and wandered across the frozen stony ground towards the camp. Outside a rickety shelter made of rotten timber and ragged sailcloth a boy was sitting on the ground, trying to light a fire with an old flint that refused to spark.

'Here.' Tal knelt down and struck his stolen flint. The fire caught. The boy blew on the sparks and the wood glowed and flickered into flame. Gaia and Tal stretched out their hands to the heat. The boy glanced at them.

'Thanks. Not seen you two before. Just arrived?'

Gaia nodded. 'We haven't got papers.'

'Nor've the rest of us. Why d'you think we're sitting outside?' He added a couple of sticks to the fire.

'So why come at all?' Gaia asked.

'Freehaven's the last chance. And there's ways of getting in, if you're lucky...'

'How?'

He gave her a wry smile. 'Determined, are you? Well, hitching a ride by boat works, sometimes, or mixing with a big crowd...' He broke off, looked sharply towards the gate, and swore. Ranks of men in grey livery were marching out of the city and across the rough ground towards the tents.

'Arctos! Better move.' The boy jumped up and hurried away from the camp, across the open ground and onto the road. Gaia and Tal followed him. They dodged out of sight behind a large wagon piled high with wood, stopped, and looked back. The men in grey were tearing the camp to pieces: they heaped up the old timber and canvas, and flung lighted torches into the middle of the pile. The flames hesitated, caught and roared into the cold, damp air.

'That's that, then,' said the boy.'

'What'll you do now?' asked Tal.

The boy shrugged. 'Same as everyone else. Go away for a bit, come back, try and get in again.' He paused. 'I'll tell you what, though. If you've got a place to go to and folk that'll look after you, you'd be stupid not to go back to them.'

He raised one hand in farewell and plodded away. Under the walls, there was nothing left of the camp except the bonfire. They watched until it had died to smouldering embers, and the grey men had gone back into the city. Tal turned and started trudging back along the road. Gaia ran after him and grabbed his wrist.

'We're not going home! We're *not*, Tal. We've got here. All we have to do now is get in.'

'All?'

'Mum might be in there, Tal!'

'I know that! I just don't know what to do.'

'There *has* to be a way!'

Gaia looked at the frozen ground and the ruined camp; along the road to the impassable gateway, and then at the multi-coloured swirling river. She stepped off the road and walked to the water's edge. Downriver, she could see the walls and towers of the city. A little way upstream, a couple of boats were moored at a jetty.

'Those boats...' she said.

'What about them?'

'If they're going into Freehaven, maybe we could hide on board.'

Something could go wrong at every stage of that plan, Tal reckoned: getting aboard, getting ashore, and all the moments in between. But he didn't have a better idea. 'Worth a look,' he agreed, and they strolled up the bank, in time to see one of the boats cast off. The steersman called back to the remaining barge. 'I'll see you in Freehaven! When are you coming in?'

Gaia nudged Tal.

'Tomorrow morning,' the bargeman answered. 'That's when they want them delivered. And buy me a very large drink, will you? I hate carrying these things. They give me the creeps.' He lifted a hatch cover on the deck, peered inside it, dropped it shut again and sketched the shape of the crescent moon in the air.

The other man laughed across the water. 'Good money, though, isn't it? Carnival business. I reckon you should be buying the drinks.' He waved and swung his boat out into the middle of the river. Gaia and Tal walked on up the bank.

'Well?' Gaia said. 'That man's going to Freehaven. If we could hide on his boat...'

Tal was silent. 'We could try,' he said at last. 'But I don't like the sound of what he's got in there.'

They loitered on the bank until evening, pacing up and down for warmth, frozen hands shoved deep into the pockets of their coats. The bargeman sat glumly on the cabin roof, casting frequent uneasy glances towards the locked hatch on the deck. Shortly after sundown, he stood, stretched, and set off along the towpath. Gaia and Tal waited for a while, but he didn't come back.

'Gone for the evening, d'you reckon?' Tal asked.

'Looks like it.'

'Might as well give it a go, then,' he said. She couldn't see his face clearly, but his voice sounded as if he was struggling to keep it steady.

They felt their way down to the jetty and onto the barge. It lurched under their feet, and the water slapped softly against it, but otherwise there was stillness and utter silence. They crawled along the deck to the hatch and Tal explored it with his hands.

'Padlocked,' he said through chattering teeth. 'The frame's rotten, though. I can get these screws out easily.' He levered the hasp out of the wood, and eased the hatch ajar. Gaia tensed, waiting for a response from the things in the hold.

Nothing.

Tal heaved the hatch wide open, and they peered inside. The hold was full of big shapes, huddled and motionless in the darkness. It was impossible to see what they were.

'They aren't moving or anything,' Gaia whispered. 'D'you think they're alive?'

'Sounded like it, the way he was talking about them.' Tal screwed up his eyes. 'Just wish we could see...'

'I'm going to get in,' Gaia decided. She ignored Tal's alarmed, 'Wait!' and lowered herself down into the hold. She landed on something soft. It didn't stir, or make a sound, but it was definitely alive: she could feel it breathing. She felt it with both hands. A big strong, feathered body, a long neck… As her eyes got used to the darkness she made out a faint gleam of white.

'Tal! I think they're *swans.*'

'Are you sure?' He slid through the hatch to join her and felt the creatures for himself. 'You're right. Just swans. Why haven't they woken up, though? I've trodden on at least three of them.'

'He was scared of them, wasn't he? The boatman. Maybe he gave them something to make them sleep.'

'Maybe.' Tal let out a long sigh of relief. 'Sleeping swans. Well, that's alright.'

They pulled the hatch shut, wriggled into the innermost part of the hold, and curled up among the big sleeping birds. Warm and hidden, they slept too: waking at last to the sway of the boat, and the steady rippling of water beneath them. Around them, the swans slept on, even when the barge slowed, bumped against something, and rocked as someone stepped aboard.

'Papers,' said a voice overhead. 'What's your cargo?'

'Swans, for Carnival. You want to look?'

'I'd better.' The voice sounded reluctant, and the hatch was raised and closed again quickly. 'That padlock's loose. Better watch out for that. You coming ashore?'

'Not staying with that lot a moment longer than I have to.'

There were footsteps on the deck overhead, the boat lurched, settled, and was silent.

'He's gone, hasn't he?' Gaia said at last.

'Think so.'

They crawled over the sleeping bodies, shoved the hatch open, and climbed cautiously out onto the deck. Gaia rubbed at her dazzled eyes. It had been dark in the hold and they had climbed out into a bright day, with rare glimpses of blue sky and sun through the racing clouds. The brilliant colours of the river swirled around them. The boat was moored against one of the central piers of a long, high arched bridge.

'We're stuck in the middle of the river!' Gaia said.

'No, we're not.' Tal pointed. An iron ladder fixed to the stone pier led up to a network of thick wooden beams beneath the arches. 'We can cross those.'

They shut the hatch on the swans, jumped off the boat, and climbed up into the beams. Dizzied by the height and by the flow and swirl of the multi-coloured river beneath her, Gaia concentrated on each movement of hands and feet, and breathed out with relief when they reached another ladder fixed to the pier at the far end of the bridge. Halfway down, there was a broad ledge, where they paused to catch their breath. Tal lay back with his head on his hands, staring up into the gloomy shadows under the bridge.

'This'd be a good hiding place.'

'Yes.' Gaia thought for a moment. 'Tal, if we ever get separated, I'll wait for you here. The first morning of every quarter.'

He looked startled. 'Wasn't thinking of losing you.'

She grinned, and then was suddenly solemn. 'Nor me. But just in case.'

They climbed down from the ledge onto the broad base of the pier. From here, a narrow flight of slippery stone steps led up the high embankment wall which rose sheer from the river. They scrambled up the steps onto a broad, paved riverside terrace, climbed a wide marble stair onto the bridge - and stopped, astonished. The roadway across the bridge was seething with a densely packed crowd of people; gilded carriages and sedan chairs forcing their way through the jostling and hustling pedestrians. Gaia had never dreamed there were so many people in the *world*.

'Busy.' Tal spoke lightly, but he looked as giddy as she felt. She reached for his hand.

'Where now?' she asked.

He thought. 'We need somewhere to sell the amulet. It was all houses over there, wasn't it?' He gestured at the steep hill on the far side of the river. 'Let's try this way.' They plunged into the crowd and let it carry them into a vast square, bordered by huge buildings of white stone, dominated by the high tower and the silver dome that they had seen from outside the walls. They wandered, stopping to watch a puppet show, a juggler and a fire eater, and staring hungrily at the stalls selling sweets, cakes and tea.

'Wish we had some money for those cakes,' Tal said.

A sudden shout seemed to echo him - 'Cakes! Carnival cakes!' - and the air breathed with the rich smell of warmth and spice. Men in bright liveries wove through the crowd, throwing handfuls of brilliantly coloured things as they went. Tal jumped and caught one. It *was* a cake: orange, about the size of his fist. They kept falling: a shower of colour: emerald, turquoise, gold, daffodil... Gaia caught a blue one and bit into it. It was the best food she had tasted since Nouldewood: spicy, moist and sweet.

'Grab as many as you can,' Tal said. 'We might need them later.'

They stuffed their pockets, but soon the cakes stopped coming. The liveried men drove the crowd back to clear a broad path; there was a loud fanfare, and a procession of heavy silver carriages lumbered across the square, festooned in banners of dark green, magenta, brilliant blue...

'Sallender!' hissed Tal, but Gaia was watching the creatures pulling the carriages. They were monsters: huge and thick-set with strong limbs, scaly skins and long tails that trailed behind them.

'What're they, Mum?' a small boy next to her asked.

'Dragons,' said his mother.

'Those aren't dragons...' Gaia began, and stopped: because they were, but they were all wrong. There were stumps where their wings should have been, and they were breathing hard, but with no fire or smoke.

'What's wrong with them?' she asked the boy's mother. 'They haven't got wings. Or fire.'

The woman gave her a strange look. 'Of course not,' she said. 'They're Fellowship dragons. Their wings and firelines are cut. They wouldn't be safe otherwise, would they?'

Gaia stared. Dragons had blazed through her nightmares at home, but she couldn't look at these maimed, ruined creatures without feeling sick at what had been done to them. Another dragon hauled itself past them, straining for breath. Gaia looked angrily up into the carriage that it was pulling - and caught Parhelion's eye.

He started, she was sure of it, and kept his gaze fixed on her, turning to look back at her as his carriage drove on. She ducked her head, and tried to shuffle backwards into the crowd.

'What's the matter?' whispered Tal.

'Parhelion. On that carriage. He saw me.'

'He can't have *recognised* you, though.'

'I think he did.'

They stared after the carriage. Parhelion was still looking back.

'You might be right,' Tal said. 'Let's move.'

They pushed back through the crowd, and found themselves at the foot of the steps to the huge silver-domed building. Tal flopped down onto the bottom step, leaned back and closed his eyes, feeling the unusual dryness of the air and the faint warmth of the winter sun on his face. Gaia sat next to him, and drowsed too, letting her eyes drift over the crowd, watching the faces dreamily; strangers' faces... Except... She gasped.

'Tal! The Crabbits!'

Quarrelling, the Crabbits were winding their way through the crowd. They were getting closer and closer.

'*Arctos!*' said Tal. 'Quick! Before they see us.'

They fled up the steps and in through the massive open door of the silver-domed building.

The Company

They halted on the threshold. An immense space unfolded before them: the stone pavement reached far away under a forest of thick pillars, under a roof that soared up into shadowy heights. Brilliant banners of many colours hung from the roof, and round stained-glass windows in the side walls splashed coloured light onto the white marble floor: blue, turquoise, emerald, gold, yellow, orange...

'Are we allowed in here?' Tal whispered.

'Think so.' Gaia gestured at the people walking to and fro, talking in low voices, looking tiny under the soaring roof. 'Let's have a look round.'

The building had a wide central nave, and two broad side aisles that were cluttered with towering monuments: giant marble figures - on horseback, standing, sitting, lying peacefully in death. Country visitors clustered around each statue, and Gaia and Tal loitered at the back of one of the groups. A man wearing a midnight blue gown was saying, 'It's the memorial to the late Lord Lanneret... The inscription? It says: *Sacred to the memory of Cedric Attarius, Lord Lanneret, Anointed of the Moon Idalia, Fellow of the Lords of Liberty, Upholder of the Republic of Assalay, Guardian of Freedom, Defender of Justice, Merciful and Bountiful Friend of the People...* And this is his son, the present Lord. May Idalia and all the Moons watch over him and grant him long life.'

'Grant him long life,' murmured the crowd, and they shuffled away. Gaia and Tal stayed where they were.

'Lanneret?' said Tal, staring at the open, generous marble hands and compassionate marble face. 'But John said...'

'He took his usual tribute. No matter that there was famine.' Gaia turned abruptly, and headed up the aisle. Tal dodged through the crowd to catch her up.

'Where are you going?'

'I want to find Parhelion.'

They carried on along the aisle, gazing into the marble faces above them, until they reached the statue of a tall man, looking pensively into the distance, one hand resting protectively on the marble shoulder of a boy about Jason's age. Tal caught Gaia's sleeve.

'Hang on. That's him, isn't it?'

They stared up at the statue. The heavy set of the figure and its strong features were familiar, but the kindness and courage and intelligence in the face made it almost unrecognisable.

'Yes,' Gaia said. 'He looks different, though.'

'Nicer than he really is.' Tal's voice was too loud. Gaia shushed him and darted a quick anxious glance over her shoulder. Most of the blue-gowned officials were busy with sight-seers; but a tall man dressed in the same deep midnight blue had been hurrying past them as Tal spoke, and he stopped, put his finger to his lips, and flashed them a swift wink before walking on.

'*Tal!* He *heard* that! Remember what John said.'

'Sorry.'

'It's alright. He looked friendly.' She considered the statue again. 'You're right. Much nicer. What d'you think the inscription says?'

'Shall I read it for you?' One of the officials had approached without them noticing.

'Oh!' Gaia startled, and steadied herself. 'Yes. Please.'

He took a deep breath, and read:

Stop! Humble stranger and admire
The noble brow, the seeing eye
Bright with intelligence's fire
Compassion, courage, and mercy!

Great Lord of our Republic blest
From north to south, from east to west,
May Lusinia's rays shine freely on,
Our wondrous Lord Parhelion.

'Thank you.' Gaia could hardly speak and Tal was shaking with barely suppressed laughter. She clutched his arm, and pushed him to safety at other side of the building before she dared to meet his eyes. They laughed themselves weak, holding onto one another for support.

'But honestly,' she said, when she had recovered. 'It's not funny. It's just a *lie.'*

They dawdled back to the massive entrance doors, past more Fellowship statues, pausing to look at Sallender and his handsome son ('He's probably hideous. In real life,' Gaia guessed). From the doors, they peered out into the square. The procession was over. The stall-holders had packed up and were wheeling heavy hand-carts away. Sweepers were clearing up abandoned cakes, empty papers and broken bottles. Another group of workers were building a giant pyramid of dry wood: felled trees and old rafters and beams.

'What's that, d'you think?' asked Gaia.

'Don't know,' said Tal. 'Don't care. We're meant to be finding somewhere to sell your amulet.'

They crossed the square, and took a narrow road between two of the high white buildings. A turn to the left and another to the right plunged them into a labyrinth of winding cobbled streets. They passed a few dingy shops, but every door and dusty window was shut and barred. As the sky overhead began to darken, they meandered on, aimless and lost: twice, they came back to a small three-sided square where there was a fountain topped with a leaping copper dolphin; the marble basin beneath it overflowed with rainwater. When they came to it for the second time, they stood and looked at one another helplessly.

'Let's try that way,' said Tal. 'Don't think we've been there.'

They started along a winding backstreet. At the first bend, Tal stopped, spun round and peered back into the shadows.

'What?' said Gaia.

'Shh. I thought... Did you hear something?'

'There's nothing,' she said. 'Come *on,'* and they carried on into a shadowed alley where the buildings almost touched overhead, blocking out the fading evening sky. Tal walked hesitantly, squinting through the failing light, while Gaia went ahead of him.

'Tal! Look!'

'Shhhh!' He hurried to catch her up. She was pressing her face against the grimy window of a narrow-fronted shop. The windowsill was a mess of untidily piled silver boxes, mirrors spotted with age, blackened filigree frames - and carved panels.

'Look!' Gaia said again. 'Those are moonswood, aren't they? And they're like the amulet.' She took it out and they leaned over it, looking from it to the scraps of moonswood in the window.

'The shapes on yours look different,' Tal said.

'That's the only difference, though. Do you think they're worth a lot? Those other things... the silver things... they look really valuable.'

He caught her enthusiasm: suddenly hopeful, he said, 'I know. They do.' He glanced up at the scrap of dimming sky between the houses. 'We should get back to the bridge while there's still enough light. We can sleep there. Come back here in the morning.'

'Let's go back to the square first. See what's going on.'

'No. Too risky. We need to keep out of sight.'

'Alright. Suppose so.'

She turned away from the window and froze. A skinny boy was standing behind them, leaning against the wall of the house opposite, close enough to have heard every word they said. He was tall and gangly, with grubby fair hair, and though his clothes were shabby and threadbare, he looked oddly elegant in them. He grinned.

'Wotcher.'

'I *knew* there was someone!' Tal glared at him.

Gaia tucked the amulet back into its pouch. 'This is our business. How dare you ...'

The boy held up his hands. 'Woah. Keep your hair on. Whatever business you've got with old Fossick, it ain't nothing to do with me. Just wondered if you needed help.'

'Help?'

'Yeah. Two kids, on your own, from out of town... Spotted you in the square. You stuck out like a dragon on a beach. Thing is... Freehaven's a hard place to get by, if you don't know the dodges, and if you ain't got papers.'

Gaia glanced uneasily at Tal and said nothing.

'So... You ain't got papers?' The boy pursed his lips in a silent whistle. 'You'll have the Watch on you before night's out, if you don't get a bit of help.'

'What sort of help?' Gaia couldn't stop her voice shaking. 'Who from?'

'Me. Jinx.' He held out his hand. Neither of them moved to take it. 'It's not only me. There's a gang of us. Kids without papers. We help each other out.'

'We don't need help,' said Tal.

'Sure about that, are you? Got somewhere to sleep?'

'Yes.'

'Somewhere not known to the Watch? Or to slavers? You know about slavers, right?' He looked from Tal to Gaia, and back again. 'Honest. Come with me, and I'll show you our place. Not luxury. But it's sheltered, and it's *safe.*'

'Tal?' said Gaia.

'No.'

'Fair enough,' said Jinx. 'Take it or leave it.' They watched him saunter away down the alley and out of sight, but a moment later he came pelting back, grabbed hold of Gaia and shoved Tal ahead of him, bundling them both down a steep flight of steps into a dark low cellar underneath the road.

'What...' Tal began.

'Shhh!'

Heavy footsteps echoed in the alley above and stopped. A voice said, 'I thought I saw someone come up here.'

'Well, you were wrong, weren't you?'

The footsteps sounded again, became fainter, and died into nothing. After a few moments of silence, Jinx crawled out of the cellar and back up the steps. At the top he considered Gaia and Tal with a slight smile.

'Still think you don't need help?'

'Tal,' Gaia said.

His shoulders slumped. 'Alright,' he said. 'If you want... Alright.'

'Good!' Jinx draped his arms round their shoulders. 'Welcome to the Company!'

He led them swiftly through the twilit streets, always keeping to the darkest side, ducking out of whatever light gleamed from doors and windows. They took a long winding route and by the time they reached the main square, night had fallen. Globe lanterns cast pools of coloured light on the marble pavement. The square was crowded again, hundreds of people gathering around the high stack of wood. Gaia stopped. 'Jinx? What is that?'

'Swan fire.'

'*Swan fire?*'

'Stop and see if you like. Safe enough, with this many people around. Tag onto a group that looks allowed. Families are good. Here.' He stopped alongside a group of grown-ups and children, the adults talking together, and occasionally breaking off to go after a child who had strayed too far among strangers in the darkness.

'This'll do,' said Jinx. 'Hang on. I'll be back in a bit.' He slipped away, leaving Gaia and Tal hovering uncertainly at the edge of the group. Lighted torches were flung into the huge stack of wood. Someone shouted, 'Burn the swan!' and the cry was taken up by one person after another, echoing from the high walls around the square.

Burn the swan!

Burn the swan!

A red glow spread through the woodpile, brightening into orange and white, illuminating a puppet perched on top of the fire: a human figure with a white bird's head. Towering flames leapt up around it, sending sparks scattering into the sky. The coloured lamps wavered behind the heat haze; the white walls glowed orange; reflected flames flickered in the windows. The swan-man slumped sideways and collapsed into the burning heart of the fire.

'Alright?' Jinx reappeared from the darkness, holding three steaming cups. 'Here.' They took a cup each, folding chilled hands around the warmth, and burying their faces in the hot scent of fruit and spices.

'Do they give these away too?' Gaia asked. 'Like the cakes?'

'Little innocent.' Jinx winked at her. 'No. The cakes are the only things that come free.'

'You bought these? But we haven't...'

'Gaia... The Company don't do buying.' He winked again, raised his cup to them and drained it. A big log fell in the fire. Bells sounded from the high tower. 'Curfew. Come on, kiddiewinks. Bedtime.'

They followed him down a passageway between the big white buildings and round into the road that ran behind them. Behind one of the buildings there was a yard, guarded by a rough stone wall.

'Reckon you can climb that?' Jinx asked.

They nodded, scaled the wall, and lowered themselves down into the dark yard on the other side. The building loomed above them: a face of blank stone, broken only here and there by tiny windows. Jinx stooped down and lifted a loose grating at the base of the wall.

'In here. Just sit and let yourselves drop. It's not deep. Look. I'll go first.' They followed him down into utter darkness. Gaia held onto Tal while Jinx replaced the grating. She felt him reach past them and heard the faint click of a latch, and the squeak of hinges opening.

'Through here. Bend your head.' Jinx steered Gaia through a low opening. Inside, she stood blinking into the darkness: she felt the warmth of stuffy air, smooth stone under her feet, and Jinx and Tal stepping in alongside her. She heard the squeak and click of something closing softly.

'Where are we?' Tal asked.

'Shhh!' Jinx caught hold of Gaia's hand and guided it onto a polished wooden rail. 'Down here.'

Gaia clutched the rail, shuffled forwards and felt the edge of a step underfoot. She fumbled down one step, then another, and another. The stairs spiralled down into the darkness, and she climbed blind: guided only by the wooden rail under her hands; hearing the tread of Tal's feet and his shallow breathing behind her. At the bottom, she turned, reached for Tal's hand and held it tight.

'This way.' Jinx caught her free hand and she stumbled along in the dark between him and Tal. At last, they stopped. Jinx gave a soft whistle. A faint glimmer showed ahead of them, moved closer, and brightened, and in the sudden light Gaia saw that they were standing at a locked iron gate. On the other side a girl with a lantern was peering at them through the bars.

'Who's this, Jinx?'

'New members, Lizzie. Gaia and Tal. Open up.'

'Who?'

'Gaia and Tal.'

'Funny names.' Lizzie unlocked and opened the gate, and they stepped through it into a room crowded with high shelves that reached from floor to ceiling, forming a maze of narrow passageways. Jinx led them along a complex route of sharp turns to left and right, halting at the end of a blind alley where there were shelves on either side and ahead of them. He and Lizzie hauled a couple of boxes off one of the bottom shelves, and Lizzie crawled through the gap they had made.

'In you go,' Jinx said. Gaia hesitated, took a steadying breath, and crawled through. On the other side there was enough light for her to see that she was in a small square room crowded with children who were watching her, curious but welcoming. They were all snuggled - she looked carefully - under *paper*: sheets and sheets of yellowing parchment, curly at the edges with age, covered with spidery writing in faded brown ink. Other crumpled sheets were burning in an iron basket, sending out a smoky warmth. A couple of lanterns stood on upturned boxes, with the ends of some bread and cheese, wrinkled apples and a dozen colourful Carnival cakes. Gaia turned, bewildered, to Jinx. He grinned.

'Welcome to the Nest.'

'Yes, but…Where *are* we?'

'Basement of the National Archive. It's where the Fellowship keeps all their old papers.'

'It's a *Fellowship* building? Are you allowed…?' She caught the beginning of a laugh in his eyes. 'What if they find you?'

'Nah,' he said. 'No-one ever comes this far down. Anyway, you saw. We rearranged the shelves. They'd never find us.'

'What if they did?' she insisted.

Jinx kicked some stray papers aside and heaved up an iron lid set in the stone floor. Peering in, Gaia felt a rush of cold, foetid air, and saw the oily glimmer of water a long way below.

'Escape hatch,' Jinx said. 'Main drain. Goes to the river.' He let the lid fall shut and grinned at her again. She picked up a crumbling, yellowed piece of paper and fingered the wax seal and ribbon that were attached to it. They were both brittle with age.

'What are all these papers, anyway?'

'Search me. We've never had a Reader in the Company.' He shrugged. 'Go on. Help yourself to a heap of parchment and snuggle down… make yourselves at home.'

'But there are no windows.' Tal had been looking round the small room, and he said again, hoarsely, 'Gaia, there aren't any windows. We're out of the moonsight.'

She stared, wildly. No windows, not even a slit, no opening through which the moon could keep watch over them. She looked at Jinx with outraged panic in her eyes. 'There aren't, are there?'

'No.' Jinx held up a hand to stem her protest. 'But it's *safe* here. Sure, the moon could see you if you were out on the streets, but so could the Watch and the slavers. And a bit of moonlight comes down the back stairs…'

'We can't see the moon, though, can we?' said Tal.

'No. But I bet the moon can see you. You think walls can keep gods out? We've all been here for ages. And we're *fine*.'

They weren't convinced. They lay awake for a long time, listening to the rustle of papers as the Company children turned over in their sleep and when at last they slept themselves, they dreamed uneasy dreams until Jinx woke them and told them it was morning.

'See?' he said. 'You're fine. Now, I reckon I better learn you Freehaven.'

Outside, in another day of clear sun, they dodged through the Carnival crowds, across the square and onto the bridge. Jinx settled himself comfortably on the parapet.

'Right. Over there' (he waved a hand at the steep hill on the other side of the bridge) 'is High Side. Stay away from it. It's all Fellowship houses: guarded streets, unfriendly slaves, and vicious dogs. You stick this side of the river. The big square is Liberation Square. The building with the dome's the Basilica. The others are Fellowship offices. It's really busy there now, because of Carnival, but it's always a good place if you need to get lost in a crowd.'

He jumped off the parapet. 'Coming?' he said, but Gaia was staring down at the multi-coloured river below them. A flock of swans was swimming into sight from under the bridge, to a clamour of booing and hissing from the crowd on the bridge and the riverside terraces.

'What's going on?'

'Swanning. Second day of Carnival.'

A small fleet of boats was rowing hard after the swans; their oarsmen dressed in bright liveries of the same vivid colours that swirled in the water. The birds were panicking: swimming this way and that, even turning back towards the boats in their confusion.

'Why don't they fly away?' asked Gaia.

'Can't,' said Jinx. 'Their wings are clipped.'

The boats were in the middle of the frightened flock now. The man in the dark green boat dropped his oars, leaned out, and seized one of the swimming birds. He wrestled with it and after a moment's struggle, the big white body slumped limp in his arms. A roar rose from the crowd.

'He's *killed* it!' Gaia exclaimed.

'S'what happens.' Jinx shrugged. Gaia saw another swan caught and killed; and after that she couldn't bear to watch anymore. They were probably, she thought, the same swans that had kept them warm on the night before last.

'You were going to show us around,' she reminded Jinx, and they left the shouting crowd on the bridge, crossed the square, and wound through the twisting streets behind the Basilica, to the harbour and its tall ships. The steel blue sea stretched to a clear horizon.

'You never seen the sea before?' Jinx asked.

They shook their heads, staring.

'Pretty, I suppose, but don't get distracted. You've to be careful down here. The watch, slavers… and some of these captains ain't above grabbing kids for cheap labour on the ships. Only come here if you need to. Let's go and nick some lunch,' and he swung away from the quayside up a stepped passageway back into the city.

Next morning, on the last day of Carnival, they clambered out of the Archive window to find a cold rain lashing down.

'S'usually dry for the whole three days,' said Jinx. 'Mind, the weather's mad this year.' A shivering crowd had gathered to watch the final Carnival celebrations. In the sky above the square, a big, white, bird-shaped kite was flying. Thirteen archers dressed in the colours of the Fellowship aimed at it; ribboned arrows struggled through the rain and the kite collapsed to the ground in a mess of soggy paper.

'A swan again?' Gaia asked.

Jinx nodded. 'Last day. Downing of the swan.'

A fanfare sounded and there was a clamour of beating wings. Brilliant, exotic birds, like flying jewels - emerald, lapis, magenta, scarlet, gold and more - filled the grey sky.

'What are they?'

'Just doves,' Jinx said. 'They dye them' - and, in the rain, the colour was streaming out of their feathers and spattering in rainbow pools on the pavement. The colours ran into one another, and mixed into a muddy brown.

'Well,' said Jinx. 'That's it. Shame about the weather. There's usually good pickings on the last day of Carnival. May as well go back to the Nest.'

The following morning was the first day of Arctos, the start of the year, but Gaia woke with the sense of something ending. Today the Freehaven shops would open again, and Jinx had promised to show them the way back to Fossick's shop. Today, she would sell the amulet. She crouched in her paper bed, the light fragment of moonswood nestling in her palm.

'You ready, Gaia?' Jinx asked.

'I don't know.'

'Gaia!' Tal exclaimed.

'Just...' She turned the amulet over in her hand. 'Even if we sell it, we still don't know how to find Mum...'

'As to that,' said Jinx, 'there might be ways.' They turned to him hopefully. He held up a warning hand. 'No promises. But there's ways of getting the High Side gossip. Shop boys. Seamstresses. And you said Tal looks like her?'

'Very,' said Gaia.

'So we could show you around a bit.' He grinned at Tal. 'See if anyone recognises you.'

Gaia ran it over in her mind. Sell the amulet. Stay safe in the Nest. Put out the word on Jinx's spider's web of gossip. It was *possible*. She pulled on her coat and buttoned it with determined fingers. 'Let's go then. No point hanging about.'

It was still raining hard. In the three-sided square, the dolphin fountain was overflowing onto the wet cobbles. Jinx slipped into a sheltered alley between two houses to wait and made the sign of the crescent moon to wish them good luck. They climbed the narrow street. The window and door of Fossick's shop were unbarred, and a faint light glimmered inside. Gaia took a deep breath, and pushed the door open.

The shop was crammed with locked glass cases, and overflowing, dusty bookshelves filled the walls from floor to ceiling. A tall man was leaning against one of the shelves, flicking through the yellowing pages of a small leather-bound book. He looked up as they entered and Gaia recognised the man who had overheard them in the Basilica. He gave them a puzzled smile.

'Excuse me...' Gaia's voice faltered. She swallowed hard. 'Are you Mr Fossick?'

To her disappointment, he shook his head and gestured to the counter at the back of the shop. A thin, sandy-haired man was watching them narrowly. He was dressed from head to toe in brown and his skin was as dry as old parchment. Gaia gripped Tal's hand and pulled him with her to the counter.

'Yes?' the man asked. His voice, too, was thin and dry.

'We... We've got something we want to sell,' Gaia stammered. He looked sceptically at her, and she fumbled at the pouch around her neck. 'It's carved moonswood. Like the ones you've got in the window.' She tugged the amulet free and laid it down on the dusty counter.

Fossick caught his breath with a gasp like the wind through dried reeds. With a trembling finger, he reached out and traced the carved symbols on the amulet.

Nervousness made Gaia babble. 'Will you buy it? How much is it worth? Enough to redeem a slave?' A sudden thought struck her, and she continued, 'It is *mine*, honestly. We didn't steal it. I had it from my father, Athanasius. I mean, he's dead now, but Mum gave it to me last birthday...'

Tal squeezed her hand and mouthed at her to shut up. She fell silent, watching Fossick's face. His eyes were worlds away. At last he wrenched his gaze away from the amulet and looked at her. There was an odd expression of mingled astonishment and shame in his eyes.

'What's your name?' he asked.

'Gaia.'

'And I'm Tal,' said Tal. Fossick ignored him.

'Gaia? *Gaia?*'

He looked at her, wonderingly, then his face seemed to close and harden. With a wintry smile he said, 'I ... Look... I need to ... check something.' His hand hovered over the amulet, but Gaia snatched it up and clutched it tightly. Fossick frowned. 'Wait here,' he said. He ducked through a low door at the back of the counter and pulled it shut behind him.

'Run.'

The man from the Basilica was standing close behind them. Gaia swung round to face him.

'What?'

'Whatever that thing is, it's in Old Script. It's a Prohibited Object. He'll be sending for the Watch now.' He bundled them towards the door. 'Go. Run.'

Gaia stared. 'What do you mean, *Old Script?*'

'Prohibited?' asked Tal. 'Like a prohibited place?'

The tall man nodded. 'Exactly. And with the same penalties.' He pushed them to the door and out into the street. 'Just go. Get as far away as you can.'

'But I don't understand…' Gaia began. Tal tugged at her.

'Never mind! Let's just *go*, Gaia!'

They backed away, turned and broke into a run, skidding on the wet cobbles and almost colliding with a man coming the other way. Dodging around him, they pelted down the sloping street into the square. Jinx was lounging in the shelter of a doorway. They hurtled towards him.

'What's up?'

'Got to get out of here!' panted Tal.

Jinx nodded, and plunged headlong into the maze of streets. They pounded after him along a crazy winding route that finally brought them to the big bridge; scrambled up the ladder to the ledge and flopped down, breathless and exhausted.

'What in the name of moonshine was all that about?' asked Jinx.

On the Run

Fossick had given one last troubled and curious glance at Gaia and Tal before retreating into his private rooms, and closing the door behind him. His face set, he crossed to the corner where a heavy rope disappeared into a hole in the ceiling. He followed it in his imagination up to the bell, sheltered in its iron cage on the rooftop. 'Anything odd,' the city officials had told him when he first set up shop. 'Anything prohibited - especially anything prohibited - you let us know. And if you don't...'

He closed his fingers round the scratchy fibres of the rope. One sharp pull would do it. It had happened once before. He knew how it would be. His calling bell would set other alarm bells ringing above the rooftops, summoning the Watch. They would be here in moments. They would destroy the strange little square of carved moonswood. That glimpse he had just had of it would be all he would ever get. And those children...

He closed his eyes and remembered. He had made himself find out what had happened to the man he had reported, and he had a vivid recollection of fresh earth heaped carelessly over a criminal's grave. That would be where they would end too: buried. That boy (he had forgotten his name) and the girl. Gaia. He fingered the frayed ends of the rope, pondering what a coincidence it was that a child with a name out of the Old Times should be carrying an object from the Old Times.

Then it hit him, with a jolt like treading in the dark on a stair that isn't there: the thing he had heard and not heard. Her father's name. Her father's name was Athanasius. He let go of the rope and steadied it, afraid that he might have set some fatal vibration travelling upwards to stir the bell. His thoughts were in turmoil -

It's not possible.

It might be. That might be who she is.

- and instinctively, to the core of his being, he felt sure that the impossible thing was true. But he was a scholar. It had to be

112

properly proved, and the most important piece of evidence was out there, in the shop, clutched in Gaia's frightened hands. The first thing to do was to take another look at it.

They were gone. The tall man was leaning against the shelves, reading again, carelessly blocking the way to the door. Fossick stopped short behind the counter. 'Where are they?'

The tall man raised his eyes from his book. 'Who? Those children? Oh. They left.'

Fossick pushed past him, flung open the door, and hurried down the alleyway. In the fountain square he stopped in confusion. They could have taken any one of the three roads, and there was no-one to ask: the relentless icy rain had driven everyone indoors. Fossick swore to himself and trudged back to the shop. The tall man raised an eyebrow. 'No luck?'

'Damn you, Gabriel.' Fossick slammed the door shut.

'For pity's sake,' the other man protested. 'They're *kids*. You were about to get them arrested and killed.'

'I *wasn't*.'

'Oh, come on,' said Gabriel. 'You were going for the alarm...'

'No.' Fossick seized Gabriel's arm and dragged him out into the street. 'Listen,' he snapped. Rain hammered on the rooftops and seagulls cried in the wet sky, but there were no alarm bells pealing out across the city. The two men stepped back inside, and Fossick picked up a moonswood panel from the window. He turned it over in his papery hands, staring out at the wet street.

'I don't understand,' Gabriel said. 'It's your duty to report those things, isn't it?'

'Well,' Fossick said, avoiding Gabriel's eyes. 'Like you said. They're only children, aren't they?'

Gabriel looked out into the pitiless rain. 'I hope they're going to be alright.'

'Well?' Jinx asked. 'What was all that about? You come flying down that alley like you just nicked something.'

'We weren't stealing.' Gaia tucked the amulet away.

'Weren't selling either, by the looks of it,' said Jinx. 'Wasn't old Fossick interested?'

'No. He was. Only there was someone else in the shop. He told us it was a… a prohibited object.'

'What!? How in the name of Aquilon and all his dragons do you two…' Jinx glanced up into the hidden heights of the bridge, and lowered his voice. 'How come you've got a *prohibited object?*'

'I told you,' Gaia said. 'My father left it to me. I didn't know it was prohibited.'

Jinx scrambled to his feet and they stood to go with him, but he held up his hands. 'Oh no. No way. You're in big trouble. You'll be papered by tonight…'

'Papered?' asked Tal.

'Your pictures, descriptions… they'll be everywhere. Pick up a scrap of paper from the street tomorrow and a dozen to one you'll find yourself looking out of it. Whole city'll be after you. You can't come back to the Company. You're too much of a risk.' His voice softened. 'I'm sorry. But I got the others to think of.'

'So what can we do?' Tal wiped a shaking hand across his mouth.

Jinx sat down again, uneasily. 'You got to get out of Freehaven. They won't stop looking till they find you, and you can't hide for ever.' He breathed out deeply and shook his head. 'You can't go through the gates. Risky without papers at the best of times, and with that thing… But there is a way. Downriver. We've got kids out that way, when the city got too hot for them. Look.'

He pointed across the river. 'Over that side, the embankment runs on past the city wall. Wait till dark. Climb the embankment wall. Not on the top. You'd be seen. Along the side. It's tricky, but doable. Once you're past the city wall you can cut back inland. Get as far away as possible…' He put one foot on the ladder.

'Wait!' Gaia caught hold of his arm. 'Couldn't I throw it away? Chuck it in the river, or…'

He shuddered. 'For pity's sake, Gaia, don't do that. If they find it on you, it's death, but at least it's clean and quick. If they find you, and you don't have it, and they know that you did, they'll want to know where it is. And even if the truth is that you chucked it in the river, they won't believe you: not till they've checked every last person you've so much as brushed against since you got here.' He shuddered again. 'For your sake and ours, Gaia, don't get rid of it.' He looked at her sharply. 'You tell Fossick your name?'

She nodded miserably.

'Then make up a new one. Be ready to give it. Best, don't get into any scrape where you *have* to give it.' He dug in his pocket and chucked a couple of bread rolls onto the ledge. 'Here. Stay hidden today. Get out tonight.' He gave them a troubled smile and left. They listened to the ladder reverberating under his feet until it fell still and silent. Gaia looked at Tal.

'I'm sorry. This was my stupid idea...'

He said nothing.

'I'm *sorry,*' she said again.

'Not your fault. And we've been lucky so far. Maybe we'll get out.' He didn't sound convinced.

'Maybe,' she said. She sat against the solid stonework of the bridge, hunched up against the cold, and he pressed next to her. The river surged and eddied beneath them: no longer multi-coloured, but a single deep mournful dark green. Rain shattered the surface of the water. They waited. The cold day dragged past. As evening started to close in, Tal stirred.

'Time to go.'

'It's not dark yet. Jinx said...'

'We're not going on the *road*. We'll cross the beams, like we did before.'

They climbed the ladder, and crawled along the wide beams that ran between the thick stone piers of the bridge, high up underneath the arches where dark had already fallen. Climbing down the ladder on the far side, they were startled by a clamour of bells pealing out across the city. Gaia grabbed Tal's ankle.

'Have they seen us?'

'I don't know...' He paused, tilting his head to listen to the pattern of the sounds. 'I don't think so. It's curfew, isn't it?'

They climbed down to the broad base of the pier, and huddled against the stones, waiting for silence and darkness. After the last curfew bell, they worked their way to the wall, and peered at it in the fading light. It was built of massive square blocks of pitted stone: easy to grip hold of, and Tal felt suddenly hopeful. This was *nothing* compared to scrambling up rocky slopes at home. 'It's alright, Gaia,' he whispered. 'This is going to be *easy.*' They edged along the wall, leaving the bridge further and further behind them; the lanterns along the roadway grew smaller and fainter until they were almost swallowed by the darkness. The river was wider now, and there was a salt smell of the sea. Maybe this really was possible...

Tal came to a halt.

'What?' Gaia whispered.

'Shh. Don't know. Look.'

There were shadowy figures moving on the opposite shore, and the distant murmur of voices. Tal moved cautiously forward; then a wide beam of brilliant light shone out across the water, hitting the wall ahead of them, pitilessly searching out every detail of every stone.

'Back!' Tal hissed.

They scrambled, panicking, back the way they had come, fumbling for finger- and foot-holds in the darkness. Tal's hands felt slick with cold rain and fear: at any moment, he thought, the beam of light would swing round, pinning them to the stones. At last, far back into the sheltering darkness, he stopped and looked back. The light hadn't moved, but it was still shining, and it was as impassable as any physical barrier, with the guards keeping an unblinking watch from the other side of the river. They were trapped in Freehaven.

For a while they clung to the rough wall, but then the icy rain began to fall again. 'Gaia,' Tal whispered. 'We have to go back. We'll freeze otherwise.' With dull despair, they made the long climb back to the hidden ledge, where they sat close together: clothes and hair soaked with rain, the savage winter cold biting into their bones. Downriver, the light shone all night. It grew faint in the grey dawn, and was extinguished as day broke.

'We could try again tonight,' Tal said. 'They might not have the light every night... or we might be able to get round the guards on the road.' There was no real hope in his voice. 'We should get some rest, anyway.' They closed their eyes; worn out by the night and hopelessness, they fell into a fitful cold sleep. The rain pitted the green river, and drummed on the bridge above them.

At noon that same day, Fossick locked his dark narrow shop and set out for his usual lunch in a dark narrow tavern on the far side of Liberation Square. With his head bowed beneath the steely rain, watching his footing on the wet cobbles, lost in thoughts of Gaia and her amulet, he didn't notice the other man hurrying up the alley towards him. He was startled out of his day-dream by a hand on his arm, and a dry voice:

'Babbington Fossick!'

He looked up, astonished, into the face of an old Academy friend. Years had passed, but he recognised him straight away.

'Cosmo Scrimp!'

They shook hands.

'Heard you'd set up shop here,' said Scrimp. 'Thought I'd look you up.'

'I was on my way to eat,' said Fossick. 'Will you join me?'

'Gladly,' said Scrimp, and they fell into step, side by side, along the meandering streets. Liberation Square was almost deserted, except for a few passers-by hurrying through the rain, and a sodden stall selling loaves and tea in the lee of the Basilica wall. Fossick led Scrimp down a steep road towards the quay, and into a dimly lit tavern where a miserable fire smouldered in a giant hearth. A pale, rather expressionless girl sat at the fireside, embroidering a grubby pillowcase. She greeted Fossick with a casual 'good-day,' opening her eyes wide with surprise as she realised that he wasn't alone.

'Hello, Sassy,' Fossick said, as she stood up to make room for them at the fireside table. 'Soup and bread. For two, please, and maybe some wine?'

'Definitely wine,' said Scrimp. 'I'm on holiday today.'

'On holiday from what?' Fossick asked. But Scrimp had loosened his coat, revealing its indigo lining, and Fossick answered his own question. 'You're working for Lord Parhelion.'

Scrimp nodded. 'I'm his new Treasurer. Accounting. Collecting tribute. That sort of thing.'

Fossick studied his old friend closely. Cosmo had always been ambitious to make his way in the world, and an important post in a Fellowship household was about as high as you could get. He had made it, and it showed in his clothes. Fossick compared Scrimp's good overcoat and new leather shoes with his own threadbare cloak and badly mended boots.

Cosmo Scrimp and Lord Parhelion. An odd match: Parhelion was rumoured to be vain, spendthrift and very stupid. And Cosmo was clever: he had vied with Fossick for first place at the Academy. Fossick would have given a month's takings (which, admittedly, wasn't much) to know what Cosmo really thought of his new master.

'Have you seen his new statue in the Basilica?' he fished.

Scrimp blushed. 'Oh. Yes.'

'Cosmo!' Fossick had a sudden flash of intuition. 'You didn't write that... poem?'

'Part of the job. I *know*... But you try finding a decent rhyme for Parhelion!'

'Impossible, I'm sure.' Fossick dismissed the poetic dilemma with a nonchalant gesture. 'Was his Lordship pleased?'

'He *loved* it.' Gloomily, Scrimp poured himself a second glass of wine; drained it; peered at Fossick through the smoky dimness, and seemed to make his mind up.

'I was coming to see you yesterday, Babbington, but something rather strange happened.'

Fossick thought of his own strange yesterday, and said, 'Oh?'

Scrimp hesitated before he went on. 'There are Parhelion lands in the Arimaspian Mountains. They've never been worth much, obviously. Except one village. They mined gold there, for years: it was a decent source of tribute while it lasted. But the mines dried up - thirty years ago, or more - and the late Lord stopped bothering with the place. It's a long journey, terribly dangerous. Dragon country.' He poured himself another glass of wine.

'Despite all that, we went there, in Brumas. A slight... er ... cash-flow problem. His Lordship hoped they might have started mining again. It's a pit of a place: stinking, uncivilised, leagues from anywhere, and of course, there was no gold. They've scraped by for years, goat-herding, and they had precious little to give. We took goats and slaves mostly.'

He hesitated. When he spoke again, it was more slowly. 'There was a widow's daughter. She offered us a strange object as tribute: she called it an amulet. Parhelion refused it - said it was worthless. I wasn't sure. It was a square of moonswood about so big. Inscribed. It... It wasn't Free Script.'

Fossick gave a cautious look round, but the tavern was deserted apart from Sassy. 'Old?'

Scrimp looked round as well. 'Maybe. Anyway, the really strange thing is... I saw her again. Yesterday. Running down the alley from your shop. There was a boy with her: her brother, I think: there was a brother, up in the mountains. I tried to follow them...'

'Where did they go?' Fossick interrupted eagerly.

Scrimp looked at him, narrowly. 'I lost them. There was another boy with them; typical Freehaven street urchin. They gave me the slip in that confounded maze of streets you live in.' He leaned forward. 'They'd been to see you, hadn't they?'

Fossick nodded. 'They tried to sell me the amulet.'

'And?' Scrimp asked.

Fossick lowered his voice. 'You were right. It was Old Script.'

Scrimp exhaled a long breath of disbelief. 'How in the name of all the moons does a peasant kid from the wilds of Arimaspia come to own a piece of moonswood in Old Script?'

'Good question.' Fossick picked up his wine glass, turned it between his fingers and drained the last mouthful. 'You've got connections nowadays, Cosmo. Could you get me into the Closed Archive?'

'What?!' Scrimp choked on a mouthful of wine. 'You must be joking. You need permission of the Fellowship given in full council to get in there. Why, anyway?'

Fossick chewed at the skin around the edge of his thumbnail. 'I need to check a couple of things.'

Scrimp shook his head. 'Babbington, if this is to do with that girl and her amulet, then forget it.' He looked at Fossick in horror. 'Wait a moment. They haven't been papered; there've been no search parties out... You didn't report them, did you?'

Fossick shrugged.

'You're on dangerous ground, Babbington,' Scrimp warned. He stood and buttoned his coat. 'Drop it.'

They stepped out into the gusting rain, and Sassy put down her pillowcase, and stood at their abandoned table, running through all the details of their conversation in her head.

Late afternoon. The grey light was fading to dimness, but under the bridge it was as dark as if night had already fallen. They had slept a little, but cold and hunger nagged at them now, keeping them miserably awake. Gaia sat hunched over a gnawing in her stomach that was part dread, part emptiness.

'Tal,' she said.

119

He didn't reply. The icy rain was still falling: in the freezing wet, tonight's climb would be difficult and dangerous, and there was no hope of it ending in anything except another panicked retreat from the light across the river.

'Tal,' Gaia said again.

'What?' He forced his gaze away from the mesmerising rain.

'Let's go and get some food.' She stood, paced to the edge of the ledge, and back again.

'Are you mad? Jinx said *stay hidden.*' He sat back against the stone pier and clasped his arms round his knees. Gaia crouched in front of him.

'Come *on.* It's pouring. There won't be many people about.'

'No.'

'We can't not *eat.*'

'No, Gaia.'

She stood up again. 'Well, I'm going.'

'Fine,' he said. 'You go. I'm staying.' But as she started down the ladder, he called, 'Wait!' and climbed down after her, catching her up on the riverside terrace.

'You don't *have* to come,' she said.

'Let's just get it done, shall we?' He trudged up the broad marble steps to the road. The bridge and the square were almost deserted. The relentless rain had driven people indoors, and the few passers-by hurried along with their heads hard down against the weather.

'Told you,' Gaia said.

'Alright,' he said. 'Food. Where do we try?'

'Behind the Basilica?'

They skirted the square and dived into the tangle of streets that led down to the harbour. An icy wind drove the rain into their faces. Water ran over the cobbles, and dripped heavily from the eaves of the buildings on either side. Every shop they passed was firmly closed against the weather. At last, Gaia stopped outside a bakery and put her hand on the door.

'No!' said Tal. 'Remember what Jinx said? Don't go into shops.'

'Where else?' she asked angrily. She pushed hard at the door. It slammed open, letting out a roll of air that blossomed with the warmth of newly baked bread. Someone said, sharply, 'What do you two want?' but Tal was already grabbing at Gaia's hand, dragging her out of the shop and pulling her into a run; alert for pursuing footsteps, and shouts of 'You! It's you, isn't it….!' After a headlong flight through the crazy streets they stopped and leaned against the back wall of the Basilica to catch their breath. The giant silver dome gleamed dully above them in the rain.

'Idiot,' said Tal.

'Well, have you got a better idea?'

'Yes.' He pushed himself upright. 'I'm going to hide, and stay hidden.' He started back along the towering side wall of the Basilica, and Gaia trailed after him. As they came out into the square, she caught his hand and hissed, 'Look!'

A solitary stall selling tea and bread stood near the Basilica steps. Rain and wind savaged the flimsy canopy; hunched beneath it, the stall-holder looked cold and bedraggled. Tal looked at it, and the vast deserted square beyond.

'No way, Gaia. We'd stand out like black goats in the snow.' His words were drowned in the clamour of bells from the Basilica tower and an answering peal from smaller bells all over the city. His heart lurched momentarily, but they were just ringing the end of the working day. People poured out from the white Fellowship buildings, and the stall was suddenly crowded with customers, buying tea and buns, wrapping cold hands around hot cups and trying to find shelter under the awning.

'We could try *now*,' Gaia said.

'I don't know…' he began, but she had already burrowed into the bustling crowd. He swore under his breath and followed. When he reached the stall he found himself separated from her by a group of men who were huddling close together, sipping hot tea. He loitered behind them, next to a tray of damp buns. The stall-holder was busy with another customer. It'd be easy… Tal leaned against the counter and worked his hand out of his pocket…

'Oy! Thief! *Thief!*'

He startled, and whirled round, but the shout was nothing to do with him. *Gaia* was running, trying to dodge through the crowd that had become a mass of arms reaching, grabbing, clutching at her. She ducked past a snatching hand, and ran headlong into a big man who held onto her, pinioning her arms at her sides. She kicked and struggled but he held her tight. A circle of curious spectators gathered round. Tal fought his way frantically to the front of the crowd and stopped.

The stall-holder pushed past him and halted in front of Gaia. 'Thief!' she said again. Her face was raw with cold and anger. She wrenched Gaia's hand out of her pocket and forced her fingers open. Fragments of sticky dough tumbled to the wet pavement. Someone said, 'Best call the Watch,' and a skinny boy standing a couple of paces from Tal piped up, 'I'll go!' and scudded away across the square. Tal met Gaia's eyes.

'Go,' she mouthed.

He should go to her, he knew he should: should cross the empty space between them, and take his place beside her. But making those few steps felt as impossible as walking to the moon. He didn't - couldn't - move.

'Go,' she mouthed again, and this time he took a single step backwards.

'What's going on?' A couple of burly men, wearing the grey livery of the city Watch, shouldered their way through the bystanders.

'Alright, you lot, shove off. You got nothing better to do than stand here in the rain? Show's over. Go.'

People began to drift away until only Tal and a handful of other curious onlookers remained. One of the watchmen fished a dog-eared notebook out of his pocket and Tal remembered Jinx's warning: 'You'll be papered.' A cold surge of fear passed through him. But the Watchman only said, 'What's she done?'

'Been thieving from me,' the stall-holder complained.

'What she take?'

'Buns.'

'Only one,' Gaia said.

'One or a hundred,' said the Watchman, 'thieving's thieving. Only her, was it?'

'Yes,' Gaia said clearly. She mouthed 'go' again, and this time, Tal dropped his gaze, and shuffled backwards and sideways so that he was hidden behind a large man at the front of the crowd. The Watchman shoved his notebook away.

'We'll take her now,' he said, and each of the Watchman took one of her arms and marched her away. They walked close to Tal: so close that he could have reached out and touched her; close enough for him to imagine that he could hear her breathing. He stood silently with his head down as they passed him. Then they were gone: out of reach, out of sight behind the hurrying townsfolk heading for home.

He stood and stood; alone in the rain.

Fellowship Justice

Tal was close enough to touch, and every scared lonely fibre of her ached to reach for him. But she allowed herself to be walked past without a word or sign to give him away. She waited until he was out of sight before she started to struggle, kicking and twisting in the Watchmen's grip.

'None of that,' one of them said, and they held her tighter, half carrying and half dragging her across the square. Through a blur of rain and tears she saw the shimmering marble of the pavement, dancing raindrops, hurrying feet, looming white walls, a lamplighter carrying light to the big coloured lanterns. The rain clung shining in his hair, and she heard him murmur, 'poor kid,' as they passed him.

They stopped at a wicket gate in a pair of big wooden doors. The Watchmen pushed Gaia inside, and through an arched entryway into a cramped messy office. A skinny young man was leaning back, balancing his chair on two legs, and batting scrumpled balls of paper across the room, aiming for the overflowing wastepaper basket.

'Hope you ain't wasting Fellowship stationery, Bill,' said one of the Watchman. The young man started. His chair rocked alarmingly backwards and forwards and finally landed with a thud on all four feet.

'What can I do for you, Brandon?'

'Another one to sign in. Theft.' Brandon turned to Gaia. 'Papers.'

'Lost them,' she said.

He looked at her disbelievingly. 'Never had them, more like. Better add vagrancy to that charge sheet, Bill.'

The young man opened his desk, heaved out a leather-bound volume, thumped it down, and flipped it open. Picking up a pen with blue stained fingers, he dipped it in the inkwell, and scratched a few lines in the ledger. 'What's your name?' he asked Gaia.

Lie, Jinx had said. 'Umm...' she fumbled. 'Ummm... Elsa.'

'Elsa what?'

Her mind spun. At the harbour, they had seen big white birds in the sky, far out at sea, and she'd asked Jinx if they were swans too, but he'd said no...

'Seagull,' she said.

Bill looked at her doubtfully, but entered the name in his book.

'Going to search her, Brandon?'

She took an instinctive step backwards. Nestled in its pouch, the cool, light square of moonswood felt suddenly as hot and heavy as molten gold.

'Take your coat off,' Brandon told her. She shrugged her arms out of the sodden fur and let it fall heavily to her feet. Brandon picked it up, felt the lining, dug his hands into the pockets, swore, and wiped the sticky sweet paste from the stolen bun from his fingers. He threw the coat back to her.

'Nothing.'

'Better check the wanted list,' said Bill.

'Right.' Brandon adjusted a lantern and light flared into the shadowy room, drowning the firelight and darkening the windows. A harsh beam fell on Gaia. She kept her head bowed.

'Put your head up,' said Bill, and through the blinding light, she watched him wrench a thick file down from a shelf. He leafed through it, one page at a time, occasionally glancing up at her with a frown before turning to the next page. She squinted to see what he was looking at, and felt a rush of fear. The file was full of roughly sketched faces. *You'll be papered.* So this was what Jinx had meant. She held her breath, waiting for the inevitable discovery. The room seemed to have become very small. Her ears were full of the pounding of her heart and the drumming of Brandon's fingers on the mantelpiece and the lashing of rain against the window...

'Nah.' Bill forced the bulging file shut. The bindings broke and a sheaf of drawings poured onto the floor. With a shock, Gaia recognised one of the Company children, whose face she had last seen looking at her from a nest of parchment.

'Right, you.' Brandon took her arm and pushed her back out into the archway, and for one crazy moment, she thought that they were headed out again, back to the open square and freedom. But they turned the other way, crossing a wide courtyard towards a hall whose lighted windows wavered behind the rain.

Tal stood, staring at the place where she had disappeared into the crowd. The square was almost deserted now. He was roused by the rumble of wheels: the stall-holder had packed up her goods and was dragging them away in a handcart. She gave Tal a questioning glance as she passed, him, halted, and looked back. 'Ain't you got a home to go to?'

'No. Yes. I'm fine,' he stammered.

She looked at him closely. 'You look half starved. Here,' and she dug into a bag on the cart, pulled out a loaf and thrust it into his hand. *No,* he thought, *no.*

'No-one ever teach you any manners?'

He managed a dry-mouthed, 'Thank you.'

'Hmm.' She gave a curt nod and carried on across the square. He watched her for a moment, and ran after her. 'Excuse me! That girl... The one who was stealing from you. Where will they take her?'

She looked at him questioningly, but she only said, tersely, 'Court,' and gestured at one of the big white buildings looming over the square.

'Thank you,' he said again. He hurried away into the rainy dusk.

At the far end of the hall, a strange lantern made of thirteen coloured spheres cast a harsh light on a raised dais where there was a table, covered with a silver cloth, and two chairs. Below it, in the body of the hall, there were rows of benches, crowded with ragged men, women and children, shackled at wrists and ankles. Brandon steered Gaia between them and she glanced into the ranks of faces as she passed: faces pinched with hunger and cold, some fearful, some defiant, some beyond expression altogether.

Near the front of the hall, Brandon pushed her down into a space on a bench, fastened heavy chains to her wrists and ankles, and left her. She twisted round to watch him go, picking his way out of the hall and disappearing out into the rainy night.

'What're you here for?'

Gaia turned. The girl sitting next to her was wearing patched and torn country clothes. Her fair hair was tangled and filthy and there was a deep scar on her left cheek.

'Stealing,' Gaia told her. 'And… what's it called… I don't have papers.'

'Vagrancy,' the girl said. 'Me too. Been done for it before.' Her fingers strayed to the scar on her cheek.

'What…' Gaia stopped, swallowed, and went on shakily, 'What'll happen now?'

The girl shook her head. 'Last time they said I'd be in trouble if they caught me again. Don't know what that means. Don't know what happens if you've been caught stealing, either.'

'You'll be sent out east. Both of you,' said the big man who was sitting on the other side of the girl. He was sprawling casually, seemingly at ease in his chains. His shirt was stained and he smelled of old wine. Gaia looked at him doubtfully. 'Trust me,' he said. 'I'm an old hand. Seen a hundred trials. In here almost every quarter. Brawling, drunk, out after curfew. I've been done for the lot.'

'So why haven't you been sent away?'

'Because,' he said with an exaggerated wink, 'I'm useful. You hear things…' He mimed drinking, and winked again. 'Their Lordships like to know what's going on.'

'You're a spy?' Instinctively, awkwardly because of her shackled wrists, Gaia tried to pull the fur more closely around her, to hide the amulet.

'I do what I have to.' He fell silent and turned away.

Out east. Gaia tried to picture John's map, but it was a blank. Tal would have remembered, and thinking of him almost made her cry. Through unshed tears she stared at the harsh light of the hanging lantern, and the silver-clothed table on the platform beneath it, and the grey-gowned officials bustling to and fro with armfuls of paper. As she watched, another officer burst through a door at the back of the dais and summoned the others to him. They held a brief whispered conversation. Someone called, 'Silence! *Silence!* The court will stand for Lord Lanneret!'

'Lanneret?' said the big man, loudly. 'Should be Parhelion, this evening. What happened? Pressing meeting with a game of cards and a bottle or two of wine…?' His voice tailed off. Every official in the hall had turned to look in his direction.

'Just a joke,' he said. The colour had drained from his face. 'Didn't mean anything by it...' But one of the officials on the platform had already given a muttered order to two guards. They hauled the man to his feet, unlocked the shackles on his ankles and pushed him towards the dais. 'It was a *joke*,' he said, again. His voice rose into a wail. 'You know who I am, don't you? I'm *Badger*, I'm your tavern spy...' The guards halted in front of the officials.

'You know what to do,' one of the grey-gowned men said.

'Please...' the spy begged, 'Please!'

The guards hauled him through a small side door. For a little while, his terrified voice could still be heard, protesting, over and over again, 'I'm Badger! I'm your best spy!' Then there was silence. Gaia stared where he had gone, remembering John's warning. 'Don't even make a joke...'

One of the guards prodded her in the back and hissed, 'Stand!' and she struggled to her feet as a tall man strode through the door at the back of the dais in a flurry of emerald robes. Lord Lanneret, she thought: just about recognisable from his statue in the Basilica. There was a boy with him, dressed in the same green. He hung back on the threshold, blinking into the light. Lanneret summoned him into the hall with an impatient gesture and an usher bowed to him.

'So you've come to sit in on a court, my Lord. I hope you'll find it interesting.'

The boy's expression said quite clearly that he doubted it. He gave a sulky nod.

'Nothing out of the ordinary, though, my Lord,' the usher said to Lanneret. 'The usual run of vagrants and thieves.' He set a thick pile of papers on the table. Lanneret sat. He gestured at the empty chair next to him, and the boy slunk into it, looking out at the hall with hollow eyes. Lanneret took the top sheet from the pile of papers, asked the boy something, frowned at his answer, and passed the paper to the usher.

'Carrie Beckett!' he called.

The fair girl gasped, 'Yes!' Guards unshackled her ankles and pushed her forward to stand at the foot of the platform.

'You've been tried and sentenced before for vagrancy,' Lanneret said. 'This is your second offence. *Hope's End.*' The usher made a note on the paper, and tossed it into a tray on the table. Gaia

128

caught a brief glimpse of the girl's frightened and confused face as she was bundled out through the door where they had taken the spy.

Hope's End?

Name after name; one ragged figure after another stumbling to the front of the room; the pale boy tracing patterns with his forefinger on the silver cloth, called to attention by a fierce whisper from Lanneret. The benches around Gaia emptied, but when the usher called, 'Elsa Seagull!' she didn't recognise herself, and said nothing.

'That's got to be you, hasn't it?' a guard said, and she looked round and found that she was the only prisoner left. The guard released the chains from her ankles and she walked to the foot of the platform, shaky, partly from standing so long with the weight of the chains on her legs, but mostly from fear.

Hope's End?

'Elsa Seagull?' Lanneret said.

'Yes,' she said. The boy jerked his head up and stared at her. The guard hissed, 'My Lord.'

'Yes, My Lord.'

'Theft and vagrancy.'

She waited for the usual brief dismissal, but Lanneret said nothing. Puzzled, she squinted at him through the glare of the light. He had a hard face: proud and certain, blue eyes like dark ice.

'Were you acting with anyone?' He hadn't asked anyone else that, and the boy darted him a questioning glance, and turned to stare at her again.

'No,' she said quickly. 'I was alone. My Lord.'

Lanneret nodded and beckoned her closer. She took a couple of unsteady steps forward.

'The thing is –' Lanneret placed his palms together and touched his forefingers to his lips. His voice was quiet now, confiding. 'We know there are criminal gangs of children working in Freehaven. Vagrants. Responsible for a string of thefts.'

She could feel the boy watching her. She flicked him a quick look. His eyes were bright with tense interest.

'Our problem,' Lanneret continued, 'is a lack of information. We know the gangs exist, but it's been impossible to pin them down. What we need is a child on the inside...'

'A spy,' she said.

'An informer. Yes.' Lanneret leaned forward across the table. 'Now. If you help us, we'll help you. You'll be protected from the usual penalties for your crime, and given appropriate payment.'

Gaia looked wildly behind her to the door of the hall.

'Absolutely,' he said. 'Agree to help, and you walk out of here now.'

She closed her eyes. Tal was out there, somewhere, alone in the rain, and she was here, alone, and all it would take to mend that was a single word. *Yes.* It was all she had to say, and she could go and find him. They would have permission to stay, and money to live off. If she said yes, they could carry on looking for Mum...

'I can't wait for ever.'

She opened her eyes. Lanneret had picked up a sheet of paper and was tapping it impatiently against the edge of the table. Paper. In her mind she saw the drifts of parchment in the Nest, sheltering Jinx's lost and desperate children. She saw the burning camp outside the walls, deserted farmhouses in starved fields, the slave market at Trebburn and Jason in chains. If she said yes, she set herself with the Lords who had made that land.

'No,' she said. She was full of tears - for Tal, for herself - and through the shining mist she looked at the boy, and saw an astonished, horrified triumph in his eyes.

'Hope's End.' Lanneret flung the parchment aside and summoned the guards with an impatient gesture. He stood, and pulled the boy to his feet. 'You'd better see what happens to a convicted thief.'

Tal hurried across the square towards the Courthouse. It had only a few, tiny, high-up windows, and the solid wooden doors were firmly closed. A bell-pull hung alongside them; in reckless desperation he tugged at it, and a bell clanged somewhere deep inside. He waited, half hopeful, half terrified for an answer, but no-one came. Perhaps there was another way in at the back... He set off at a run, head down, and collided with a lamplighter, his clothes and hair shiny from the rain. The man put out a hand.

'Careful, son. You alright?'

'I need to get into the Court,' Tal said.

The lamplighter gave a short laugh. 'Folk generally want to get out, not in.' He looked closely at Tal. "Who is it?"

'My sister… She stole a bun. She was *hungry*…'

'If she's been arrested for stealing, son, there's nothing you can do. She'll be taken out east.' He glanced up: the sky was blue-black behind the tearing clouds. 'Almost night. You best get home.'

Tal nodded, unable to speak, and ran away into the shadowy alley between the Courthouse and the Archive.

The door led onto a blind corridor, stone underfoot, stone on either hand. Flickering torches threw smoke and nightmare shadows around her as she walked. She stumbled along the passage, down a winding staircase and into an antechamber where an inky-fingered clerk sat at a desk. In the uneven light the ink looked like blood. Lanneret drummed his fingers on the desk. 'Quickly,' he said. Hands gripped her: pinning her arms to her sides. She sought out the boy's face. He looked white and sick, his eyes wide in the half darkness. Someone pulled her head back. There was a flash of steel in the torchlight; once, and again; a cry in a high voice that might have been hers; the rusty smell of blood; a sensation like an unbearable high pitched note that distilled into pain. A wet warmth spilled down her cheek. The boy put a shaking hand over his mouth, and Lanneret cuffed him round the head and said, 'Get used to it.'

There were no lights in the alley. Tal groped along, blind, shuffling over the uneven cobbles, guiding himself with a hand on the wall. At the end of the alley, he paused. To his right was the back yard of the Archive; the warmth and safety of the Company… He turned left: to the back of the Court building. There was a walled yard here, too, and he tried to scramble up the stones, but they were smooth-faced and slippery with freezing rain. Again and again, he slithered to the ground; finally he gave up, hammered his fists against the wall and leaned his forehead hopelessly against the wet stone. Then there was a glow of light in the yard and a shout of 'Let's go!' Iron bars rattled. A pair of wooden gates swung open.

Pain engulfed her. Sick, dizzy, blinded: she clutched her hands over her head; digging her fingers into her scalp; rocking herself, trying to comfort the pain away; but it sliced through her: two slicing cuts across her cheek: those cuts were her, everything; there was nothing outside them; no time or space that wasn't pain. When someone shouted it was years away, a shout from beyond the moon; and the rush of cold rain and the wooden floor where she fell; the sudden swaying and lurching: everything was nothing; there was only pain.

Tal watched the gates open, and saw a line of caged wagons and the huddled shapes of people inside the bars. He couldn't see Gaia but he followed anyway, slipping along behind the last wagon. At first he was careful, tiptoeing through the shadows under the walls, but soon the horses began to canter and the wagons careered along the streets, and he broke into a run. He didn't care if he was seen now: all he wanted to do was reach her, talk to her, *go* with her...

It was useless. The horses were so fast that he couldn't keep up with them and he shouted. A single shout, at the top of his voice, the way he used to shout for her at home, in summer, across the long shadows on the mountains.

'*Gaia!*'

Pain. A freshening in the air. A tang of salt. The wind stung against her face. She was hauled to her feet and dragged through darkness; forced down a steep ladder into a place out of the wind. Eyes gleamed in the low light of a lantern. She crawled to a space on the floor and lay down; hands pressed against her cheek. The floor rocked and swayed. The boards were rough and sodden. The air was icy. The cold sliced to the bone.

Pain and cold.

Nothing else in the world.

Nothing.

Only - next to her - someone else was breathing; dragging in frozen, shuddering breaths. Gaia forced her eyes open. In the weak lantern light, she recognised the girl from the court: Carrie, in her threadbare, thin, useless clothes. Gaia remembered winter nights at home; sleeping curled up with Mai and Tal for warmth.

'Carrie?' she said.

The girl didn't answer.

Gaia struggled up onto hands and knees and pushed at her. 'Carrie! You need to get warm. Here.' She sat up, unbuttoned her coat with shaky fingers, and opened her arms as wide as she could against the chains on her wrists. Carrie crawled towards her, under the chains; twisting round to sit with her back against Gaia's chest. Together, they tugged the heavy fur around themselves. It was better straight away, like it is when you find a sheltered place out of the wind. Slowly, the cold eased a little. Their breathing settled into the rhythms of uneasy sleep.

When she woke, grimy daylight was seeping through a round window over her head. She moved, and Carrie started awake too, with a frightened, 'What is it?' In the faint light, Gaia saw that there was a new cut on Carrie's cheek, parallel with the old scar. She lifted her hand to the throbbing cuts on her own face. Her fingers came away smeared with blood that looked dark in the dimness. She stared at them.

'It's how they mark criminals,' Carrie said. 'Didn't you know?'

'No.'

'No? Where d'you come from?'

'Long way away.' She pressed her hand to her cheek again. Beneath her she could feel the deep judder of machinery, and the swaying she had felt in the night had risen into a pitching and rolling.

'Let me up. I want to see.' She wriggled out of Carrie's arms and struggled onto her feet. The window was so crusted with salt and grime that it was like trying to see through quartz, but she could see enough to realise that they were on a ship, heading out to sea. In the distance, she could just make out Freehaven harbour, and the white buildings above it, and the dark green stain where the Leathy flowed into the sea. She watched as Freehaven - and her chances of ever seeing Tal again - receded, and shrank into nothing.

Tal Alone

Dusk and clouds were gathering over the mountains and a dragon swept lazily overhead. Tal shivered. It was time to go home, and he couldn't find Gaia and the goats. He called, again and again, and at last he saw them: tiny in the distance, climbing the cliff to the snowfield below the peak. But it was an impossible, sheer climb, and as he watched, one of the goats lost its footing and fell. It seemed to fall for ever, turning over and over like something weightless in the frozen air. Gaia turned, slipped, scrabbled for a handhold, and he yelled, 'Hang on! I'm coming,' but he knew that he couldn't get there in time and as he floundered through the snow he saw her slip again...

He woke with a start from one nightmare into another. He was lying on the ledge under the bridge and the memory of yesterday swept over him with the sudden chill of a cloud across the sun. Gaia arrested; and his own useless and helpless self: too frozen with fear to do anything until she was gone. Following the wagons had been pointless: he had run after them to the harbour, but there they had disappeared into a high-walled compound, and the gates had slammed closed before he could try and dart through them. He had waited outside: it was hours and hours after curfew, but he hadn't tried to hide: he had almost wanted to be taken by the Watch. Somehow, he had passed the night without being found. At dawn a ship had sailed from the harbour and he had known that she was on it. He had found his way, blindly, back to the bridge and fallen into a troubled sleep.

He sat up. It was another drear day, but the quality of the light and a painful, gnawing hunger told him that it must be late morning. Shamefully, he pulled out the bread that the woman had given him yesterday and chewed at it. Each mouthful tasted like dust.

What now? He stared at the swift green waters. His thoughts swirled like the current; this way, that way, leading him nowhere. *Just go home*, the lamplighter had said, and he could see the mountains, still vivid from the dream; he could see Ambrose holding out warm arms to welcome him home; could hear him asking 'Where's Gaia…?'

No. Going home was not to be thought of.

He was roused from his thoughts by a muffled clang. Someone was climbing up the ladder and he remembered that this was where Gaia had told him to wait, if they got separated. It couldn't be her. It wasn't possible. He held his breath and …

'*Tal!* You still here?' said Jinx.

He closed his eyes and nodded.

Jinx stepped onto the ledge and sat down. 'Thought you'd be long gone. Where's Gaia?'

'Arrested.' He could hardly get the word out.

'Oh, no!' Jinx winced and gestured to his neck. 'Because of…?'

'No. Stealing. We were starving.' A terrible thought struck him: *worse and worse.* 'She still had the amulet though. What if they find it?'

'Maybe they won't,' Jinx said. 'If she was arrested for nicking food, they maybe won't look too close. And you ain't been papered, you know.'

'Oh.' It no longer seemed to matter.

'Dunno why. Should've been. Holding a prohibited object's about as bad as it gets. Seems old Fossick didn't report you, but… You hungry, by the way?' He turned out his pockets, handed over a wrinkled apple and sat watching thoughtfully while Tal ate.

'Tell you what,' he said at last. 'Five days' time. Meet me here, at noon. If you ain't been papered by then, it's probably safe for you to come back in.' He gave a worried smile and swung himself down the ladder. Tal listened to his footsteps fade into silence, and went back to staring at the rain falling into the green river.

Fossick pulled his chair closer to the tavern fire and held out his dry cold hands to its weak warmth. 'Soup, Mr Fossick?' Sassy asked. He nodded distractedly and she went out to the kitchen, returning a few moments later with a steaming bowl of broth and some bread. She placed the dishes on the table, retreated into a corner, and spread her messy embroidery on her lap.

Fossick cut up the bread into precise cubes, and built them into a neat pile. He took the cubes from the top layer and pushed them around his plate, making them stand for possibilities in his theory. If this and this and this (he lined up three cubes) then almost certainly that (he placed another alongside the line of three) and if that, then... He knocked the big piles to pieces, scattering bread across the tabletop; caught Sassy's eye, and smiled a wintry, apologetic smile. Without using the bread this time, he carried on, turning the theory over in his head. He shook himself. If he couldn't get into the Closed Archive, theory was all he had: possibility; speculation. And that was probably how it would stay. Cosmo clearly didn't want to take this thing any further.

He dipped his bread into the hot soup. The door banged open and an icy draught brought Scrimp in with it. He dragged a chair up to Fossick's table, and slumped into it. 'That *man*. That stupid, impossible...'

'Calm down, Cosmo. Who?'

'Parhelion, of course. Idiotic, bone-headed, mindless...'

Fossick made a warning gesture. 'Keep your voice down!'

'What? Oh, it's safe enough here, surely.' Scrimp turned and caught Sassy's eye. 'Bring me some soup or something.'

She nodded, laid down the pillowcase and went silently into the kitchen. Scrimp leant his elbows on the table and put his head in his hands. '*Idiot.* Thinks I can conjure silver out of moonlight, and if I did, he'd only lose it at cards. Wish I didn't work for him. Wish I could *leave.*'

'Well,' said Fossick. 'That's the drawback, isn't it, of working for the Fellowship? Job for life. Fine from one point of view...'

'But only if you don't want to get out,' said Scrimp. 'You know, I envy you, Babbington. The way you've kept your independence.'

'It's not been easy, said Fossick, as Sassy placed bread and soup on the table. 'Constant security checks, watched all the time, impossible to get permission to travel... Thanks, Sassy.'

She said, 'Welcome,' retired to her dingy corner, and picked up the pillowcase and her needle again. Fossick and Scrimp ate without speaking. At last Scrimp pushed back his dish. 'Babbington, this amulet...'

'Yes?' Fossick gave a cautionary glance around the room, but he and Scrimp were the only customers in the tavern.

'You think it's important, don't you?'

'I do.'

'But why?'

'I think,' said Fossick, 'that it might show there's a truth about our past - about the history of Assalay - that's been hidden for hundreds of years.'

'Yes... I can see that would matter to you, as a historian. But for the rest of us? It can't be that important, can it?'

'Oh, yes, it can.' Fossick trailed his finger around the rim of his empty glass. 'Because if I'm right, this truth will shake the Fellowship to its very foundation.'

Tal sat huddled against the pier of the bridge, waiting. If Gaia had somehow - impossibly - managed to get away then it was here, to their agreed place, that she would come to find him. But as the daylight faded, so did hope. She would not, could not, be coming, and he was a fool even to think of it. The emptiness of the ledge seemed to mock him, and at last he couldn't bear it any longer. He left the bridge, and climbed up from the terrace into Liberation Square as the first curfew bell rang. Crowds of drably dressed people, heads bowed and coats buttoned up against the cold, hurried for home. The lamplighter wove his way between them, leaving a trail of light in the globe-shaped lanterns. Tal leaned against the wall of the Basilica and watched him. The lamplighter had been kind, yesterday: perhaps he could ask him for help? But before he could make up his mind, the man was gone, swallowed up by the evening.

The wind strengthened, and the rain became a cold sleet. Tal climbed the steps of the Basilica and sheltered under the porch, then he noticed that although the big wooden doors were firmly closed, a smaller door, set into one of them, stood ajar. He edged across to it, gave it a tentative push, and crept inside.

When he had been here with Gaia, it had been busy, and full of movement and light. It was very different now. The nave and aisles were in darkness, and the statues of the Fellowship seemed to have shrunk into a huddled, formless mass: faceless as rocks in the night at home. But beyond the darkness, at the far end of the nave, there was a pool of light where a group of people dressed in midnight blue were sitting in a crescent of chairs. Scared of being seen, Tal pressed himself against the wall and sidled along in the shadows until he came to one of the statues. There was a narrow gap between its marble plinth and the wall and he squeezed into it to hide.

As he crouched against the wall, the door that he had entered by banged open again. Quick footsteps echoed on the stone floor and a voice that was somehow familiar rang out. 'Good evening, everyone!' Tal peered out from his hiding place to a see a tall man hurrying up the nave. He could only see his back, but he thought he was the man they had seen first in the Basilica and again at Fossick's shop. The man stopped in front of the group; he said something that Tal couldn't catch; a single note flew into the height of the vaulted roof, and then they were all singing.

It was the saddest tune he had ever heard: full of the kind of sadness that changes the world for ever, and he strained his ears to hear the words. He recognised the story: Ambrose had told it to them on long cold Aquilon evenings: the tale of Salyxis and his dead son. '*My son, my son.*' The voices wove together in sorrow, and then came the plea that harsh Aquilon had denied: heart-stoppingly clear at first above the other voices, then taken up by them, one after the other. '*Lord, give him life and let me die.*' Tal leaned against the wall and closed his eyes, and the music sobbed around him.

'What d'you think you're doing here?' An angry voice cut through the singing, and Tal looked up in alarm, into the harsh glare of lantern light reaching into his hiding place. A Basilica guard was standing over him. Tal wriggled backwards, but the man seized his arm and hauled him out into the nave. He pushed him into a chair that shifted under him, scraping noisily against the stone floor.

'It's after curfew,' the guard said. 'You've no right to be here. Where do you live?'

'What's all this noise? What's going on?' The singing had stopped and the tall man was striding down the nave towards them. The guard held up an apologetic hand.

'Sorry, Gabriel. This little bit of low-life riff-raff was hiding behind the statues. Out after curfew. *And* I'll take odds he hasn't got papers. I'll take him over to the Watch now.' He hauled Tal to his feet.

'No. Wait,' Gabriel said. The guard stopped short and Tal looked up in surprise. 'There's no problem. He's... um... the son of an old friend. They were in town for Carnival. I promised I'd try him out for the choir.' He dropped his voice and said, confidingly, 'Just as a favour. I don't suppose he'll be any good.'

The guard looked uncertainly from Gabriel to Tal and back again. 'Why was he hiding? Why didn't he tell me who he was?'

'Did you give him a chance?' Gabriel put a hand on Tal's shoulder and, reluctantly, the guard let him go.

'Come with me,' said Gabriel. 'We're nearly through. I'll see to you when we're done.' He steered Tal up the nave, and told him to sit on the choir steps. They had finished the song of Salyxis, and the piece they sang now filled the building with joy: Tal listened, rapt, to the fanfares of brilliant chords and the exhilarating fast phrases that seemed to chase one another like birds round the vaulted roof above the choir. Then it was ended and there was just a group of twenty or so people scraping chairs, rustling papers and talking and laughing as they got ready to leave. Suddenly aware that he was an object of curiosity, Tal ducked his head and looked hard at his wet and filthy boots.

'Tal?' The singers had left and Gabriel sat down next to him on the steps. 'That is your name, isn't it?'

Tal nodded.

'I've been wondering whether you were alright or not.' Gabriel gave him a quick head-to-toe look. 'You're not, are you? I can help... I will help, but...' He gestured down the nave. The guard who had found Tal was leaning against one of the broad stone pillars, watching. 'Since I've told him this is an audition, we'd better make it look like one.'

'An audition?'

'I just need you to sing for me.'

'Oh. Is that all?'

'That's all.' Gabriel stood, and Tal followed him up the steps and stood waiting in front of the crescent of empty chairs, while Gabriel opened the lid of a little wooden box on legs. 'Sing what I play,' he told Tal: his fingers moved lightly and a few thin notes floated out and sounded in the air for an instant before dying away. 'Try and sing that back to me. Listen, I'll play it again.' He spoke reassuringly, but it was easy: nothing to it: a simple rise and fall of notes. Tal took a steadying breath and sang out, and the vast, shadowed space echoed back a clear strong voice that he had hardly known he owned, and in spite of Gaia, in spite of everything, he smiled, because this was a building made for singing in, and not all the sorrow in the world could quench the simple physical joy of it. But Gabriel was looking at him oddly.

'Is something wrong?' Tal asked.

'No,' said Gabriel quickly. 'No. Nothing's wrong. Try this one for me.' He turned back to the little box, and played a more complex phrase. Tal recognised it: it was part of the joyful piece that had ended the rehearsal. He nodded and sang it back confidently.

'Good,' said Gabriel. '*Good*. Now this.' He played the next phrase of the piece: a soaring exultant rise to a last bright high note. Tal sent it flying into the shadows in the height of the dome, hanging onto that shining, exalted note for the sheer glory of it.

Gabriel's face broke into a broad smile, almost a laugh. 'Can you put them both together?'

'Yes,' and he did, feeling the joy of that lovely upward flight again.

'Yes!' Gabriel raised his hands in delight. 'That's it. Well done!'

'Thought you said he wouldn't be any good?' Neither of them had noticed the guard, who had walked up the nave and was standing, listening, at the bottom of the choir steps. 'You'll be taking him, I daresay, Gabriel?'

'I hope so.' Gabriel glanced at Tal, and nodded thoughtfully. The guard retreated towards the main doors, his footfalls echoing from the stone walls. His lantern cast a little moving pool of light. The big statues gleamed as he passed them, and receded into darkness again. Gabriel bundled together a handful of papers, stowed them in a scruffy satchel and slung it over his shoulder. 'Come on, Tal.' He gestured to a door in the side wall.

'You mean... Come with you?'

'Yes. I said, didn't I? I'll help.' But Tal, his thoughts a wild muddle, stood uncertainly where he was. Further down the nave, the guard had stopped to study one of the statues. There was still time to run, to dodge past him and out into the night... *Don't trust anyone*. It was what he had decided when they had run from the Crabbits and Linnet's father. But his heart sank at the thought of returning to the cold empty ledge under the bridge. He wanted to trust Gabriel. He *did* trust him: he had trusted him instinctively, unhesitatingly, when he had told them to run from Fossick… He looked up in confusion, and met Gabriel's bright blue, gently enquiring gaze.

'I'm not going to turn you in, you know,' Gabriel said quietly.

Tal felt a sudden weak relief, as if a tangle of knots in his stomach had undone themselves all at once; and then guilt, sharp as ice, because it wasn't *fair*, that this luck had come to him and not to Gaia. He followed Gabriel wordlessly out of the Basilica, along one side of a cloistered courtyard, and through another door into the warmth and light of a kitchen. Gabriel dropped his satchel on a chair and stooped to kiss the little girl who was sitting at the table, and the woman who sat next to her.

'Hello, Allegra. Connie, this is Tal. He needs something to eat.' The woman darted a quick, bright-eyed look at Tal.

'Another one of your waifs and strays, Gabriel?' she laughed, but her voice was kind.

'No,' Gabriel protested, pulling out a chair and beckoning Tal into it. 'No, this one's a singer. A bit waifish and strayish, perhaps. But a real singer.' He took two faded blue bowls from the dresser, rummaged in a drawer for some knives and spoons, found two mismatched glasses, and set everything on the table.

'Let's eat.' He sat opposite Tal and lifted the lid from a pot that stood on the table. A rich, mouth-watering warmth filled the room. Gabriel filled a bowl with soup, and pushed it towards Tal. He stared down at it. There was a tight hard knot in his throat that made it impossible to swallow.

Connie stood, took Allegra's hand, and led her quietly out of the room. Gabriel picked up a spoon, and turned it between his fingers, watching it catch and reflect the light from the lantern above the table. 'I'm guessing,' he said, 'that something's happened to your sister.' He stopped turning the spoon and looked directly at Tal.

Tal closed his eyes. 'She… She was stealing food. She was arrested…'

'I see,' said Gabriel gently. But Tal shook his head, because Gabriel didn't see. He *couldn't*, because there was so much more that Tal couldn't bring himself to tell him. *He* should have done the stealing, and he *would* have, if he hadn't been so furious with her, because she had been bound to get it wrong: clever, clumsy Gaia whose hands always betrayed her. But he hadn't, and when she was

141

caught he had ducked his head and held his tongue while she was led away... To what? Was she even still alive or had he left her to go alone to her death?

The Choir

Tal could hear distant singing, the faint scrape of a chair, and the muffled clink of a table being laid. A child's voice asked loudly, 'Why is he still here?' and someone else said, 'Shhh!'

He opened his eyes. Allegra was watching him with a solemn gaze as bright blue as Gabriel's, and Connie was setting cups and plates on the table. She smiled at him.

'Sorry. Didn't mean to wake you. Gabriel said you fell asleep with your head on the table last night.'

'Did I?' He sat up. He had been sleeping in his clothes, wrapped in a blanket, on two armchairs that had been pushed together as a makeshift bed. Allegra was still studying him curiously.

'What's his name?' she asked Connie.

'You can ask him. He won't bite.'

Allegra looked at him.

'It's Tal,' he said.

She gave him another long, serious look. 'That's a funny name.'

'It's a nickname. It's short for Telemachus.' He felt a brief catch in his throat. It was Gaia who had called him Tal: it had been all she could manage of that mouthful of a name when she was very small.

'That's a *really* funny name.'

'*Allegra.*' Connie paused and listened. The distant singing had ended. She beckoned Allegra and Tal into chairs at the table, and a moment later the kitchen door was flung open.

'If those altos miss that b flat again...' Gabriel threw his satchel onto a chair, ruffled Allegra's hair, and picked up the kettle from the stove. 'Morning, Tal. Sleep well? Hungry?' He poured out cups of honey tea, and Connie sliced a loaf of bread, fresh from the oven. The warm sweetness made Tal's mouth flood with hunger, and he ate eagerly, until the thought of Gaia choked him to a halt. He shoved his plate away unfinished.

'Done?' Gabriel asked.

Tal nodded.

'Let's go, then.'

'Go?'

'You wanted to try and find out what had happened to Gaia, didn't you?'

'Oh. Yes.' He pushed his chair back and stood up quickly.

'Tal,' Gabriel said. 'I told you, didn't I? I can't promise that we'll find out. And even if we do … there's really no chance of getting her back. You do understand that, don't you?'

'Yes,' he said, but he buttoned up his coat quickly and hopefully and followed Gabriel through the cloistered courtyard and into the Basilica. Early morning gleamed through the round windows in the side wall, casting a dark green underwatery light onto the white marble. Tal halted, puzzled.

'Gabriel? I thought those windows were all different colours. When we were here before…'

'Yes.' Gabriel hurried him through the Basilica. 'They're only multi-coloured at Carnival. For the rest of the year, they're a different colour each moon, according to which Fellow's moon it is. That's the only window that's multi-coloured all year round.'

He gestured quickly up at a massive window above the doors (thirteen huge circles of glass, in all the Fellowship colours), and ushered Tal out and down the steps into the cold drizzle. They crossed the square to the Court, where Gabriel leaned against the white, faceless wall, and scanned faces in the morning crowd. Tal stared back across the square at the big window above the Basilica doors.

'Gabriel? I don't understand what you mean… About which Fellow's moon it is.'

Gabriel glanced at him in surprise. 'You don't know about the patronal moons?'

Tal shook his head.

'Well, it's simple enough,' Gabriel said. 'There are thirteen Fellows and thirteen moons. Each Fellow has a moon that's special for them: their patronal moon. Arctos is Anserine's, so all this moon there'll be celebrations for him; and the river's his colour, and the glass and banners in the Basilica. In Clamynto they'll be magenta, for

Hallion; bright blue in Galanthus for Sallender; crimson in... Hang
on. Here he is.'

He stepped forward to intercept a man with floppy fair hair
falling into his eyes, who was sauntering towards the Courthouse, a
cup of hot tea in one hand.

'Hello, Philip.'

'Gabriel,' said Philip. 'Is this an accidental meeting, or were
you waiting for me?'

Gabriel laughed. 'Waiting. Wondered if I could ask a little
favour.' He gestured towards Tal. 'Tal's lost his sister. She was
arrested for stealing food. He wants to know what's happened to her.'

Philip gave the bell-pull a tug. 'She'll have been sent to one of
the slave farms, of course. What more do you need to know?' The
door swung open and he set one foot over the threshold. Gabriel
caught his arm and held him back.

'Can you find out where, exactly?'

'Maybe. But what's the point?'

Gabriel glanced at Tal. He scuffed the toe of his boot against
the shiny wet marble. 'I just want to know.'

'Very well.' Philip shrugged, tipped his tea into the gutter and
guided them through the door and into a little side office where a
lanky young man was balancing his chair on its back legs.

'Bill,' Philip said. 'Do me a favour. I've spilt my tea. Get one
for yourself while you're at it.' He flipped a gold coin onto the desk;
Bill pocketed it, and headed out into the square. As soon as he had
gone, Philip pulled a heavy ledger from the desk, checking details with
Tal as he flipped through the pages. 'Day before yesterday? Evening?
In the square? Right... this is the list we need. Keep an eye on the
door, Gabriel.' He read out a list of names rapidly, and looked at Tal.

'Is that all?'

'Yes.'

Tal swallowed. 'She's not there.'

'Wait a moment,' said Gabriel. 'What about other arrests that
evening?'

'You said theft... Alright.' Philip read rapidly.

'And that's it?' Gabriel asked. 'That's all the other arrests?
Vagrancy and breaking curfew? No other offences?'

'*No*, Gabriel. What is this?'

'Just checking.' But it was pointless. Her name wasn't there, anywhere, and, dazed with disappointment, Tal followed Gabriel back out into the rainy square. He was reminded of going to see Penn Scrivers. Then too, he had hoped for an answer, but Mum had become a name on a list, her real self vanished, and now Gaia had disappeared even more completely. Suddenly, he understood.

'She gave a false name,' he said. 'Ji... Someone told us not to give our real names if we got into trouble.'

'That makes sense.' Gabriel thought for a moment. 'Did any of those names remind you of her?'

Tal stared hard at the shiny white pavement. 'No. So that's that.'

'Well,' Gabriel said, 'At least we know she wasn't arrested for having a prohibited object.'

'That's why you asked about the other arrests,' Tal realised. 'Thanks.' He gave Gabriel a pale smile, shrugged, and turned away. Gabriel caught hold of his arm. 'Hang on. Where are you going now?'

'Don't know.'

'I meant it, you know. When I said you could stay.'

Tal lowered his voice. 'But I can't. I'm not supposed to be in Freehaven. I don't have papers or anything...'

Gabriel waved an impatient hand. 'Oh, that's nothing. All choir members are given papers automatically.'

'*Choir members?*' Tal stared at him. 'You mean... stay and join the choir?'

'Why not?'

'But... I don't know anything about music.' It seemed impossible, but something inside him lifted at the thought of it. 'Could I?'

Gabriel's eyes crinkled in a smile. 'Of course. You can learn. And you've got the thing that can't be learned.' His expression softened. 'I know it's not what you planned. But it's a way of keeping safe. And you'll be in Freehaven: you might find out something about your mother, at least.'

A place to stay, a chance - a very faint chance - of finding Mum; singing. It was three times more hope than he had had yesterday morning. 'Alright,' he said. 'I mean, thanks.'

'Good,' said Gabriel. 'Let's get your papers sorted out.' He guided Tal towards the far end of the square, away from the river, asking questions as they went. 'From Arimaspia, right? And you're how old? Twelve? When's your birthday? Himalios? So's Allegra's. She's five. And your name... Telemachus? Family name... Athanasius?' He stopped and gave Tal a close, questioning look. 'Gaia and Telemachus. And Athanasius. They're...'

'Odd names,' Tal finished for him. 'I know. We've been told over and over, ever since we came off the mountains.'

'Well,' Gabriel began, 'old-fashioned, maybe...' then the Basilica clock called the hour, a rapid peal of falling notes through the drizzly air, and he glanced up at the tall bell tower. 'Not much time. Come on.' They hurried across the square, down a narrow alley, and through an obscure side door into a badly lit corridor. Gabriel set off at high speed, through a maze of identical passageways.

'What is this place?' Tal asked. 'And how do you know where you're going?'

Gabriel laughed. 'Watch Office. And I know where I'm going because I've been here a hundred times before. Permission to work, to travel, to stay, to go: it's all given from here. Right, this is the room we need.'

He opened one of many faceless doors, and they entered a long room which smelled of dust and old paper. Tal followed Gabriel to a counter that ran all the way along one wall.

'I need papers for a new choir member,' Gabriel said to a bored-looking young man behind the counter. The man nodded, pulled a ledger down from a shelf and dipped a pen into an inkwell.

'Name and place of birth?'

Gabriel hesitated for an instant. 'Tal Marcus,' he said. 'From north of Nouldewood. Fairwold.' Tal opened his mouth, but Gabriel trod lightly on his foot, and he closed it again. The man checked one ledger after another and filled in form after form with inky, dusty fingers. Finally he handed something to Gabriel, and they made their way back along the endless corridors to the street. In the shelter of the doorway, Gabriel said, 'Here you go,' and passed Tal a small, folded piece of parchment, covered with official stamps and a lump of sealing wax holding a grey ribbon in place. 'Your papers. Congratulations. You're now a free citizen of Freehaven. Three rules, though.' He counted on his fingers. 'Don't lose your papers. Don't stay out after curfew. Don't go into any prohibited streets. Stick to those, and you'll stay out of trouble with the Watch.' He started striding back the way they had come.

'One more thing,' he said as they walked. 'Don't ever be late for an office or a rehearsal, or you'll be in trouble with *me*.' They reached the square. The drizzle had become a steady rain. 'Any questions?'

'Yes,' Tal said. 'Why did you lie about my name and where I come from?'

Gabriel didn't answer until they were back inside the Basilica. Then he halted at the door and said in a low voice, 'It's that moonswood. I don't think Fossick's reported it, and I don't think he's going to. But if he ever does, I don't want anyone to be able to trace a line from it to you.'

'I still don't understand why it's prohibited,' Tal said. 'You said something about old... something...'

'Old Script.' Gabriel nodded. 'What you'll learn to read...' Tal looked doubtful, and Gabriel said, smiling, 'It's not that difficult, honestly. What you'll learn to read is called Free Script. Free Script replaced Old Script ages ago. Anything written in Old Script is meant to have been destroyed.'

'Why?' asked Tal. 'And you knew it was Old Script. Gaia's amulet, I mean. Does that mean you can read it?'

'No-one's allowed to read Old Script,' Gabriel said. 'Come on. Rehearsal time. Let's see how you get on.'

'Can't I just watch for now?' Tal asked as he followed Gabriel up the nave.

'Got to start sometime. Might as well be now. Come and meet the others.'

The rest of the choir were already waiting, sitting on the steps, or leaning on the semi-circle of chairs. Tal observed them, apprehensively: about twenty people wearing dark blue cloaks like Gabriel's, some a lot older than him, others about his age, but...

'No girls,' he said.

'No,' said Gabriel.

'Why not?'

'Tradition.' He raised his voice and called, 'Good morning again, everyone. Places, please. Oh, and this is Tal. He's joining us from today.' He gave Tal a little push forward. 'Go and sit with Sam. He'll look after you.'

Tal dropped into the chair that Gabriel had indicated. It was made of dark, heavy, intricately carved wood. Beneath his feet, the floor was inlaid in tiny squares of coloured stone, and the vault above his head was set in silver. He felt suddenly awkward. He didn't belong in a place like this; but the boy next to him was saying in a friendly voice, 'What did Gabriel say your name was?'

'Tal.' He looked into a pair of puzzled blue eyes, in a freckled face, under curly red hair. 'I know. Odd name.'

The boy shrugged. 'A name's a name. I'm Sam... Come on.' Everyone else was standing and Sam pulled Tal to his feet. They started to sing straight away, and Tal felt his nervousness ease: this was simple: repeated patterns of notes, working higher and higher. He relaxed into the singing, feeling his voice loosen into the sound, enjoying it, sorry when it came to an end. There was a pause while Gabriel rummaged among a pile of papers. Tal stared at the floor. The tiles made a picture, with ships and houses... It was a *map*, he realised. There was the Leathy and Freehaven and the open sea. He tried to follow the coast to the east, to see where Gaia had gone, but Sam was pushing something into his hands: a sheet of parchment covered with a bewildering pattern of lines and dots. Tal stared at it. Sam took it from him with a grin and turned it the other way up.

'You don't read music?'

Tal blinked at the paper. 'No.'

Sam winked. 'Nor could I, when I started. Share with me: I'll show you where we are.' As the singing started he ran his finger along the paper and Tal began to see how the printed patterns mirrored the patterns of sound. *Up where the music goes up, down where it goes down,* he thought, watching Sam's finger tracing the line. Sometimes, he heard Sam holding a long sustained single note, and then the pattern would be simple: a single open circle. But more often, the music was complicated and rapidly changing, and here Sam's finger darted along (and once or twice got lost in) a pattern of densely written black dots and tails. Concentrating hard on the music, Tal hadn't noticed the words at all, but as soon as the last notes died away, a tall boy opposite him shot his hand into the air. He wasn't dressed quite the same as everyone else: there was a stripe of bright blue in his dark blue cloak.

'Gregory?' said Gabriel.

'This is... I can't believe this is an *approved* text.' He read out the words that Tal had been too busy to hear.

Under the shining moons we are but one:
Lord Arctos breathes his cold on great and small,
On rich and poor Coranto's showers fall,
Melisto's sweetness blesses each and all.
We are but one.

He put the parchment down and stared angrily at Gabriel. 'The choir exists to uphold the Fellowship, but this... This is *sedition.*'

Gabriel returned the boy's furious look coolly. 'Thank you, Gregory. I'm aware of the choir's responsibilities. They include making fine music, which is why I chose to look at this piece, because it's rather a good test of one's ability to sight-read the difference between b and b flat. After this morning, I thought it might be a useful exercise. That's all.'

Sam - and several other people - laughed. The tall boy flushed angrily.

'Let's put this away now,' Gabriel said, 'And...' He was interrupted by one of the Basilica guards, proffering a note which he took and read swiftly. 'Ah. We're required to sing a special office for Lord Parhelion tomorrow. We'll need this... this... this...' He pulled out a sheaf of papers and handed them round. 'Let's get to work.'

'Look after Tal,' Gabriel said to Sam at the end of the long rehearsal. 'He can have the room along from yours, and find some clean clothes for him. Oh, and maybe a bath?'

Sam led Tal through the cloister and into a large room furnished with a long wooden table, a scattering of battered armchairs, and an iron stove which gave out a welcome heat. From a large cupboard in the wall he pulled out a towel, a shirt, trousers, a jacket and a dark blue cloak. He bundled it all into Tal's arms, and led him back into the cloister, through a side door, across a narrow yard and into a small circular building. Inside there was a deep round pool, and it was warm, despite the icy rain that hammered against the window in the roof. Tal could feel heat rising from the green-blue water.

'There,' said Sam. 'I'll wait for you in the dining room. You can find your way back there, can't you?'

Left alone, Tal bolted the door and stood for a while, breathing in the steamy air. Then he stripped off his filthy clothes - the old woollen tunic and trousers from home - and climbed down into the green pool. He sat on a low step with the water up to his neck, letting the heat fold round him, easing away the cold that seemed to have settled into his bones. Taking a deep breath, he closed his eyes, and slid down to the bottom of the pool, rubbing his hands over his face and hair, feeling the water wash away the filth of the streets. It felt good except -

Except that nothing in the world could wash away *time* and take him back to that moment of decision in the square. Nothing in the world could wash away what he had done. He climbed out of the pool quickly, dried and dressed. The new clothes felt comfortable against his skin: not scratchy, like the old home clothes, and the cloak fell in generous folds around him. Ill at ease, he took it off, slung it over his arm with the damp towel and found his way back to the dining room.

Sam was crouching on the floor opposite another boy, frowning over a wooden board marked into squares, one finger poised on a black counter. He pushed it tentatively forward, moved it back, and sat back on his heels staring at the board.

'You've lost, Sam,' said the other boy.

Sam nodded slowly, and tipped the board so that the counters slid off onto the rug. He noticed Tal watching, and gestured at the board. 'Sheep and Wolves.'

'We play at home,' Tal said. 'Only we call it Goats and Dragons.' He knelt down and arranged the counters in their starting positions, thinking of Gaia: playing against Jason on the day of the summer dragon...

'Dragons?' said the other boy. 'Are there dragons where you come from?'

Tal nodded.

'Wow,' said Sam.

'So you must be from Arimaspia,' the boy said. 'No wild dragons anywhere else. You ever *seen* one?'

'Yes. Lots.' The other boys around the stove were all listening now, except the tall boy called Gregory who was sitting in one of the armchairs with his face hidden behind a book.

'Really? How close've you got to one?'

151

'Close enough. Only once though.'

'And do they…?' Sam's opponent started to ask, but he was interrupted by a boy who put his head round the door and said, 'Extra rehearsal. For tomorrow. On the hour. Don't be late.'

Sam jumped to his feet. 'I haven't shown you your room yet, Tal.' They hurried out into the cloister, and the boy who had asked all the questions called after Tal, 'Can you tell me some more about those dragons later?'

'That's Davy,' Sam explained. 'Wild about wildlife.' He grinned, and led Tal up an uneven staircase onto a long corridor, with doors along one wall and windows along the other, looking out onto the cloisters, the high wall of the Basilica and its silver dome. Sam opened one of the doors.

'This is you.'

Tal stepped into a narrow room, furnished with a bed, a chest, a table and a chair. It had a high window, so high that all he could see through it was sky: a good window for moonlight. Someone had left a folder on the table. He picked it up. It contained a few sheets of music: that bewildering confusion of lines and dots. If he half closed his eyes, the rising lines of notes reminded him of flocks of birds, flying up and over the mountains.

'We should go.' Sam dumped an armful of sheets and blankets on the bed. 'This happens from time to time. One of the Fellowship asks for a special office, and we have to learn things quickly.'

Tal glanced down at the mystifying piece of music again. 'Don't worry,' Sam said. 'Gabriel won't leave you out.'

'But I can't…'

'There'll be some you can learn by heart. You've *got* to join in,' Sam insisted. 'Otherwise you'll miss the tip.'

'Tip?' Tal felt more mystified than ever.

'Money,' explained Sam. 'Whenever we sing a special office, we get a tip from whoever it's for. Day after tomorrow I'll take you to the best cake shop in Freehaven.'

Money. Tal felt a faint hope, like a scrap of yellow in a storm-covered sky. If he sang and sang and sang, would there be enough money in the end to buy Mum's freedom?

152

'Going away?' Fossick asked.

'A tour of the estates. Raising tribute. I'm sorry, Babbington. We leave first thing tomorrow. So there's no time to do anything about... you know.' Scrimp glanced over his shoulder, but once again, they were the only customers in the dingy tavern.

'Damn.' Fossick gave Sassy a brief nod as she set a basket of bread on the table before them. 'How long will you be gone?'

Scrimp grimaced. 'Who knows? A couple of moons? It can't be less.'

Fossick sighed. 'And you can't do anything to get me into the Closed Archive until you get back?'

Scrimp shook his head. 'Is it so urgent?'

'Oh, I suppose not. The secret's kept for hundreds of years. It'll keep a few moons more. I'll have to wait. Unless I can find those children. I've asked every street urchin I could find. None of them knows Gaia Athanasius. Or if they do, they're not saying.' He stared into the dull embers in the grate, then he said with sudden excitement, 'Maybe they've gone back to Arimaspia! If you're going there, you could look for them. And that amulet; and if they're not there, talk to the others. Histories, local tales... Someone must know something, even if they don't know what they know...'

Scrimp held up both hands. 'Hold on. We probably won't even go there. Even if we do, there aren't exactly many opportunities for cosy chats with the locals on these occasions. I'll *try*. That's all I can promise.'

'I suppose that'll have to do. By the way...' Fossick reached into his satchel, took out a thick book and dropped it onto the table with a dull thud. A shower of brown dust drifted from the crumbling leather cover.

'Brought this for you. Call it a going away present. Well, loan. A bit of bedtime reading for all those tedious evenings ahead of you.'

'Thanks. Looks jolly relaxing.' Scrimp opened the volume at random, and the blood drained from his face. The yellowed paper was printed with symbols that meant nothing to him. Beneath each line there were neatly hand-written words in Free Script.

'Is this...?'

'Old Script.' Fossick nodded.

'But that means...'

153

'It's a prohibited object. Yes.' Fossick flipped back to the front page. On the inside cover was a large official stamp and underneath it, in a faded official hand: *Removed from the library. To be burned. By order of the Fellowship.* Fossick ran his hand tenderly over the page. 'I rescued it.'

'But what is it?' Scrimp picked up his glass and gulped a large mouthful of water.

'Official history of the Liberation.' Fossick flicked affectionately through the old pages. 'What do you know about that, Cosmo?'

'The what?'

Fossick gave a dry smile. 'Have you never wondered, Cosmo, why we have a main square called *Liberation Square* in a capital city called *Freehaven*? Why the highlight of our Carnival is the burning of an effigy of a man with a swan's head?'

'Not really,' said Scrimp.

'Economists,' said Fossick in disgust. He pushed the book across the table to Scrimp. 'Read it. It's an interesting tale, but the devil is in the detail. Read it, Cosmo, and *tell me what's wrong with it.*'

Spying and Slavery

Sassy sat for a long time by the fire with her grubby embroidery, running her finger over a corner of the cloth where puckered uneven stitches made an ugly flower. Two children, a boy and a girl. A girl called Gaia Athanasius, from Arimaspia, carrying an object engraved with words in *old script*. A dusty book: a history of something called the Liberation. She sat thinking until the fire had almost died on the hearth. Late in the afternoon, she bundled up the cloth and stuffed it into the pocket of her apron. Throwing a cloak over her head, she stepped out into the rain.

Lord Lanneret was dining alone at the Fellows' club; sitting at one of the tall windows which overlooked the wide street and the green river beyond it. The evening was beginning to close in and the steady rain which had come with the new year was still falling. Arctos was usually a dry moon. Lanneret turned away from the window to the warmth and light of the room. A generous fire roared in the hearth, and chandeliers glittered silver overhead. Long-dead Fellows frowned down from the portraits on the walls. Lord Teredo and Lord Anserine were talking quietly together at a table near the fire; Parhelion was hosting a loud drunken party at the other end of the room. Lanneret turned to stare out at the rain again.

'My Lord?' One of the club officials had crossed the room on soft feet, and was murmuring at his elbow. 'There's a young person asking for you. A young *female* person, my Lord.'

'Did she give a name?' Lanneret interrupted.

'No, my Lord. She asked me to give you *this*.' He held out a grubby piece of embroidery, held fastidiously between the tips of his forefinger and thumb.

A slight smile played around Lanneret's mouth.

'Show her into the reading room. And see to it that we aren't disturbed.'

'Well, Sassy?'

She had been studying the ancient Carnival portrait above the mantelpiece, which was so blackened with age and smoke that you could hardly make out the white feathers of the dead swans in the Lords' arms. Startled, she turned to face him as he closed the door noiselessly behind him. She moistened her dry lips and tucked her trembling hands beneath her apron.

'Well?' Lanneret said again. 'What have you got for me?'

'I'm not quite sure...' She shivered.

'You're cold. Sit.' It was an order, not an invitation, and she dropped into a chair at the fireside. She looked at the flames and seemed to gather her courage. 'I'm not quite sure, My Lord, what it's about. But you told me to tell you, if I heard anything odd. Could I have the pillowcase, My Lord?'

'The - ? Oh. Here.' Lanneret handed over the dirty cloth. He sat opposite her, and leaned back, studying her with narrowed eyes as she traced the threads and gathered her thoughts. She had been a good find, this girl: pale and so insignificant that she was almost transparent against the background she inhabited, and gifted with that uncannily exact memory. Not that this tale seemed to be going anywhere. Fossick he knew as a dusty, pedantic antiquarian, though the connection with Parhelion's treasurer was interesting. But *this...* Lanneret sat forward. '*Gaia Athanasius?* Are you sure?'

She nodded, and blinked her pale eyes as he pulled his chair closer to hers, and held a warning finger to his lips. 'Go on.'

She ran over the threads again, and unfolded the rest of her tale in a whisper. When she had finished, Lanneret sat as frozen and white as marble.

'My Lord. Did I do something wrong?'

He shook himself. 'No. No, Sassy. You've done very well.' He took two serafs from his pocket and handed them to her with a wan smile. 'Never trust a historian, Sassy. Come. I'll see you out.'

He escorted her back to the street and watched until her slight, unremarkable figure was lost to sight in the busy homeward crowds. Returning to the reading room, he gave orders that he was not to be disturbed, and sat behind the locked door until late, gazing into the dying fire. Fossick... Parhelion's treasurer... a prohibited object in old script... a boy and a girl called Athanasius... the history of the liberation... the Closed Archive.

He smiled a thin smile. The Closed Archive. A windowless room, four storeys underground. It was the perfect rat-trap, and he would watch the rat all the way into it before he pounced.

Leaving the club the next morning, he crossed the bridge, and paused in Liberation Square to watch a flying carriage which winged its way out to sea, banked steeply and wheeled inland to head north. Parhelion. Well, that would put an end to his treasurer's plotting, at least for the time being. In the meantime, Lanneret would keep a close eye on Fossick, and he must - above all - find those children. *Gaia Athanasius.* Now more than ever he needed a reliable spy among Freehaven's street urchins. If only that girl hadn't proved so intractable the other evening. He trusted that she was regretting her stubbornness by now.

Nearby, two boys had also stopped to watch the carriage. Lanneret cast a quick suspicious eye on them, but they were both wearing the dark blue cloaks of the Basilica choir school, so he wasted no further time on them, and continued his journey across the square.

'Well, there goes Parhelion.' Sam dug in his pocket for the seraf that had been Parhelion's tip for yesterday's long office. 'Shall we go and spend this?' He tossed the coin, spinning it in the air before catching it again. Tal fumbled in his pocket, took out his own seraf and studied it curiously. It was the first money he had ever held: a tiny thing, no bigger than a man's thumbnail, bright gold, embossed with thirteen tiny moons. He tucked it away and they left the square by one of the narrow streets that ran down to the harbour. Sam stopped in front of a familiar door: it was the baker's that Tal and Gaia had looked into and fled from only four days ago.

'Here?' said Tal.

'It's the best. Believe me.'

Tal hung back on the threshold, his eyes down, and the same voice that had shouted after them said, 'What'll you have, boys?' It sounded as warm now as the smell of bread that filled the shop.

'Tal?' Sam gestured at the laden shelves behind the counter, and Tal let his gaze flicker upwards. He met the baker's eyes. There was no trace of recognition in them: he was just another choir school boy: nothing to do with the urchin who had stumbled in out of the rain and run away.

'So?' Sam asked. 'What're you having?'

Tal took the glittering seraf out of his pocket again. He wasn't sure about parting with it.

'It's alright,' Sam reassured him. 'You'll get more. There's always a tip when we sing a private office for one of the Fellowship. We got a whole silver radiant each from Lord Philemot once. And everyone else gives more than one seraf. Parhelion's a -' He checked himself, blushed as red as his hair, and glanced nervously at the baker.

'Careful, Sam,' the man said.

'I didn't mean…'

'It's fine. I didn't hear a thing. Now. Tal. That your name? What do you want?'

Tal left the shop with a bag stuffed with cakes and a pocket rattling with change: seven dull brown rens. As the baker shut the door behind them, he winked at Sam. 'It's fine,' he said again. But Sam remained unusually silent and ill at ease as they made their way back up the steep street. As they reached the square a sleety drizzle started to fall.

'Ugh,' said Sam. 'Not again. I was going to take you down to the river, but I suppose we'd better go inside.'

'There's a ledge under the bridge,' said Tal. 'It'd be dry there.'

'Oh, I know. Good idea.' They hurried to the river, and climbed the ladder. The rungs were ice cold under Tal's fingers, but the ledge was sheltered and his choir school cloak was as warm as John's fur coat. They settled down against the stonework to eat.

'By the way.' Sam swallowed a big mouthful of cake. 'What I said about Lord Parhelion… I don't know if you know, but it's really important. You must never say anything bad about the Fellowship…'

'Not even a joke.' Tal nodded. 'I know. Someone told us.'

'Good,' said Sam. 'Us?'

'Me and my sister,' said Tal. He told Sam, but not everything: he couldn't tell him, any more than he'd been able to tell Gabriel, that he had watched Gaia being arrested and done nothing. He changed the subject. 'What about you? Before the choir?'

'Nothing that exciting. Dad's a ship's carpenter. Gabriel heard me singing when he was passing the workshop. Just as well.' He gave the quick grin that was like a flash of sunlight and showed Tal the back of his hand. There was an old white scar across his knuckles. 'Chisel. I was hopeless. Probably wouldn't have too many fingers left, if I was still working with Dad.' He scrumpled up the empty bag, and got to his feet. 'Time to go. Midday office.'

It was raining harder now, and they climbed the shiny marble steps to the road with hoods pulled tightly over their heads. Halfway up, someone passed them, turned back, and said, 'Tal?'

'Jinx!'

'I was coming to look for you.' Jinx frowned. 'You've got new togs. That's a choir school cloak. *Good* disguise. No-one'll look twice at you…'

'It's not a disguise.' Tal explained, and Jinx's face relaxed into a relieved smile.

'Gabriel's a good man. Any news of Gaia, or your mum?'

'No.' Tal thought of something suddenly. 'I'm going to wait for Gaia, though. Here. First of every quarter: it's what we arranged.'

The look in Jinx's eyes told him what Gabriel had told him: *no chance of getting her back.* But all he said was, 'Good idea. I'll keep you company, if you like?'

Back in his room, Tal climbed onto the table and looked out of the window at the city roofs, the harbour, and the wide sea: a grey wash in the rain. He felt a slight lifting of his spirits. Gaia was gone, but there was some comfort in the decision to keep faith with her, and wait for her in their agreed place. He kept staring at the sea until Sam hammered on his door

'Tal? Time to go.'

Tal jumped off the table, picked up his music, and hurried out to join Sam. They ran along the corridor, reaching the top of the stairs at the same time as the tall boy, Gregory. Tal took a step ahead of him, but Sam grabbed hold of his cloak and hauled him back. Gregory eyed them coldly.

'Teaching your little peasant friend some manners, Sam Gutter-Snipe? About time by the looks of it.' He swept on down the stairs.

'Stay out of his way.' Sam was red-faced. 'It's Sallender; you get used…'

'*Sallender?*' Tal had winded himself once, falling from the path by the waterfall and he felt the same now: every scrap of breath knocked out of him.

Sam scowled. 'Only a third or fourth cousin or something; not that you'd know it from how he...' But Tal was already tearing down the stairs. He pelted along the cloister and caught up with Sallender at the door into the Basilica.

'Wait! There's a slave called Mai. In your family. I need to know... Where can I find her?'

Sallender looked at him in icy bewilderment. 'How in the name of all the moons should I know?' He pushed through the door and let it swing shut in Tal's face.

'Tal?' Sam had caught up with him. 'What's going on?'

'Mum was sold to the Sallenders. I thought he might be able to help.'

Sam slumped against the doorframe. 'Oh darkness and damnation. Not Sallender. He won't help.' He glanced at the cloister clock, and said, apologetically, 'We're going to be late...'

Tal followed him wordlessly and slumped into his seat. It was like falling through darkness: it had been the best hope yet, but it had ended, like all the others, in empty nothing. He stood listlessly as Gabriel took his place at the front of the choir. They sang the simple hymn that Tal had learned yesterday; and when he was singing there was no time or space to think about anything else. The music was a forgetting, a refuge from despair, a place of glory and light.

Grimy light dawned through the porthole of the crowded hold and faded again to darkness. They counted the passing of days, wrapped in Gaia's coat, and told their stories.

'I'm Gaia, really, not Elsa.'

'Funny name,' said Carrie.

From time to time, they stood and looked out, but the blurred view was always the same: grey sea and sky, and a thin undulating line of coast in the distance. At last, after days at sea, the ship changed direction and heeled in towards the land. There was a change in the feel of the water beneath the ship as the swell of the sea gave way to a smooth calm. Pressing her face to the salty porthole, Gaia saw towering grey buildings along the water's edge. The ship stopped. Mooring chains rattled. The hatch above the hold was pushed back with a sudden burst of daylight.

160

'Hope's End prisoners!'

With a dozen or so others, Gaia and Carrie clambered up the steep ladder onto the deck. The day was fading, and a misty rain was blowing, but after so long in the dim hold, even the grey end-of-day was blindingly bright.

'Where are we?' whispered Carrie.

Gaia blinked her dazzled eyes clear. The ship had docked in a wide river, alongside a jetty which was crooked and slimy with age and decay. The huge buildings on the bank were ancient and ruined too: crumbling shells of stone. The window glass was long gone, window- and door-frames had rotted away, and roofs and floors had fallen in, leaving the walls open to the sky. As Gaia stared, a chattering flock of black birds flew up from inside the ruins, and wheeled across the river. They seemed to be the only living things in this massive, broken, deserted place.

'Move!' The guards were chivvying the prisoners off the boat. Gaia stepped onto the rotten boards of the jetty and stopped: her legs were unsteady after days on the rocking sea, and she was dizzied by the glimpses of swirling water below her. Alongside her, Carrie halted too, and gasped.

'Move, you two!'

'Take it easy,' Gaia said, 'and don't rush.' It was what Tal always said, climbing at home. But Carrie wasn't looking at the fall to the river through the holed planking. She was staring downstream, at two big white birds gliding along the dark water under the trees.

'Swans,' she whispered. Clumsily, with her shackled hands, she made the sign of the crescent moon, hurried across the jetty and retreated as far as she could go, pressing herself against the grey wall of one of the big buildings. Gaia followed her slowly.

'They're only birds,' she said.

'They're *swans.*' Carrie made the crescent sign again.

'Well, they're behind you as well.' Gaia pointed: on the wall, slightly above head height, there was a worn frieze of carved swans. Carrie recoiled from the stones as if they had burned her.

'What *is* this place?'

Gaia shook her head.

'We can't be staying here, can we?' Carrie shivered.

'Don't know. Doesn't look like we're moving, does it?' Gaia shivered too: the drizzle was driving straight up the river and into their faces, and she sat down on the ground in the lee of a pile of timbers, caught Carrie's hand, and pulled her down next to her. The other prisoners had slumped down on the quayside too, and the guards stood around with an air of impatient expectation. The ship's captain came to stand near Gaia and Carrie: he seemed as edgy as the others, casting frequent glances along the quay, and up at the darkening sky. One of his men came to talk to him and Gaia strained her ears to hear their muttered conversation.

'They're very late, Captain.'

'I know.' The Captain looked up at the ruins, grimmer than ever in the fading light.

'What if they don't come tonight?'

'Aquilon and his dragons! They'd better. I don't fancy a night at Swanhaven...' He swung round, startled by a sudden commotion along the quay. Four carts careered along the broken cobbles and slewed to a halt. Their drivers jumped down to soothe the shivering and wide-eyed horses. There was a moment of shocked silence, then another terrified horse galloped onto the quay, a driverless cart swinging wildly behind it. One of the drivers made a flailing grab at the reins, but the horse swerved past him, galloped the length of the dock, found its way barred by the pile of timbers, and reared up. The Captain and the sailor cowered against the woodpile. Gaia pressed herself against the wall. Carrie scrambled to her feet and stepped calmly towards the horse.

'Shhh,' she said. 'Woah.' She raised her shackled hands to stroke the horse's trembling, sweating neck, caught the reins, and gathered them in.

For a moment no-one moved or said anything. Then the driver of the first cart, a small wiry man with red hair and sharp features, hurried along the dock and took the reins from Carrie. 'I'll take him now. Thanks.'

Carrie sat down again. Gaia looked at her, open-mouthed.

'How did you do *that?*'

'I told you,' Carrie said. 'I grew up on a farm. I've been around horses all my life.'

'And you're scared of swans?' Gaia joked. Carrie didn't laugh.

Alongside them, the Captain had recovered from his fright. 'Where in the name of Arctos have you been?' he demanded of the red-haired man. 'And why are all these carts empty? You were meant to bring food for my sailors... the other prisoners... It's a halfmoon's journey to Deepdene.'

The man's face darkened. 'Don't blame me, Barghest.'

'You're in *charge*, Superintendant Fox. Who else should I blame?'

'Bandits. They ambushed us. Stole everything.'

'Then let's take a party of men and get everything back!'

Fox gave a short dismissive laugh. 'Not a chance. I know this lot: they've raided us before. They give the food away. It'll be stewing in a hundred cottage stockpots and filling a thousand hungry bellies before tomorrow's out.'

Barghest wiped a hand across his face. 'I'll have to report this. To their Lordships. What am I going to tell them?'

'Try telling them the truth, Captain! Tell them the Fellowship's writ no longer runs in Estmoor.' Ignoring Barghest's protests, Fox turned impatiently away, looked at the driverless cart, and then at Carrie.

'You know about horses. Could you drive this cart?'

'Yes, but...' She held up her shackled hands.

'I've got the keys for those.' He gave an unexpected smile, took out a bunch of keys, and unlocked her chains. Carrie shook out her numb hands, climbed into the driver's seat and picked up the reins. Fox watched her for a moment, nodded, and barked an order along the dock to the other drivers. 'Time we were going! Get this lot loaded up!'

Gaia found herself herded away from Carrie, and hauled up onto one of the other carts. She landed on her knees on the muddy boards, and a woman whom she vaguely recognised from the court leaned down to help her up. They sat close together. It was cold, and the daylight was almost gone; a single swan drifted white on the dark river. Fox worked his way along the carts, slamming the tailgates shut and lighting the lanterns. Climbing into his own seat, he called, 'Let's go!' and they moved off along the old paved road, jolting over the gaps in the broken cobbles. The lanterns cast dancing pools of light. Gaia looked back at Carrie.

'You two together?' the woman asked.

'Yes,' Gaia said. 'I mean... I didn't meet her till the court. I don't know much about her, just that she grew up on a farm.' She paused, remembering the story Carrie had told her during the long cold days at sea. 'When the famine came, her brother went to Freehaven to look for work. They never heard anything, so she went to look for him. She was arrested as a vagrant and sent home, but when she got there the farm was shut up and her parents were gone. She thought maybe they'd gone to Freehaven too, so she went back, and she was arrested again, and...' She shrugged. 'You know the rest.'

'Yes,' said the woman. The lantern light cast deep shadows around her eyes. 'I know the rest. Lost parents, lost children. Damn this rotten land.'

She put an arm round Gaia and held her close. The carts trundled on into thick darkness and drizzle. Later, the rain stopped; the clouds cleared the moon and in the white light Gaia saw that they were travelling up a broad flat valley where the road and the river ran side by side. The river shone silver, and the road was marked here and there by white stones that gleamed like swans in the moonlight, but further ahead everything was lost in a dark mass which filled the valley bottom and spread up the hills on either side, as if some of the thick night had been left lying there when the moon appeared.

Gaia knelt and leaned forward, screwing up her eyes to stare at the darkness, wondering, fearfully, if that was where they were heading, and what it was... But before she could make it out, the carts changed direction, swinging off the paved road onto a rough track bordered by high thorn hedges. The track zig-zagged steeply up the side of the valley and the horses slowed, straining against the slope. Halfway up the hill, Fox's cart lurched sideways and stopped, one wheel sunk deeply in the wet mud, and the prisoners were made to climb down and help dig it out. Among them, Gaia saw a boy casting for a way to run; but the hedges were thick and tangled and there was no way through. When the wheel was free, he climbed unhappily back into the cart with everyone else.

At the top of the hill, the land opened up into a bleak windy moorland. The track travelled straight across it, bringing them to a pair of tall gates set in a stone wall that ran like a line of darkness across the silvered moor. The ironwork of the gates threw strange moonlit shadows on the rough grass.

'That you, Superintendant?' A man with a lantern emerged from the shadows, and with a rattle of locks and chains, the gates swung heavily open. The carts passed through; the gates shut again behind them.

Hope's End

Inside the gates, the track wound between big ploughed fields: down a slight slope, through a shallow stream, and uphill again into a dimly lit farmyard where the carts stopped. A cold wind chased between the buildings, and Gaia huddled, shivering, into her rain-drenched coat.

Fox jumped down from his cart. His red hair gleamed in the lamplight. 'Well, this is Hope's End,' he said. 'I'm not one for speeches, and it's late and cold, but there are some things I'm obliged to tell you. You've been sent here because you've broken the laws of the republic. You'll be making recompense for your crimes by doing useful work. Farming. And you'll be doing it till the day you die, or the day that you're pardoned.'

'Some chance.' A sarcastic voice rang from the darkness.

Fox gave a wry, tired smile. 'Two rules. Don't run. Do as you're told. Follow those and you'll be... Well. Things won't get worse. Now...' He pulled a paper from his pocket and held it close to read it in the weak light. 'Carrie Beckett!'

'Yes.' Carrie raised her hand.

'Oh, that's you, is it?' Fox gave her a quick smile, and beckoned her to his side.

'Simon Garth!' The boy who had been looking for a way to run in the lane dragged himself to stand with Carrie.

'Elsa Seagull!'

That was her, Gaia remembered. She slid clumsily down from the cart, found her way to Carrie's side and felt for her hand in the darkness, holding tight to her icy fingers.

'You three go with Mr Hawkins.' Fox gestured at a big man with a bunch of keys jangling on his belt. They followed him out of the yard. The clouds were closing in again and in the fitful moonlight Gaia could make out the dark shapes of other buildings resting on the moorland like sleeping dragons. Hawkins led them across a stretch of rough grass, stopped at one of the buildings and unlocked and opened the door.

'Kids' hut,' he said. 'In you go.' He shoved them inside, slamming and relocking the door behind them. Gaia looked round at a low room, where piles of straw were heaped up in makeshift beds on the earthen floor. But all the beds were empty. A couple of dozen kids were crowded beneath the single high window in the end wall where a girl was standing on a boy's shoulders to look out, gripping the windowsill to steady herself. Someone said something, and there was a burst of laughter.

'Shut up!' said a tall girl. 'Can you see him, Jenny?'

The girl at the window said, 'Not yet,' over her shoulder and went back to looking. Gaia, Carrie and Simon threaded their way through the heaps of straw to join the back of the group.

'He's coming!'

Jenny jumped down from the boy's shoulders, and a bulky package, tied with a cloth whose ends were coming loose, flew through the window and landed on the floor. A gang of kids scrabbled for it, but the tall girl was there first: she snatched it up and held it out of their reach. 'Wait! You'll have it in a moment.' Everyone turned back to look at the window. A hand appeared on the ledge, and a boy hauled himself up, wriggled through the narrow gap, and swung himself down into the room.

'What d'you get?' someone asked.

'Have a look.' He shoved his hands in his pockets and stood aside as the other kids clustered around the tall girl, who was already unwrapping the cloth. 'Bread,' she said. '*Ham.*' Carrie stood on tiptoe to look too, but Gaia pushed her way through the crowd to the boy's side and caught hold of his hand.

'*Jason!*'

Working alongside him in the pale cold light of the next morning she felt a catch of tears and laughter every time she looked at him. Her oldest and best friend: the same old Jason, swaggering in with a load of stolen food…

Except… he wasn't quite the same old Jason, not completely. As they worked - grubbing for stones in the frozen earth and chucking them into the basket that sat on the ground between them - Gaia watched him, remembering the simple history he had told her last night. He'd been sold to Baladine's agent at Trebburn and set to work in the kitchen of his house in Imber province. A halfmoon of taking orders had been enough for him. He had run, stolen food from a market stall; been caught, tried and packed off to Hope's End. A simple history. It had changed him though. He was skinnier than ever: the bones stood out in his face and wrists. But it wasn't only that. Gaia had curled up next to him last night - he slept apart from the others in a spot under the window that no-one else wanted because it was too cold - and in the middle of the night she'd heard him wake with a shaky, frightened catch of breath. She'd listened to him breathing deeply, trying to calm himself; it had been a long time before he'd fallen asleep again. There was something in his eyes, too, when he didn't know he was being watched: a sort of defeated bitterness under the swagger...

He looked up, caught her eye, gave the old grin, and winked.

'Reckon this is full again?' He jerked his head at the half-empty basket.

'Reckon.' Between them, they hefted the basket from the ground and carried it to the dump of stones that was piling up in the lee of the field wall. As soon as they were out of earshot of the other prisoners and the bored guard who was watching them, they picked up their interrupted conversation.

'How did you think you could you afford to free her, though?' Jason asked.

'Remember the amulet?'

'Oooh, now let me think,' he teased. She thumped him. 'Yes, Gaia. I remember the amulet. Did you ever find out what it was?'

'Well, not exactly, but...' She explained.

'*Prohibited?*' The laughter had gone from his eyes and he stared at her in horror. 'So what happened? Where is it now?'

She moved a hand instinctively to her neck and his eyes widened.

'You haven't still got it? Gaia, you have to get rid of it!' His voice rose in alarm; he checked himself, looked round, and continued in a harsh whisper, 'If they find you with it... It means *death*.'

'I know,' she said. He was right, of course. It was a risk to keep it, and a pointless risk. What possible use could it be to her now? But she still loved it, in spite of everything: her pretty, mysterious, dangerous little talisman. She couldn't get rid of it. She looked at the heaps of stones that ran alongside the field wall. Some were old, covered in moss.

'Do they just leave these?' she asked.

He nodded, and she crawled behind an old, settled heap of stones and pulled a few mossy flints loose. She lifted the amulet from her neck. For a moment, she crouched, holding it, feeling the shape of the moonswood through the worn leather.

'Hurry up,' Jason whispered and she shoved the amulet into the pile, replaced a couple of stones to hide it, crawled out, and picked up the empty basket.

'Will it be safe there, d'you think?'

'That's not the point. *You'll* be safe if it's there.'

At midday they rested next to the pile of stones for a lunch of water and flat bread. As she ate, Gaia stared across the farm: the big rain-sodden bare fields, the smaller walled plots near the stone farmhouse, the wooden barn, the stark grey stone wall around everything. Outside, the moor reached away into the distance. The dark mass that she had seen in the night was a forest. Gaia stared at the distant trees, chewing on the hard dry bread.

'Helps if you dip it in the water,' said Jason. 'And here. Have this.'

He slipped her a slice of white crumbly cheese. It was strong and salty.

'Where d'you get this?'

'Nicked it with the rest of the stuff last night.'

'Jason… What happens if you get caught?'

He didn't answer. When she looked at him, the defeated expression was back in his eyes. 'Jason?'

'Reckon he knows. Fox, I mean. He knows I do it. He knows it's me.'

He stood up. Head down, he trudged back across the frozen soil to join the other prisoners, who stood, hunched up against the sleet, while Mr Hawkins gave out orders for the afternoon. He beckoned Jason and Gaia to follow him, and led them through the big bare fields to one of the enclosed gardens near the farm buildings. Four long beds of earth ran the length of the garden, empty, except for a few brown stalks whose hanging rotten leaves dripped in the rain. Mr Hawkins settled himself on the fence, pulled his hat down and collar up, and started to whittle at a piece of wood.

'What are we doing?' Jason asked him.

'Planting.' Hawkins jerked his head at some wooden trays resting on the ground by the gate, and went back to his carving. Gaia crouched by the trays. They were full of – well, what? Unfamiliar little things. Small. Dry. Hard. Drab brown and black. She frowned up at Jason, who was leaning against the fence, watching her.

'What are these?'

'Seeds.'

She looked blank.

'You stick them in the earth and things grow from them. And die, mostly, here,' he added, with a glance at the dripping brown stalks. Gaia gave him a long, doubtful look, pressed a finger into one of the trays and stared at the fragile pale husks sticking to her fingertip.

'You're kidding, aren't you?'

'No,' he protested. But he was laughing, and she said, half laughing too, 'Oh, come on, Jason. These can't turn into *plants*. They're ... *nothing.*'

'I don't know how it works. But it does. Honestly. Moons' own truth.'

She rubbed the seeds between her thumb and fingertip, remembering the forest: the leaves and fruit that were rich with juice and scent when you broke them open. It was impossible to imagine that all that flourishing life had grown from something like this.

'Go on, then. What will these grow into?'

'No idea. We just stick them in and wait to see what comes up.'

'Those are lettuces.' Carrie was leaning on the gate. She came into the garden and crouched down next to Gaia. She had spent the morning in the stables, and she smelt of hay and horses.

'Onions... beans... carrots...'

'Show me.' Jason squatted down next to her, and she recited the list again, pointing. When she had finished, Jason seemed impressed.

'Maybe we'll actually manage a decent crop with you here.'

'Doubt it. It's not a good place. Too windy. No shelter, and this ...' Carrie fingered the wet, stony, thin earth and grimaced. Gaia

169

picked up a handful of soil and rubbed it between her fingers, feeling the sticky grittiness of it. She plunged both hands into the bed, up to her wrists.

'Haven't you ever seen *earth* before, Gaia?' Carrie asked.

'No.' Gaia picked up a heavy clod and weighed it in her hand. 'Not really. Where we come from it's all rock.' She broke the clod apart and crumbled it between her fingers.

Jason watched her with a slow smile. 'She's always been like this...' he said to Carrie, but Mr Hawkins had jumped down from the fence and was striding towards them.

'You three are meant to be getting on with some *work*. Enough chat! Where d'you think you are? Fellowship garden party?'

'Sir!' Jason picked up a tray of seeds. 'You better show us what to do, Carrie.'

'It's a doss, gardening,' Jason said. 'One guard for all the gardens, so they leave you alone for ages.' Mr Hawkins had moved off to supervise work elsewhere, and Carrie and Jason were sitting side by side on the fence, while Gaia crouched at their feet, digging a patch of earth. She paused, looked up at Jason, started to speak, stopped, and frowned.

'Uh-oh. She's thinking,' Jason said.

She flicked a piece of earth at him. 'I was *thinking* that they leave us alone a lot. You got out of the hut last night... and they weren't watching us too closely this morning, either. I mean, it must be easy to escape, mustn't it? Climbing that wall'd be simple...'

Jason cut across her, harshly. 'Getting out's not the problem.' He jumped off the fence and stood with his back to them, leaning on the rail and gazing across the fields to the wall and the moor beyond it. '*Being* out's the problem.' He swung back round to face them, touching a hand to the double scar on his cheek. 'This gives you away, whichever way you run. And whichever way you run, there's people who are keen to earn a quick seraf or two by turning in any idiot slave who thought they could make a break for it.'

'You tried.' Gaia knew it suddenly, for a certainty.

He was silent, remembering. Jumping down from the cart in the yard, listening to Fox giving out his rules. *Don't run...* But Jason's eyes had already been straying across the farmland to that oh-so-climbable wall and the open moor beyond it. He had run on his second night. Easy. Couldn't have been easier. Morning had brought him to a wretched cottage by a copse of twisted trees at the top of the long slope down to the coast. He'd seen the sea that morning, for the first and only time in his life: huge, grey and restless under the winter sky. As he'd stared at it, a woman had come out of the house. He'd turned to run, but she'd said, 'Don't be afraid.' She touched her cheek lightly. 'You're from the Farm. You must be hungry.'

'Yes.' He was tired too, from a night of alternately running and walking, desperate to put as much distance as possible between himself and Hope's End before dawn. She'd taken him into the smoky house and given him bread and sour tea. 'Rest,' she told him and, dog-tired, he'd put his head on the greasy tabletop. As his eyes closed he'd caught an expression in hers that he couldn't read. Later he thought maybe it was shame.

He'd woken to find himself bound, hands and feet; fresh air on his face; the swaying of a cart beneath him; the Hope's End gates stark against the sky.

'Do I get my money?' the woman had demanded of Fox, and he'd handed over a couple of serafs and waved her wearily away. Unable to meet Jason's eyes, he'd said, 'This is ordered by the Fellowship, Jason. I've no power to alter it...'

And Jason's mind stopped: refused to follow the track of memory any further; flinched away from it with a shiver that Gaia saw.

'Yes,' he said. 'I tried.'

'What happened?' Gaia asked, but he shook his head. He'd run from Baladine in a stolen brown jacket that was too big for him, baggy around his shoulders and too long in the sleeves, and he looked lost in it. She stood up and put her arm around him. He shook her off.

'The thing is, Gaia - you can survive here. It's hard work, and you'll be cold and hungry most of the time. But if you stick by the rules, Fox is alright. It's survivable. Best you can hope for, if you're a criminal slave of the republic. I'm going to get on with some work.'

He pulled a fork from the pile of tools lying on the ground, trampled across the beds to the other side of the garden and assaulted the row of dead stalks, wrenching them out of the ground and flinging them aside.

She should never talk to him about escaping again: that was obvious. His bad dreams were worse that night. A cry in the darkness woke her, and she lay, listening to him, her body tensed for his next long shuddering breath. When he had, at last, relaxed back into the rhythms of deep sleep she was stark, staring awake, her mind racing. She sat up and stared into the darkness and the bleak future. For the whole of the rest of her life, this was all that was left to her; this dull patch of land inside its grey walls: locked gates, a locked door at night.

Tal caught a bird once, at home, and tried to keep it in a box, but it battered its wings against the sides, and then crouched at the bottom, hunched up, ready to die. In the end he had let it fly away. They had watched the life returning to it as it soared up into the air.

So next day - even though she hated herself for doing it, even though Carrie darted her a fierce look and mouthed, 'Shut up! - next day, as soon as they were alone in the garden, she said, 'If you did escape…'

'Forget it, Gaia.' Jason's voice was unsteady but she pressed on anyway.

'If you did escape, you could hide in the forest, couldn't you? We were in a forest, Tal and me. It was fine.' She smiled, remembering the sheltering trees and the plenty of things to eat. But Jason looked at her, hard-eyed.

'Are you crazy? That's Nouldewood, Gaia. Mean anything to you? It's a prohibited place. If they find you there, you're *dead*.'

'Nouldewood? It can't be. That's where Tal and I were…'

'*What?!*'

'That's the forest we came through, but it's *moons* away from here. All that time to Freehaven, and then on the boat…'

Jason gave a thin laugh. 'Don't try and escape, Gaia. You've got no sense of direction.' He squatted down and sketched a rough map in the earth. 'Look. Arimaspia's here, in the north. Here's Freehaven. You say you came along the Leathy River?' She nodded. 'That runs through the west of the forest. When they brought you here, you came all the way along this coast and up this one,' he sketched in another line, 'and round to here. You're at the eastern edge of Nouldewood now. You've come round the side of a circle. Didn't you realise?'

'No.' She studied the map. 'How d'you know all this?'

'Worked part of it out, got someone to explain the rest, before I ran. Thought I'd go back to Arimaspia. Reckoned I better know the way first.' He scrubbed the map out with his foot. 'Stop thinking about it. Just get back to work.'

Gaia dug at the bed of earth in front of her, but her thoughts were still in the forest. Nouldewood. The kindest of places. She could survive there. But then Mr Hawkins walked into view and her eyes refocused on him, on the stark grey line of the boundary wall, on the bleak stretch of moor before the forest edge. There were so many risks. She might be caught getting out, crossing the moor, or, worst, entering the forest…

She turned her frustration to the earth, digging hard and deep into the soil, forcing a spade through the sticky clay, wrenching it free, slicing into the earth again. Then she threw the spade aside and picked up a fork, chopping, stabbing, twisting. She began in a fury, but there was an unexpected, strange peace in the rhythm of the task: dig, turn, pull; dig, turn, pull. She worked on, breaking the soil down and down until she had made a fine tilth that ran freely through her fingers. Before the afternoon started to darken, she had a bed ready for planting.

She picked up a handful of seeds and took them to Carrie. 'What did you say these were?'

'Onions.'

'How do I plant them?'

'I'll show you.' Carrie knelt on the wet earth, next to the bed that Gaia had made ready, made a hole, dropped in a couple of seeds, covered them and marked the place with a twig. When she had finished, she sat back on her heels and looked warily at Gaia.

'Were you really in…?' She nodded towards the forest.

'Nouldewood? Yes.'

Carrie flinched and made the crescent sign. 'It's an evil place, Gaia. It's out of the moonsight.'

'It's not,' Gaia said. 'It's… It's the Moons' own wood.'

She knelt down and did as Carrie had showed her: making neatly spaced holes for the seeds, planting and covering them, marking where they were with pieces of stick. Utterly absorbed, she forgot everything except the earth; Jason's voice, when he called, seemed to come from a long way off.

'Gaia… Gaia, that was the bell. It's time to go in.'

She sat back and pushed her hair out of her eyes with a muddy hand. Jason and Carrie were waiting for her at the gate. There was one last unplanted patch of earth. 'You go. I'll just finish planting this.'

Jason shook his head. 'You're not allowed to stay out after the bell. Anyway, I'm not leaving you on your own. Don't trust you not to do something stupid.'

She frowned at him, and followed his gaze over the wall, across the moor to the darkening trees. 'Oh. That.' Nouldewood seemed far away now, as distant as the moon. 'I wasn't going to. I wanted to plant these.' She held out her hand. Half a dozen seeds rolled on her grubby palm.

'Tomorrow'll do for that,' said Jason.

He held the gate open for her and as he followed her up the path, he turned back for an instant to look across the moor at the dark forest, remembering again. After it was all over, Fox had said, 'Don't run again, Jason,' and defeated, he had agreed, 'No.' That night he'd climbed out of the hut and crossed the farmland to the wall. He'd stared out over the open country, and battered his hands against the wall until his fingers were bleeding. Then he'd turned his back on the outside and taken a long, long look around at the farm. This was it, now.

Until Gaia, this afternoon, had carelessly planted that little seed of a chance. 'We were in Nouldewood. It was fine...' He stared across at the forest, feeling a slow tipping in the balance of risk, from hopeless to almost, maybe, faintly possible. When she ran, he decided, he was going with her.

But she didn't talk about it again. The ice in the earth melted, sleet became rain, Arctos waned and gave way to Clamynto, last of the winter moons. Gaia tended her frozen garden; she seemed, strangely, more at peace than Jason had ever known her.

Spring

At midday on the first day of Galanthus, Lanneret stepped into the Basilica, and cast an eye around for Sassy. If she had news for him, she would be sitting at the end of the last row, pretending to pray. But her place was empty. Lanneret walked up the nave, looking along each row of chairs and into all the shadowy corners alongside the statues. There was no sign of her anywhere.

The choir were gathering for rehearsal, and he leaned on a chair and watched them, caught up in his own gloomy thoughts. There was still no news of those children: the boy and girl from Arimaspia; the children with that uncommon, resonant surname and their little fragment of moonswood and Old Script. Lanneret had done what he could to find them. He had pulled in every stray street child he could find; he had gone through court and watch records in case they had been arrested or had somehow managed to get permission to stay... Nothing. They had vanished like shadows in the moonlight.

'Uncle!' Gregory Sallender ran down the choir steps to greet him. 'Happy new moon, Uncle! I mean... My Lord.'

Lanneret gave a cold nod.

'Will you be at Uncle Miles' new moon dinner?'

Lanneret nodded again.

'So will I,' Gregory beamed.

'Till this evening, then.' Lanneret waved Gregory back to the choir and listened as they began to sing: a single treble voice sounding alone before being joined by all the others. 'That was fine, Tal,' Gabriel said when they finished. 'Just like that. Even quieter on the high notes if you can.' The boy who had been singing nodded, and scrawled a quick note on his music. Lanneret walked away down the nave, pushed open the door and scowled at the rain dancing in the puddles. On top of everything else, he thought sourly, he was apparently doomed to spend the evening celebrating the new moon with that odious child Gregory.

175

Spring

Tal stared at the new glass in the side windows, and the new banners above the nave. He was getting used to these changes: dark green for Anserine's moon, magenta for Hallion's, and now bright blue for Sallender's. Sam sighed exaggeratedly and Tal turned to him.

'He's going to be unbearable. For this whole moon.' Sam nodded across the choir at Sallender, resplendent and arrogant in the family regalia that he would wear throughout Galanthus: a long cloak of silver and lapis blue.

'He's always unbearable,' Tal muttered.

'I know. But he'll be worse than usual.'

'Worse?' Tal grinned. 'Are you sure that's possible...?' He broke off, feeling Gabriel's eyes resting meaningfully on him, and dropped his gaze to the floor as Gabriel said, 'I want to have a first look at the Coranto liturgy. Come and take a copy, please. And anyone who's never sung this before had better *concentrate*.'

'He's joking,' Sam whispered. 'It's easy. We hardly sing anything; just a bit at the end.' Back in his place, Tal flipped through the music and saw that Sam was right. The lower voices - alto, tenor and bass - sang for three or four pages before the trebles joined them. Tal settled in his chair to listen.

He had known this story all his life, of course: the first of the Coranto stories: Ambrose had told it to them every spring. But hearing it now, it struck him with a savage pitiless intensity; he felt as if he had never understood it before.

Now Areos and Elimar were brothers
Born of the same blood...

'The same blood, the same blood, the same blood,' echoed from one voice to another, and Tal closed his eyes and listened to the story of his own shame.

They guarded their flock at the edge of the wood
And each to the other swore:
Brother thou art
And to the end of danger
I will follow thee.
But a wild beast came out of the darkness.

176

Spring

And Areos fought but Elimar fled
Deep under the trees where no moon shines.

Tal felt Sam tugging at his sleeve. They had reached the
moment where the trebles joined the rest of the choir. He stood,
fumbled to the right page and sang the bitter words.

New born Coranto weeps,
One brother dead,
The other false and failed and fled,
Lost in the dark where no moon shines.

He was crying as he sang; his nose running, hot tears splashing
onto the page in front of him. He scrubbed his face with the sleeve of
his cloak. But there was no stopping these tears: they ran like a spring
that has finally forced its way through frozen ground. As the last note
died to nothing, Gabriel darted him a troubled glance. 'That's enough
for now, I think. Let's finish there.'
Tal bolted for the door.
'What's the matter with *him?*' Sallender's voice followed him as
he plunged out into the cloister. 'Oh, maybe a *goat* died.'

He reached his room and climbed onto the table to look out
to the empty sea where she had gone. He had been hiding from this: it
had been possible not to think about it, when his days were so busy
with singing that he tumbled into bed at night, dizzy with tiredness
and ready for dreamless sleep. It had been possible to lose himself in
the wonder of the music, in its curious trick of lifting him from
sorrow into glory.
Until now. *A brother false and failed and fled...* He worked and
sang his way numbly through the rest of the long new moon day,
avoiding Sam, not meeting Gabriel's eyes. But at the end of the
nightfall office, Sam and Gabriel stopped him at the door to the
cloister.
'Tal. Come.' Gabriel led them into his kitchen and they sat at
the table under the warm light of the hanging lantern. Tal ran his
finger along the tabletop, tracing the grain in the wood.
'What's wrong, Tal?' Gabriel asked.

'Nothing...' he began; but this shame was so heavy it was impossible to carry it alone for another moment longer. He raised his head and made himself meet Gabriel's eyes.

'Areos and Elimar.' He swallowed hard. 'It... it made me think of Gaia. What I did.' He looked from Gabriel to Sam to Connie, and down at the tabletop again. 'I never told you properly. When she was arrested... I was *there*. With her, and I didn't do anything... I... I just let them take her.'

He stopped, unable to say any more. Connie said, instantly, 'She'd have wanted you to be safe, Tal. She wouldn't have wanted you arrested too.'

He said, remembering, 'She told me to go.'

'There, then,' said Connie but he shook his head, fiercely. 'She told me to go but she didn't really want me to.' He could still see it: everything: her hair and coat soaked by the rain, her eyes terrified. She had whispered, 'Go,' but he had known that all she wanted was for him to go to her and put his hand in hers.

Sam said, 'Bet she did. She'd have wanted you to keep looking for your mum, wouldn't she?'

'But *Mum* would've wanted me to stay with Gaia.'

Gabriel had listened carefully but had said nothing. Now he reached down four cups from the dresser and filled them with tea from the kettle on the stove. He picked up his own cup and cradled it in his hands, breathing in the sweet steam.

'Gabriel?' Connie said.

Gabriel put his cup down, and looked directly at Tal.

'I think you did the wrong thing.'

'Gabriel!' Connie said.

He gave her a quick glance and turned back to Tal. 'You had to make a quick decision in a moment of fear and panic. I can't imagine how scared you were; I shouldn't think any of us can. There are a hundred excuses for what you did, but it was the wrong decision.'

'Gabriel!' Connie protested again, but he said, 'Tal knows it, perfectly well. I'm not telling him anything he hasn't told himself. Am I, Tal?'

'No.' Tal let out a long, shaky breath. Connie and Sam had been kind, trying to make him feel better, but Gabriel's simple acceptance that he had been wrong felt more real, and strangely more hopeful. He waited, hungry for what Gabriel was going to say next.

'I can see why that story got to you.' Gabriel winced. 'A brother who runs away leaving the other to face death alone. You must have felt as if it had been written for you.' He leaned back in his chair. 'But the problem with these stories is that they only show us a slice of people's lives.' Sam looked at him doubtfully. He smiled. 'Look at Elimar. What is he to us? A man who made one cowardly, fatal decision. But what about before? If he'd always been a coward, Areos wouldn't have taken him into danger. And afterwards... Who knows what he faced and conquered in the darkness?'

'I thought he died,' said Tal.

'That's not what the story says.' Gabriel leaned forward across the table. 'Tal. You've done something you'll regret for a long time. But there were a hundred choices before that one. There'll be who knows how many hundreds to come. What you are is the sum of all those choices, not only that one bad one. It won't ever be nothing. But it's not all there is.'

Tal was silent for a long time. He felt as though someone had opened a window onto a darkened room. The main outlines of things were the same, but they looked different. Lighter, less frightening.

'Here.' Gabriel pushed his tea towards him. 'Drink it before it's cold.' He stood up and crossed the kitchen to look out of the high window at the night. 'Wherever Gaia is, Tal, the moons watch her, just as they watch you. Remember that.'

Gaia pushed open the garden gate and stopped short. It had happened. The thing she had been waiting for with a patience that would have astonished Mai and Tal; the thing she had still, until today, not wholly believed to be possible. Dozens of pale green shoots had forced their way out of the earth, all over the beds she had planted. She caught Jason's arm.

'Look!'

'Told you.' He grinned at her.

'You've got green fingers, Gaia.' Carrie looked round the empty beds in the rest of the plot. 'Yours are the only ones that have come up so far.'

Gaia crouched on the soaking earth and touched one of the tiny plants with marvelling fingers, astonished at the life pulsing through it, pushing it out of the ground. She worked her way along the new shoots. Leeks, carrots, cabbages...

'What's *that?*' shouted Jason.

'I think it's an onion.'

'Not that!' He hauled her to her feet and pointed into the cloudy sky. *'That.'*

She stared. In and out of sight between the hurrying clouds, something was winging its way out of the west: a silver body below innumerable beating wings.

'No need to ask what that is, Jason.' She looked at him, and the memory of the fatal day in Brumas hung between them. The carriage was moving fast: it was already close enough for them to see the tethered eagles, beating hard against the strong moorland winds. Descending rapidly, it swept over the farm buildings, wheeled round, and hovered for a moment before setting down in the centre of the farmyard.

'What's going on?' Gaia asked.

'Only one way to find out.' Jason shoved open the garden gate, and they hurried up the path, joining a crowd of curious and apprehensive prisoners. Two unfamiliar wagons had halted outside the farmhouse, and a dozen strangers in black livery stood around the yard. A young man stepped down from the eagle carriage. He had fair hair and he was dressed entirely in black except for the bright threads of silver in the long cloak that fell in folds around him.

'Lord Helminth,' murmured Carrie.

'Let me through,' Fox said from behind them. They shuffled aside to make space for him, and he crossed the yard and knelt in the wet mud at Helminth's feet. Helminth pulled a scroll of parchment from inside his cloak. He handed it to Fox.

'Read this.'

Fox unrolled the paper, ran his eyes across it, and jerked his head up.

'Seditious speech against the republic?' His face was white under his copper hair. 'My Lord, I swear... This isn't... I haven't...'

'We received a report from Captain Barghest,' said Helminth. Fox closed his eyes briefly. 'He reported you as saying that the Fellowship's writ no longer runs in Estmoor.'

'That was meant as a *warning*! Banditry's out of control here; there've been…'

'Fox!' Helminth cut across him. 'Don't make it worse.'

'Can it be?' Fox gave a wry, sad smile. Helminth shook his head, and two of the black-liveried strangers seized Fox's arms, hauled him to his feet, marched him to one of the wagons and bundled him inside it. Helminth climbed back into the carriage, and signalled wearily to his driver. Gaia watched the birds rise into the air, but Jason was tugging at her hand. Someone had climbed out of the other wagon, and was standing, surveying the yard: a tall, gaunt man with a streak of white in the long dark hair that was blowing around his face in the wind from the birds' wings.

'Who's that?' Gaia whispered.

'New Superintendant, I guess.' Jason turned to gaze across the moor towards Nouldewood.

'So now we've got a madman in charge,' Jason said some days later, as they worked the garden in the spring drizzle.

'What d'you mean?' Gaia asked.

'Superintendant Stearne, obviously. What did you say he made you do, Carrie?'

Carrie frowned. 'Put white stones outside the stable doors. That doesn't make him mad, though, Jason. We did it at home; it keeps evil away from the animals.'

'That's crazy,' said Jason.

'It's not,' Carrie said. 'White's like moonlight, isn't it?'

'But swans are evil,' said Gaia.

'Yes.' Carrie flinched and sketched the sign of the crescent moon in the air.

'So that doesn't make sense, does it? I mean, swans are white too, so why aren't they like moon…'

'Gaia!' Jason hissed. She looked up. Stearne was leaning on the fence, watching them. He opened the gate, came into the garden, and cast his eyes over the four long beds. His gaze rested on Gaia's carefully tended earth. The first green shoots had grown taller, unfolding leaves that shivered in the falling rain.

'Who grew these?' Stearne asked.

'Me,' Gaia said.

'Your name?'

181

'Gaia.' He looked at her narrowly and she felt a lurch of panic. Were they looking for her outside Freehaven now: the girl with the odd name carrying the little moonswood fragment that meant death? 'I mean...' she stammered. 'Elsa. Gaia's a... a nickname.'

'A strange nickname.' Stearne turned to look at the plants again. 'Why have yours grown better than the others?'

'I don't know. Luck, I suppose.'

'Growing things is like that,' said Carrie. 'Some people have a feel for it. A gift; like a kind of magic...'

'She works harder than anyone else.' Jason cut across Carrie. 'That's all.'

Stearne frowned, turned away from them without a word, and left the garden. As he climbed the path to the farmhouse, Gaia noticed that he was sketching the protective sign of the crescent moon in the air. She looked at Jason and Carrie.

'What was that about?'

'I'm not sure,' Jason said. 'You want to watch him, though.'

But, in the days that followed, it was as if Stearne was watching *her*. She looked up, often, from her work to find him leaning silently on the garden fence, studying her, and if she looked back, she found that he would retreat, sketching the crescent as he went.

Towards the end of Galanthus, planting a fresh crop of beans alongside Jason and Carrie, she glanced up to see him inside the gate, standing, watching. She stared back at him, willing him to go, holding his gaze - and watched, bewildered, as his eyes flickered past her and widened into an expression of horrified terror.

'No,' he whispered. 'That's not...'

Gaia spun round. A huge heavy creature was flying low, riding the air above the rough moorland on strong leathery wings; swooping to and fro, scanning the ground for prey. Somewhere on the farm, someone screamed, and the dragon turned with a loud flap of its wings and flew fast over the farm wall and the outer fields. Carrie gave a choking cry and started to run. Jason grabbed hold of her and pulled her to him; wrapping both arms round her and holding her close.

'Don't move. It's too close. It'll see you if you run. And keep quiet. Understand?'

Carrie swallowed and nodded. The dragon swept closer.

'Don't run,' Jason was muttering, 'Don't run....'

'I know,' Gaia whispered, only he wasn't talking to her, but to the dozens of prisoners who, in fields and gardens all over the farm, had thrown down their tools and were bolting for the farmyard. The dragon banked and swept down in a long dive. There was a burst of fire, a high scream of pain and terror; silence. Carrie sobbed and pressed her face into Jason's shoulder. The beast swept up and down again, landing in the farmyard. It looked starving - its bones stood out sharply under its loose scaly skin - and lost and bewildered: a mountain creature, a long way from home. It crawled across the yard, peered into the barn, and shuffled inside. Jason let go of Carrie, dashed across the garden, hurtled up the path, slammed the barn door shut and yelled across the fields:

'Get to the huts! Now!'

Gaia grabbed Carrie's hand and ran, joining the stampede of terrified prisoners. From the door of their hut, she looked back at the farmyard. The wooden barn was ablaze; smoke and flames leaping and pouring into the rainy sky; as she watched, the dragon burst out of the roof in a shower of sparks, soared up into the clouds and was lost to sight.

After the attack, Stearne watched Gaia more closely than ever: it seemed that whenever she looked up it was to find his pale eyes on her. If she met his gaze, he flinched as if he had been scalded, scanned the skies over the farm and sketched the protective crescent against his chest, again and again.

This morning, though, a few days after the new moon of Coranto, there was for once no sign of him. Jason had been sent to one of the top fields with a message for Mr Hawkins. Gaia knelt next to Carrie on the wet earth and worked her way along a bed of seedlings, tugging up the weeds that had sprouted around them.

'Gaia!'

She startled and looked up. Jason was tearing down the path between the gardens. He vaulted the fence into their plot, ran across three beds of plants and halted, doubled-up and out of breath. 'The stones... Top field...' He hauled in a long breath. 'Stearne's having them moved.'

Gaia leapt to her feet and fled, out of the garden, up the path, and across the furrowed fields, stumbling on the rutted ground, ignoring the stalks snapping beneath her feet. At the boundary wall, she found gangs of prisoners pulling apart the settled, mossy piles of old stones, supervised by Mr Hawkins.

'What are you doing here?' he asked.

'Left my coat here. Can I fetch it, please?'

He grunted. Gaia wriggled behind the pile of flints, plunged her hand in among the stones and retrieved the pouch, feeling the edges of the moonswood square through the worn leather. Shakily, she hung it round her neck and tucked it out of sight. She took a steadying breath and sauntered back to Mr Hawkins.

'Not there,' she said. 'Must've left it somewhere else.'

'Hope you find it before it's pilfered. It's a good coat, that.'

'Mmm.' She watched the work on the stones. 'What's going on here, anyway?'

'Getting ready to rebuild the barn. Least, that's what some of us are doing. That fool's more interested in finding white stones to ward off spirits and demons... ' He broke off. 'Don't tell anyone I said that, will you?'

'Course not,' she assured him. She ran back down the slope to the garden.

'Did you get it?' asked Jason.

'Get *what?*' Carrie demanded.

Gaia laughed. 'It's just an amulet.' She took out the moonswood and showed it to Carrie. 'I had to hide it. There's a bit of a problem with it...'

'A bit!' exclaimed Jason. 'An almighty great dragon-sized problem...'

'What?' Carrie asked.

'Well, the thing is...'

'What's that you've got there?'

Intent on the little fragment of moonswood, none of them had noticed Stearne until he spoke from behind them. Instinctively, Gaia put the amulet behind her back. She looked up at him defiantly, but for once he held her gaze.

'Show me.'

She darted a rapid look past him. The fence, the boundary wall, the guards in the fields: nowhere to run. Reluctantly, she held out the amulet. Stearne took it from her, a strange light in his pale eyes, and studied it in silence for a long time. When he finally spoke, he uttered a single word.

'*Swansprite!*'

Shadows

Gaia laughed.

It was so unexpected, so *ridiculous* that she laughed, but Jason was murmuring 'Gaia,' and Carrie looked as pale as death. She looked from their frightened faces into Stearne's stone eyes, and her laughter faltered and died.

'I'm not a... a *swansprite*. That's...' Her plants were shivering in the slight wind, rain dripping from their leaves to the earth, and she breathed in courage from them. 'That's just *stupid*...'

'So what's this?' Stearne held up the amulet in his gloved hand.

'It's nothing,' she said, but her voice faltered. *It has power*, Mai and Ambrose had said; it was a prohibited object; what did she really know about it? But it hadn't done anything. *She* hadn't done anything. She darted a panicked look at Jason and Carrie.

'Please,' Carrie said. 'She isn't...'

'Oh, but she is,' Stearne answered. 'You said it yourself. A kind of magic. Those were your words, weren't they?'

Carrie looked as dizzy as if the ground had tipped under her feet. 'I didn't mean... not a *swansprite*. Not that...'

'And what about you?' Stearne rounded on Jason. 'You were quick to try and defend her. Are you part of this too?'

'He hasn't done anything,' Gaia shouted. 'Neither of them have!'

'Only you, then.' Triumph gleamed like cold fire in Stearne's eyes. He seized hold of Gaia's arm, his fingers pressing tight into her flesh. Jason took a step forward. Gaia shook her head furiously. 'Don't,' she mouthed. She let Stearne walk her out of the garden, up the path, across the yard, and into the farmhouse, across the stone-flagged hall and into a large square room. He pushed her into a ring of white flowers on the floor. 'Stay there,' he told her.

She glanced around. In Fox's time this room had been kind and unfussy: whitewashed walls, old furniture, the shutters folded back as far as they would go to let the rainy light in. Now, the shutters were locked and bolted, and the walls were painted a deep blue that was almost black. The only light came from a low fire on the hearth. Something - the flowers or the fire - was sending out an acrid scent that caught in her throat and made her eyes water.

There was a flare of white light as Stearne lit a lantern on the mantelpiece. He studied the amulet for a long time, before raising his eyes to Gaia.

'So I've found you. *Stay in the circle!*'

She had stepped forward, instinctively. She retreated inside the ring of white flowers, wild thoughts growing and blossoming in her mind. He had been *looking* for her, then? Because of the moonswood? Had Tal been right all those moons ago, thinking that it was a swansprite's thing? Was *that* why it was prohibited? But she had felt no magic in it, ever: no mystery except its age and the touch of all those generations of hands on it before hers.

'Why...' Smoke, or the flowers, made her throat tight and her voice cracked. 'Why were you looking for me?'

'Oh, I didn't know it was *you*, to start with.' He placed the amulet on the mantelpiece, took off his coat and gloves and laid them on a high-backed chair. 'But there had to be someone. The rain, the raids on the farm carts, that dragon. *Someone* had to be causing all that bad luck.'

'But it's *not me*...'

'*Of course* it's you, Gaia. There's that garden of yours, to start with. That's what first led me to you. You see, nothing grows well here, and yet, there are those plants of yours, flourishing. And your strange nickname, and your eyes, every time I looked at you. Cursing me. Summoning the dragon...'

'I didn't *summon* the *dragon!* They're wild. No-one can...'

'And now this. The final proof. The one thing I needed to find to be sure.' He gestured to the amulet. 'The charm, the magic-worker, the spell-maker...'

'It's not magic,' she said, but her voice was unsteady and she was uncertain despite herself. 'It's just old. And I'm not a swansprite.'

He gave her a look of mingled pity and triumph. 'Oh, Gaia. You *know* that's not so. Look.' Taking a deep breath, he picked up the amulet. As it touched his skin he gave a savage high scream of pain and hurled it away from him. It hit the wall and crashed to the stone floor in three pieces.

'No!' Gaia shouted, and she stumbled out of the circle of flowers and across the room. Stearne was doubled up, pressing his hand between his arm and his side, moaning, as if he had snatched a burning log from the fire. She hesitated for an instant before touching the moonswood, but when she gathered up the fragments they were as cool as ever beneath her fingers.

Jason waited in the garden. Around him, Gaia's plants danced in the warm rain, daylight shining on their wet leaves, but the warmth and the light could not touch him: all he knew was fear, as dark and cold as a pit in the earth. At last, the farmhouse door opened, and Stearne dragged Gaia out.

'Jason,' said Carrie.

He didn't move or speak.

'Jason!' She pulled at his hand. 'We have to find where he's taking her.'

'I know where he's taking her.' He watched Stearne hauling Gaia across the farmyard and into the stables. They passed out of sight. But he knew the rest; the memories battered at him and he couldn't stop them now.

'Where?' Carrie tugged at him again.

'There's a hole in the ground.'

'In the stables?'

'You wouldn't have noticed. It's covered with a slab of stone. It's right underground. Out of the moonsight. That's where he'll be putting her.'

He remembered. The remorseless darkness, the confusion of night and day, the terror of being hidden in the blind earth. He had been savaged by waking nightmares in which he seemed to himself to have become his dead father, trapped for ever under stones and earth. And Gaia would have those nightmares too...

Only when they had finally pulled *him* out, half mad with terror, shaking, freezing and filthy, Fox had been there, and he had been kind. He had lent Jason a warm coat and taken him outside as darkness fell and the moon rose among the clouds. He had waited with him for hours while Jason stood with his face turned to the sky, feeling the moonlight seeping back into his soul. But what would be waiting for Gaia, when they got her out?

'Carrie,' he asked, 'what do they do with swansprites?'

She whispered the answer, so quietly that he had to ask her to say it again. 'They burn them,' she said, and he felt the pit of fear open beneath his feet.

Two days before Coranto full moon, returned from the long tribute raising tour of the estates, Scrimp shut himself in his cubbyhole office in Parhelion's High Side house, bolted the door, and hid his head in his hands. Desperate faces haunted him. On every estate, the starving and ruined had handed him the last scraps of their livelihood in tribute: a miserable seraf or two that Parhelion would lose before the moon was out.

Scrimp held their faces in his head as he took Fossick's book out of his satchel, laid it in his lap and opened it. It had terrified him, this volume, when Fossick had first given it to him: with its sinister prohibited stamp on the inside cover. More than once he had wondered whether to burn it. But then he had started to read - peering at Fossick's tiny neat brown ink words underneath the printed Old Script.

The title of the first chapter had intrigued him. 'Of the state of the kingdom of Assalay in the year before the Liberation.' Kingdom? he had wondered, and after that, every page had revealed a hidden history that made him feel like a man discovering a whole corridor of unknown rooms in a house where he had lived all his life. An Assalay before the Fellowship…

He had read the book twice. On the second reading, he had found one, tiny mistake (fourteen here, thirteen there); but he couldn't believe it was the thing that Fossick had meant him to find: the rift in the foundations that would bring the whole Fellowship crashing to destruction. He closed the book, tucked it out of sight behind a set of old tax ledgers, and set out to find Fossick.

It was noon, so he headed for the dingy tavern behind the Basilica. As usual, Sassy was sewing in a corner, while Fossick daydreamed at his table. Scrimp sat down opposite him.

'Babbington.'

Fossick started. 'Cosmo! You're back. Did you read it? Where is it?'

'Hidden,' said Scrimp. 'And yes. I read it.' He gestured to Sassy to bring a jug of wine.

'What did you think?'

'Astonishing,' murmured Scrimp. 'I never knew...'

'Why would you?' Fossick poured glasses of wine, and pushed Scrimp's towards him across the table. 'We've always been told that Assalay began with the Fellowship. The kingdom's a well-kept secret. But did you spot the mistake? The thing that doesn't make sense?'

Scrimp frowned. 'I don't think so. There was one thing. I'm mean, I'm sure it's not it...'

'Tell me,' Fossick said.

'Alright. The book says the Fellowship was formed from the King's Council, after the fire. But in the list of the King's Council there are fourteen names, and only thirteen in the list of the Fellowship. Like now. Palamon's missing: he's in the Council, but not the Fellowship.'

'Hah!' Fossick's face shone with delight. 'I knew you'd notice it, Cosmo, you old number-cruncher. That's it. Fourteen councillors to the King, but only thirteen Fellows of the republic.'

'Does it matter?'

'Course it matters.' Fossick got up and paced restlessly to and fro in front of the empty fireplace. 'It's a hole. Something not explained.'

Scrimp looked unconvinced. 'But he probably just died, or something.'

'No.' Fossick shook his head. 'If he'd died, it would have said. I think there's more to it.'

'And you think the answer's in the Closed Archive?'

'Who knows? But if it's anywhere, it's there. Can you get me in?'

Scrimp poured himself another glass of wine. 'I'll try.' In her dingy corner, Sassy shook out a grubby tablecloth, hesitated over a bundle of tangled thread, and drew out a skein of bright scarlet.

Tomorrow night Coranto would be full, and at dawn on the following day Gaia would die. Everything was ready. Jason had seen the ominous stack of wood in the farmyard, covered in sacking to keep it dry. He sat on the fence in the garden and stared unseeing at Gaia's flourishing, fatal plants. He was going to get her out. He would run to Nouldewood, and he would take her with him. He just didn't have a clue how he was going to manage it.

'Jason?' Mr Hawkin's voice roused him.

'Yes?' He waited for Hawkins to snap at him to get off the fence and get on with some work, but when Hawkins spoke again, his voice was unusually soft.

'Come to bring you something.' He held out a pouch of worn leather, fastened with a string. Horrified, Jason shook his head.

'That's Gaia's amulet. I can't...'

'Thing is...' Hawkins rubbed a hand over his head, and cleared his throat. 'She asked me to give it to you. To give to her brother. After ... You know.'

'But I don't know where he is.' *And she can't die.*

'She told me where you'll find him. She said, there's a big bridge in Freehaven. There's a ledge under it. Same side as the main square. He'll be there. First morning of every quarter.' He held out the amulet again, and reluctantly, Jason took it from him.

'Help me get her out,' he said. '*Please.* You know she hasn't done anything wrong.'

'No-one gets out of Hope's End, Jason. *You* know that.' Hawkins' gaze flickered sideways, and Jason followed it to see Stearne standing silent and watchful at the gate. Jason tucked Gaia's amulet into his coat pocket, dragged himself across the garden, picked up a fork and started turning over the soil, seeing nothing except darkness. Hawkins watched him for a while; pulled his handkerchief out of his pocket, blew his nose loudly, and walked away. When he and Stearne had both gone, Jason dropped the fork and sat with his back against the fence. He took out the amulet, loosened the string of the pouch, tipped the pieces of moonswood into his hand and sat for a long time, cradling them.

'Jason?' He looked up to see Carrie standing next to him. 'What's that?'

191

'Gaia's amulet,' he said. 'She gave it to Hawk, for Tal...' He choked to a halt. Carrie knelt to put her arms around him, and gave a sudden cry.

'What?' he asked.

She scrabbled in the earth, and held up the thing that had hurt her.

'Hawk's knife.' Jason took it and turned it over, watching the blade gleam in the dull daylight, wondering if Hawkins had dropped it on purpose. A knife was better than no knife, but he couldn't see what use it would be. Carrie took it from him and studied the length and slenderness of the blade.

'I've got an idea.'

Tonight was Coranto full moon, and the early morning office had been elaborate and long. Sam nudged Tal and slid a sheet of music towards him. *Cake?* said a scrawled note in one corner. Tal nodded. He'd *need* cake by the time this was over. He felt in his pocket for the seraf that had been Parhelion's measly tip for yesterday's service of thanksgiving for his return to Freehaven.

Almost done. They had reached the last prayers, chanted by a single voice, for the moon's blessing on each Fellow. *Grant oh great lady Coranto, long life and good fortune to our noble Lord Filarion; give him the blessing of your light; shine on him...*

Tal yawned, and let his eyes wander past the marble statues to the end of the nave. It was early, but the Basilica was already crowded with people, their hushed conversations rising in a whispered echo behind the ringing prayers. He watched idly. Then a girl stepped out of the shadows and the flash of bright colour from her green-blue cloak caught his attention. A Fellowship girl, though he couldn't remember which family wore that colour. She walked with the confident pride of the Fellowship, but there was an air of defiance about her too; the look of a child deliberately doing something forbidden. She was on her own. Perhaps that explained the defiant look: young ladies of the Fellowship weren't encouraged to wander Freehaven unchaperoned. He imagined her, slipping early out of one of the big High Side houses, meandering through the city streets alone, wondering what to do with this snatched moment of freedom...

Oh. Not quite alone. There was a woman following her: drably dressed, but with a slash of green-blue in her costume that marked her as the girl's slave. He let his attention wander from the mistress to the maid, and she turned slightly, so that he glimpsed her face for an instant before she turned away again. Only a half heartbeat's glimpse, but it was enough to set his heart racing and to make the flow of his blood crescendo to a roar in his ears. He kept his eyes fixed on them, but they moved out of sight behind one of the solid stone columns.

...and give us, great Lady, humility, obedience and thankfulness in our hearts... Sam kicked Tal's ankle. That was the end of the prayer, and everyone else was standing, ready to sing. Tal scrambled to his feet, catching a warning look from Gabriel. They had reached the final blessing - a simple 'Watch and guide us this day, Lady, and keep our feet in the proper paths.' Gabriel had chosen a long, complicated setting of the hymn today, with phrases that grew and twisted and intertwined in the air like tendrils on a crazy vine. But the first few bars were easy, and Tal knew them by heart. He lifted his eyes from the music and past Gabriel's hands keeping time, and looked down the nave.

They were there again! The girl was looking up at the thirteen coloured moons of the huge north window, while her maid waited beside her. Tal kept his eyes glued on them, missed Gabriel's slowing beat, and found himself awkwardly out of time with the rest of the choir. Gabriel glared at him. He forced his attention back to the music, darting hidden glances at the two figures at the end of the nave. They moved to the door. With a brief flourish of her green-blue cloak, they were gone, and the choir reached the last note of the hymn. A sustained note: a long slow return from the sacred to the everyday. At last they were allowed to move and speak. Sam turned to Tal.

'What's up with you?'

'Look after this, will you?' Tal thrust his music into Sam's hand.

'What about breakfast?'

'Got to do something.' He ran down the choir steps. Ignoring Gabriel's 'Tal? A word?' he pelted down the aisle and out through the door. The dawn showers had stopped, leaving the white marble wet and glittering in the rare sunshine. Tal's eyes, used to the heavy crimson Coranto light inside the Basilica, flinched at the glare, and the square was confusingly busy too, thronged with early morning crowds. Dazed, he turned one way, then the other, set off in one direction, changed his mind, came back again... *Think,* he told himself. They must have come from High Side. Maybe the girl would be heading back now, trying to get home before anyone noticed she was missing. He made up his mind, and dodged through the crowd towards the bridge.

They were there! - climbing into one of the light, swift carriages that ferried paying customers up and down the hill to High Side. He saw the girl's bright cloak, like the flash of a bird's wing; the door slammed shut and the carriage set off at a brisk trot. Tal broke into a run.

Scrimp hurried along the road from Parhelion's house, his hand clutched round thirteen letters of authority, one from each Fellow, giving him permission to enter the Closed Archive. He had forged them last night. He had rifled through Parhelion's correspondence for letters from each of the Fellows, had copied the signatures, prised the seals loose with a hot knife and refixed them to the forgeries. His fingers were still ink-stained and blistered. At the junction with the long road to the bridge, he hesitated.

He could still turn back. So far all he had done to draw attention to himself was to borrow the thirteen different coloured inks that had been needed for those letters, and he could concoct some excuse for that. He could burn the letters, burn the book...

But - no. He couldn't forgo the chance to find out what lay at the root of that tiny, inaccurate detail that both Fossick and he had spotted; to find out what all this had to do with that girl - with Gaia Athanasius and her name full of echoes and her little square of moonswood.

He couldn't forgo the chance of an end to the Fellowship.

He clenched his fist around the forged papers, and carried on down the hill to the National Archive, where Fossick was pacing to and fro on the steps.

'Cosmo!' Fossick's face lit with surprised pleasure.

'You thought I wasn't coming,' Scrimp guessed.

'I wasn't sure,' Fossick admitted. 'Have you done them?'

'Yes.'

'Convincing?'

'They'd better be.' Scrimp shuddered, and Fossick took his arm, and ushered him inside, into a plain hall full of silence and the smell of old books and paper. The Archivist sat at a desk, guarding the wooden gate that led to the stairs. Fossick crossed the hall alone, showed his dog-eared ticket and was waved casually through. Scrimp counted to thirteen and approached the desk himself. He put on his curtest, most official, most *Fellowship* manner.

'Good morning.'

The Archivist frowned. 'Mr Scrimp, isn't it?'

'Yes. On Fellowship business.' Scrimp lowered his voice and leaned forward. 'This is all rather confidential. There's a document in the Closed Archive that their Lordships have asked for.'

The Archivist blinked. 'I can't open that for you. Not without the proper permission. Have you got a Council order?'

Scrimp shook his head. 'They're in a rush. No time. They've signed and sealed separate permissions for me instead.' He laid the forged letters on the counter, and watched dry-mouthed as the Archivist studied them, frowning over the ink and the signatures and the seals.

'It's needed for this afternoon,' Scrimp said. 'There'll be trouble if I'm late.'

The Archivist made up his mind. 'Very well.' He unlocked a drawer, took out a ring of keys, lit a lantern and led Scrimp through the gate. After four twisting flights of stairs and a long narrow corridor they stopped in front of a locked and barred door. One by one, the Archivist fitted the keys into the rusty locks, forced them open, and swung the door back. Scrimp followed him into a long low room, filled from floor to ceiling with packed shelves. Crates of documents were stacked up on the floor, surrounded by heaps of loose papers. Dust had settled thickly on everything: the slightest movement sent it billowing into the air. Scrimp's shoulders sagged. This was impossible.

'What are you looking for?' The Archivist pulled a file at random from one of the shelves. Scrimp took it from him.

'I'll manage by myself.'

The Archivist hesitated.

'The permissions given are for me alone,' Scrimp said. 'Their Lordships won't be pleased to hear of any interference or *curiosity* on your part.'

The Archivist paled and backed hastily out of the room. Scrimp listened to his footsteps receding along the corridor. Before they had completely died away, Fossick put his head round the door.

'Impressive, Cosmo. Ice cold. I could hear you from round the corner.'

'Shhh!' Scrimp pulled Fossick into the room and shut the door softly. 'There's so much of it.' He gestured helplessly at the overflowing papers. 'We haven't a hope of finding anything. And this door doesn't lock from the inside...'

'Cheer up, Cosmo. You're as gloomy as a wet Carnival.' Fossick picked up the lantern and circled the room, reading the labels on the shelves and taking in deep breaths of the stale dusty air. He came back to Scrimp and sat down on the edge of a crate.

'We don't have much time, Babbington,' Scrimp reminded him anxiously.

'I'm *thinking*. None of this is what we're looking for.'

'*What?*'

'Too recent. We're looking for something older, something from the very beginning. The difference between thirteen and fourteen.'

'*One,*' Scrimp muttered.

'Or in this case, quite possibly everything.' Fossick gazed around the room again, with narrowed eyes. 'Now, if they'd asked me how to lose an old document in an Archive, I'd have told them to wrap it in new parchment and stick it on a shelf. But an old friend of mine - he's dead now - was Teredo's librarian...' Fossick got up from the crate, put his hands on one of the broad uprights that supported the shelves, pressed it, shook his head, and moved to the next. 'He taught me an old Fellowship trick... Ah!'

A panel in the upright swung open. Beaming at Scrimp, Fossick felt in the hollow space and pulled out an ancient, yellowed scroll; fragments of dry parchment drifted from it to the dusty floor. He knelt on the floor, and unrolled it. Looking over Fossick's shoulder, Scrimp frowned at the unreadable text.

'Old Script.'

'Mmm.'

'Why did they stop using it?'

'That's obvious isn't it?' Fossick answered without looking up from the paper. 'They wanted to blot out the past, Cosmo. They wanted people to forget that Assalay was ever a kingdom; that it had even existed before the Fellowship. So they made the past unreadable, literally unreadable...Wait a moment...' He sat back and breathed out. 'Sweet moonlight. So *that's* what happened. I knew I was right...'

'*What?*' demanded Scrimp.

'This is a memoir.' Fossick laid a finger lightly on the parchment. 'Written by Teredo. An account of Palamon's treachery and of his trial by the Fellowship.'

'Treachery?' Scrimp asked, but Fossick was reading on, frowning over the faded words.

'They tried him in his absence. They couldn't find him, but they declared him guilty, every man of them. They sentenced him to death, if he should ever be found. They ordered the slaughter of his family. They stripped him of his lands and titles. There's even a charming little note to say that every statue or painting or effigy of him should be destroyed: burned, smashed, melted down, whatever it took. They wanted him obliterated, Cosmo.' He thought for a moment. 'Someone made a big mistake, writing that history, forgetting to take his name off the Council list. I suppose they just lifted it from a royal record and stuck it in and no-one read it carefully enough to notice until it was too late and it had already been printed...'

'Never mind *that,*' said Scrimp. 'What exactly did he do?'

Tal had never realised how *impossible* High Side was: a labyrinth of twisting streets between towering white walls. He had kept the carriage in sight across the bridge and up the broad main road. But then it had swung into a side street and by the time he had turned the corner, it had disappeared. He ran along the side road, came to a junction and took the right hand turning, but a little further on the road was gated and guarded.

'This is a prohibited street,' the guard told Tal. 'You got a pass?'

'No.' Tal trudged back to the main road and sat on a low wall to think. A couple of carriages passed him, and a pale girl with a dirty cloth tucked under one arm. A cloud swept across the sun. He glanced up at the sky and - of course. *Of course.* High Side's walls and houses were all uniform white stone, but each roof was the heraldic colour of the family who lived under it and he could see that brilliant green-blue: up the hill and to the right.

Fixing it as precisely as he could in his head, he dived back into the maze of streets. But as soon as he turned off the main road, a series of gates forced him downhill. He followed the road further and further down, his spirits sinking with it, and came to another junction. From here, one road ran steeply uphill, giving him a glimpse of that green-blue roof, high above him - but like every other uphill road he had passed, it was prohibited. Tal stopped and stared over the gate. The guardhouse was a little wooden hut, close inside the gate, but there was no sign of a guard.

'Hello!' he called.

The only answer was the echo of his own voice, bouncing back to him from the walls. He made up his mind, climbed the gate, and started uphill. But the road snaked bewilderingly left and right and when at last he came to a big white house behind a fence of iron railings, he had so lost his sense of direction that he had no idea if it was the house he was looking for. What colour was the roof? That would settle it.

But seen from this close, the colour had gone. The roof glass simply reflected the grey pall that had gathered over the sky.

'Oy!' A stout man was hurrying towards him, and Tal had time to note, with a pang of disappointment, that his livery was scarlet. Then he turned and ran.

'Sweet heavens.' Scrimp held his head in his hands, as if the thing that Fossick had just read to him was too heavy for his brain. *Enough to bring the Fellowship crashing to destruction.* Fossick hadn't been exaggerating. Scrimp felt dizzy and slightly sick.

'Cosmo? We should go.' Fossick rolled up the scroll and weighed it in the palm of his hand. 'What about this?'

They could slip it back into its hiding place and walk away, thought Scrimp, and over many years it would crumble into silence. If they took it and were caught... If they took it and somehow miraculously got away to tell its story... He felt giddy again.

'What do you think?'

'Safest to leave it here,' said Fossick.

'But it's the past. Her past, that girl's. All of ours...'

He whipped round. The door was swinging open. Fossick stuffed the scroll inside his jacket. A boy stepped over the threshold.

'Wotcher.' He grinned at them: a lanky, bright-eyed boy, ragged and improbably elegant. Oddly familiar, Scrimp thought, though he couldn't place him. 'Thought you might want to know,' the boy continued. 'Lord Lanneret's upstairs, with a division of the Watch. Come to find whoever's been in the Closed Archive without permission...'

Flight

'Cosmo,' Fossick stammered. 'I'm sorry.'

'No,' Scrimp shook his head. 'No, I knew what I was doing. I wanted to...'

'Woah,' said the boy. 'This ain't the time for talking. If you're going to get out...'

'No chance of that.' Scrimp turned his hands upwards in a gesture of defeat. Above them the silence was shattered by the thunder of heavy footsteps on the stairs.

'Might be a chance,' the boy said. 'If you come with me. But *now*, gents. We ain't got all day.' He picked up the lantern and held the door open for them. They exchanged a look, and nodded; the boy hustled them out into the corridor and along a twisting low-ceilinged passageway that ended at a spiral staircase. Scrimp started up the steps. The boy caught his sleeve and pulled him back.

'Other way.'

'We need to get *out*,' Scrimp protested. 'There's no point hiding; they'll turn this place upside down to find us.'

The boy rolled his eyes. 'I'll *get* you out. But climb that stairs and you climb straight into his Lordship's arms.'

The sounds of the arrest party were surging like fire through the building. Back along the corridor, voices were calling, and doors were being opened and slammed shut again. Lantern light reached along the walls.

'*Now!*' the boy urged, and, clinging onto one another, they half ran, half fell down the uneven stairs, and stumbled along a dark corridor that ended at a locked grating. With a hollow lurch of fear, Scrimp thought *trapped!* But the boy was rattling the bars and calling softly, 'It's me!' and a pale girl carrying a lantern emerged from the darkness inside the locked room. She threw a puzzled look at Scrimp and Fossick.

'Jinx?'

'Let us in, Liz. Quick.'

Jinx bundled Scrimp and Fossick through a labyrinth of shelves that ended in a blind alley where a few boxes of papers had been shifted from the bottom shelf. He waved at the gap - 'After you, gents' - and they squeezed themselves through, landing on all fours in a sea of papers, under the curious gaze of a dozen or so ragged children.

'What's going on, Jinx?' someone asked.

'Lanneret's men. After these two. We need to fly. You know the drill.'

One of the girls righted an upturned crate that had been used as a table; others gathered armfuls of scattered papers and stuffed them into it. The girl who had let them through the gate grabbed a scuffed leather satchel and filled it with scraps of food. Another girl replaced the boxes in the gap on the shelf.

'Carefully does it,' Jinx warned her. 'Let's make it as difficult as possible for them. Ready to go, gents?' He turned back to Scrimp and Fossick, who was sitting on the floor, scanning a sheaf of abandoned papers in the lantern light.

'Fascinating...' he murmured. 'Look, Cosmo, these are all trial records from...'

'Babbington!' Scrimp snatched the documents from him. 'This isn't exactly the time for the history of the criminal law! We need to get out.' He glanced round the solid walls, and turned back to Jinx. 'How, though?'

Jinx kicked a pile of papers aside, and heaved up the solid iron lid that he had uncovered. There was a rush of foul cold air into the room. Scrimp recoiled from the smell, but outside someone was rattling the bars of the grating and shouting for the keys.

'*Quickly.*' Jinx swung himself into the dark hole in the floor. 'Follow me. There are rungs set in the wall. Bit loose, some of them. Watch how you go.'

Scrimp helped Fossick into the hole, and lowered himself onto the ladder. He descended into blind darkness, fumbling from one rung to the next. Below him, he could hear water running, but at the bottom of the ladder his feet met solid ground.

'Alright?' Jinx whispered.

'Yes.' Scrimp's voice echoed hollowly in the darkness.

'Shhh! Listen, we're on a narrow ledge. You won't kill yourself if you fall, but it's a bit mucky. Be hard to pass you off as a clean living citizen if you took a tumble. Hold onto the wall.'

Beneath his palm Scrimp felt the roughness of brick, coated in something foul, damp and clammy. Breathing shallowly to try and keep the stench out of his nostrils and lungs, he inched along the ledge. After a few, shuffling paces, something scurried across his foot and leapt into the water with a loud splash, and he started, almost lost his balance, calmed himself and set off again. Ahead, Jinx was murmuring encouragement: 'good going, not too far now…' Behind him, he could hear the muffled thud of falling shelves, the scurry of feet on the ladder, and a faint dull ring of iron as the drain cover was eased back into place.

The dark and the stink seemed endless. At last, from somewhere ahead, there was a whisper of clean air and a glimmer of grey light. Rounding a corner, they saw the mouth of the tunnel, and groped their way out of the drain and onto a narrow strand of shingle at the riverside.

Legs trembling, Scrimp flopped down next to Fossick and breathed in deep draughts of the fresh air, blinking at the bright crimson river. But Jinx wouldn't let them rest.

'Soon as they realise you're not inside any more, they'll be scouring the city for you. We need to get you out of Freehaven.'

'How?' Fossick asked.

'Not sure,' Jinx admitted.

'If…' Scrimp hesitated and shook his head. 'No. I don't think it'd work.'

'Spit it out,' said Jinx. 'Any idea's better than none.'

'Parhelion's garden wall is part of the city wall,' Scrimp explained. 'There's a locked gate out onto the cliff path. I've got the key. But it's the first place they'll look.'

'Worth a try. Wait here a moment.' Jinx hurried up a flight of steep slippery steps to the riverside terrace. They watched him out of sight.

'Well.' Fossick sat back down on the damp shingle. 'So far so good.'

'Good?' echoed Scrimp. 'What's good about it?'

'We found the *truth*, Cosmo.'

Scrimp snorted. 'And it's likely to die with us, if you ask me, quite soon probably. We aren't out of this, Babbington, not by a long way. Even if we get out of Freehaven safely...' He choked on the word. *Safely.* There would be no more safety for him, ever again. As long as the Fellowship lasted, all that lay ahead of him was a life of waiting: for the accusing hand on his shoulder, the dawning recognition in a stranger's eyes, the slow opening of a door in the night-time. He paced to and fro, the shingle crunching under his feet, until a low whistle made him start. Jinx was leaning over the parapet of the terrace.

'Up here!'

They struggled up the steps to join him.

'No sign of anyone searching the square,' Jinx said. 'They're probably still turning the Archive over. Got any money?'

'Money?' Scrimp queried.

'Well, we could walk to High Side, but a carriage'd be quicker, and quicker means safer.'

Scrimp dug a seraf and a handful of rens out of his pocket, and they hurried along the terrace and up the marble steps to the queue of carriages waiting on the bridge. Jinx bundled Scrimp and Fossick into the first carriage, handed Scrimp's loose change to the driver, jumped in himself, and slammed the door. The carriage jolted into movement, gained speed as it crossed the bridge, and slowed into the laborious pull up High Side. Jinx leaned back in his seat and grinned at the unlikely pair of fugitives opposite him. 'Reckon we might do it.'

'In which case, you've saved our lives,' Fossick said. 'We owe you...'

'Nah. Don't owe me anything. I don't like Lanneret.' Jinx scowled. 'Taken too many of my kids. Couldn't miss the chance to diddle him.' The carriage rattled round a corner onto a narrow steep road where the air smelt of the sea, and Jinx turned to look out of the window. Seeing him with his face half turned away, Scrimp started and slapped his hand to his forehead.

'I *knew* I'd seen you before!'

'Me?' Jinx turned back to him, puzzled.

'You were with that girl - with Gaia, and her brother. Running away from Babbington's shop. Moons ago; at the beginning of Arctos.'

'*You know her?*' Fossick stared at Jinx. The carriage halted. Scrimp swung the door open, jumped heavily onto the pavement and pulled Fossick after him. He fumbled among his keys, opened a side gate into a chilly garden of long gravel paths and sodden empty flowerbeds, and gestured towards the low door in the end wall. But Fossick was still staring at Jinx.

'You *know* Gaia Athanasius? Can you give her something for me?' Fossick pulled the stolen paper from his jacket and thrust it towards Jinx.

'This what you two nicked?'

'Yes.' Fossick waved the question impatiently aside. 'Can you get it to her? Tell her it'll explain her name... who she is... *Everything.*'

'I can't. I mean she's not here anymore. She was arrested.' Jinx hesitated. 'I know her brother, though. He's...'

Fossick raised his hand. 'Don't tell us. The less we know, the better.' He pushed the scroll towards Jinx. 'Give it to him. It's his story too.'

Jinx looked doubtfully at the parchment in Fossick's hand. A yellowed, crumbling, ancient piece of paper. A *dangerous* piece of paper. 'Not sure I want to be carrying that around. Or saddling him with it... Alright. Hand it over. And you better go.'

'Thank you.' Fossick looked as if he was about to say something lengthy and solemn.

'*Go.*' Jinx gave him a little shove. He watched them hurry along the gravel paths, and safely out through the city wall. Then he shut the garden door, tucked the scroll under his jacket and sauntered down the hill.

Tal had dodged the fat man in scarlet. But in his dark blue cloak he was easily recognisable as a choir school boy and as he vaulted over another gate, he heard the man shout something that ended '... tell Gabriel!' Doubly in trouble, then. He had broken the rule about avoiding prohibited streets. As well as that, he had been dimly aware of the Basilica bells tolling the hours, and knew that he had missed a whole rehearsal this morning, the full moon ceremony and most of the afternoon rehearsal.

What now? he wondered. All these houses were hedged about by one protection after another, hidden behind their white walls at the end of guarded streets. And even if he got past the gates and the guards, he wouldn't know when he reached the right house, because of that curious trick by which the coloured glass roofs became a blank mirror when you got too close.

One more go, he thought. He took a turning that he hadn't tried yet, and bumped into Jinx.

'Tal! What're you doing here?'

'Jinx! I... Nothing really. You?'

'Long story. You should hear it though. And I've got something to give you.' A maid and a footman, both in Baladine's orange livery passed by, giving Jinx a long curious look. 'Let's get off High Side, though.'

Tal hesitated. 'Alright. Might as well.'

'Well, this is no good.' Jinx leaned on the parapet of the bridge and stared down at the river. Boats full of Watchmen were rowing up and down, stopping to search the fishing skiffs moored at the water's edge, and the trading boats at anchor in the middle of the stream. As Jinx and Tal watched, a small detachment climbed down the narrow stairs on the embankment wall, and up the ladder under the bridge.

'Best go somewhere else.' Jinx led Tal up the broad steps and into the square. As they crossed it, there was a sudden pealing of bells that sounded on and on, a harsh warning clamour that was taken up and answered by bells all over the city. Wincing at the din, Tal followed Jinx into one of the narrow streets behind the Basilica. There were more Watchmen at work here, scattering printed pamphlets that blew along the wet cobbles and caught against the front walls of houses. Tal snatched up a damp sheet of paper and frowned at the sketched portraits.

'That's Fossick! And that looks like... It *is*. It says. Scrimp. Parhelion's treasurer. "Wanted for seditious plotting and treason against the republic." Treason? Those two? That's crazy!'

'It's not. I'll tell you... Not here though.' Mystified, Tal followed Jinx downhill, and into a narrow lane behind the harbour; up a rotten wooden staircase and into the empty attic of a disused warehouse. A square window looked out onto the masts of tall ships in the harbour and beyond them, the grey sea. Jinx sat down with his back against the wall and considered Tal with an uncertain look.

'You said you had something for me,' Tal reminded him.

'Don't know. Don't want to get you into trouble.'

Tal sat down next to him, and scuffed his feet against the dusty floor. 'I'm in trouble anyway. Missed two rehearsals, *and* the full moon office.'

Jinx gave a short, mirthless laugh. 'I'm not talking about a telling-off from Gabriel, Tal. This is… Well. Life or death. Maybe I shouldn't have taken it. But they said it was important. They said you had to know. You and Gaia…'

'*What?* I don't understand. *Who* said?'

Jinx took a deep breath. 'Fossick and Scrimp.'

'*What?*'

'They blagged their way into the Closed Archive. Stole this.' He pushed the tightly rolled scroll across the floor towards Tal. 'Lanneret knew they were there - someone's likely been spying on them. I went to give them a word of warning and ended up getting them out. They nipped out Parhelion's garden onto the cliff. They ain't got a clue. I give 'em about a day.'

'What about this?' Tal had unrolled the scroll on the dusty floor, and was holding it open with both hands on the top corners and one knee on the bottom edge.

'Dunno. Fossick said it would explain… Everything… What does it say?'

'No idea.' Tal lifted his hands and let the scroll furl itself shut again. 'I can't read it.'

'Thought Gabriel had taught you…' Jinx began, but his words were drowned in another clamour of bells across the city. Tal recognised this call: the familiar three consecutive falling notes that ended each day.

'Curfew! But it's not nearly dark yet!'

'They ring it early sometimes. Easier to track people down in empty streets.' Jinx jumped to his feet. 'Got to go. Check the kids are alright.'

Tal rolled up the scroll and tucked it inside his belt, under his cloak. 'Where? You can't go back to the Nest.'

'There's another place. Past the Basilica. I'll come back with you.' Jinx opened the door, glanced left and right, and nodded. They ran down the wooden steps and along the alley, but at the corner, Jinx pulled Tal to a halt.

'No go.'

A short way ahead, a rough barrier of wooden rails blocked the street and a couple of Watchmen were stopping everyone who was trying to get past. They were checking papers, Tal realised, which meant trouble for Jinx, but that wasn't all. They were searching people too, making them turn out pockets and bags, and take off cloaks and coats and jackets. Grim-faced, Jinx pulled Tal silently back into the alley.

'Best give me that scroll. Get yourself home.'

Tal put a hand on the scroll, and withdrew it again. 'No. It should be me who takes it. They meant it for me.' He darted another look out of the alley. 'Maybe they'll go soon.'

'No chance. They'll be on every street, up to curfew and after.'

Tal fought to keep his voice steady. 'So how do we get back?'

Lanneret entered the club and climbed the stairs heavy-footed under the stony gaze of the ancestral Fellowship portraits on the walls. In the dining room, Filarion's Coranto full moon party was still in full flow. Lanneret glanced in briefly, taking in the glittering lights, the ring of silver on china and crystal on crystal; the confident voices and laughter. He turned away with a sense of shadowed foreboding and made his way to the reading room where Teredo was waiting.

'Elverton. Sit.' Teredo nodded him into the chair on the other side of the hearth. 'I got your note. A break-in at the Closed Archive, eh? You were onto it commendably quickly.' Teredo raised his heavy-lidded eyes to look at Lanneret. Age had not blunted the fierceness of his glare or his mind, and Lanneret shifted in his chair, waiting for the inevitable question.

'How long had you known about it?'

'I ... That is... A spy gave me warning of the possibility, a few moons ago.'

'*Moons?*'

'I thought... Catching them in the act... I didn't see how they could get out. I still don't see: four storeys down and a locked gate...'

'Fool,' said Teredo. 'There's only one way with treachery, Elverton. Stamp it out early. You've taken the usual measures to track them down, I assume?'

Lanneret nodded.

'Then cheer up. We've a good record when it comes to catching criminals.' He gave a wintry smile and poured himself a glass of thick red wine. 'And, frankly, most of the stuff in that room is harmless enough; it could be blowing around Liberation Square and not do us any real damage.'

'I don't know,' Lanneret said slowly. 'Did you know there was a Teredo cache in there?'

'In the Archive? No. Are you sure?'

'Absolutely. They left it open. This was in it.'

Lanneret pulled a folded scrap of ancient parchment out of his inside pocket, handed it to Teredo, and watched his face change as he read it.

'What in the name of all the moons was the oath doing in the Closed Archive?'

'I thought you might know that. It's a *Teredo* cache, after all...'

'Oh, don't try and make this my fault, Elverton! You're the fool who let them get away!' Lanneret flinched. Teredo turned the paper over in his fingers.

'Wait a moment. If this is the oath, then where... I mean, it was always kept with...' He looked fearfully at Lanneret.

'There was nothing else there,' Lanneret said quietly.

Teredo's face drained of blood; the glass slipped from his fingers. Spilled wine seeped like dark blood into the carpet.

'So they've taken the Palamon Trial.'

'I think... Probably. Yes.'

Teredo got heavily to his feet, leaning on his ruby-topped stick. 'Then whatever searches you've started, double them. Triple them. Whatever it takes.'

A journey out of nightmare: a crazy, twisting, turning scramble across the hostile city. Jinx and Tal headed for the harbour, planning to take one of the smaller roads back into the centre. But the docks were swarming with Watch patrols, so they climbed a wall, dodged a barking dog in the yard behind a workshop, leapt another wall into a tavern garden, climbed into a warehouse yard and came out through an unlocked side gate. The street they reached was narrow, empty - and a dead end. They climbed another wall into a lane between rows of houses which brought them to a wide street, just above another checkpoint, and dashed across it into another blind alley while the watchmen's backs were turned. Here, they paused to catch their breath.

The second curfew bell sounded.

Jinx and Tal climbed another wall, crossed a shed roof, jumped down into a passageway that led to a courtyard of tumbledown houses and walked out onto the main street. There were busy checkpoints above and below them, and they retreated back into the courtyard.

The third bell sounded. They could be arrested simply for being out-of-doors now, and there was none of the protective darkness that usually came with curfew, just the grey and drizzly end of a late spring afternoon.

Tal had no idea how long that confused zig-zagging through alleys and passages and across gardens and roofs went on. But he could tell that, even with all the diversions and doubling back, they were heading in roughly the right direction and at last, as evening began to fall, he realised with a surge of relief that they were in one of the streets behind the Basilica. He tiptoed to the corner. From here, he could see the back door of Gabriel's kitchen, a glow of lamplight in the high window. He glanced left and right. No-one. He took a step out of the shadows. Two steps. Just another dozen to go...

'Oy!'

Lantern light caught him; heavy boots thundered on the cobbles. Tal darted back into the street, and grabbed Jinx; they skidded round a corner, and dived down a set of basement steps. There was a cramped hollow beneath the steps, half hidden behind a scant stack of firewood, but Jinx was pushing open the wooden trap door to a cellar. 'Quick!' he whispered. 'And lose that scroll!' Tal tugged the scroll out of his belt and stuck it among the wood pile. On the street above, the footsteps echoed closer and closer. Jinx slithered into the cellar. The footsteps slowed, and stopped.

It was the decision of a heartbeat. Tal shut the cellar door as quietly as he could behind Jinx, crouched down in the useless hiding place behind the woodpile, closed his eyes and waited. Footsteps descended the steps. A big hand gripped his shoulder hard, heaved him to his feet, and hauled him back up to the road.

'You're one of Gabriel's boys.' The Watchman studied him in the lantern light.

'Yes,' Tal said, hopeful that the man would just take him home. But he marched him away, past the Basilica, across the square and up the steps of the Watch Office. They halted at a long desk in the entrance hall. The man behind it looked up impatiently.

'What?' he said.

'Out after curfew,' said the Watchman.

The man at the desk sighed. 'Well, there's no-one around to deal with him now. Everyone's down at the harbour. Someone reported them there...' He sighed again. 'Stick him in the back for now. And shift yourself down to the docks.'

Tal sat on a bench in a bare room, watching the window. Daylight faded into darkness; the clouds blew and parted and a fitful moonlight flickered between them. He felt hollow and dry-mouthed. Last time he'd been in this building, collecting his papers, Gabriel had given him a few simple rules for staying out of trouble with the Watch, and now he'd broken almost all of them. He wrapped his arms round the hollow in his stomach that was partly hunger but mostly fear, swallowed hard, and fixed his eyes on the moonlight. After hours of silence there were voices and footsteps outside, and the door was flung open by a burly watchman. Tal stood up from the bench, his mouth drier than ever.

'Out after curfew, eh?'

Tal nodded.

The man looked at his dark blue cloak. 'One of Gabriel's boys?'

Tal nodded again.

The man smiled grimly. 'You'll be singing by the time we've finished with you...'

Then there was another, familiar, voice in the corridor: courteous and firm; and the sweep of a long dark blue gown in the doorway; a quick conversation... 'Yes... yes... probably best if you deal with him. We've enough to do this evening...' and a hand on his arm, guiding him away, out, into the fresh wet evening air of the square. In the multi-coloured light of the big lanterns, Tal glanced up, but Gabriel's face was stony, and Tal dropped his gaze again.

Don't ever be late for a rehearsal or an office or you'll be in trouble with me... And he had missed the whole day. They crossed the square in silence. In the Basilica the choir were gathering, ready to sing the nightfall office.

'Go and wait in your room,' Gabriel told Tal. He fumbled his way blindly into the cloisters, and bumped into Sallender at the foot of the stairs.

'Oh, it's you, riff-raff.'

Tal clenched his fists. 'I'm not riff-raff.'

'No? It's what you'll look like when Gabriel's slung you back out into the gutter where you belong.'

Slung out? Unable to muster an answer, Tal stared numbly after Sallender. He waited in the cloister, listened to the singing start, and climbed the stairs to his room; flopped onto his bed and stared into the dark with hot unseeing eyes, straining his ears for the distant music. When it ended, there were the cheerful sounds of running feet along the corridor, laughter, and talking. Someone tapped on his door, and he heard Sam saying, 'Tal?' He curled into a ball on the bed and didn't answer. Sam's door closed sadly. Silence fell. Then there was another knock on the door, and another voice calling his name. Gabriel, at last.

Tal got up heavily to open the door.

'Come with me,' Gabriel said, and Tal followed him unwillingly downstairs and into his kitchen. Connie flashed him a reassuring wink, but Gabriel was still grave and unsmiling: he sat at the table, leaving Tal standing.

'Well?' he said.

'You're going to throw me out, aren't you?' Tal said miserably.

'Not necessarily,' said Gabriel. Some of the usual warmth had returned to his voice and eyes, and Tal felt a tiny flicker of hope. 'I would like an explanation, though,' Gabriel continued. 'Perhaps you'd like to start with why you ran off this morning? Before we get on to playing about in prohibited streets on High Side and being arrested for breaking curfew?'

Tal closed his eyes and swallowed hard. 'I saw my mum.'

211

Night and Dawn

Tal felt Gabriel guide him gently into a chair. 'What happened?' he asked, and Tal stammered out the shimmer of the girl's bright cloak in the early light, the shock of recognition, and the forlorn chasing of hope and its dissolving colours through the impossible turnings of High Side. 'Which family wears that greeny-blue? I couldn't remember.'

'It's called halcyon,' said Gabriel. 'It's the Philemot colour.'

'But she was sold to the Sallenders. I tried asking Gregory about her, ages ago, only...' His voice tailed off.

'Mmm.' Gabriel frowned. 'Slaves get moved round quite a bit, you know, Tal. Given as presents. Wagered. Swapped.' He sounded angry again, but this time Tal knew that it wasn't with him, and he watched, hopefully, as Gabriel rummaged in the dresser drawer for a pencil and paper. He worked rapidly for a moment, and put the paper on the table in front of Tal. It was a rough sketch map.

'This is how you get there. It's easy enough, if you know the way. Up the main road to High Side, along here...' he traced the pencil along the paper, 'and this is the Philemot house.' Tal stared at the simple, straightforward route that was nothing like today's mad twists and turns.

'Go and find her tomorrow,' Gabriel said. 'Miss as many rehearsals and offices as you need to.'

'Can I?'

'Of *course*, Tal.'

Tal picked up the map with shaking hands, folded it unsteadily and tucked it into his pocket. He managed to say 'thanks' but his throat felt too full for him to say anything else, and he watched wordlessly as Gabriel got up from the table, washed and dried some cups, filled the kettle and stood it on the stove. By the time it had boiled the shakiness had passed a bit. He took the cup that Gabriel offered him and wrapped his hands round it. Gabriel sat down opposite him.

'There's one thing I don't understand, Tal.'

'Yes?'

'About this afternoon. When the early curfew rang, why didn't you come straight back?'

'Oh.' Tal stared into his tea. 'I...' He stopped and blushed. 'It was...' He halted again: it was impossible to explain without mentioning Jinx, and Fossick and Scrimp, and their stolen parchment: that wretched scrap of unreadable paper, still hidden in the woodpile: it would be best if it rotted there. 'I...'

'I can tell you,' Connie said, unexpectedly. 'Jinx told me, after you'd rushed off to bail Tal out.'

'You *know* Jinx?' Tal looked from Connie to Gabriel.

Gabriel nodded. 'It was Jinx who told us you'd been arrested. Go on, Connie. Tell me.'

'Jinx and Tal met up in the afternoon,' she said. 'They'd got themselves saddled with... um... something they shouldn't have had. Anyway. Once the checkpoints were up, Jinx was in trouble, of course: no papers. He offered to take the... thing, so that Tal could come straight home. But Tal insisted on sticking with him, and of course, all the streets were closed, so it took them ages to get back. They didn't get anywhere near here till well after curfew.'

Gabriel gave Tal a long look, but said nothing.

'They nearly made it,' Connie went on. 'But they were seen and chased, and they took cover in a basement. Jinx got into the cellar, but Tal didn't. Deliberately. So that he'd be found, and Jinx wouldn't.'

'Did you?' Gabriel asked quietly.

Tal looked at his feet and shrugged. 'Well... I've got papers and he hasn't. He'd have been in more trouble than me, wouldn't he?'

'You'd have been in trouble enough, if they hadn't been busy with other things,' Gabriel said grimly. Then his face relaxed into a smile. 'That was a brave thing to do, Tal.'

The words hung in the air for a moment, and in them Tal felt a feeling that was like moonlight and birds flying upwards and music. He ran his finger along the woodgrain of the tabletop.

'You must be starving, after all that.' Gabriel got up and turned to the dresser. Connie half rose from her chair. 'Oh, and by the way. What was this thing you couldn't be found with?'

He lifted the lid from the bread bin. Connie stood up.

'Gabriel…'

'Ah.' Gabriel reached into the bread bin and pulled out a scroll of yellowed parchment.

'Jinx brought it,' Connie said. 'He said he'd been told it was important for you to have it, Tal.'

Gabriel blew a few crumbs off the parchment and brushed a cobweb from it with gentle fingers. 'This looks ancient. Can I have a proper look?'

Tal shrugged. 'Course. It's not mine. I just got landed with it.' He watched as Gabriel unfurled the scroll and laid it on the kitchen table, holding it open with the empty tea cups. He leaned over it, and the blood drained from his face. 'Where in the name of moonlight did this come from?'

Tal explained, watching Gabriel's face turn whiter still. 'It's not my fault!'

'I know, Tal.'

'What is it anyway?'

Gabriel glanced, instinctively, at the door before answering in a low voice, 'Old Script.'

'Great,' said Tal. 'So it's stolen *and* prohibited and we can't even tell what it says.'

'Mmm,' Gabriel murmured. He lifted the cups and let the scroll furl itself shut. 'Tal, will you let me hide this? I'll give it back, if you ever need it, I promise. But I don't want you keeping it. It's too much of a risk.'

He hadn't wanted the scroll, but now he remembered that it had been meant for Gaia, as well as him. He had to keep it safe: getting rid of it would feel like giving up on the chance of ever seeing her again. 'You're only going to hide it? Not do anything else with it?'

'Such as?'

'I don't know… Burn it. Turn it in. Give it to someone else.'

'None of those things, I promise.'

'Well… Yes. Alright.' It was a relief to share the secret and the burden of it. 'You keep it.'

Above the eastern provinces, the moon tossed in a bruised sky. Jason sat awake, turning things over in his mind. They had a rough plan: too full of gaps, but there was nothing he could do about those now. From what he could glimpse of the moon's height between the racing clouds, he judged that it must be just after midnight. It was time.

He put a light hand on Carrie's shoulder and whispered her name. She started up instantly, and he guessed that she hadn't been asleep either. They tiptoed to the window; Jason heaved Carrie up onto the sill and scrabbled up after her in bare feet, his boots slung around his neck. Giving one last look at the sleeping room, they dropped silently to the soggy ground outside.

Jason stepped into his boots, laced them, and straightened up. The night was tricksy: the blowing clouds across the moon cast shifting light and shadow on the uneven ground. He took Carrie's hand and they ran behind the farmhouse and round to the back of the stable block. The big building stood solid and dark in the changing moonlight.

If only she was a swansprite, he thought, stupidly, *it would be easy*. He imagined the walls falling to dust, the building opening to release her, the guards turned to stone... Angrily, he told himself to stop it. She had no magic: she was simply a scared girl, his best friend, trapped in the darkness and if she was going to get out it was his wits and his hands - his and Carrie's - that would have to manage it.

They edged along the stable wall and he peered round into the farmyard. Alongside him, he felt Carrie give a little start. 'What?' he whispered.

'Down the track. There's something...' He turned to look, but there was nothing, just the quick change from light to shadow. 'Trick of the moon, Carrie.' He turned back and squinted into the farmyard again.

No guard. The farmyard was empty, and he felt a sudden lift of hope. The stable doors would be locked, of course, but he had tested them earlier: the wood was soft with age, and Hawkins' sharp knife would make short work of cutting the lock free from the door. He took a step out of the shadows into the yard.

Carrie seized hold of his sleeve and pulled him back.

'*What?*'

'Shhh!' She was pointing up at the farmhouse, at the long upstairs window which commanded a broad view over the yard and the fields beyond.

Stearne. White-faced, motionless in the moonlight, keeping an unblinking watch. Jason ducked back into the shadows. Carrie had already turned away; he followed her, feeling his way along the stable wall to the low square window of the storeroom. 'You did leave it open?' he whispered, and Carrie nodded, but when he slipped the knife between the frame and the window he couldn't lift the catch; it must have been padlocked again after Carrie had left. He thumped the wall in frustration. He had been depending on getting in through this window. He could break the glass, but the sound would shatter the night silence, and Stearne was already awake and watching. Could he ease the glass out with Hawk's knife? He wasn't sure. And what if it fell and smashed anyway?

'I left the skylight open too,' Carrie whispered. 'They might not have thought of that.'

Jason stepped back to consider the climb. The rough stone walls were manageable, but it would take time and what if...

What if, what if... He could lose the night - and every chance - in *what ifs*, and Carrie was climbing already, feeling for hand- and footholds, pulling herself steadily up. He started after her. It should have been easy, but nerves and the damp night made the stones slippery under his hands and he almost lost his grip a couple of times before reaching the eaves safely.

The wet slates of the roof reached steeply up to the little skylight. From here, it was a horrible climb: hardly any purchase for hands or feet and a long fall to the ground. He was forced to go slowly, feeling time falling away from him: half the night seemed to have passed before he finally got a hand on the wooden frame of the skylight and pulled himself up. The wet wind had strengthened: it battered around him as he clung to the roof, and chased moonlight and shadows across the fields. For a moment he thought he saw figures moving in the field below the stables, but then the shadows gathered again. A trick of the moonlight, he thought. He reached down and heaved Carrie up alongside him.

The window was unlocked. Jason eased the catch open with Hawkins' knife and folded back the skylight. He and Carrie dropped down into the hayloft and crept down the loft ladder.

Jason hadn't been in the stables since his own imprisonment. He had always made excuses to avoid the place, and as they tiptoed through the building, he was shaking, his breath catching in his throat.

He felt savaged with his own, old terror; with the new raw fear for Gaia. Carrie, alongside him, seemed calm, her hand cool and steady in his. But at the end of the stable, she halted and recoiled.

The clouds had cleared the moon again. A strong shaft of white light fell through the high barred window, shining on the stone trap-door, and a circle of something around it. Something as white as the moonlight, laid carefully in an unbroken ring around Gaia's prison.

'Swanflowers!' Carrie whispered.

'So what?'

'They're unlucky. You can't cross them.'

Jason gave a silent, derisive laugh. 'Is that why Stearne thought he didn't need a guard? Well, if he thinks that's going to keep me out...' He stepped over the flowers into the circle.

'*Jason!*' Carrie whispered. He ignored her and bent to grasp the iron handle of the stone cover.

He hadn't reckoned on it being so heavy - though, now he made himself think about it, he remembered that the guards who'd moved it to give him food and water when he was in here had always found it hard to lift. There was no way he could open it by himself. He could barely shift it in its frame, let alone raise it wide enough to let her out. He let go of the handle. Carrie was standing with her back to the wall, as far away as she could get from those *stupid* flowers without abandoning him altogether.

'Carrie,' he said, 'I can't do this. I need your help.'

She shrank against the wall. She was shaking her head, mouthing, 'I can't, I can't.' He crossed the flowers again, out of the circle, and grabbed her arm hard.

'She's my *best friend*... Your friend too, and she's going to *die*... she's going to *burn* if we don't get her out. Or maybe you don't really want to? Maybe if you're stupid enough to believe you can't cross those flowers, you're stupid enough to believe she really is a swansprite.'

Carrie whipped her head up as if he had slapped her. 'No!'

'So *help.*' He was almost in tears. Slowly, very slowly, she took one step forward, another and another, into the circle of flowers.

At first, one thought anchored Gaia to the world beyond the darkness. Tal must have the amulet. She made herself practise, over and over again, the simple directions by which Jason would be able to find him: a ledge under the bridge in Freehaven, near the big square, on the first day of each quarter. She recited them endlessly, a prayer to ward off madness: so that when at last it was Hawkins who lifted the slab to give her water, she was able to pass him the pouch and speak with a steady clear-headedness that astonished him.

That done - the amulet passed on - the darkness invaded her. She curled up, pressing herself into the filthy wet soil at the bottom of the hole to try and escape it. But the darkness was as heavy as earth over the dead: it was everywhere: it clung to her skin, pushing against her closed eyelids, smothering her mouth and nose, driving the last drops of moonlight out of her soul... Then the slab above her was lifted again, and she looked up into a shaft of light falling around Stearne's tall figure.

'Not long now.' He smiled his terrifying smile. 'Next time we come, it'll be to take you to the fire. It's a kind burning, Gaia. To free your troubled soul.' He let the stone fall shut on her again, and all her childhood nightmares of fire returned to her and she prayed, to every moon, that she would die of the darkness before she died in the flames.

'Let me die of the darkness, let me die, let me die of the darkness...' But the stone was lifted again; she looked up into brilliant light and fear seared through her; the brightness blinded her; her own screaming filled her ears. Then, faintly, as if far away, someone was saying *Gaia, Gaia, Gaia,* and there was a body alongside hers, squashed into the little hole with her, familiar arms around her, his hands stroking her hair.

'It's alright,' Jason was saying, 'you're alright; we've come to get you out.' He lifted her up, out of the hole, climbed out after her, and helped her to sit on a bale of hay. The light was moonlight, not day, and he was kneeling in front of her, holding her cold hands in his, saying, 'Gaia, it's me; it's Jason. It's alright.

'I thought... He said... Fire...' Fear stopped her voice in her throat.

'No. We'll get you safe. I *promise.*'

'It was so dark...'

'I know,' he said. 'I was in there too.'

She held onto him, as if she would never let him go. He freed himself gently. 'We need to get moving. Let's get that stone back, Carrie.'

Together, they hefted it back into place and stepped out of the circle of flowers. 'Do they look right?' Jason asked, and Carrie made herself look, and bent forward to adjust a branch with shaking hands. Jason smiled at her, and lifted Gaia to her feet. But she could barely stand, and every step was terrifyingly slow: even the tiny journey through the stables seemed to take hours. In the store-room, she slumped to the floor while Jason and Carrie eased the window open. She hung heavy in his arms as he half lifted, half heaved her onto the windowsill and down onto the wet grass of the paddock.

He raised her up again, and the night burst open with the sound of a single angry bell, calling from the farmyard, on and on and on and not stopping. There was light everywhere: in Stearne's house, in the guards' hut, in moving pools of lamplight as the guards ran out across the farmyard and the fields.

'What's going on?' someone shouted, and Jason tensed.

'Bandits!'

He peered into the shifting moonlight and darkness. Along the track the farm carts were moving: the wagons that had been standing ready for tomorrow's journey to Swanhaven, the journey that Stearne had hoped would be blessed with luck by a swansprite's death. They thundered through the gate and along the rough moorland track, dark, swift shadows in the moonlight. As they disappeared, there was a shout close at hand; the paddock gate swung open, and the field was full of guards.

There was no time to think of running. Jason simply crouched down in the shadow under the stable wall and pulled the others close to him, and waited to be found. But the guards rounded up the horses, mounted, and rode away into the night, leaving silence behind them.

'They didn't find us,' Jason whispered.

'They've taken all the horses,' Carrie said.

'All of them?' He stared, in despair, at the empty field. They had counted on stealing a horse to carry Gaia to safety across the wide fields and the moor. 'Alright. We'll have to walk.'

'We'll never do it.' Carrie's voice held all the doubt that he felt, and by the time they had crossed the paddock and the first field, he was frighteningly certain that she was right. The paddock was boggy and pitted with deep hoofprints and the field had been ploughed for planting: the furrows between the ridges were flooded from the heavy spring rains, ankle deep with sticky wet clay. Supporting Gaia between them, Jason and Carrie staggered forward as if claggy hands were dragging them back at each step. At the field end, they heaved her over the fence. She fell to the ground, and didn't move when Jason tugged at her.

'Come on, Gaia.' He glanced at the sky. It was still dark, but they had been hours already: it couldn't be long before the first traces of daylight began to show. 'Get up!'

'Just get yourselves out.' Gaia's voice was empty, utterly weary.

Suddenly angry, he said, 'I'm not going anywhere without you. You can go back if you like, Carrie.' Carrie shook her head. 'Then we'll make it together, or not at all.' He lifted Gaia onto his back, and started off again across the wet earth.

Clumps of mud clinging to his feet, her inert weight on his back, the heavy fear at his heart, he struggled across one field, another, and another. He walked with his head down, Carrie silent at his side, reaching out to steady him when he stumbled. At last the boundary wall loomed up before them in the darkness - only, it wasn't quite dark now. That struggle across the farm had taken ages. The moon had paled, and a faint grey glimmer was beginning to lighten the eastern sky.

What hope now?

Grimly, he helped Gaia over the wall, climbed over himself, and silently lifted her onto his back again. He set off in a hurry, but it was impossible to rush across the waterlogged, uneven ground. Every step was a stumble. A few paces away from the wall, he fell, and after that he made himself slow down. Going steadily was better, faster in the end than having to keep picking himself up, but it was a huge effort to go so slowly, when the sky was lightening with every breath, and his nerves were on edge for the clanging bell that would tell him they had been discovered.

It was going to be a beautiful day, he realised bitterly, a rare, beautiful day. Pelting, blinding rain, or the white mist that often hung about the moor: that's what they needed. But instead they were going to get clear sunshine, and the first guard who so much as glanced in this direction would see them.

Sunrise gleamed gold out of the grey; he felt a faint warmth on his face and hair. Carrie urged, 'Jason, *hurry!*' and he lifted his eyes to see the trees looming over him. Not far now. He could hear birds calling in the forest. But not for long, because the bell started again, drowning out the birdsong, drowning Carrie's frightened 'Quick!' drowning even his own terrified blood beating in his ears. He started to run, fell, staggered up and struggled on.

Tal woke as usual to a knock at his door just before dawn. Time for the daybreak office, the break, maybe, of the best day of his life. He dressed quickly and climbed onto the table to look out of the window. A faint light was rising over the sea; up on High Side, all the roofs were the uniform dull grey that had made him despair yesterday. It didn't matter today. He walked Gabriel's simple route in his head again; jumped off the table, and opened his door to find Sam waiting for him on the landing.

'Are you alright?' Sam asked. 'What happened?'

In a muddle, Tal poured out the events of the day before.

'You've found your mum?'

'Yes!' He ran down the stairs with hope and joy soaring higher than birds above the mountains, and found himself face to face with Sallender at the door into the Basilica.

'What happened to you yesterday, peasant riff-raff? Hasn't Gabriel slung you out?'

'Ignore him,' Sam murmured.

'You keep out of this, you filthy little bit of gutter-bred low-life!' Sallender's voice was resonant and carrying, and everyone seemed to be staring in their direction. And because Sallender's family had bought Mum as if she was a thing, and casually got rid of her when they didn't need her anymore; because Sallender had never said a word to Sam that wasn't loaded with contempt; because Sam had turned bright red and was staring furiously and unhappily at the floor - because of all that, Tal said, 'Don't speak to him like that.'

'What?' Sallender looked at him dangerously.

'I said, don't speak to him like that. I don't care whose fourth cousin you are, Sallender. He's a hundred times better than you'll ever be.'

For a moment, Sallender looked as if all the words had been knocked out of him. Then he stammered, 'You'll be sorry you said that.'

'I don't think I will,' said Tal.

Daybreak, and the long full moon morning office. He was alert and watching throughout the prayers. There was no halcyon flash at the end of the nave, not this morning, but it didn't matter: Gabriel's map was safe in his pocket and his head, and the last hymn was a fanfare of triumphant hope.

'Good luck,' said Sam.

'Remember,' said Gabriel. 'Don't worry about being late.'

He nodded his thanks, and ran; out into the daylight, and through the rain up the long hill to High Side. Following Gabriel's directions, he came to a set of gates in a white wall. He shook them, but they were locked, so he pressed his face to the bars and looked through. There was no guard on the gate and the front door of the huge white house beyond the wide gravel drive was firmly shut.

There was a bell-pull mounted on one of the gate-posts and he put his hand on it, but he didn't dare tug it, not yet. Later, he promised himself. If there wasn't any other way, he would dare it later, but for now he decided to walk around the walls. There might be a back gate; an entrance less imposing and off-putting than this one, and with luck a friendly gardener within hailing distance.

He set off resolutely along the road. Climbing plants, full of deep blue flowers, tumbled out of the garden and the shining wet pavement beneath his feet was bright with fallen blue petals, like fragments of summer sky. After a while, he found himself in a road where a long row of trees ran alongside the wall. At least he could look into the garden, he thought. He swarmed up the trunk of the nearest tree, hauled himself astride the first branch, and froze.

Close by, just out of sight on the other side of the wall, someone was singing. For a moment, he rested his back against the tree and closed his eyes and listened. A lilting tune, as familiar as his own breathing.

Night and Dawn

Far above the summer pastures,
Golden in the setting sun,
Fly the flocks that tell you, dearest,
I'll be home when day is done.

High above you when you're sleeping

The singer faltered and started again, and this time he sang too. Quietly at first, whispering the words to himself, but joy would not let him be quiet for long.

High above you when you're sleeping
In the silent winter night
Hangs the single star that tells you
I'll be home before it's light.

At the end he was singing alone and as the last note died away, he could *feel* her listening, like a shivering on the air. Finally, she whispered, 'Who's there?' and then, with impossible hope, 'Tal?' and he clambered along an overhanging branch, lost his grip, and tumbled onto the wet lawn at his mother's feet.

The Heart of the Forest

She held him so close he could feel her breathing as if it were his own, and when she let him go, it was only to take his face between her hands, and look and look at him.

'How did you get here? Are you alright? You are, aren't you?' - and then the question that he had dreaded. 'Where's Gaia?'

'She... I don't know...' As he fumbled for the right words, a voice called across the garden, 'Mai?' and a girl in a long green-blue dress came hurrying towards them. He recognised her from the Basilica: she wasn't as old as he'd thought; probably about Gaia's age, only much taller. She stopped short when she saw him. Her bright, green-eyed glance darted from him to Mai and back again. 'You... Are you *Tal?*'

Mai nodded, and the girl said, 'Oh *Mai,*' and gave her a quick hug, before turning to him with a grin. 'She said you could sing.'

Baffled, he said, 'What?'

She pointed at his dark blue shirt, stained with damp green from the tree. 'That's a choir school shirt.' She thought for a moment. 'If you're at the choir school, you'll know my cousin. Gregory Sallender.'

'Oh. Yes.' He kept his voice deliberately level, polite.

She grinned again. 'Bad luck,' she said, and suddenly she was apologetic. 'I'm sorry. I'm interrupting. Sorry...' and she ran away across the garden, like a long-legged bird. At the steps to an upper lawn, she turned back. 'Mai. Have a holiday. Go and hear him sing.' Then she was gone.

Tal looked at his mother in bewilderment. 'Who was that?'

'That's Rachel. Rachel Philemot.'

They left the garden and meandered through the confusing High Side streets and down the long hill. He told her his story, and found the courage to tell her about Gaia, and asked, 'What about you?'

'I've been alright,' Mai said. 'The Philemots have been kind, especially Rachel. It's been a hundred times better than it might have been. Except for looking out at the sky every night and wondering where you and Gaia were and what you were doing. I guessed you wouldn't stay at home.'

'That was Gaia's idea.'

She laughed. 'I guessed that too. She was always looking over the edge, wasn't she? Leaving would have been easier for her than anyone, but I bet she couldn't have done it without you looking after her.' She put her arm round his shoulder and hugged him close.

'Didn't look after her that well, did I?'

'She wouldn't say that, Tal,' she said. 'I know she wouldn't.'

They were halfway across the bridge, and he stopped and leaned on the parapet. He looked down into the swirling crimson river, at the long wall which they had tried to climb to safety, and out to sea where she had gone, to the thin empty horizon against the sky. 'She wouldn't,' Mai repeated. 'Ask her, when you find her.'

He was about to say it was impossible, but... sometimes you could find lost people again, and he held her hand tightly as they crossed the bridge into the square. A crier was announcing a reward for information about Fossick and Scrimp, and the Watch were still out too, working the crowd, stopping people, searching and questioning them. As Mai and Tal neared the Basilica, an officer halted them and handed them a printed sketch.

'You seen these men yesterday? Or today?' He looked more closely at Tal. 'Oh, it's you. You got off lightly last night, didn't you?'

Tal mumbled 'Mmm,' shook his head, handed the sketch back, and the watchman moved them on.

'What was that about?' Mai asked.

'Nothing.'

'What did he mean, you got off lightly?'

'Nothing, Mum, honestly. It's fine.' She was still looking at him doubtfully, so he said quickly, 'You wanted to hear the singing, didn't you?' He caught her hand and hurried her into the Basilica. Just past Parhelion's statue, she tugged him to a halt.

'Are you sure this is alright, Tal?'

'*Yes.* Come *on.*'

'I mean... shouldn't I listen from here?' she asked, and he understood. The rows of seats ahead of them were kept for the

225

Fellowship and their families, and she was a slave. She was scared to go further forward. As she hesitated, the cloister door banged open and Gabriel hurried through it. He caught sight of them, and strode down the aisle to join them.

'Gabriel,' Tal said, 'This is...'

'Your mum. I'd have known her anywhere.' Gabriel smiled. 'I'm so pleased to meet you.' He held out his hand and Mai took it uncertainly; and Tal thought that probably no-one, except maybe Rachel, had treated her like this for a long time: like an equal human being. 'So pleased he found you,' Gabriel was saying. 'You must have missed him; he's certainly missed you.'

His warmth seemed to give her courage. 'Thank you so much,' she said, 'for looking after him.'

'A pleasure. He's a good singer.'

'I know.' She looked at him with a fierce pride.

'You'll want to hear him, won't you?' Gabriel ushered her up the aisle, found a spare chair and helped her into it. He gestured the choir to stand but Gregory remained sitting, his eyes fixed on Mai, taking in the drab clothes with the bright seam of halcyon that marked what she was and who she belonged to.

'Gregory?' Gabriel said. 'On your feet, please.'

'But she's...' Gregory's face was taut with outrage. 'She's a...'

'A guest,' Gabriel said. 'I think that's probably the word you're looking for.' His voice was mild but there was steel in his eyes, and Gregory got reluctantly to his feet, flushed with anger at being made to stand while a slave sat. Sam nudged Tal delightedly, but Gregory and Gregory's fury were as far away from Tal as a dragon flying so high above him that it was out of sight. All he could think about was Mum, and the music he would pour around her like a shower of moonlight.

'We need to get further in,' Jason kept telling them. There had been no sign that they had been seen; no sound of pursuit, but he wouldn't let them stop. As morning strengthened overhead, they followed a rough track deeper and deeper into the trees. Finally, at the bottom of a long slope, Carrie said, 'Can't we rest now?'

226

'You two can. I'm going to explore a bit.' Jason felt wide awake despite the exhausting struggle across the moor: alive with a dawning triumph. He walked further on and shoved through a patch of dense bramble, coming out into a clearing, where a big man was leaning against a tree-trunk. Jason startled, and turned to bolt, but he wasn't quick enough. The man grabbed him by the arm and held him.

'Oh no, you don't,' he said.

Jason struggled to break free, kicking and twisting, but the hands holding him were too strong. 'Don't take me back,' he stammered. '*Please*. Don't take me back...' A shudder ran through him.

'Hey!' The man gave him a little shake. 'Do I look like I'm in the business of taking folk back to Hope's End?'

Jason looked up. The man had laughing dark eyes, and a black beard that couldn't quite hide the familiar, double scar on his cheek.

'My name's Daniel. And none of us are going to take you back there, son.'

Us? Jason glanced round the clearing. The stolen Hope's End carts were standing under the trees. The horses dozed on their feet, and around them half a dozen ragged, scarred men and women were beginning to wake, sitting up on the dried leaves.

'Mind you,' Daniel was saying. 'You took a risk, running. If you'd been caught...'

'I know.' Jason shivered. 'But we had to. Because of Gaia. Stearne thinks she's a swansprite.'

'*Who?*'

'Stearne,' Jason explained. 'He's the new superintendant, he's mad, he...'

'Not Stearne,' Daniel said. 'The girl. *What* did you say her name was?'

'Gaia. Why?'

'What's going on?' Carrie pushed her way into the clearing, Gaia trailing wearily after her. Daniel stared. Across the clearing, one of the other men was blinking and rubbing at his eyes.

'In the name of all that's wonderful...' Daniel took a step towards Gaia and Jason darted in front of him.

'You're not going to hurt her!'

'No,' Daniel said, 'Oh, no, no, no. Not for anything in the world.' White with tiredness, Gaia rocked on her feet, and Daniel stepped forward and caught her in his arms.

'Come on, little swan. Let's get you home.'

Faintly she was aware of someone lifting her and lying her down, of the sway of a cart beneath her, of Jason slipping the amulet back around her neck, cradling her head in his lap. Then she slept, all through the long journey into the sheltering heart of the forest. When at last she woke, she was lying on a bed of leaves and rough blankets.

It was night: moonlight filtered through clouds and branches, and fell around her like lace. At first she thought she was sleeping in a grove of trees, but the moonlight was gleaming on a white stone floor, and crumbling stone walls rose above her. There were fragments of pictures on the walls: hands, the sweep of a long cloak, running animals, a wheel... Her eyes grew heavy and the images dissolved into a confused dream.

She woke again to the warmth of day and the enfolding forest. Through half opened eyes, she saw slanting shafts of apple-coloured light falling around her. She smelled the freshness of damp leaves and heard the whisper of breezes through the branches, the call of a bird, the low murmur of water.

'Are you sure she's alright?' Carrie whispered.

'She's fine. She just needs to rest.'

Gaia opened her eyes properly. The woman who had spoken was tall, her long brown hair plaited in a thick braid, her eyes like water: grey-blue, with flecks of green and hazel. Gaia sat up, pushed back her blankets and looked warily at the strange woman.

'It's alright,' Carrie said. 'Kay's been looking after you.'

The woman took both of Gaia's hands in hers, and looked into her face with a strange intensity. 'Welcome,' she said.

'Thanks.' Embarrassed, Gaia glanced down. The night-time vision had not been a dream: her bed of leaves rested on a floor of white marble between broken white walls. The floor was old: green with moss and lichen and cracked by the tree roots that had grown beneath it. Gaia freed her hands from Kay's, slipped off her bed and walked between the walls, stopping to study the carvings of horses and riders, fleeing deer, dogs, a city on a hill... She came to an empty doorway and went through it into a wide courtyard where saplings had forced themselves up through the broken pavement. In the centre there was a cracked marble basin, and poised above it a marble swan which must once have been a fountain: its wings spread and its beak open.

Gaia wandered round the courtyard, peering through arches and doorways into vast roofless chambers overgrown with trees and creepers. On one side, the wall had collapsed into a jumble of carved stone. She picked up a fragment that showed the head and wing of a bird, tracing the intricate details of its feathers with a wondering finger. It was perfect. She laid it back where she had found it and made her way back to Carrie and Kay.

'What is this place?'

Kay smiled. 'That's a long story. Let's have breakfast first. You must be starving.'

She led them along long wide corridors and through a towering archway, down a flight of broad steps, to a terrace overlooking a fast running river. A fire was burning on the weathered pavement, the smoke blue against the green of the forest, and in the talking, laughing group gathered around it, Gaia saw Jason.

He looked different. He'd taken off the brown coat that was too big for him, and he looked taller, but it wasn't only that: he had his old ease back and the shadows had gone from his eyes. He hadn't just rescued *her*, Gaia thought: he had rescued himself. She ran down the steps to greet him, and he broke off the conversation he had been having, and took her in his arms. For a long time she pressed her face against him. He smelled of rain and earth and woodsmoke. At last they let one another go, and she looked round the gathered company and started in surprise at the sight of a man who was standing aside from the others, watching her.

'You!' She turned to Jason. 'He helped us… Me and Tal, when we were in the forest in the winter.' Her voice caught on Tal's name, and Jason caught her hand and held it. 'Tal's good at looking after himself, Gaia. Bet he's alright.'

'Maybe,' she said uncertainly. She turned back to the stranger. 'I'm sorry we ran away. We'd had some bad times. We didn't know who to trust.'

'I understand,' he said. 'And by the way, my name's Aldon.'

She frowned. 'What happened to forest rules? No names, and all that?'

'Ah,' he said. 'This is the heart of the forest. There are no secrets here. This is where all things are revealed.' He looked into her face, and she read the same swift changing emotions in his eyes that she had seen in Kay's: a solemn wonderment and dawning excitement. 'I told you I'd seen you before, didn't I?'

She looked at him blankly. 'What do you mean?'

'Oh.' He glanced at Kay. 'Hasn't she shown you yet?'

'Shown me what?'

'Ask her.' He shook his head and turned to Jason. 'You ready?'

'Ready for what?' Gaia demanded.

'Going hunting,' Jason said, but there was a look of suppressed adventure in his eyes. 'We'll be gone a while. Don't know how long.' He gave her another quick hug, and ran after Aldon up the steps, turning at the top to wave to her before slipping away into the trees. She stared after him, lost and cross. *No secrets*, Aldon had said, but that conversation had been nothing but mysterious half hints. She crossed the terrace to join Kay and Carrie in the circle around the fire, full of questions.

'Here.' Kay handed her a slice of warm sweet soft bread folded round a juicy freshly grilled fish running with hot oil... and she forgot everything except the sudden realisation that she was starving; hollow with hunger. She ate, aware only of the rich flavours in her mouth and the warmth in her stomach. When she had finished, she licked the oil off her fingers.

'There's more,' Kay said, and Gaia looked at the fish lying on the grill over the fire. They were big and plump, with mottled green and brown skins. She frowned.

'Those are Fellowship fish, aren't they?'

Kay laughed. 'Yes. But there are no Lords in the forest. We eat what we like here.'

One of the men sitting round the fire rubbed his hands. 'Pigeon for dinner...'

The big, black-bearded man whose name was Daniel said, 'You've got a job to do first, Christopher, before you go hunting. Deliveries to get ready.'

230

'On my way.' Christopher stood and followed Daniel up the steps.

Gaia picked off a fragment of fish that had stuck to the grill and ate it. 'Deliveries?' she asked.

'The Hope's End crops,' Kay explained. 'It's Dan's scheme: he started it. He was a prisoner there. A few years ago he got out, and like you he had the sense to realise that he'd be safest in the forest. He found this place, and survived on his own for a bit, but he had friends who were still stuck in Hope's End, and he'd had his big idea. So he let himself be caught and taken back.'

Gaia shivered.

'Anyway,' Kay went on quickly, 'As soon as he could, he broke out again with a dozen or so friends. They came back here, and they started their scheme of raiding the Hope's End carts, and delivering the crops round the local villages. Between taxes and the rain, people barely make a living from the land here. A bundle of food on the doorstep, once a moon, can make a big difference. It's risky, but Dan's a fighter. He couldn't have sat here safe and done nothing. It's his own private war, against the thieves and murderers who call themselves the Fellowship.' She caught Gaia's surprised expression, and said, 'It's not only the food rules that don't apply here, Gaia. There are no prohibitions on what you say, either. We tell the Moons' own truth.'

'Some of those crops are the ones I grew,' Gaia said. 'I'm glad they're going to people who need them.'

She looked at Kay thoughtfully. 'You're not all from Hope's End, though, are you? Aldon doesn't have this.' She touched the scar on her cheek. 'Nor do you. How did you two end up here?'

'Aldon's just a wild man,' Kay said. 'He'd lived rough in the forest for years before he joined us. As for me... I came because of that.' She gestured at the old white walls, half hidden behind the close growing trees.

'What is it?' Gaia asked.

Kay stood up. 'Come and see.' Gaia and Carrie followed her, back up the broad steps and through the high doorway. They wandered through massive stone-flagged rooms full of green light from the trees overhead, along endless passageways where dead leaves lay in drifts, past fallen walls and stone stairs that led to nothing except empty air.

'What do you know about the history of Assalay?' Kay asked as they walked.

Gaia shrugged and shook her head, but Carrie said, promptly, 'Assalay was founded by the Fellowship.'

'That's what we've always been taught, Gaia,' Kay told her. 'That the southern provinces were a land of peaceful farmers until invaders came, and then the farming villages grouped together under the leadership of thirteen families. The Fellowship. They drove the invaders out, and built Assalay into a great and powerful land. Like Carrie said: the Fellowship was there at the very start.'

They turned a corner into another courtyard, where the statue of a flying swan was set on a tall pillar. They walked to the bottom of the pillar and looked up at the shape of the big bird, silhouetted against the leaves and the light.

'I think it's all a lie,' Kay said. 'I think there was Assalay before the Fellowship; an older history that we've never been told. And I think - I'm not sure, but I think - it might have something to do with you, Gaia.'

'Me?'

'Yes. Nothing's written down - but people remember things. They remember things they don't even understand. For me, it was a child's rhyme.'

'A rhyme?' Carrie said doubtfully.

'Yes. A stupid little rhyme. We played clapping games to it when we were kids. Then, after we were grown up, one year...' She took in a long unsteady breath, sat down on the plinth at the base of the pillar and stared hard into the distance. 'It was summer tribute time. The village was full of Teredo's men, and my fool of a brother got drunk and went out into the street and sang our little kids' song. I was away. We were cloth traders. I was at market. I never saw him again.'

'What happened to him?' Gaia asked quietly.

'He was killed. I would have been too, if someone hadn't told me what happened and warned me to run. I spent a long time running. When I finally stopped, I thought, why would Teredo kill someone for singing a nursery rhyme? I thought about what it said, and I travelled, and I listened. Ours wasn't the only song. There were scraps everywhere. Songs, poems, riddles, stories: little bits of a truth that the Fellowship have kept silent for hundreds of years.'

'So what was the song?' Carrie said.

'It goes like this,' said Kay.

King Telemachus
And his daughter Gaia
Slept in the palace
Died in the fire,
The king and the queen
And all their little childer
Big swans and little swans
Burned to a cinder
And that was the end of
The heirs of Athanasius
Who – comes – next?

'That was our version. The others are different, but the same: the same names, all the time: Athanasius - Telemachus - Gaia - and always a fire.'

'No,' Gaia was whispering, 'No, no, no.' She got to her feet and spun round. The walls enclosed her on every side.

'*Gaia,*' Kay said, 'I didn't think… I'm sorry.' She held out a hand, but Gaia pushed past her, and ran. She dived through a doorway whose empty arch towered high above her, and she saw leaping flames; great wooden doors ablaze and crumbling to ashes. She ran through vast chambers open to the sky, seeing the roof timbers burning and falling around her. She ran and ran, until at last Kay caught up with her and held her, folding her arms around her. She held her for a long time.

'I'm sorry,' she said again when Gaia had stopped shivering.

'It's … Hope's End. Stearne…He…'

'I know.'

Gaia swallowed and freed herself from Kay's arms. They were standing in the middle of a vast chamber. There were leaves and birdsong overhead, carved swans and portraits on the stone walls and two stone chairs on a high dais at the end of the room. She climbed the steps onto the dais. There was something on the wall behind the chairs: a carved panel, discoloured with age. At first, she thought it

233

was stone, but as she came close she saw that it was moonswood in a stone frame. She reached out her hand and touched it.

At the bottom of the panel a square had been cut away, and she put her hand over the space. She knew it without thinking: it was as if her very skin recognised it.

'That's my amulet.'

Mending

She took out her broken pieces of moonswood and slotted them into the empty square in the panel. They fitted perfectly: the stone frame held the three fragments together, even when she took her hand away.

She took a step backwards. The big panel was streaked with grey where the rainwater had run down it, and covered with green lichen. Her little square was cleaner and lighter, but it belonged. There was no doubt of that. She remembered what Ambrose had said, that its power would be revealed when it was read in the right place, and even though she was sure it wasn't magic she shivered slightly. But there was no thunder and lightning, no tumult of earthquake and falling stone: only the murmur of a breeze in the trees above the roofless walls, the calls of birds, and Kay saying something to her.

'Gaia.' Her face looked whiter than the moonswood in the green light. 'Where did you get that?'

'From Mum. My father left it to me.'

'Where did he get it from?'

'His father. It's been in our family a long time.'

'By all the sweet Moons and their stars, Gaia... Can I show you something else?'

'I suppose.' Unwillingly she allowed Kay to lead her down the hall, to Carrie, who was staring at one of the stone portraits: the carved face of a girl.

'There.' Kay put a soft hand on the portrait.

'What?' Gaia said.

'Gaia. When did you last see yourself in a mirror?'

'I don't know. Why?' She looked at the stone face, and, unbidden, an image from last summer came into her head. The day before the dragon came, she had been swimming with Tal and Jason in a still brown pool among the rocks. She had ducked her head under water, so that her usually tangled hair had been sleek against her head. The girl in the portrait had her hair pulled back like that.

'So?' she said. 'I look a bit like her. So what?'

'A *bit*?' Carrie said. 'She could *be* you.'

'It's true,' Kay said. 'It's why Aldon thought he knew you, in the winter. He didn't realise why until it was too late.'

'It's just a coincidence,' Gaia said.

'Coincidence?' Kay said. 'One thing maybe. But your face, your name, your brother's name, your father's name, that little piece of moonswood. I think you're Assalay's past, Gaia, come back to us; the thing that's been lost and hidden and lied about...'

Gaia ran her fingers round the contours of the stone face, and then, wonderingly, round her own.

'She's so like you,' Carrie whispered. 'Your flesh and blood. It must be...'

'But she died.' Gaia looked at Kay. 'That's what it says. Your song. *The king and the queen and all their children.* They all died in the fire.'

She shuddered again. She could *see* that girl, panicking, turning this way and that, and meeting rising flames and thick smoke whichever way she turned until she was overwhelmed by them. She had been trapped, here, between these old destroyed walls, and she had *burned*. Gaia snatched her hand away from the carved face. Sickness rose in her throat.

'It's impossible: she died! I can't be... They all died. They were all burned...' She pushed blindly past Kay and Carrie and ran the length of the chamber: she ran as if she was running from flames, through the endless corridors, under the high arch, down the broad steps and into the forest. She wanted to run and run, to put all Assalay between herself and the burned ruins. But imprisonment and fear had weakened her; she stopped and slumped down onto a fallen tree trunk with the walls of the palace still visible between the trees. She hid her face in her hands and tried to steady her breathing.

'Gaia!'

She looked up to see Carrie, standing uncertainly before her.

'I'm not staying there!' Gaia wiped her hands over her face. 'I can't. I'm going away.'

'Why?'

Gaia saw flames and death and pressed her hands into her eyes again. 'Because I hate it. All of them thinking I'm something to do with that girl, and I'm not. I *can't* be. She died. I'm not going back.'

'But... You can't go away.'

'I can. I'll live in the forest.' She hadn't known it until she spoke, but she felt better for the idea. She had managed here before, and at the worst time of year. Under the cool green of the trees, surrounded by growing things, she might find her peace again.

'You've left the amulet behind.'

'I don't care. I don't want it.' She had loved it when it had been a mysterious, pretty thing; the feeling of her father's hand in hers. But now it belonged to a place where a girl had suffered and died horribly. Now she would happily leave it behind. She stood up from the log.

'What about Jason?' Carrie asked, and Gaia closed her eyes. Stupid. If she fled into the forest, Jason would never find her when he came back from wherever he and Aldon had rushed off to this morning. She had already lost him once, and after that she had lost Mai and Tal too. Finding Jason had been a miracle of hope: it was unthinkable, to lose him again. Defeated, she sat down on the fallen tree again. 'Alright. I'll stay. But only till he's back.'

Returning to that doomed building was the hardest thing she had ever done. She waited until dusk was falling before she dragged herself back through the trees. Kay and the others were on the terrace, talking; hoarse as if they had been talking excitedly all day. They fell silent when they saw her, and in their eyes she saw awe and astonishment - and hope. She understood. For them she was Assalay without the Fellowship - an ancient Assalay, but not destroyed, not dead; still there, like a low fire that can be blown into life again. She shivered.

'I know what you think.' She came onto the terrace and stood among them, looking at the faces that the Fellowship had scarred, and finally turning to face Kay. 'Your stories and songs. You think there was a time before the Fellowship, don't you? When Assalay wasn't ruled by them, but by the people who lived here. Athanasius. Telemachus.' She glanced behind her at the walls, looming dark and sad in the dusk, and shivered again. 'Maybe you're right. But you can't pick one bit of the story and forget the other. They died in the fire. I can't be anything to do with them. I can't.'

'That moonswood, though.' Daniel looked unconvinced. 'Your amulet. Generations old. Surely that proves…'

237

'It doesn't prove anything!' Gaia said. 'It could have come to us a hundred ways... Maybe treasure hunters came here and took it, and it got swapped and bartered till it ended up with a goatherd in Arimaspia. That makes more sense than believing that a girl who died in a fire passed it on to children she didn't live to have.'

'But...' Kay started.

'Forget it!' she shouted. 'They're dead! They're not coming back!'

She pushed away from everyone and ran up the steps. She had a vague idea of going to her bed in the corridor and hiding there until Jason returned, but she couldn't pass the threshold of the entrance hall. She froze in front of the high doorway. The hall beyond it seemed to be full of the bright roar of flames, and she shut her eyes and put her hands over her ears because, somewhere, someone was screaming.

It was her. Slowly, she became aware of Kay's firm cool hands on her shoulders and her voice saying, 'Gaia, shh, Gaia,' hushing her, calming the nightmare like Mum would have done. Together, they walked away into the trees. They sat, and Kay held her. 'I can't go in there again,' Gaia said. 'I can't go back. I *can't*...'

'I know.' Kay wrapped her cloak around Gaia's shoulders, found her a sheltered place under a thick tangle of leaves, and sat with her till she slept.

Morning woke her with cool wet air and green light. For a long time she lay breathing in the scent of earth and things growing, reluctant to move, but there was something she needed to know. She forced herself back to the terrace, and faced the curious, disappointed, hopeful eyes again.

'Is Jason back?'

He wasn't. She sat aside from the others, missing him more than ever. Her best friend; her oldest friend; the only person here for whom she wasn't someone extraordinary. The one person for whom she was just Gaia: clumsy, a bit dreamy, quite clever, argumentative, not much good at anything... Except that wasn't true anymore, because in the most improbable place in the world, she had found the thing she could do. She thought of her garden at Hope's End: in her mind she paced step by step along the beds, stopping to touch her plants with a gentle finger.

She disappeared after breakfast, and in the middle of the morning, Kay asked, 'Where's Gaia?'

Carrie shook her head, and Dan said, 'She borrowed some tools. A pick, a spade, a fork. And she said, can we leave her alone?'

Kay looked uneasy. With those tools, you could smash a moonswood panel into unreadable fragments and bury them, or obliterate the face of a carved portrait. 'I'll just have a wander round,' she said. But the vast chamber was deserted, and the panel and the stone face as peaceful as they had been for centuries.

Gaia reappeared in the evening: hot and grubby, a little calmer. 'Is Jason back?'

She said nothing in answer to Kay's 'not yet,' and went downriver to bathe in a place where there was a deep pool between smooth rocks. She returned for supper, but at night she went back into the forest to sleep alone under the trees. Days and days passed in the same way, and each day she was stronger: more peaceful and more certain of herself.

'Is Jason back?' she asked as usual one morning, and when Carrie answered 'No,' she said, 'Sweet Hesperal! How long can hunting take?'

She caught the surprised look in Carrie's eyes. 'Are you alright, Gaia?'

'I think so, now.'

'Where've you been?'

'Can't you guess?'

Carrie looked blank.

'Come and see.' Gaia glanced up. Kay was standing to one side, not part of the conversation, but close enough to have heard. 'You can come too, if you want. I mean... I'd like you to.'

She led them along a path where the branches had been cut back to make a way through the forest; into a wide clearing. 'We felled some trees here, a couple of years ago,' Kay said. 'Dan said there was no point giving people food if you didn't give them firewood as well. But it was completely overgrown last time I was here.'

The space between the trees had been cleared. Old tree stumps and roots, small saplings and brambles lay in a heap at the side, and the soil had been patiently dug into a fine tilth. Four long earth beds ran the length of the space, with paths of beaten earth between them.

Carrie smiled. 'You've made a garden.'

'Yes.' Gaia crouched down, picked up a handful of earth, and crumbled it in her fingers. Whoever she was, whatever blood flowed in her veins, whatever anyone wanted to make of her - slave or swansprite or queen - it was here, working the garden, that she had found her peace and her place: had found herself.

'Daniel,' Gaia asked. 'Where's Kay?'

He looked up from the arrow that he was whittling, and waved a hand at the ruined walls. 'Inside. Everything alright?'

She nodded, and climbed the broad steps towards the huge empty doorway. Over the last moon, she had lost her terror of crossing this threshold: the ruin still felt steeped in sadness, but it no longer roared with imaginary flame every time she entered it. She wound confidently through the corridors until she found Kay in the huge chamber of the stone portraits, running a finger thoughtfully along the join between Gaia's amulet and the rest of the moonswood panel.

'Not gardening?' Kay asked.

'We were...' Gaia hesitated.

'What's wrong?'

'Nothing, really. Only... I think we've found something.'

'We thought we'd make the garden bigger.' She led Kay along the tangled path under the trees. 'There's that overgrown patch at the back. There aren't any big trees there, so we thought we could clear it.'

They came out from the green shade of the trees into the brighter light of the garden. Gaia pointed to a rise in the ground at the far end: a hummock of dark leaf mould where Carrie was sitting, waiting for them. The ivies, bushes and brambles that had covered it lay aside in a heap. 'I thought it was a lump of earth,' Gaia said, 'but we tried to level it out, and it's not. There's stone underneath.'

Kay crossed the garden and knelt to look, clearing the leaf mould with her hands. There was a big block of stone, with stone supports at either end of it, and a gap beneath, as if it was the top of a doorway. It was impossible to tell how deep the space inside was, but the cold and stale air of somewhere long undisturbed breathed from it.

'What is it?' Gaia asked.

'I don't know.' Kay put her face to the narrow opening, and stood up, brushing the earth from her hands and knees. 'I'd like to find out, though. Is that alright, Gaia?'

Gaia nodded. Whatever secret this earth held, she felt instinctively that it needed to be uncovered, and she watched and helped as Kay and the others worked to dig the soil away from the stones. By the third morning, they had uncovered a square, windowless building. The low door was guarded by an iron grille which had rusted almost to nothing: it broke away from the stone and fell into the building with a clang when Dan pushed his weight against it. But the rainy light could not penetrate the darkness; whatever was inside the building remained obscure and secret.

'Who's going in?' asked Kay.

'Not me,' said Dan, and Gaia shook her head and backed away. Kay lit a lantern, and crawled through the low doorway. 'There are steps here.' Her voice sounded hollow, otherworldly. Crouching to peer in, Gaia saw the lantern-light dance on smooth stone and then fade and disappear, leaving only darkness. She stood up and tilted her face to the daylight. They waited, until at last Dan couldn't wait any longer: he stooped down and called through the doorway.

'Kay! Are you alright?'

'Yes!' she called back.

'Are you sure?'

'Yes. I'm coming back...'

They clustered round her as she crawled out, blinking at the brightness. She looked round the circle of faces, found Gaia and held her gaze. Her eyes were dancing, many coloured. 'There's something here that you have to see,' she said. She reached out and took Gaia's hand. 'Come.'

Inside, there were centuries of darkness. Gaia halted at the top of the steps and would have turned back. But there had been that strange excitement in Kay's eyes. Fighting down the memory of the terror of Hope's End, she allowed Kay to guide her down the steep steps into a square rocky chamber. There were shelves cut into the walls on each side, and shallow boxes of stone on each shelf.

'Look.' Kay held Gaia's hand and lifted the lantern so that its beams fell into the two long stone boxes on the right hand wall. Gaia peered through the light and recoiled. There were bones in the boxes. Big, grown-up human bones, dry, dead and broken. After the first instinct of fear, she felt pity more than anything.

'And here.' Kay had turned to shine the lantern on the other wall. The boxes there were smaller, some of them tiny. *The king and the queen and all their little childer,* Gaia thought, *big swans and little swans,* and she said, 'No,' and hung back, tugging against Kay's hand. She thought of the girl again, her namesake, running and dying in the fire. 'No,' she said. 'Please. No.'

'It's alright,' Kay said. 'I *promise* you.'

Gaia followed her reluctantly across the narrow chamber, and looked into one of the boxes. She started, reached a hand in, picked up what was there and let it run through her fingers. Sand. Gritty sand, like tiny smoothed pebbles, black and brown and grey: the same sand that she trod underfoot when she went to bathe in the river.

They all went in and out after that, and in the afternoon they gathered on the terrace. Gaia turned her back on the excited conversations and stared at the ruined walls and the trees beyond them.

'Gaia?' Kay took her arm, and led her aside from the loud, laughing group. They leaned on the crumbling stone balustrade and looked down into the fast running river. A weed had taken root in one of the cracks in the stone and grown wild, tumbling in a green fall to the water. Gaia took one of the stems gently between her fingers and felt it.

'You understand why this matters, don't you?' Kay asked her.

Gaia traced the outline of a leaf with her thumb and said nothing.

'You've seen Assalay, Gaia. You've seen what it suffers.'

Gaia remembered the starved fields and the empty houses, the refugees under the walls of Freehaven, and the distant pain in Carrie's eyes. *Lost children, lost parents. Damn this rotten land.* She nodded.

'It's time for a change,' Kay said. 'Time for the Fellowship to go, time to be ruled by justice and fairness. But it's hard for people to imagine that change when as far as they know there's never been anything different. *Really* hard for them to imagine getting rid of men who claim to be the moons' anointed rulers. But... If they knew that the Fellowship hadn't ruled from the very beginning. If they knew that there'd been a different past, that wasn't dead, but still living among us... Then maybe people would have the courage to fight.' She smiled. 'That's why we wanted to believe in you, Gaia, even when it seemed impossible. You arrived among us with that name and that face and that little bit of moonswood out of the past, and you gave us the possibility of a different future. And now... It's possible, isn't it? There's no dead child in that tomb.'

'You still can't prove it!'

Kay looked surprised. 'Do you doubt it?'

She shouted, 'I don't know!' startling a bird out of the trees, and against the clatter of its wings, she whispered, 'No.'

'So...' Kay began.

'But you can't prove it. What have you got? This place that no-one will come to because it's prohibited, and some missing bones, and a bit of moonswood and a person with an odd name. If I was Fellowship I could easily show that it was all a fake. We could have destroyed the bones, cut the moonswood from the panel ourselves... And all the rest's just kids' stories. We could even have made up my name. As far as Lanneret's concerned I'm called Elsa Seagull. There's no proof.'

She walked away from Kay, up the wide steps and through the ruined doorway, through the green light falling from the trees overhead, into the vast room with the stone chairs on their dais. She paused to look at the face of the girl who - maybe - hadn't died, and climbed the steps to run her fingers round the edge of the little square of moonswood that she had - maybe - brought away with her when she escaped. She turned away and wound her way through the broken empty corridors, out into the trees, and along the path to her garden.

Plants grew fast and strong in the wet rich forest earth: the lettuce seeds that she had planted had already sent out leaves, brilliant green against the red soil. She knelt down on the earth and started to pull out the weeds that had sprouted around them. This work - tending the things she had grown - had calmed her at Hope's End, but today she couldn't settle to it: her mind was full of the low tomb at the end of the garden; the court in Freehaven, and her decision to stand against the Fellowship, the triumph in the unhappy boy's eyes; the rhythms of Kay's little rhyme. *Slept in the palace, died in the fire....* *Who comes next?* It was impossible to concentrate with all that spinning in her head. She left the weeds to grow, and dawdled back along the path towards the palace. Then she heard someone shout, 'Aldon!' and she broke into a run.

They were standing in a tight circle on the terrace: Daniel and Kay and the others, looking down at something on the ground. She couldn't see Jason, but she recognised Aldon by the bow slung over his shoulder and she ran to him and grabbed hold of his arm.

'Where's Jason?'

He smiled a greeting, and gestured towards the ruins.

'Inside. Looking for you.'

She started towards the steps.

'Gaia Athanasius!' The voice was oddly familiar, and she turned back. Two men were sitting on the ground in the centre of the circle, their town clothes damp and dirty with leaf mould and rain. But the man who had spoken was, unexpectedly, smiling at her.

'Mr *Fossick*?' She glanced at his companion, and her voice sharpened. 'Kay, that's Scrimp. *Parhelion's* treasurer...'

'Not anymore.' Scrimp shuddered. 'If Parhelion - if any of them caught up with me - with us - now... We've been on the run, for moons, at sea, lost in the forest...'

'So you came home, Gaia?' Fossick interrupted him.

She looked at him warily. 'What do you mean?'

'The heir of Athanasius. In the palace that Athanasius built.' He nodded towards the ruined walls against the dark trees.

'Wait!' Kay crouched down to face him. 'How do you know who she is?'

'Because of her name,' said Fossick. 'Because she had an object in Old Script that no peasant child from Arimaspia should ever have had. Once I found out that Telemachus' children escaped the fire, it was obvious.'

Kay rocked on her heels. 'Escaped...? That's what we think too... But there's no proof.'

'Oh, yes, there is,' said Fossick. 'Her brother's got it.'

'My brother?' said Gaia. '*Tal?* How...? Where is he? Is he alright?'

Mending

There was a call of 'Gaia!' from the palace doorway, and she swung round to see Carrie and Jason hurrying towards her. Carrie: her eyes alive with delight, and Jason: grinning in triumph, and...

'Tal!' she shouted, and she ran up the steps and into his arms.

The Palamon Trial

'I'm sorry,' he kept saying, 'I'm sorry.'

She held her fingers to his lips to hush him.

'I know,' she said. 'It's alright.'

He looked at her doubtfully. It hadn't been alright, he could tell. She was skinny, there was that cruel double scar on her cheek that made his guts clench and her face had the dark shadows of nightmare. But her eyes were shining. He stopped trying to speak, and held her wordlessly, with a fierce determination never, ever, to let go of her again. He would have kept his arms round her till nightfall, the next morning, the next *moon*. But Fossick, followed closely by Kay, had climbed the steps to join them, and he was tapping Tal on the shoulder and saying, 'You said you'd brought it. Where is it?'

Tal half let go of Gaia, keeping one arm round her shoulder, and reached into his satchel with his free hand. He pulled out a long thin parcel, wrapped in carefully stitched canvas, and offered it to Fossick.

'Thank you.' Fossick smiled slightly and inclined his head. 'My Lord.'

'What? I'm not...' Tal looked from Fossick to Gaia and caught something in her eyes that made him fall silent.

'Yes, you are.' Fossick handed the parcel to Kay. 'Here. Here's your proof.'

Kay sat down on the steps with the package balanced on her lap, took out her knife, cut the stitches gently and took out the parchment. Fragments of brittle paper, like scraps of dried leaf, fell away from the edges as she unrolled it. Tal looked over her shoulder as she bent over the faded, illegible script that had baffled him in Freehaven.

'I can't read it.' Kay frowned up at Fossick.

'Shall I?'

They sat in a circle around him, and when they were all settled, he began to read.

I, Teredo, Lord of Southdene, set down here for my own remembering a true record of the treachery of Palmyr Palamon, inasmuch as he did swear loyalty unto us in our great enterprise and did break his oath...

'I don't get it,' Jason interrupted. 'What's *our great enterprise?*'

'Just wait,' said Fossick.

'Alright.' Jason shrugged. 'But I could do without all the untos and inasmuches.'

'Too bad,' said Fossick.

It fell in this wise. In Aquilon, in the fourteenth year of the reign of King Telemachus...'

Tal started.

'What?' asked Fossick.

'Telemachus,' said Tal. 'That's my name.'

Fossick laughed. 'You see, Cosmo? The past returns to us.' He found his place on the paper and read on.

'*... there was great distress in this our fair land of Assalay. For the King took to himself much power and showed himself no respecter of the ancient rights and traditions of the most noble families of the kingdom. So we did form our Fellowship to protect and preserve our due liberties. And we were myself: Lord Teredo, the Lord Anserine, the Lord Querimon...*'

Fossick interrupted himself. 'This is just a list of the Lords of the Fellowship. No surprises here.' He paused and gave a secret smile, his eyes dancing. 'Well, only one. The members of the Fellowship were also the members of the King's council, and there were fourteen of them. Not thirteen. There was another Fellow. Lord Palamon, the King's Chamberlain. Anyway, they took their oaths to one another, and then...'

Our Fellowship did go unto Telemachus and said to him, "Great King, we are the first among your subjects and from generation to generation we have had rights and privileges and powers which no King has authority to take from us. Yet you seek to strip us of these rights and powers and to make us equal to the least of your subjects." And we demanded of him that he did not so. For otherwise, we said, the King would be no King, but a tyrant in the land. And Telemachus swore that he would ponder on what we had requested of him...

'Clear?' Fossick asked Jason.

'I'm not *stupid*,' he said.

And at sunset on the same day, the King did call us unto him and said, "I love you all as my brothers and as my worthy counsellors, yet I cannot do as you have asked of me." Then he did speak great foolishness, saying how there were many that suffered and were in distress in the kingdom, and he would not have it so. And that for many to be poor and weak when a few were rich and strong was a disgrace and a shame and a foulness to spoil the fairness of Assalay. And he requested that we would not speak of these matters again.

So we did meet privily together again, and said one to another, what do we do now? And Palamon said, we must ask again. But I said, "Fool. The King's scribes and lawmen are even now writing the laws that will change our ancient ways for ever. Delay, and we will find our armies and our courts, our taxes and tributes, even our lands, taken from us by his command. And think on this. A true King guards the usages of his land. But a King who strives to change and overturn tradition is a tyrant, and there exists no law against the slaying of a tyrant...

Gaia imagined them: gathering in secret; arguing; and Teredo, speaking that fatal word: calling up the idea of murder...

Then spoke Lord Helminth, saying, "Truly, my Lord, a happy notion. For Gaia is yet young, and a young queen may be easily guided."

But I said, "No. Let us have no more kings in Assalay. A King is a dangerous thing: too powerful, and a prey to foolish notions. Let there be an end to the house of Athanasius. And let us govern, and we shall preserve the ancient ways."

And Palamon said, "You propose the murder of a noble King; I shall have no part in this." And he made to leave, but we drew swords and prevented him, saying, "You have taken your oath, Palamon." And he protested no more, and we laid our plans for the next day.

But Lanneret said secretly to me, "I do not trust Palamon," and he sat that night at Palamon's door with sword drawn. In the morning we met together again. "What is the appointed hour?" Palamon asked and we told him "Tonight," and he said, "Then I shall away, and spend today hunting, the better to accustom myself to the shedding of blood." And Lord Hallion and Lord Parhelion took wagers on his returning...

'Typical,' muttered Scrimp.

... And at evening he had not, and we went without him to the King and Queen in their private chamber, and we said, "Your Majesties, a word." And Telemachus said, "If this concerns your liberties, my Lords, I have spoken my final word." And I said, "You have, your Majesty," and I & Anserine drew swords and slew him and Lanneret & Mallander likewise slew Queen Aglaia. That done, we said, "Let us finish this night's good work," and we went to the children's chambers. The nurse sat in the ante-room and we said to her, "Are the children within?" and she answered, "No."

And Parhelion said - for it had been his task to watch the children and be sure that all were within the Palace - "You lie, woman, for I have followed them all day."

But she said again, "Telemachus' children are not here." And she opened the chamber and within we saw royal clothes empty on the floor and a gaggle of kitchen and stable brats in rags, and Lanneret said to Parhelion, "Fool..."

'Typical,' said Scrimp again.

... Then Demersal said, "We could kill these anyway," but I said, "For what? This blood is not worth the spilling." And we asked of the nurse, "Where are Gaia and her brothers and sisters?" But she would only answer, "Gone. You will never find them. You will not quench the blood of Athanasius." And I cursed that I had not thought to guard Palamon's window as well as his door. Again I demanded an answer of the nurse, and again she said nothing, and Lanneret in his fury ran her through with his sword and killed her. And Hallion said, "Now she will never tell what she knows..."'

Fossick was silent for a moment, then he said, 'That's it, really. That night there was a fire in the palace and the next day, the Fellowship gave out that the king and all his family had died and that from now on the Lords would rule Assalay. Over time, they started to talk about the kings as tyrants and bad rulers, and the fire as a heaven-sent liberation. Later they tried to wipe out the memory of the kingdom altogether, destroying everything that had been written about it, changing the script...'

'But this survived?' Kay put a hand lightly on the scroll. 'How?'

'By accident, I imagine,' said Fossick. 'Hidden away, in a forgotten part of the archive...'

'What about Palamon?' Gaia interrupted.

'He got away. With the children.' He gave her a quick smile. 'The Fellowship never found him. There's a note at the end of this document: recording how they tried him in his absence. They condemned him to a traitor's death, killed his family and divided his lands between themselves. And wiped his memory from the records; forgot the fourteenth Lord, claimed that they had always been thirteen... *Moon-anointed.* Huh.'

He rolled the scroll shut and passed it to Kay. 'There you are. Proof.'

'Gaia?' she said. But Gaia had her face hidden in her hands. She was imagining that girl, woken from sleep to undreamed-of danger, hurrying in the darkness to an agreed hiding place, trying to calm her terrified brothers and sisters, waiting for dawn and the man who had sworn to help them. And the long journey with fear in her tracks all the way. Had she ever felt safe enough to stop looking over her shoulder for her father and mother's killers?

'I wonder what happened to Palamon,' Kay was saying thoughtfully.

'I doubt we'll ever know,' said Fossick. 'Let's hope he lived long and happy. He deserved it.'

Winter too, Gaia thought: bitter cold, and snow thick on the mountains. She knew that journey from somewhere. And there was something else…

'You said something about Palamon,' she said to Fossick. 'He was … not just a counsellor. Something else?'

'Chamberlain.' Fossick started to explain. 'It means he was head of the royal household. He would have been responsible for…'

But Gaia wasn't listening. A title, then: not a name. Chamberlain. Mai had got that wrong, and so had all the other tellers of the tale, maybe from the first time it was ever told. Almost without realising it, she was crying.

'He didn't live long.' She wiped her face with the back of her hand and met Tal's puzzled look. 'Chamboleyne,' she said. Mum's favourite story: the one she always told if you gave her a choice. The story she had told moons ago, on the day of the summer dragon.

'Gaia, what's this about?' asked Kay. So Gaia told her about the little line of children trailing down from the snowfields to the village, and the dying man who had led them, and the gold that had fallen from the cliff where they left his body.

She was very quiet after that, as Kay led them down the steps and through the forest to the garden. At the uncovered tomb, Fossick read the inscription over the doorway. '"Sacred to the eternal memory of Telemachus, last of the kings of Assalay, and of his Queen Aglaia and of their children. The moons watch over their souls among the stars and we revere their memory for ever." Huh!' He gazed distantly into the green of the forest. 'It was a hard winter. The hardest for years, and the day they buried them was worse than any other. Hours after they had sealed it, the tomb was almost hidden by snow.'

'It sounds as if you saw it,' Kay said.

'There was a book I used to have.' He glared at Scrimp. 'It'll have gone the way of most other old things by now, I don't doubt. But this is still here. Can we go inside?'

They crowded into the little space, and Tal touched the ancient bones with wondering fingers: dry bones from which his living flesh and blood had sprung. Their smooth wornness reminded him of the moonswood, and once they were out in the light again, he asked, 'Have you still got the amulet, Gaia?'

It was Kay who answered, 'Come and see,' and she led them to the throne room where Tal climbed the steps onto the dais and stood in front of the panel. He ran his fingers along the grooves of the carved letters. 'What does it say?' he asked Fossick.

Fossick squinted through the green shadowy light. 'It's a regnal list, I think,' he said, finally. 'Yes. These are the names of the Kings and Queens of Assalay, from the earliest times, and along the bottom, there's something... I can't make it all out, but it ends, *to rule with humility and justice under the moons*. Your amulet is the end of the word *moons*, Gaia.'

'Back in the right place,' Tal said.

'What?' asked Kay.

'That's what the story said. At home. That it would bring our family honour and wealth and greatness, but only when it was read in the right place.'

Kay looked at Gaia. 'You didn't tell me that.'

'No.' Gaia scuffed her toe against the worn stone floor. 'I don't want any of this! The kingdom, honour: all that stuff. I just ...' She turned away and stared down the long green-shadowed hall. Tal. Mum. Jason, Carrie, a square of earth to care for: that was all she wanted, not a whole country. But...

But a long time ago, a brave man had taken his stand against the Fellowship, and because of that, he had died, and she was alive. And she realised, suddenly, that in his last frail hours, this moment was what he had hoped for. *Save them, and one day they may save you.* In the village, they had always thought that meant the gold, but that was nonsense: how could he have known about that? No. What he had known was what Assalay would become under the Fellowship, and he had given his life to save the faintest of hopes for a different future.

And as for her... whatever she felt about the long dead kingdom, she knew her mind about the Fellowship. She had declared it many moons ago, in the loneliest moment of her life, when she refused to spy for Lanneret.

'Gaia?' asked Kay quietly.

In the court at Freehaven, she had had only an unhappy boy's eyes to comfort her. But now a whole circle of friendly faces were waiting for her decision. Fossick and Scrimp, who had risked their lives to find this truth. Kay, Daniel, Aldon and the others. Her best friends, Jason and Carrie. And...

'Wait a moment,' she said. 'I need to talk to Tal.'

She took him outside, through the trees to her garden. They sat on the roof of the tomb, and she took his hands in hers.

'You know what this is all about, don't you?'

'Sort of,' he said, uncertainly.

'They want to fight the Fellowship.' She was thinking it out as she spoke. 'And they'll do it by telling this history. By saying that things were different once, and because of that, they can be different again. By saying that the old kingdom isn't dead.' For a moment there was something in her eyes that made her almost a stranger, but then she was just his sister again. 'I don't want to be a queen. I want to be a gardener. But for now...There's too much that's wrong.'

He thought of the starving winter, the raid on the village, Mum. Especially Mum: still a slave in Freehaven, not free to come to her lost daughter. While the Fellowship lasted, none of that would be put right.

'The thing is,' Gaia was saying, 'I can only do this if you agree. It's going to be dangerous. For you too. You're the same blood. They'll want to destroy you as much as me. I won't do it, if you don't want me to.'

Heavy clouds had gathered, and the trees were an intense green against the dark grey. In the long silence before he spoke, the first thunderclap sounded, and big drops of rain started to fall.

'Do it,' he said. 'I'll be with you. To the end.'

They went on sitting, the rain hammering on the trees above them, until they heard voices calling for them. Jason and Carrie dashed into the clearing, huddled together under Jason's coat.

'You're getting soaked, you two. And there's supper.'

Gaia stood up, headed for the path and turned back. She crouched down on the wet earth and pulled up her crop of lettuces, shaking the rain from their brilliant green leaves before bundling them up in her skirt and hurrying after the others.

The storm had driven everyone inside. They had gathered in the throne room, around a big fire in the middle of the floor. The flames hissed in the rain that dripped through the branches overhead. There was a smell of grilled fish, and, piled by the fire, mushrooms, roots and berries harvested from the richness of the forest. Gaia put her wet lettuces on top of the pile.

'They might be the last things I grow for a while.'

They had been waiting for her to speak, and they understood straight away. She watched joy spread from face to face like a fire catching. Dan took her hand and tried to lead her to one of the stone thrones.

'No,' she said. 'I'll sit with the rest of you.' She settled down next to Tal in the circle around the bright fire, and while the storm crashed and flickered above the trees, they talked and ate. There were moons to catch up and they talked until it was dark. But after nightfall, she lay down next to him, and was silent while the conversation continued around her and turned to the future.

I can go home.

I can look for Mum and Dad.

I can come with you.

She fell asleep, lulled by hopeful voices, and woke to a day washed clean by the heavy rain. The air was fresh and the sky above the leaves was a clear pale blue. She had slept late. The hall was deserted, though close outside, she could hear Tal singing. A tune she didn't know: a tune that left you no room to doubt that the world would be well.

Because there was no-one to see her, she climbed the steps to the dais, hesitated, and sat in one of the stone thrones. She sat with her legs drawn up to her chest and her arms huddled round them, resting her chin on her knees. Somewhere through the moving clouds of the future, she thought she could see a fair land where life flourished on the kind earth. But the clouds were very thick, and it was impossible, really, to know what lay beyond them.

Assalay's Calendar : Moons and Fellows

Arctos: Lord Anserine (dark green)

Clamynto: Lord Hallion (magenta)

Galanthus: Lord Sallender (lapis blue)

Coranto: Lord Filarion (crimson)

Hyrondal: Lord Querimon (yellow)

Idalia: Lord Lanneret (emerald)

Lusinia: Lord Parhelion (indigo)

Melisto: Lord Philemot (halcyon blue)

Astia: Lord Demersal (burgundy)

Brumas: Lord Baladine (orange)

Hesperal: Lord Malander (gold)

Aquilon: Lord Teredo (scarlet)

Himalios: Lord Helminth (black)

Coming soon…

Assalay Volume Two: The Singing War

Lightning Source UK Ltd.
Milton Keynes UK
UKOW02f1355061116
286984UK00002B/49/P